SHOOTER IN THE SHADOWS

TIM HERBERT

This novel is entirely a work of fiction. The names, characters, organisations, and incidents portrayed in it are the work of the author's imagination. Any resemblance to actual persons, living or dead, events or localities is purely coincidental.

Copyright © 2011 Tim Herbert

The moral right of the author has been asserted.

All rights reserved.

ISBN 978-1-463-64923-4

For

BREN

CHAPTER 1

The plane touched down at Heraklion Airport, on the north shore of Crete. A flurry of passengers - businessmen on junkets, tourists on package holidays, young couples with children - rose in unison and prepared to disembark.
Michel checked his watch and adjusted it two hours ahead. Slowly the stream of passengers trickled off and for the first time in four hours he left his seat. As Michel stretched, a large shaven-headed man elbowed him out of the way. Michel lost his balance and fell backwards. The middle-aged couple that flanked him remarked upon the rudeness of the burly brute, but Michel did not reply.
An angry sun welcomed the newcomers and forced them to shield their eyes. Behind a cloud of diesel smoke, the last of the packed buses ferried the passengers from the plane to an unobtrusive-looking terminal building.
The airport officer, attractive, brown-eyed and dark-haired, probed mischievously, 'Michel Trebeh, the nature of your visit, please?'
'Pleasure,' Michel replied, curious as to why he was singled out.
'You may go.' She handed him back his passport, delaying her release ever so slightly.

Once outside he hailed a taxi. It was an excessively hot day, oppressive even for locals. His clothes were stained with perspiration. He was thinking about the shaven-headed man.

With a gasp of brakes, the taxi pulled up in front of the Elizabethan Apartments. The slightly overweight receptionist set aside her half-eaten pastry and asked for his passport. She gave him a set of keys and let out a yell. Immediately a young man, with stubble-tacked chin, appeared from behind the staff-room door. Wearing jeans, a linen shirt, and an iPod dangling around his neck, he led the way to room 206.

Michel gave the porter a tip and closed the door behind him. Moments later the noisy air-conditioning kicked in, and the room temperature dropped a few degrees. Gingerly he kicked off his sneakers and walked barefoot over the cooling tiles to the windowless bathroom and turned on the light and stood in front of the mirror. A boyishly handsome face filled the darkened glass; brown hair, a discreet scar on his forehead, softly tanned skin, and emerald green eyes. After dabbing his face with sun-cream, he removed his clothing and generously applied the cooling substance to the rest of his thick, muscular body. He lifted the complimentary drink from the table and made his way out onto the balcony. The poolside was laced with medical students celebrating the end of their exams. Some were talking, while others were stretched out paying homage to the sun. When he had finished his drink he dressed in a pair of flip-flops and black swimming trunks.

He arrived at the larger of the two pools and lifted a sun-bed from the rickety pillar. The scent of lotion hung thick. He spread the towel on the sun-bed and stood for just a moment facing the water.
His dive was perfection; with a powerful thrust, he skirted the bottom of the pool. Twenty lengths later he placed his hands on the poolside and lifted himself out. On his way back, he noticed a blonde girl staring at him, perhaps fancying him or just appreciative of his repertoire of swim strokes.

He returned to the apartment and put on a pair of khaki shorts, pulled a green T-shirt over his head and slipped his feet into a pair of sandals. His eyes searched the room and settled on a cheap print hanging in the alcove. After removing the back of the frame, he inserted three white envelopes, and then he restored the print to its original state and position. He took three identical envelopes from his toiletry bag and popped them inside the safe-deposit box.

An orphan since the tender age of seven, both Michel's parents had died when their family saloon collided with a campervan travelling on the wrong side of the road, he was the only survivor. A philosophy moulded in foster homes, and shaped by long periods of isolation, gave him a strong sense of self-awareness, as well as a heightened consciousness of those around him. The more he observed the behavioural patterns of diverse peoples, both men and women, the stronger his belief that society suffered greatly under the strain of two great qualms: the first, fear of death, and the second, problems with loneliness. Troubled by neither of these, he was determined to tackle life head-on. A self-taught programmer, he sold his first technology start-up, which attracted funding from a Silicon Valley venture capital firm, for one million dollars when he was just sixteen. And with that seed capital, he built a global business empire.

In front of him lay a sheaf of documents requiring his signature. He browsed the first document, Nuclear Reactions without Uranium; written by Professor Vladimir Kerzhakov, a scholar he met while negotiating a deal in Russia. The professor's work was of paramount importance to his next venture, but for now he was satisfied to leave it simmering on the backburner until a more recent foray into the world of energy bore fruit. Leafing through the next document, he momentarily paused to reflect on the small picture stapled to the bottom of the page. He was glad that he had been briefed about May Franks.

Prior to leaving the apartment, he jerked a short strand of hair from his head and slotted it between the door and the frame.
The sun was beginning to lower.

At a junction, he waited patiently on the hard shoulder. Hurriedly, he crossed the busy road linking Hersonisus to Heraklion.

A motorcycle rattled past.

Michel veered onto an up-and-down road, and he came to a whitewashed bungalow surrounded by a multitude of plants. Through a gap in the hedgerow, he had an unobstructed view beyond the house to where an elderly woman laboriously tilled with rustic tools. Dressed traditionally, all in black, the thickset woman stooped over, so low, she appeared to kiss the red earth. She did not look up.

As he neared the beach, he passed a hotel, five stars, and he made a mental note of the archery range located within the outer perimeter of the grounds. He walked along the recently paved promenade.

On a jutted out section of coastline, he came across a tiny orthodox church. It had just received its annual whitewash, a brilliant white, broken only by the blue of the small windows. A tranquil atmosphere infused with incense welcomed him. Inside, the floor was composed of cream marble slabs, with a raised granite altar and on this stood a large cross of brass. He went forward and bowed his head reverently. After a few minutes, he left in a relaxed mood.

A stone's throw from the church stood a sign, Archaeological Dig. A series of disinterred knolls and tunnels covered by a makeshift galvanised roof and fenced off with chicken wire. Nylon tarps, strung out over the excavation site, fluttered and flapped like sails. He stood on the southern edge of a mound and surveyed the site. Tomorrow, he would find out more.

He hauled himself away and he carried on towards the village.

On the far side of the pavement, several shops were still open for business, selling everything from English newspapers and cheap T-shirts to fresh fruit. Leaving the promenade, he ducked inside a camera shop and purchased two mini-crossbows and a pair of Kershaw amphibian knives.

An Irish pub stood at the end of the road. He went inside.

The barman rearranged his spectacles and pulled a pint. Two-handed, he passed the overflowing glass to Michel.

Michel entered the lounge and sat down on a cane chair. On the big screen, there was a football match. He noticed a group of men and women huddled around a table littered with empty crisp bags and other rubbish. On his way to the bathroom, he recognised the shaven-headed man who had shoved him on the plane.

Michel sauntered over. 'You owe me an apology.'

'I don't know you. Piss off,' the burly man bellowed in a strong Geordie accent, his face weather-beaten.

The chubby woman sitting beside him intervened. 'Wait! Harry, stop it, you promised you'd behave.' It was wishful thinking.

'You owe me an apology,' Michel repeated grimly.

Harry, bigger and heavier than Michel, got to his feet and shook his fist in Michel's face, cursing him, then bellowed, wanting to intimidate him: 'For the last time, PISS OFF!'

The others watched, delighted. 'You heard him!'

Harry threw the first punch. Michel sidestepped the telegraphed swipe. His gladiatorial eyes were unwavering as he clenched his right fist. With the speed of a scorpion strike, he delivered a one-knuckle punch with precision and power. A crack filled the air. He followed up with a second strike. And he was prepared to deliver a third, fourth, and fifth blow. Harry buckled, gritting his teeth. One look at his face signalled the end. It all happened so fast that when the chubby woman looked up from helping him, about to plead for mercy, Michel was nowhere to be seen.

After splashing seawater over himself, Michel, buoyed up by the afterglow of confrontation, jogged at pace back to the apartment. His exploits made him a mite peckish, so he ordered room service: mousaka, salad, and a small bottle of ouzo. He let the food digest and went out onto the balcony, yawned, and took out a filter-tipped cigar. He lit it and drew heavily.

Introduced to martial arts during a period of residency at a highly unorthodox foster home that belonged to a robed descendant of the great sensei, Yoshida Shoin, Michel became hooked when it helped him turn a bullying situation around. And, in spite of an unsettled lifestyle, he attained a black belt by the age of fifteen. He capped his education by learning about Bushido. Although linked to martial arts, Bushido was not a fighting discipline but rather a way of life, the way of the warrior. And it gave him a heightened sense of things.

From a ready stance, with heels apart, his hands and elbows became a blur as he repeated karate forms at top speed. Then he unleashed a twenty-minute salvo of fists and feet to build endurance. There was a time when he would spend four hours or more practicing every day. As he sat cross-legged on the floor, meditating, with his back straight and his eyes closed, the telephone rang. He did not answer. After a while he opened the shopping bag and removed the crossbows and the knives. He armed the first crossbow and set it down on the bedside locker nearest the door. The second, he placed on the leather chair. A knife, he left in the bathroom, the other, he stuffed under his pillow.

The extreme precautions he regularly employed when on foreign soil had paid dividends in the past. A few years ago, in Port Harcourt, a corporal in the Nigerian army had been assigned to protect an expensive piece of drilling equipment, imported by Michel and scheduled for transportation. Unfortunately, while on sentry duty, the soldier had fallen asleep and was subsequently demoted. Under the cover of darkness, the vengeful soldier had gained entry to Michel's hotel room. Alerted by the scent of the soldier's aftershave, Michel jumped from the bed, knife drawn. Even though the soldier possessed advanced fighting skills, and was heavily armed, Michel quickly fought him off.

Inside the apartment it was warm, the air-conditioning off hours ago. Michel lay on the bed, sparked a cigar and watched the plume of smoke waft upwards. His thoughts were tinged with regret. Nonetheless, he was delighted to have curbed his anger and not dealt Harry a more serious blow. He drifted off in semi-sleep, always alert, always ready.

CHAPTER 2

May had spent much of the day browsing her favourite stores, Selfridges and Harrods, and flexing her plastic friend. At 5ft, with a slim petite figure, she was spoilt for choice. Ably assisted by Celia, a personal shopper, she chose a Betty Barclay designed pink dress suit, a Dolce & Gabanna white blouse, etched with diamond effect beads, and rounded it all off with a pair of Louboutins peep-toe shoes. In the fitting-room, Celia considered May's outfit and then she disappeared. She returned with a ruby brooch and pinned it to May's lapel. Satisfied with their collaboration, the girls hugged and parted. On her way to the checkout, May noticed an insipid looking mannequin decked out in lingerie.

May wore no bra, as her pert firm breasts did not need support or embellishment. Also, she preferred the smooth contouring effect of a g-string and, as an afterthought, she added a royal blue g-string to her basket. Positively glowing, with her carrier bags in hand, she stopped off at Snips Salon for a wash and blow dry.

In the mood for a manicure and pedicure, she took a detour down an elegant boulevard. The beautician, a tall sandy haired woman, gassed non-stop while she stroked gingerly May's nails.

By the time May got home, Jenny, her flatmate, had already gone out on a date. It had been a long and tiring day, but nothing that

May could not wash away in a hot bath. Afterwards she brushed her teeth and rinsed her mouth. Next she filled a glass with mineral water and carried it into her bedroom. Then she crawled into bed and pulled the pink duvet over her head. At last she fell into a blissful sleep.

A foghorn of an alarm heralded the morning awakening of May Franks. She tried to open her eyes but they were stuck fast with sleep. The alarm clock had been buzzing for some time before Jenny boomed in from the adjoining room.
'Will you turn that useless thing off, or I'll throw it out the window. I'm going to get you the mother-of-all-alarms, with booster speakers, for your birthday,' she yelled.
Jenny, first in consternation and then in mounting fury, slammed the bedroom door.

They had shared the second-floor apartment, on the corner of Queensway and Westbourne Grove, for three years. Jenny had already spent two years in college before May, upon seeing an advertisement in the evening standard, arrived with her father to inspect the apartment. In spite of their disparate upbringings, the girls clicked instantly and became best of friends.

Born with a silver spoon in her mouth, May's parents were not a couple lacking principle and they had resisted the temptation to spoil their only child. Unfettered by protective wrappings, May never backed down from a dare and when barely out of her teens she completed her first bungee jump, and two years later, she demonstrated her burgeoning aerial prowess by pulling off a uniquely audacious parachute jump. Although frustrating at the time, her upbringing stood to her and made her shrewd beyond her years and kept her feet firmly on the ground. When the time came for her to move to London her parents took a softer line and substantially increased her allowance. Her wardrobe, unnecessarily compliant with the latest fashion, featured labels in the vein of Prada, Dior, Armani, Balenciaga and Versace.

Jenny, on the other hand, did not have an extravagant stipend at her disposal. She had the kind of childhood that did not revolve around the hottest fashion because she was too busy dealing with the harsh realities of life and her background toughened her up for the trials and tribulations of student life. She had to supplement her college grant by working in a bar at night and in a café on Saturday mornings. The product of an arranged marriage, she was one of five children, three older brothers and one younger sister. They grew up in the borough of Lambeth, initially residing in Brixton before moving to Streatham and finally settling down in Clapham. On the day that Jenny celebrated becoming a teenager, her mother died of breast cancer. Marked with a mature sadness, Jenny assumed a more maternal role, comforting her grieving sister and looking after her dad and her older brothers. After finishing her A-levels, she gained a place in College and left the crowded family home. Her sister took up the mantle of managing the house but called upon Jenny whenever a crisis loomed. As a result of her childhood experiences, Jenny espoused a very conservative approach to life, evident in the way she dressed. Seldom seen out and about in a skirt or stepping out in a pair of high heels, her tall frame was usually covered by a long flowing dress and her feet clad in a comfortable pair of moccasins. The relationship enjoyed by May and Jenny had blossomed into an older-younger sister bond. Although their friendship endured peaks and troughs, the girls set great store in loyalty and in times of trouble always turned to each other for help.

In the coming weeks, May would turn twenty-two and was looking forward with apprehension to starting her first real job. Her curriculum vitae, composed in the week after her last exam, held no account of part-time or seasonal work. In spite of this lack of worldly experience, she had been offered a plum position in the Information Technology department of National Bank plc. She believed with perfect certainty that her highly acclaimed thesis,

"Access control and biometrics", was the reason for her appointment.

Jenny, already an employee in the bank, earned a crust as a software developer. She had handed May's curriculum vitae into human resources and was thrilled when May got the call.

May finally silenced the alarm, stretched her arms above her head and kicked the duvet from off the bed. She stood up, touched her toes and did twenty star jumps before leaping onto the floor. Still trying to shake off her bed hair, she flipped open her mobile phone and checked for belated good luck messages.

One new message ran across the small screen.

She read the text: *Knock them for six, love mum and dad.*

She toddled off to the bathroom and performed her ablutions whilst humming the latest nightclub floor-filler.

Meanwhile, in the kitchen, Jenny, the early riser, was fully functional, rattling a saucepan or two, preparing breakfast. A technique she used oftentimes in the past to wake her sleepy brothers. She heard the toilet flush and a few minutes later May glided into the kitchen, barefoot and wearing a flannelette tee shirt that flopped modestly about her knees.

May exaggerated her breathing with the sensibility of a jester and then, with the back of one hand, she blocked her nostrils.

'Is that burnt toast I smell or is it a new perfume?' she joked.

'Damn it, remind me to buy a new toaster, that's the second slice I've burnt this morning,' Jenny said.

She flicked aside her side-swept fringe and used a knife to dislodge the shackled slice.

'Throw me on an egg, please, pretty please with sugar on top.' May, adept at getting her own way, deployed her bubbly charm.

'Okay, but only because it's your first day at work,' Jenny retorted blithely, and then, with menacing politeness, she continued, 'you're not even dressed, stop skiving and get a move on or you'll be late and I've no intention of waiting for you.'

Jenny waited until the moisture had evaporated from the boiled egg and then she yelled out. 'Your egg is ready.'

May, resplendent in her new finery, exercised her artistic talents by putting on her makeup. Her thoughts wandered affectionately to that of her mother, who had recommended the brand. She applied a touch of eye shadow to accentuate the blue of her fluorescent eyes, which stood out a mile, and then she brushed her long raven hair that reached down to the cleft of her buttocks. She painted her lips with a matte lipstick, and then dabbed a sprinkling of Paloma Picasso on her cleavage. Not yet satisfied, she selected a pink blusher from her vanity case and smiled widely in the mirror. She patted lightly the fullest part of her cheek. All done, she put her small white vanity case into the camel-haired briefcase, a family heirloom she had borrowed from her dad. She returned to the kitchen.

Jenny looked up from her breakfast and smiled, as a mother would do to her favourite child.

What a beautiful creature, Jenny thought, without a hint of jealousy. Not a blemish on that porcelain skin. The observation caused her to reflect upon a wearisome chore. In the quiet of the morning, while May slept, she had stolen into the bathroom and arduously plucked the dark hairs from under her nose, which if ignored, would in no time, form a thin, noticeable moustache. She promised herself a course of electrolysis and allowed a small sigh to escape her lips.

'Something wrong?' May enquired with a look of puzzlement.

'Nothing darling, what's with the briefcase?' Jenny asked.

'Image dear, it's all about image,' May laughed.

She opened the briefcase and showed the contents.

'What on earth? You're wearing makeup?' Jenny exclaimed.

This was the first time she had ever seen May with makeup on.

'Oh that! Image dear,' May repeated airily.

'You should wear a bra?' Jenny suggested diplomatically, not wishing to undermine May's confidence.

'Don't fuss so.' May scrutinised her cleavage. 'Why?'

'You know, an office environment and all that, you can clearly see the imprint of your nipples,' Jenny stated matter-of-factly.

'All I can say is, I don't have a bra, and yours won't fit, so the rest of them will have to grin and bear it,' May kidded.

'I'm sure they will,' Jenny commented ruefully, 'the men, definitely.'

'Are you in the mood for a game of squash this evening, after work?' May asked.

Jenny called out on her way out of the kitchen. 'No I'm meeting Tony and we're going to the movies. You're more than welcome to join us. I know you're going to like each other.'

'Whoa, your new boyfriend, you mean you're putting him before me, anyway you know the old saying: two's company, three's a crowd,' May said.

She gulped down the last of her egg.

'You haven't met him yet.' Jenny scratched her head and winced.

'Gooseberries are my least favourite fruit. Anyhow, you've only been going out with him for a couple of weeks,' May teased.

Within the hour the girls walked at go-getter pace up the west side of Queensway lined with luxury retail outlets and posh restaurants. They passed a red phone booth where a man in his early twenties was gluing pornographic cards above and below the handset. He lifted the handset and pretended to make a call. Distracted by him, Jenny walked into one of the posts supporting the glass-awning that covered the entrance to Bayswater tube station.

In the vortex of an up-swelling draft, she stopped to nurse her shoulder but May hadn't noticed, and kept on walking.

Jenny, still massaging her shoulder, managed to catch up with her halfway down the long flight of stairs.

'Hold on, May! That bloody fool caused me to bang my shoulder,' she said breathlessly.

'You should've just ignored him, like I did,' May told her as they passed under a suspended Bayswater sign, crowned with green and yellow horizontal bars.

They were herded down an aisle.

Quarter ways down the congested platform Jenny jerked May back from the anti-suicide pit. Her nervousness stemmed from the time a crazed man, who had been standing beside her, jumped in front of an oncoming train. It was a salutatory glimpse into a society where wealth had become the principal measure of worth. Impoverished people, down on their luck and desperate for warmth, would often spend a whole day squatting awkwardly in carriages that looped endlessly an area encircling three of the busiest stations, the hub of the city's life: Paddington, Kings Cross and Liverpool Street. Sometimes, down-at-heels had a ticket, but more often than not, they were ticket-less. A circumstance that forced them to change carriages or hop off and wait for the next train in order to avoid garrulous ticket inspectors on the prowl. On that ill-fated day, downtrodden and rejected, a beggar cloaked in tattered obscurity decided to end it all publicly. Forgotten, never to be remembered, one last heartfelt act.

The low profile train rolled in with reckless abandon, whipping up the dust, packed as usual with only standing room. In the cramped conditions, bottled up commuters shuffled and etched a corridor. In the grim insanity of the early morning rush hour, the underground invariably portrayed the multi-ethnic spirit of the city's ancient order, cultivated by centuries of conquest and decades of absorption. Young professionals, habituated to discipline, decked out in pinstriped suits, perused the pink papers. Immersed in the sound of music, denizens wearing earphones closed their eyes and nodded in sync to a quietened beat. Dog-eared novels captivated the less melodious. In a world of their own, contemplating the tasks before them.

When May entered the carriage, a reprieve was granted. Both men and women made the effort. Like a miracle, her beauty conjured up mixed emotions. A woman to be seduced and adored, unspoken admiration, jealousy and lust; these were the sensations that permeated the carriage.

Sapped by a rocking motion, the novelty quickly wore off and everyone retreated into the comfort zone of inarticulate anonymity, the pithy respite lost.

It was a far cry from the environment in which May grew up. The apron strings not yet completely severed, she spent her precious weekends and holidays in the place of her childhood, at her parents' home in Wiltshire. While still only an infant, her parents, Charles and Jane, had purchased a house built in the early 1800s for a cool two million sterling and pumped another five hundred thousand into refurbishment and repair. She loved that house with as much strength of sentiment as she hated London, Harrods and Selfridges excluded.

Especially the beautiful gardens she helped tend since a young child. Even though Niall, the groundsman, was not expected to work weekends, he gambled on the likelihood May would turn up in her Wellingtons, so he always set aside a little job, which for one reason or another required urgent attention. Husbandry was a passion May inherited from her mother, who had been born and reared on the border of a river valley deep in the Yorkshire dales, surrounded by wild moors on the Eastern Pennine uplands.

Gardening and a love of animals helped nourish and maintain a youthful exuberance, which even London failed to dampen. She missed Skippy, her Alsatian. It was not practical to bring Skippy to London, so she had to be content with brief re-acquaintances afforded by weekend visits.

Over the years, she had developed an aversion to the underground; an urban fabric denuded of nature's beautiful creations, speed of transit and opportunities for self-advancement its only saving grace. Her dad pleaded with her to come and work for him, leapfrog her peers, but she refused, no short cuts. The density, the ambivalences and the absurdity of city life all infuriated May. She only tolerated this underworld unpleasantness, inherently offensive to her vision of life, as a means to an end. She relished the chance to step on the corporate ladder and climb, rung by rung, to the upper reaches of a male-dominated preserve.

Eventually, they arrived at the Embankment tube station. The girls endeavoured to stay together, so they waited for the crush to subside before exiting. They walked at a brisk pace down Villiers Street and merged with an endless stream of rail users spilling out from Charing Cross Station. The girls crossed the Strand and proceeded along Bedford Street, then cut right down King Street. They caught up with some barrow boys noisily rolling their stock through the quaint passages leading off Market Square.

The flea market, outside of Market Square, was in full swing. The faces of traders and customers, haggling over prices, presented a bizarre old-world charm.

As they walked, Jenny quizzed May. 'How's your tummy?'

'Fine, a little bit nervous. Remind me again, what's this guy Richard Gardiner like? He sounded okay on the phone, no small talk, just technical questions about my thesis, where I got my ideas from and what were my research methods,' May said.

May tried to picture him in her mind.

'I don't know much about him. We see very little of him in our area, but according to one of the girls working in the information security department he doesn't say a lot and he very rarely attends meetings. Apparently, I've not verified this mind; rumour has it that he's chairman of Secure Span. Believe it or not, Secure Span owns fifty-one percent of National Bank. So, you should feel very privileged he conducted your phone interview,' Jenny joked.

'Privileged?' May queried.

'Yes, normally they don't do phone interviews. Usually, interviews are conducted with a three to four person panel. When I did my interview, there were three, one from human resources and two from the computer programming department.'

May laughed. 'They probably saw my curriculum vitae and decided we must have her at all costs before some other company snaps her up.'

'May, you better stay in the job for at least six months or I'll miss out on my two thousand pounds finders-fee. After all, it was I who handed in your curriculum vitae.' Jenny reminded May, having already spent the money in her mind: a new entertainment centre, a nice little holiday abroad, and a small sum left over for the electrolysis job.

She wondered if Tony would be interested in a vacation, but she thought it prudent to wait and see how things develop before broaching the subject.

'Well, it's not really a national bank if it's owned by another company, and I won't be railroaded into anything.' May backtracked hastily.

'True, but when privatisation became our government's core policy; our esteemed leaders were prepared to gamble with state assets. It was the first state owned organisation floated on the stock exchange,' Jenny expressed herself in high-flown terms.

'Did you buy any shares?' May looked perplexed.

'I didn't have any spare cash at the time,' Jenny replied.

'You should have told me. I would have bought some,' May said in a strangled voice.

'I would've, but you were on holidays, and I had no way of contacting you,' Jenny answered haughtily.

'Fair enough, that must have been when mum and I went to Aspen.' May regretted the missed opportunity.

  They stood in front of the tall glass building that dominated all other structures on James Street. The bronzed letters THE NATIONAL BANK Plc hovered above the formidable entrance. May betrayed not the slightest hesitation and she took a deep breath. But it was daunting clambering into the biggest revolving doors she had ever seen, continually rotating with a steady influx of employees. Across the marble-tiled floor, beneath a ceiling sheathed in cameras, loomed an elevated security desk. Three security guards manned from an inflated height. Jenny approached the desk, and addressed one of the guards, an officious rotund man with a walrus moustache. Jenny's eyes were trained on the man's moustache, praying the hairs under her nose would never reach such follicle strengths, roll on the electrolysis.

'Good morning, this is my friend May Franks, and this is her first day, so she needs a key- card and a...'

The guard interrupted. 'Ah yes, Miss Franks, we were instructed to phone Mr Gardiner as soon as you arrived.'

'Would you care to take a seat in the lobby. You'll find a coffee percolator with freshly ground coffee and a selection of biscuits. I'll ring Mr Gardiner, immediately.'

Jenny turned towards May. 'Would you like me to wait with you?'

'No, Jenny, I'll be fine.'

'Ok, best of luck,' Jenny said.

She ran her key-card over the reader and the light turned green. The retracted turnstile allowed her through and she made her way to the bank of lifts. She glanced in the direction of the waiting area, occupied solely by May. A thinly disguised pensive look fluttered across May's face as she munched a biscuit and placed a cup on the coffee table.

A bell chimed and interrupted Jenny's observations. The doors opened and she pressed button number four. The doors slid shut. She looked at her watch, nine o' clock and wondered what the day held in store.

 May looked at the clock hanging above the brass plate engraved with LONDON. Fifteen minutes before the hour of ten.

The flow of employees powering the revolving doors had tapered off to a trickle. A motorbike courier strode with purpose to the security desk. The walrus-moustached guard pointed to a sign, "All couriers must remove their helmets upon entering the building". The courier, with one nervous eye on May, duly obliged, and he handed a sealed package to the guard. On his way out, he could not help but stare at

May, and he almost tripped over the mat. Embarrassed, he sheepishly put his helmet back on and left post haste.

May giggled before pouring herself a third cup of coffee. She was becoming less nervous and more annoyed at having to wait. Matters were made worse by the fact there was nothing to read.

The security guard must have read her thoughts.

'Miss Franks, Mr Gardiner just phoned and asked me to give you his apologies, he has been delayed but should arrive in fifteen minutes. There are newspapers and magazines on the table at the other side of the main entrance. Sorry, I didn't mention it earlier.'

She stretched her legs and selected the current issue of Newsweek. It might look good if Richard Gardiner arrived and saw her reading a prestigious publication. Her bladder was bursting at the seams, so she crossed her legs.

She could not hold it any longer.

Desperately, she looked about for any sign of a WC. Finally, she relinquished and asked the guard where the loos were.

'So sorry Miss, I should've shown them to you earlier. I didn't realise you'd be waiting so long. Over there, to the left of the security turnstiles,' the guard said flatly.

Leaving her briefcase under the coffee table, she made a beeline for the masked door, barely discernible from the partition wall, and she rushed to the ladies. Luckily there was a vacant cubicle, otherwise she'd have peed her g-string. She pushed open the door and breathed a sigh of relief. She groped for the toilet roll and then she lingered for a while, listening to the gentle strains of piped music. She lathered her hands with perfumed soap.

She was about to refresh her makeup when she realised that she had left her briefcase in reception. Suddenly, a pounding siren, with an ominous resonance, shook the foundations of the building. Unsteadily, she entered the reception area only to be greeted by a shocking spectacle. Employees were being shepherded through an emergency exit by fire officers, wearing luminous orange jackets. One of the officers spotted May and roughly grabbed her by the arm.

He pulled her to an ordered line of vacating personnel. No sooner had they emerged, however, than they were rounded up and led off to join other evacuees, day-trippers and out-of-towners.

Approximately two hundred and fifty metres from the building, police officers were instructing the vacating crowd to remain behind the yellow-and-black tape strung across the road. Fascinated, the crowd watched the wild scenes. May strained her neck to see if she could spot Jenny amongst the throng of people whose numbers bristled with more and more evacuees from surrounding office blocks. Jenny had been ushered through an emergency exit at the back of the building and was frantically searching for May.

A girl, standing beside May, asked a policeman, 'what's going on?'

He replied in a curt tone, 'bomb alert.'

Immediately, May's thoughts switched to the courier who just delivered the sealed package.

A task force, equipped with a 20 tonne, specially designed bombproof truck laden with the latest in bomb disposal technology, screeched to a halt outside the main entrance. The crowd watched excitedly as the door of the truck flew open and officers in full protective gear lowered a robotic contraption. The officers then jumped back inside the truck. Minutes later the robot sprung to life. It whizzed around before moving forwards, staccato-like. It blazed a trail towards the entrance of the building, leaving a spoor of oil in its wake.

The robot, controlled by engineers from the back of the truck, zigzagged across the tiled floor. With no time to waste, it hunted swiftly. Guided by a camera protruding from its rectangular forehead, it quickly located its quarry. The robot honed in on the object and showed no mercy. It whisked away the offending article.

May had that sinking feeling that she was somehow responsible. She gasped, putting her hands to her mouth and squeezed tight her eyes. She was mortified. She cringed when she saw the robot whirr busily out of the building, holding in its crablike pincers something she instantly recognised. She wanted to hide, jump down the nearest manhole or take the first train back to Wiltshire, and leave the capital forever. Assuredly, the robot lowered the briefcase and shoved it inside a bombproof module. The engineers, sitting in the back of the truck, then x-rayed the briefcase. Within minutes, the engineers erupted into raucous laughter; the contents of the briefcase were displayed onscreen. Immediately, they radioed the supervising officer. He did not share their merriment.

The yellow-and-black tape was cut and the people were allowed back to their place of work. May waited until there were only a few isolated pockets of stragglers, and the streets were empty of police. She slowed her usual quick step to a snail's pace. She re-entered the building, feeling guilty and neglectful. In the lobby, the supervising police officer was arguing vociferously with a Chinese man, who remained defiant. Japanese men, wearing black suits and sunglasses, surrounded the Chinese man. The supervising police officer growled as he passed, and the oriental group, led by the Chinese man, hopped into the first available lift. The walrus-moustached security guard called May aside and explained to her what had happened.

May, visibly embarrassed by the whole fiasco, went straight to the toilets, with the briefcase firmly cosseted. She sat on the loo thinking of ways to explain the condition of the briefcase to her father. She took a few deep breaths and returned to the lobby.
After reading the sign above the seat, where she had been sitting, "Please do not leave you possessions unattended", she was furious with herself. With an appearance of normality, she picked up the discarded copy of Newsweek and flicked absentmindedly through the pages.
'None of this would have happened if that idiot Gardiner was punctual,' she muttered under her breath. She looked again under her seat to make sure the briefcase was still there.
It's really ineffective to be nervous, get perspective, a little voice whispered.

CHAPTER 3

It was morning in Crete, clear skies, no rain and very little wind. Fingers of light shaped an orb that caught every tint and shade of the pockmarked wall. Outside, yellow plumed warblers harvested the copious supply of insects and earthworms. The busy birds, demanding to be noticed, squabbled noisily over the choicest meats. A musical mimicry that liberated Michel from a restless night's sleep plagued by unpleasant dreams and horrid visions that left him in a semi-consciousness state, chilled to his bones. Never at peace, never at ease, his slumber had fallen prey to a fusion of mystical influences.

In the worst of his nightmares, an ethereal presence combed the air. A biblical figure, dressed in rags. His right arm wrapped in hardened bandages, a stump concealed. A thick mane of grey hair flailed wildly in the desert wind. In his left hand, he brandished a crooked staff and signalled gestures of despair to hordes of impish people, similarly dressed, whose arms were afflicted with open wounds that worsened as they scrimped and scraped. Michel watched a cloud of sand rise up on the horizon. An imperial legion of the roman army fanned out over the sand dune vastnesses that stretched beyond them, a view in constant motion, sliding, pulsating, gleaming. A trumpet sounded. Detached from his cohort, a centurion broke into a steady trot. The stench of decomposing flesh grew stronger. Parched and hungry, a wandering untouchable clawed at her face, awash with lesions. Over her festering sores, flies swarmed eagerly. The sand beneath her feet transformed into a pool of clear rainwater. Below the surface, a small quantity of bronze, silver and gold coins glistened in the sun, each one a link with monarchs of the past. Her feet were stuck fast, the pool deepened, she lifted her face to the sky and screamed. She was slowly sinking, swallowed up by the liquefying sands. Lying on the bed, Michel was powerless to intercede. The soothsayer knelt on his knobbly knees and lapped the water as a dog would. He drank his fill and shook his head, then turned towards Michel with saddened eyes that gradually dissolved into empty hollows. His stare cast a seditious and hypnotic spell, but Michel resisted the pull and shortened his focus. Forebodingly, the spectre raised his disfigured arm and pointed the stubbed end. A silver musket burst forth from the dirt-ridden bandages, its lethal payload discharged. Michel watched the silver bullet inch towards him. He moved to the right, but the trajectory of the bullet altered to compensate. There seemed no escape. Dropping to the ground, he noticed a gem-encrusted scroll. He reached for it. The golden transcript unfurled of its own accord and appeared to melt in his grasp. A young girl exuded from the viscous ink and handed him a gilded sword. The sword was so heavy that he had to use both hands to hold it, but even then he could not wield it. At the last possible second, the onrushing centurion, wearing jewelled armour, sprinted to his aid. Jointly they swung the sword, and parried the oncoming bullet, but when the metals clanged together the primordial mirage vanished.

Michel lazed for some time, holding his fist to his brow, chewing over the cruel apparition of apocalypse. Its meaning eluded him. Life wants me on the edge, he thought, letting his mind wander. He disarmed the crossbows and then he mused, perhaps it meant nothing at all. Sleepy-headed, naked and loose, he tottered into the bathroom, stuck a toothbrush into his mouth and took a leak. After an early morning swim, a brutal workout that left him panting, he removed one of the envelopes hidden behind the print on the wall and opened it. He stepped outside onto the balcony and shuffled a piece of paper around in the air. Sitting on the balcony rail, he tapped a string of characters into his new sat-phone. After that, breathing easier, he made a call.

The sat-phone at the other end of the link pealed noisily and was answered immediately.

'Hello Michel, it's good to hear your voice,' Richard Gardiner said at once; ready to leap like a serf to his lord's bidding. He was the most able and high-flying of all the lieutenants attached to Michel's sphere of interest, a man who always got the job done. Richard knew it was Michel, since that satellite channel was reserved for his use only.

Four years ago, Secure Span had begun launching proprietary state-of-the-art satellites exclusively for their own enterprises, which were religiously protected, even from the courting attentions of governmental agencies. Richard did indeed try to persuade Michel to offer Secure Span satellites for lease or hire but Michel was unreceptive to the idea. The crux was Michel's insistence that security far outweighed any business argument, though, in the longer term, the potential of a spin-off venture had sown the seed for a new and exciting profit model. Naturally, there was a huge rush of interest when Secure Span began to offer handpicked customers the use of their launching service. Sited in equatorial waters, it proved substantially cheaper than comparative land launches.

It was mainly communication satellites that were jettisoned into orbit, remotely controlled by operatives stationed upon an inconspicuous ship anchored six kilometres away. In the last year alone, the heavily customised oilrig had launched thirty satellites without a single mishap. Launching satellites was only a sideline for

Secure Span. With each year that passed Michel's crown of tentacles spread further. There was no withstanding him. No opportunity was wasted.

'Hi Richard, did I wake you?' Michel enquired.
'No, I'm on my way to London, should be there in an hour or so.' Richard sat slouched in the car seat, dark shadows under his purple-rimmed eyes. The slow build up to Ravel's Boléro gathered momentum. An orchestral interpretation that helped him relax.
His jaguar cruised steadily along the M60.
Rain spattered against the windscreen and muffled the swishing sound of the swaying wipers.
'Good. Is everything prepared for this afternoon's senior management meeting?' Michel asked.
'Yep, it sure is. I've double-checked your proposal and our legal department has trebled-checked every risk. We're ready to rock and roll,' Richard enthused.

He had never met anyone like Michel. An encounter with such a visionary was very rare. Five years previously, during a long tenure at a well-established accountancy firm, where he qualified as a chartered accountant, he had been assigned to Michel's account. After a few get-togethers, Richard quickly learned that Michel possessed a selfish streak, a cold-blooded nature, a dogged ability to do exactly as he pleased and a capacity to shut out the rest of the world. But Michel was also a benign and a highly refined man, a theorist and a logician, steeped in culture, and he possessed a genuine concern for his staff.
Richard realised from his involvement in the affairs of industrialists, that these were essential virtues of any businessman with aspirations of greatness. Inveterate in his prejudices, Michel was also passionate in his allegiances. Enticed by Michel's charismatic vision of building one of the world's largest business empires, Richard decided to enter Michel's service. In the years following his appointment, Richard spent a good deal of time working closely with Michel, but despite

this, he knew very little about him. However, Michel was well acquainted with every facet of the Gardiner household and indeed any person that Richard had dealings with, no matter how insignificant.

'Fine. Richard there's no need to whisper, this is a secure link. I know we've dabbled in the insurance market on a number of occasions, but the main point I want to get across is that nine out of twenty companies are borrowing to meet the exorbitant costs associated with insurance premiums. This time round we can influence market trends and be in a position to offer organisations much more competitive premiums.'
Michel outlined the scheme with verve.
'A win, win situation. How many insurance companies do you have in mind?' Richard asked.
Michel then suggested, with great fervour. 'In order to satisfy the competition authority, we'll target one major player through National Bank, and if we get the all-clear, subsequent acquisitions will be made by our South American holding companies.'
'Should work,' Richard beamed proudly, as if it was his idea.
'The second point of importance, but not in any way related, I want to make sure that our technical divisions and purchasing people complete an inventory of all hardware. Any equipment assembled with power regulators that can be traced back to Thailand must be destroyed and replaced,' Michel instructed querulously.
'Sure, may I ask why?' Richard quizzed.
After a pause, Michel said, 'don't laugh, when I tell you. A couple of employees of a leading American electronics component producer stole a formula used in the manufacture of power regulators. Unfortunately, the thieves did not copy the whole formula, so when they returned to Thailand to produce the regulators, devices throughout the marketplace began to show signs of leakage.'
Richard was in mid-reply when a juggernaut flashed its full beams. His jaguar was guilty of hogging the fast lane, much to the angst of

those behind. He glanced at the speedometer, fifty-five mph. He swerved recklessly into the middle lane. All the windows were fogged up, the rain even heavier. He flicked the wipers to full. The juggernaut roared by. The driver showed his displeasure by spewing up a torrent of muddy water. A loose stone, churned up by the car in front, ricocheted off the windscreen.

Unnoticed by Richard, a tiny fork-crack appeared at the base of the windscreen.

'Are you still there?' Michel asked.

'Sure am. Have you any idea who the culprits are?' asked a bemused Richard.

'No, I'm not concerned at the moment, but I will be if we're inconvenienced in any way,' Michel answered. Then he quickly changed the subject.

'I want to increase our share capital in National Bank to 63 percent, can you set the wheels in motion?'

'I'll look into it right away.' But Richard knew in his heart that it would prove tricky. Stockholders were reluctant to sell blue-chip shares, and forfeit enormous dividends. The bearish market would also make it more difficult for buyers to induce investors to offload their shares.

'Before close of business, can you organise a money transfer to the Minoan Ministry of culture?' Michel let his brain estimate the odds before arriving at a figure that would leave the minister in no doubt and, hopefully, act as a sweetener when it came to tendering for the contract for a large-scale energy operation.

'Who shall I make it payable to?' Richard had never heard of that particular Ministry.

'The Minoan Ministry of culture,' Michel repeated testily.

He took the Cretan print off the wall and gave it a gentle shake.

'How much do you want transferred, and to what account?' Richard queried.

'Fifteen million, ledger it as a donation.' Michel opened a second envelope and read out an account number.

'Just a moment.' Richard pulled into a motorway stop and turned off the engine.

It was lot of money, but that didn't faze him. He was used to dealing with large sums. Besides, it was Michel's capital.

Richard reread aloud the account number.

'Spot on, by the way, how's Margaret and the kids?' Michel enquired.

'Great, Esther was delighted with the present you sent her. She looked like a little doll in her first-communion dress,' a chuffed Richard replied.

'Glad to hear it, you probably won't hear from me until the day after tomorrow.' Michel was about to hang up when Richard, putting his hands on the steering wheel, shouted. 'Oh! By the way.'

'Yes,' Michel spoke abruptly.

'I'm scheduled to meet Miss Franks this morning. What's an appropriate placement for her?' Richard's voice grew hoarse.

Michel mulled over the question. He thought of Pat Hogan, who had worked his way into a position of trust within Secure Span, despite an inauspicious start, and had vindicated Chen's instinctive decision to spare his life.

'She should report to Pat Hogan and while your at it, give Declan Mills a call. Miss Franks will feel a lot more comfortable if someone she knows is about the place. Richard, be seeing you shortly.'

The link went dead. Richard placed the phone back in its cradle. He was perspiring, as was always the case after a conversation with Michel. Overburdened by demands on his attention that appeared limitless, he turned the key in the ignition and then he took a moment to reflect on his career to date.

Occasionally, he questioned the commitment demanded and energy expended in order to manage an ever-increasing workload. By the nature of his duties, he found himself working far longer hours than most, but he reckoned it was a price worth paying. It also, not coincidentally, made him a very wealthy man, but often the stress that accompanied such affluence was hard to deal with.

However, on the plus side of the argument, life was certainly exciting and to recall the last mundane day at work, an occupational hazard, he would have to think back to before he joined Secure Span. In little more than five years Richard had established himself as a key player in the city.

At the pool bar, outside in the sunlight, Michel lit a cigar, took a sip of his juice and ordered a light breakfast, and then he remembered the main reason for his visit.

After breakfast, he walked through the pool area where some holidaymakers were busying themselves reserving prime locations. Their tropical-coloured towels were unrolled across advantageously placed sun-beds.

He left the complex to gradually climb up a winding road until he reached the top of a hill. As he came over the crest, he observed labourers, without hard hats, working on an already occupied house. Even though the second storey was a roofless shell, the family had moved in the moment they deemed the ground floor habitable. It was only when the family had secured additional funding would the building of the second storey recommence.

When he heard the chirrup of his sat-phone, Michel stopped in his tracks.

'Hi Toyoko, you're bang on time, our watches must be synchronised.' He stopped on the crest of the hill and stared down.

'They must be.' His secretary scanned the list she held in her hand. Whenever Michel was abroad, she contacted him at the same time every morning, 9:00am.

'You've just received an invitation to the mayor's annual ball, how should I respond?' She already knew the answer, but hoped against hope he might ask her.

'I won't be able to make it,' he replied dryly.

'Okay. Sheikh Ra wants to know why the Warbah construction project is behind schedule.'

She coughed and blew her nose.

'Have you a cold?' he asked. 'Why don't you take the rest of the day off?'

'It's only a sniffle, besides I have too much to do,' she replied with a tiny splutter.

'Tell him there was an imbalance in the composition of the last consignment of concrete. The problem has been rectified and we should be back on course by the middle of next week,' he paused, 'to be on the safe side, tell him a fortnight.'

'Let me see, what's next?'

She crossed that item off her list and continued with typical efficiency until Michel had addressed each issue.

'Thanks Toyoko, what would I do without you?' he said with a short laugh.

'You'd manage quite all right. I'll leave you in peace,' she countered, chuckling as she hung up.

Michel set out for the five-star hotel he surveyed the previous day. The sunlight was dazzling. In no time, he arrived at the main gate. An overzealous security guard, standing between two large sandstone pillars, anxious to prevent undesirables from taking advantage of the hotel's exclusive private beach, challenged him when he tried to pass. Michel explained that he was merely calling upon a resident and allayed the guard's fears by drawing attention to the fact that he had no swimwear on his person. With a gnarled hand, the guard unceremoniously waved him through, his attention now firmly fixed on a couple of teenagers skulking along the far side of the road, their heads down, trying in vain to keep their towels out of view.

Michel walked through the open gates.

He walked through the foyer toward the reception desk.

'Hi, would you be so kind as to let Dr Cartwright know that Michel Trebeh would like to speak to her.' He then added, 'it's in relation to the Gouves excavation.'

He casually took in his surroundings.

An elaborate mahogany bookcase, towering over a large settee, caught his attention.
The receptionist checked the hotel database with her long, beautiful hands, and then she phoned Greta's room.

Greta Cartwright, a plain woman in her late twenties, examined a box file containing black and white photographs, folios, notes and rough sketches. She placed the box file on the bed and then she plucked the least filthy garment from a mound of unwashed clothing, abandoned in the middle of the room. Startled by the buzz of the phone sitting on the crowded bedside table, she dropped a pale orange jersey.
'Hey, Dmitri you're late,' Greta blurted out whilst fumbling with the collarless garment.
'Dr Cartwright, sorry to disturb you, this is Francesca here in reception. There's a Mr Trebeh wishing to speak to you.'
Francesca smiled at Michel.
'Pardon me; I thought you were my assistant.' Greta rearranged her black angular spectacles. 'Who would like to speak to me?'
'Mr Trebeh,' Francesca repeated, 'regarding the Gouves excavation.'
'I don't know anyone by that name but tell Mr Trebeh I'll join him in the lobby. I'll be there in ten minutes.'

  The name Trebeh did ring a bell, but Greta couldn't recall the context. Grumbling, she slipped into a pair of shapeless jeans and eased her head through the jersey's thin neck. She became flustered when her spectacles tumbled from her nose. Eventually, she gathered her composure. She sprayed her armpits with a lemony deodorant, and then she scrunched her feet into a pair of boots.
While she searched for her straw hat, which she found tucked away under the bed, chunks of red clay crumbled off her boots onto the carpet.
She fetched the most significant photographs, papers and sketches from the box file. Now her mind was working well. She bounced two steps at a time down the flight of stairs, almost stumbling on the

last step, and then she trotted through the corridor toward reception. Her mane of auburn hair was waving from side to side.

In reception, while attempting to prevent one of the sketches from escaping her grasp, she was reduced to muttering.

'Hi, I'm Dr Cartwright, someone rang my room saying there was a Mr Trebeh wishing to see me.'

'Ah! Yes, Dr Cartwright, I'm Francesca and the gentleman is over there by the bookcase.' Francesca pointed politely to where Michel sat.

'Thanks a million.' Greta headed for the plush suede suite, wondering if he was an emissary from one of the time-honoured institutions, perhaps seeking her consent to publish one of her papers.

Michel hesitated. Then his face softened. He closed the dusty book devoted to Greek mythology, which he had yanked from one of the crammed bookshelves, and got to his feet. With long purposeful strides, Greta reached the turquoise rug on which he stood. She threw out a hand and was shocked by the strength of his handshake. The string of her straw hat, which ringed her baby finger, unravelled. She apologised and retrieved her fallen hat. He stepped back and studied her. Before leaving London, he had reread the dossier on Dr Greta Cartwright a number of times, and he was more than pleased with the way the excavation at Gouves was being run. Archaeology was not just a job for her; it was a unique way of life. Her work ethic and enthusiasm more than made up for her lack of organisational skills and an obvious reluctance in formalising acceptable documentation. But while he was happy to identify himself, he was careful not to appear pretentious.

'Hello, Dr Cartwright, it's a pleasure to finally make your acquaintance. Allow me introduce myself, my name is Michel Trebeh and I'm the proprietor of All Materials BV.'

A flummoxed expression drifted across her face.

'The company which sponsors your noble work here in Gouves.' He spoke formally but in a friendly manner.

His words hung in the air, filled with resonance.
She could feel the warmth rising in her cheeks and she replied before it got the better of her.
'Oh, forgive me! Mr Trebeh, I'm so grateful for the generous funding we've received. You really don't know how much it means to us. Assistance from organisations such as yours makes it possible for us to solve the mysteries of the past. I didn't recognise your name, on account of always having dealt with Fobie,' she said.
Her darkening freckles enhanced the appeal of her outdoorsy face.
Michel acquiesced modestly.
She could not help but stand and stare. The resemblance was uncanny. Seven years ago, she had worked on a pyramid restoration project and, while doing so, she discovered a bust, in remarkably good condition, of an Egyptian Pharaoh, Ramses II, who ruled Egypt for 66 years. The bust had been buried in a hidden compartment deep within a tomb, his identity written on the wall.
'Please, sit down, Dr Cartwright. As you probably know, Fobie takes care of day-to-day business in Holland, and it was during one of our meetings he remarked upon your partiality for all things chocolate, so I've taken the liberty of ordering you a hot chocolate.'
He projected good-natured cordiality and invited her to sit beside him.
'Do please sit down,' he repeated.
Obediently she did as she was ordered.
They conversed in a heavy, serious way.
Acutely conscious that his eye was upon her, she did not meet his gaze. Embarrassed, she looked away. Fobie had failed to warn her of Michel's visit and to make matters worse her assistant was late. She recognised wealth when she saw it, and having no wish to loose his favour, hurried to please.
'I must confess, I indulge my penchant for chocolate more often than I should. Please call me Greta,' she pleaded guiltily, after a tremulous laugh.

She reconciled herself to making a good impression, bearing in mind that patrons were hard to come by, and when found, guarded jealously from peers. Heretofore, any application she had submitted to cover contingencies or overruns were satisfied without question or the need to justify costs. To lose her precious sponsor would undoubtedly bring the excavation to a premature end.

'Thanks Greta, please call me Michel. So tell me, how's the dig proceeding?' He deliberately used layman terms to put her at ease.

She turned to face him, her breasts puffed up, exultant, all qualms and uncertainties banished and a new conviction in place. Then, in a polite tone, she began. Her whole demeanour changed to that of a bubbly young girl, recounting excitedly events and obstacles since the dig began, delving into every appreciative detail and expressing herself eloquently. She spoke straight from the heart, nakedly and without embellishment. Michel heard the pride in her voice and it inspired him. He listened intently to her reprise of enchanted landmarks and became caught up in the infectious imagery conjured up by her animated words. Although she paused to catch her breath, her hands moved non-stop. Then, in order to emphasise a milestone, she produced a hand drawn sketch of a discovered artefact and dropped it onto his lap. It was an inspiring reminder of a time when civilisation was beginning to reveal its treasures, its intricacies and its miseries.

A waiter arrived, carrying a silver tray. In the excitement of sharing her passion, Greta forgot her manners. She gulped down the mug of hot chocolate. It was not long before the silver tray became an auxiliary store for viewed photographs and discarded notes. Michel suppressed a smile. By then, he had five sketches of decorated pottery resting on his lap, including two sketches revealing different aspects of the same vase. She had sketched the black-ink drawings on plastic sheets of graphed permatrace, creating a personal record of her discoveries. Michel was amazed by the high quality of her penmanship.

Just in case she left anything out, she frequently referred to notes, barely readable. Michel scrutinised her disjointed notes and wondered if her assistant, Dmitri, was the right man for the job.

The hours went by imperceptibly for both of them. As she neared the end of an extensive discourse, she glanced sideways and measured him carefully. He seemed genuinely captivated by her chronicled account, and her confidence grew tenfold.

A young man, with a sparse beard and an uneasy gawp, suddenly appeared. Greta discerned a presence and instinctively covered her papers to protect her work. She relaxed back into the suede wrinkles of the settee. Nonchalantly, she looked up at the man standing beside her.

Dmitri spoke sheepishly, 'I'm so sorry. My car conked out at a set of traffic lights in the centre of Heraklion and it wouldn't start, so I had to push it to the nearest car park and then I had to find a bus to bring me here.'

'Dmitri, you're here at last. Michel this is Dmitri Liberopoulos, my assistant, a graduate from the university of Athens. In truth, a godsend, so organised and so unlike me, but it seems punctuality is not his strong point.' Michel detected a trace of mirth in Greta's voice. 'He has transcribed every written word into legible English, and if you like, he can provide you with a duplicate set. Dmitri, this is Michel Trebeh, the owner of the company sponsoring our excavation.'

'If I could get a copy before I leave, that would be great,' Michel said.

Michel removed the sketches from his lap and stood up. He shook Dmitri's hand; his grip was sure and firm. Michel retracted his initial judgement

'I think there is a spare set in Dr Cartwright's room.' Dmitri then added softly. 'Thank you, for your kindness, your support means the world to us.'

Michel was about to sit down when he heard Greta's voice rocket across the lobby. 'Fobieeeeee.'

It took her two attempts to break free from the grip of the suede settee, and without compunction she legged headlong towards the tall, barrel-chested, powerfully built man. Fobie wore an effervescent Hawaiian shirt, with the collar open, which exposed a broad neck the same width as his woolly-haired head. The wraparound ray-bans disguised any emotion he may have felt when Greta jumped up and pecked him on the cheek. She admonished him for not letting her in on the surprise visit and for spreading rumours about her chocolate fixation.

He tugged on his shirt and rearranged himself. Her sloe eyes looked seriously irate and Fobie seemed momentarily taken aback by the severity of her words.

She had met the man from Uganda by chance in the Natural History Museum. It was Fobie who had petitioned the Gouves excavation upon hearing of her plight when they spoke for the first time in earnest beneath a Tyrannosaurus skeleton in the main gallery of the National History Museum. Previously, in a bid to source funding, she had poked her nose into every nook and cranny of the corporate world. Won over by her enthusiasm and energy, Fobie felt obliged to advance her cause and solicited support from Michel. Two days later, Michel arranged for All Materials BV to finance the excavation.

'Fobie, Why didn't you tell me you were coming to Crete, and, is it true, that this Michel Trebeh owns All Materials. He seems so young to own such a big company?' Greta scolded, making sure that Michel was out of earshot.

'I was asked to drop everything and fly to Crete on the first available flight. And Yes, Michel is the owner of All Materials. Don't you remember me telling you that on the day we raised the funding?'

Fobie answered, recovering from the warm yet over demonstrative reception, which he tried initially to play down.

Michel was amused by the royal welcome and inwardly smiled.
Their embrace was not the embrace of friends. The closeness between the two and their contentment as they later worked together sparked Michel into instigating a low-key inquiry. Sure enough, the satellite images, stamped for his eyes only, showed an unclad Fobie teaching traditional African dance, around a small twig fire, to a pliant and completely naked Greta on a moonstruck beach. The relationship had been flourishing for months. Michel chose to turn a blind eye.

Fobie and his older brother, Okot, had been granted refugee status by the Dutch government after they fled their native Uganda to escape the terrible legacy bequeathed by a flesh-eating despot. Shortly afterwards, Okot was killed in a car accident, leaving Fobie to fend for himself. He acquired citizenship and set about gaining an education through night classes, eventually going on to study mineralogy and geology.
Now the head of his family, he had three brothers and three sisters to provide for in his homeland. While studying, he worked on construction sites, watercourses, and dams where he learned at first hand the importance of geology when applied to engineering.
Michel, recognising a winner when he saw one, subsequently poached Fobie from All Material's closest competitor, LTMB, where Fobie had cultivated a promising reputation as an up-and-coming geologist. He trebled Fobie's salary and paid off his student loans. Fobie, together with his siblings, now lived in Utrecht, on the banks of a picturesque canal. His brothers and sisters all found work, in some capacity, in All Materials BV, and were prospering.

CHAPTER 4

Long before Richard reached his destination, the shingle-like crack had spread sizably and at such an alarming rate that he had to reduce his speed. Unsurprisingly, he was dead late but showed no signs of hurrying. He manoeuvred his jaguar squarely inside a car-parking space overlaid with the word DIRECTOR. With a rush of relief, he got out and ran his finger over the crack. He slid his sat-phone into his breast pocket and slung a laptop-bag over his shoulder before activating the car alarm. Wearing a tailored black pinstripe suit, pink shirt and an expensive silver tie, he made his way slowly through the shadow-haunted car park. Only the upper-echelons of senior management had access to the bank's underground parking facilities, where his Jaguar comfortably held its own amongst an array of exclusive vehicles: modern as well as classic, imports alongside indigenous. He smiled when he observed a dent in the back of the Mercedes belonging to Peter Sussman, a man with a propensity to belittle others. A closed circuit TV camera followed him as he dillydallied, casually inspecting the skein of parked automobiles. An unusual or outlandish purchase often indicated a change in an employee's outlook or circumstance. Satisfied, but with a tinge of regret, that everything was as it should be, he used the maintenance lift to get to his office.

The top floors were restricted to Secure Span employees, with a security guard posted at each access point. When Richard's private secretary, Larry, heard the lift door opening, he fixed his tie and stood to attention. The ninth floor was contemporary, with an accent on innate materials and traditional glazing. Its predominant feature was a stiffly posed female nude statue, fashioned entirely out of marble.

'Good morning, Sir.' His gangly secretary handed him a rolled up memo and opened the door to his capacious office, more akin to a penthouse suite than a conventional office.

An artificial tree the size of a small oak stood proudly in the corner.

'Good morning,' Richard echoed, 'any messages?'

'Bill Watson rang to confirm his attendance at today's meeting.' Larry, his quiet-spoken secretary, was not a handsome man. His nose was too long, his eyes were rheumy and his cheeks too gaunt.

'Good. Chase up Rasmus, he needs to be here. Then you can go on your break,' Richard ordered.

Larry pushed his spectacles further up his nose and softly closed the door.

'Sir?'

'Yes,' Richard shouted into the intercom.

'Sorry,' Larry said needlessly, 'Mr Tatroe on line three, shall I put him through?'

'That was quick. Yep.' Richard punched button No. 3. 'Rasmus have you laid the groundwork for the insurance investiture?'

'Sure have,' Rasmus replied simply.

'Ok, let's powwow later,' Richard said.

He removed his jacket and slotted his shiny state-of-the-art laptop into its docking station.

As always, Larry had prepared the coffee by boiling ground beans in water. Now the caffeine-filled odour beckoned. Richard had begun to develop a taste for the beverage and he helped himself to a giant mug of the brew. All of a sudden, he remembered his appointment with May Franks.

Haste made him clumsy, and he fumbled until at last he opened the cloakroom door. He examined his attire, turning left then right, in front of the full-length mirror. His head seemed too big for his body and his chin disproportionate. He wet his fingers and ran them through his jet-black hair flecked with grey. Unhappy with the outcome, he resorted to an application of gel. His rogue grey hairs, perfectly quaffed, had disappeared from view as the amorphous substance closed in on them. He pulled his shoulders back, sucked his tummy in, and then he checked his profile. After a splash of aftershave, he winked at himself and closed the cloakroom door. On his way down to reception, he thought of May, and what a fretful state she must be in after her brush with the bomb-squad.

He sought to charm her.

'Ah! The delectable Miss Franks, I was hoping you'd still be here. I'm frightfully sorry but I was caught in the mother-of-all-traffic-jams. Worse still, my windscreen was cracked.' As Richard offered his hand, he turned to the walrus-moustached security guard. 'Steve, have you organised a pass for Miss Franks.'

Richard indicated May.

May drew a sharp breath of disapproval without apparent cause. Taking note of Richard's pleasantries, hearing herself respond with equal charm, while her mind said, I suppose you consider yourself a man of import and plebes like me should be kept waiting. Hoping now to put the bomb fiasco behind her, she focused her frustration on Richard's highhandedness and haughty bearing as means to that end.

Richard did not mention the bomb-scare. In the chaos that ensued, road rage spats had increased tenfold, one of which he witnessed between a van driver and a bike courier. After an exchange of punches, both parties had returned to their vehicles to nurse superficial wounds. There, amid the clamour and fumes, the courier announced his departure with a grandstanding wheelie followed by a swift kick aimed at the passenger door of the van. He then disappeared into the warren of back alleyways snarling off Tottenham Court Road.

'I've already done that, Sir.' Steve deferred to him respectfully.
In his efforts to please, Steve knocked over a quarter-full cup of tea. Nervously, he duck-waddled round the desk and handed May her pass. Annoyed by Steve's woeful inadequacy, Richard hunched his shoulders and watched him mop up the spill. While this was going on May glowered at Richard. She had no time for ego or pomposness. Who does he think he is? She thought, letting her mind wander.

They spoke little on the lift journey. Richard, stern-faced, kept a decorous distance from May. He stole a look in the burnished surface of the lift's interior and then he gave a cursory glance at her briefcase and smirked. They stepped out shoulder to shoulder. Larry was seated at his desk reading from a sheaf of documents in front of him. He was so intent on his work that he was not aware of the approaching pair until they were less than thirty metres off.
He jumped to his feet and flew down the corridor to meet them.
'Take a break!' Richard ordered from the corner of his mouth.
Strolling nonchalantly across the ornate ninth-floor May turned heads. She was oblivious to the admiring glances she was attracting from all corners of the floor as she gave Richard her undivided attention. The closer they came to his office, the more serious her expression became.

Despite her misgivings, the office was really very comforting and welcoming. She searched for something to say and establish her composure. All the same, her nerves were not too badly on edge, else she would not have poked fun at the great fireplace, a throwback to a bygone era.
'I love your fireplace, Mr Gardiner. It's a pity the law prohibits the lighting of coal fires,' she laughed.

'It's a crying shame, just one of life's many ambiguities,' he maintained. 'Please sit down.'

'You have a splendid office, and the view is fantastic.' May sank down comfortably on her oversized chair.

He laughed with genuine delight. 'Why thank you. My wife Margaret has a life-long passion for interior design, and my office has become an integral part of her creative schemes. Quality rather than quantity has always been the tenet behind her work. In fact, if you ever get an opportunity to visit Downing Street, you'll find the exact same fireplace in the prime minister's office,' he observed modestly. 'Also, she has an avid interest in feng shui. Have you heard of feng shui?'

In reply, May remembered a lecture from Jenny during a conversation about their apartment and how best to decorate it. 'Yes, I believe it has something to do with harnessing energy. The way furniture is arranged, the colours on the walls, whether windows are big enough, south or north facing.'

'Do you have any objection to me calling you May?' he asked – not entirely flippantly - from the other side of the mahogany desk.

'No, of course not, Mr Gardiner,' she gushed, half expecting Richard to reciprocate the courtesy.

'Would you care for a cup of coffee?' He left his chair and topped up his mug.

'No thank you, I've had my fill.'

He swirled his coffee.

'To refresh, the position we're offering, as you know, is within the security division of Secure Span, and...' He was rudely interrupted.

He sat back in his high-backed chair, a little piqued.

'Excuse me, Mr Gardiner, but I was under the impression that I was joining National Bank.' She blanched, her jaw dropped and her spirits quailed.

This was an alarming twist.

Richard did not even bat an eyelid. 'Oh! Really, that's most unfortunate.'

He flicked upwards the lid of a cigar-box hidden behind a large mirror-framed photograph. The family photo served as a moralising reminder of filial obligation.

'Do you mind if I smoke,' he asked, pushing the cigar box aside.

He lovingly rolled the handmade Cuban cigar between his fingers.

Still, she viewed him with suspicion. She flashed back with her eyes fixed to the cigar. 'No, I don't mind at all. It's your office.'

May's sarcasm did not escape him. When he struck the match the flame was reflected in the windowpane. He placed the tip of the cigar to the match. She spelled trouble. He stood up and opened the window. The whiff, the echo, and the reverb from the bustling street invaded the calm of the tranquil office. A gust of wind rustled some papers on his desk. Next, from above the open window, a bird deposited a sizeable dropping. In retreat, Richard extinguished his cigar and closed the window. He dropped back on to his seat and whistled softly.

May blinked. He leant forward with his elbows on the desk and looked at her in a different way. The hush became silence. He felt a sudden frisson of excitement. His mind ranged free, stricken by the natural beauty before him. The train of his thoughts led him on, and he thought of his wife. He dropped his gaze to the floor. After a few minutes, he straightened up. He glanced at the portrait of his family.

When he compared his wife's attributes to those of the girl on the other side of the desk, his gonads chilled. It was an unfair comparison, a young woman, footloose and fancy-free, matched against a lady almost twice her age. Hot-faced, he snapped out of it.

'The Secure Span name is one of the biggest brands in security in the world.'

He continued, at a rate of knots, but he was not one to glibly offer a rosy future.

'I'm not comfortable playing God with a person's hopes, so if you prefer to work for National Bank, it can be arranged. However, I believe you'll find a career in Secure Span to be a far more challenging and much more creative prospect. In my humble view, job satisfaction coupled with greater financial rewards far outweigh the assumed advantages of a career in National Bank. Besides, I have a theory about National Bank employees. Typically they marry a colleague and set up home within the pale of the organisation, and then their household becomes an extension of this model. Their social events soon become limited to workplace celebrations. Whether or not they do a decent day's work, profits will increase. Money spawns money. I don't want to sound evangelical, but I think it's a criminal waste of talent. By this logic, it only suits the unadventurous,' he opined.

He had a nose for weakness. On and on he talked until the hapless May sighed, her inexperience was clearly evident. She failed to appreciate the offer for what it was, a chance to scale the heights and become a leading light with Secure Span. Her first instinct was to ring her dad and ask him for guidance.

As midday bonged, Richard glanced at May to assess the effect of his argument. An open-and-shut case if ever there was one, or so he thought. While the clock on the mantelshelf still chimed the strokes, he looked again more carefully and this time saw serious doubts cast over the young woman. She seemed a little perplexed as she mulled over the notion.

Her expectations had been built up. Now her plans had gone astray.

She scoffed at the idea that Jenny could somehow become institutionalised. If Jenny has a mantra, it is that *she never dates a colleague.*

What will I do, May asked herself? Jenny will kill me if she does not receive her finders-fee.

Richard detected her befuddlement but resisted probing the cause, besides he had more pressing matters ahead of him and did not wish to waste any more time in debate. Equivocations did not sit well with him. However, on the flip side, it was Michel who wanted to hire the girl.

Fiddling with his wedding ring, Richard gave way to expediency.

'Do you need some time to consider your options,' he invited.

When she recovered her tongue, she demanded, 'Mr Gardiner, I don't want you to think that I'm getting ideas above my station, but can you give me a detailed description of the various duties associated with the position, along with a brief rundown of Secure Span's trading interests? To be frank, I've never heard of the company until today.'

His eyebrows shot up as he listened slack-jawed to her request. Austere though he was, he was not without understanding.

'In keeping with the security ethos suggested by its name, many aspects pertaining to the nature of the enterprise are highly confidential. However, if it would help, I can have human resources draft a document outlining the responsibilities of the newly created post,' he said.

He smiled a thin smile and his fingers began to drum. He was about to stand up, when May forestalled him.

Desperate to unburden her qualms, she wondered aloud, 'Jenny, my flatmate, who works for National Bank, is hoping to receive a finders-fee.' She stuttered over the words finders fee and cast shyly her eyes downwards.

He tossed down his pen. 'May, that's ridiculous. Don't make a career decision based on whether or not your friend is awarded a couple of thousand pounds,' he barked irately, but then his tone changed to a more mellow pitch when a clever idea occurred to him – a brainchild far too tempting not to be put to the test.

'Nevertheless, I commend you for your loyalty. Because of the working relationship between National Bank and Secure Span, in the event of you joining Secure Span, your friend will receive a lump sum of five thousand pounds. Furthermore, it will be paid in full on the day that you commence,' he said.

Which was not entirely accurate, as there was no formal agreement in place covering the recruitment of staff.

Richard rocketed up in her estimation.

May spoke up again, plainly this time. 'Great, Jenny will be delighted.'

Despite censure, May's confidence slowly returned. 'On commencement day?' she remarked dubiously.

He shrugged and smiled.

'Yes, as it happens. New recruits are much valued by Secure Span. The firm has a good mix of older staff who have been here for years and younger ones coming through,' he said.

He relit his cigar, cocked his head backwards and took a long puff.

His words set her thinking.

'I'd like to chew on it for the remainder of the day,' she said.

Richard grunted. She had given him a tough test for his patience. A complication he could have done without. He considered the ash on his cigar before replying.

'Absolutely, I'd be disappointed if you didn't.'

Watching on with smug satisfaction, he stated, 'one more point: you'll be expected to sign a binding contract – a non-disclosure agreement - forbidding you from communicating sensitive information to anyone who does not have the proper security clearance.'

He could no longer afford to linger on in her company.

'You'll have to excuse me. I've some rather pressing engagements. But whatever you decide, let me know as soon as possible,' he suggested silkily.

She gave him a particular look, and replied, 'of course.'

'On a final note, Declan Mills was a lecturer of yours, was he not?' Richard asked expansively.

'Yes?' she answered, holding Declan Mills in high esteem, flattered by the interest he had shown in her coursework.

Richard hesitated, and then volunteered, 'Declan is one of our security advisors. It might be worthwhile consulting him, if you catch my drift.'

'That's a good idea,' she said.

She did not show it outwardly but her spirits lifted.

Richard wedged the cigar in the lip of the ashtray. Weary of prognosticating, he thumbed his braces and stood up. Refusing to take the hint, May sat where she was. He moved quickly round the desk, and he stalked to the door, leaving behind a series of blurred shoeprints in the chunky woollen carpet. He opened the door, then stood, staring at her, in the doorway. May took it as a sign it was time to leave. She gathered up her father's briefcase. While she walked, the buttons in her jacket worked loose. Her nipples bubbled under the radar, and her breasts bulged mischievously. She opened her lips to speak, but Richard narrowed his eyes. May caught the direction of his gaze, and she smoothly brought the lapels of her jacket closer together without breaking the rhythm of her stride. Shamefaced, Richard checked himself and coughed into his fist. Alas, he had never been good at resisting temptation.

Three years ago, Richard had become involved with Hilary, his former secretary. She had needed no encouragement to take up with her boss. Yielding to their mutual passion, the pair had begun to spend more and more time secluded in his office. Perhaps via female intuition, or some other unexplained science, Margaret had sensed his involvement. To allay her fears, she invited Michel to dine at the family home. Michel tried to put her mind at ease, but he himself was not sure. One crisp December morning, in snow and fog, he called Richard aside and advised him to bring a quick end to the affair. Initially, Richard refuted the allegation, arguing that the very idea was preposterous. But when Michel handed him an envelope containing photographs of a sordid nature, Richard started to sob uncontrollably. Ironically, it was Margaret who had given Michel the envelope after she had hired a private detective. As it turned out the Case Detective Agency was already on the books of Secure Span, and it had allowed Chen, Head of Security, to screen the photographs before they were passed on to Margaret. At length, when Richard finally stopped blubbering, Michel lent his voice to a couple of home truths and a reminder that everyone was expendable.

Richard took time away from the office after this rebuke. Over the days that followed, Richard spent most of his time at home, busying himself with household chores. When he finally terminated the affair, his spurned lover was transferred out of London. Chen subsequently chose Larry as Richard's assistant, a role for which his civil service training stood him in good stead.

Richard shouted out to Larry, 'can you see Miss Franks out.' Then, as something of an afterthought, he added, 'Oh! Larry, will you get someone to repair my windscreen, post-haste.'
In parting, Richard urged May to make up her mind. 'Tomorrow at the latest, you've got to be on the ball; too much dithering can be bad,' he advised.

There was much work to be done. It had been a tough week with decisions to be made, time frames to be met and budgets to be kept to. Richard immured himself in his office and logged on to the Secure Shaker System, in order to ascertain the current value of National Bank shares. His mood was subdued. He regarded the tip of his cigar with a scowl of frustration. Meanwhile, Larry complied with Richard's request and accompanied May to the front entrance. She found it remarkable that a man like Richard should choose a male secretary. Perhaps he could not hang on to a woman, she thought cynically. She stepped out onto the pavement not realising it was raining, a deluge in fact. The miserable weather brought a scowl to her face. Her lovely pink suit was about to darken in colour and was on the verge of losing its fine-pressed shape. The dark mass of heavily charged clouds showed no signs of relenting. She dashed into a novelty shop awash with trinkets and snaffled up a union-jack umbrella. Naturally, with a market of sodden people to exploit, the price was artificially inflated. Nonetheless, angry-looking customers vied with each other to snatch up the remaining umbrellas. She left the shop by the side entrance. A short while later she skidded into a large department store, feeling a little lost in the lunch-hour rush.

She shook out the tresses of her hair and purchased a brassiere, nothing fancy. As she picked her way through the aisles, drops of rain ran down her cheeks and dripped from her chin. A knot of customers shoved and wrestled with each other to reach the bargains. She slipped out the rear of the building. A No. 15 bus was waiting for her. As she slid sideways into a damp seat, she unlaced her shoes and eased off her stockings.

Two old age pensioners sat in the seat in front of her. The frailer of the two, who looked like he had been dragged through a scrubland backwards, spoke in a grated voice.

'Speaking of windfalls: I won ten thousand pounds on the Lottery. I bought myself a wide-screen television and, for the missus, a new washing machine. ACHOO!' He wiped his runny nose and coughed. 'I gave a few pounds to the grandkids and drank the rest.'

His rail-thin companion, sitting awkwardly on the seat next to him, laughed like a drain.

'I'll tell you an even better one. A good while ago, I won twelve thousand pounds on an accumulator and spent it just as quickly. I felt like a millionaire,' he said. 'You should've seen the look on the bookmaker's face. Priceless.'

The word millionaire caused May to think of her Father and how he might shed some light on the best course of action, independent of Richard's assertions. Armed with this notion, she sighed, leant her elbows on the back of the seat in front of her and stared out across the city. At the close of the rainstorm, notwithstanding the menacing skies, the sun burst forth and impaled the double-decker as it neared Marble Arch. A few minutes later, May slipped on her shoes and hopped off. She went on a long wet walk. The sun put a spring in her step and a smile on her face. Back home in her Bayswater apartment, she brooded – tetchily – on what to do. After much deliberation, though, she concluded that she would make the decision on her own and not consult her Dad, nor sound out Declan Mills.

The prevailing mood of the bank's court - also known as the board of directors, the pillar of the establishment - as it assembled to hear Richard's proposal was serene. Already sitting around the table were ten directors. Inevitably, they had got wind of it. They were all movement and questioning looks when Richard opened the door. In the milieu of the palatial boardroom - yet another room to have received a face-lift from Margaret - Richard always felt comfortable. His entourage comprised of senior company lawyer, Bill Watson, financial controller, Rasmus Tatroe, Chen, and Larry. Over the years, Richard had forged a good relationship with each one of the directors except for Peter Sussman, who was a long-standing member of the bank's court and antagonistic by nature to the point of paranoia. If there was one constant in National Bank it was that Peter would be on the opposite side of everything to Richard. He remained unbending as a dedicated campaigner of traditional banking, and was more than ready to take on Richard. Peter's old friend and colleague, Frank Stone, dressed up to the nines, had also been a difficult nut to crack, and querulous to boot. When it suited him, he often made common cause with Peter.

Richard baited their curiosity but in the end he knew that a vote would have to be taken. He rose to his feet and presented with vocal colour an overview of the insurance market and then he summarised the lucrative game plan Michel had so skilfully constructed. Even by Richard's own standards it was a presentation of unparalleled brilliance. He measured the reaction of the board. Peter seemed unconvinced, but then again he never looked at ease. Frank's resolve waxed and waned, not entirely oblivious to the changing market. He whispered to Peter in the background.

 Richard was satisfied the case he conveyed to the board had been foolproof and called for a vote. Only one hand remained on the table. The dissenting hand, inevitably, belonged to Peter. He flaunted his contempt for the proposal and, in so doing, rose with gusto. He was of the old school, renowned for his view that a bank should only concern itself with core banking activities, and he was a man who steadfastly resisted change out of sheer habit and stubbornness. Not that Richard himself was too bothered. Undaunted, Richard was quick to remind Peter that, unlike other banks, National Bank had not been bailed out by the government during the recent global crash. Even though National Bank had no liquidity or capitalisation issues, Richard was quick to point out the risk of allowing competitors to get a jump on them, a jump that could jeopardise the bank's success. On queue, Rasmus handed out a raft of projected trends to each director. Peter was drained of menace, worn down by explanatory text and figures. To add injury to insult, Richard highlighted the worst-case scenario; an overall loss of revenue caused by an economic downturn, and then he asked Peter, 'are you prepared to accept full responsibility when shareholders come baying for blood?'

Now that the end game between Richard and Peter appeared to have played itself out, Richard asked for another show of hands. He watched on in studied silence as the hand of each director rose up apart from Peter, who only half raised his arm in defence of his wounded honour. It was a bitter pill to swallow. The board was persuaded. Richard rubbed his hands with glee. Amid a chorus of bleating praise, he thanked everyone for attending at such short notice and scheduled a date for an appointed steering committee to investigate the practicalities of the undertaking. He left the boardroom basking in the glow of the court's approval and was looking forward to writing in triumph his report, which would be read by Michel.

CHAPTER 5

Greta's enthusiasm had not waned. She was full of an impressive, low-key self-confidence. Michel, as he followed the report of the excavation's progress, was struck by her thoroughness.
'As you may well know, we sent some of our artefacts to Athens for dating.' As she spoke, she spread out a crumpled slip of paper. She then briefly explained, in the simplest of terms, the technique of carbon testing, largely for the benefit of Michel.
'That's clever,' he said. He was aware of the process but effected ignorance, never inclined to exhibit the full extent of his knowledge to those outside an inner circle, a guile that often gave him an added advantage.
'Most of the artefacts are dated 1200 BC, but the alabaster storage jar is dated 1400 BC,' she announced excitedly. So infectious and appealing was her glee that Fobie was tempted to touch wood for her. He placed his bottle of juice on the floor and was first to speak. With a deep rumbling voice, he asked, 'What period would that have been, the Minoan?'
'Since when have you become an expert on the Aegean?' Michel joked.
Fobie looked down into the froth of his juice. 'There happens to be a notable overlap between geology and archaeology,' he said.

'The late Minoan era,' Dmitri interjected. 'The Minoan civilisation dominated the basin of the Aegean Sea until 1400 BC. They were a seafaring people who relied on trade to underpin a wealthy society.'

Eagerly they listened as Greta picked up from where Dmitri left off. The flame of her passion was now burning brightly. She went on to talk about a discovered artefact from a more recent period of history. Accidentally unveiled, centimetres beyond the perimeter of the excavation site, on the shore side.

Michel tried to stop his mind wandering, not entirely certain as to why he was drawn to the discovery. There was something very pure and permanent feeling about it all: the right location, the right people, and the right time. Greta sensed that he was not focused. To lend greater weight to the significance of the find, she let a photograph rest gently on his knee. With his head at a slight angle, he tuned back into the conversation. The photograph was of a scroll, almost wholly intact, which had been inserted into a dust-blackened vessel, made of goatskin, and sandwiched between two chalcedony seals. The object was clearly ancient. Michel was no archaeologist, but he could see with perfect clarity what a find the scroll had been.

Greta took out a tissue and blew her nose. She then continued. 'Unlike the rest of the artefacts, however, the scroll is a great deal younger. Dated between the year 1650 to 1700 AD.' The cadence of her voice changed, excitement was now replaced by a seriousness fuelled by doubt.

'Perhaps you're mistaken. It looks so old?' Michel queried, intently studying the photograph.

Greta paused before answering. 'I'm certain.' She went on to expound with renewed vigour. 'Now, Crete at this time was known as Candia and under the control of the Venetians.'

'The Venetians,' Michel echoed, his lazy smile suggesting surprise.

Greta turned and nodded but she saw that his smile had disappeared and now he was lost in thought once more. He began to say something but changed his mind.

The young age of the isolated artefact caused quite a stir among the small group. Afterwards Michel became restless. An inexplicable desire grew within him to hold the goatskin vessel.
'Where exactly is the scroll now?' he enquired.
'All of the artefacts, except for the alabaster storage jar, are in my room,' Greta replied enigmatically. She watched him pour a glass of water, his face stern and pleasing. He picked up the photograph that was still on the table and peered at it.

When they started to analyse the relics in depth, Michel insisted that he should study at first hand the scroll. Greta, taken off kilter, became aware for the first time of his forceful nature. At last she sighed and reluctantly agreed.
'Please follow me,' she said and led the way to the lifts. She trusted her folder to Dmitri, and they moved quickly through the lobby.

Her room was an untidy affair, except for the artefacts. She opened wide a window that faced part of the beach. Wisps of barbeque smoke were already rising into the blue. Unsettled, she looked towards the selection of artefacts, neatly arranged, like a line of soldiers standing to attention, each distinctly labelled with a brown cardboard tag. Michel made a beeline for the cylindrical container. Carefully he extracted the scroll from the goatskin receptacle. The characters on the scroll suggested an early Grecian vernacular, signs interspersed with symbols, but more significantly, the ink had a golden hue. Fobie craned his head over Michel's shoulder. For another quarter of an hour they examined the scroll, muttering an observation now and then, but for the most part quiet and absorbed.
'Will it take long to decipher this script?' Michel asked, tightly holding the scroll with both hands.
'The Linear B script was discovered in the late 1930s, but it wasn't decoded until 1952,' Greta argued, 'on the other hand, with the advent of new technology it may take considerably less time to crack.'

Michel shook his head and glared for it was not the answer he wanted. This reflected not any great annoyance but rather a preoccupation with other burdens. There was a silence. And then more silence. But something of the energy of Michel appeared to have imbued all of them. Dmitri grew uneasy and started to shuffle from one foot to the other, causing his mullet to wave in sympathy. Greta spoke quietly, but nobody heard, they were watching Michel, whose eyes remained locked on the scroll. He appeared chilled to the bone - like one of the many statues dotted around the mainland, a philosopher perhaps or just as credible, an Olympian.

This was the same parchment Michel had seen in his dream. As he gazed in fascination, unable to remove himself from the scroll, his own thought partook of the young sibyl who had offered him the polished sword, and the disfigured mystic who had fired the silver bullet. The musket played on his mind. In a kind of trance, he saw himself entering a great labyrinth and climbing the steps to an ancient mausoleum, and there, to the cheers of ancient peoples, liberating the soul of a goddess. It was enough to make him pry his eyes away in a cold sweat.

Michel, taking Fobie to one side, told him, 'I want you to stay here and make sure nothing happens to this parchment.'

Greta was presuming on Michel's generosity, and confidently expected him to pledge continued support. Instead, he started to behave as though he were an archaeologist himself. He watched her keenly, and then advised, 'it's important that you adhere to your regular schedule. Fobie is going to stay here to make sure the scroll comes to no harm or worse still, falls into the wrong hands. It's my opinion that you should concentrate your efforts in the area where Dmitri unearthed the scroll.'

Greta baulked at Michel's effrontery and was on the verge of launching a protest. He has no licence, she told herself, to recast a tried and tested approach. She looked over at Fobie in a plea for support but he warned her off by placing a finger over his lips.

Fobie had seen this side of Michel's personality once before, while attending an exhibition in Amsterdam, and pitied anyone foolish enough to cross swords with him. A group of rowdy sailors, on shore leave, had thrown a hash cake across a crowded coffee-room. The act itself had not bothered Michel so much. Instead, it was a deep-seated hatred for drugs that made his blood boil. In the ensuing mêlée, one of the sailors ended up in a canal, whilst the injuries inflicted upon the others were too numerous for the duty doctor to list without drawing a breath. Fobie remembered the fracas well, for when he went to assist Michel, a bottle came hurtling through the air and struck Fobie on the temple, knocking him out cold.

Michel now began to pace as he did in the hospital ward that night.
'Dmitri, can you get a gun?' he asked suddenly.
'What?' Dmitri's mullet seemed to rise upon his head.
'Check the daily newspapers and look up funerals announced in Sfakia. Target the older members of the congregation and discreetly cite your interest in procuring a weapon,' Michel said simply.
His knowledge of the area shone through, surprising Dmitri.
'Michel, why on earth a funeral?' Greta asked.
She studied him, as he paced from bed to door, directing affairs. In spite of her misgivings, she was fascinated by the intensity of his words.
'Crete has one of the most heavily armed populations in the world. After world war two, the Germans left behind an enormous arsenal of weapons. On occasions, such as weddings and funerals, weapons are produced and shots fired into the air.' He spoke softly and Dmitri nodded in agreement.
She voiced her concern. 'I thought it was illegal to own a gun here.'
'It is, but the authorities turn a blind eye. Cretans are determined never again to be so ill prepared or defenceless as they were during world war two,' Dmitri said.
'Why Sfakia?' Greta quizzed.

'Sfakia is a hothouse for feuds and vendettas. Almost every household has a weapon,' Michel coolly replied. 'Am I right Dmitri?'

The answer was all too readily to hand, bred of centuries of vengeance: 'it's true. There is a hard race of people living in Sfakia and they believe in an eye for an eye and a tooth for a tooth. The blood feuds are on a par with the ones you hear about in Sicily. The worst feud left a 160 people dead. More recently, riot police from Athens were deployed to Sfakia in an effort to thwart the menace of further vendettas,' Dmitri explained.

He had dated a girl from Sfakia while at university. The relationship floundered when he received a thinly disguised threat from one of her ex-boyfriends. Shortly after, his car mysteriously caught fire on campus grounds.

Dmitri was not the only one to be haunted by dreams and visions of the past. Old hatreds, flaring back to life, made Fobie reminisce. His mind was transported back to his Ugandan childhood days.

He was born in a village on a remote and dangerous plateau that provided little protection from marauding soldiery. His uncle Ruben had taught him how to strip, assemble and fire proficiently an AK47. He thought of the rifle still wrapped in greaseproof paper and buried at the foot of a gargantuan mvuli tree.

Ah! Our lovely village, he thought sadly.

Weighed down by his mission, Dmitri set off for the lobby in search of a daily newspaper. The receptionist organised for him a car-hire. Meanwhile, in the hotel room, Greta entertained conflicting emotions. Over the years she had tended to grow blasé about security, but the organisation and vision Michel brought to his endeavours defied belief. She began to fan herself. This was the only proof that she was in any way upset. Reluctantly, Michel set down the scroll. Then he asked her to book the archery range.

Greta replaced the handset. 'The range will be available in half an hour.'

'Thanks! I'll pop down now. Would you like to join me?' He did not expect a yes.

'No thank you, I'm behind and better make tracks. Besides, you advised us to stick to our normal routine,' she said, then turned her head and added, 'Fobie are you coming?' She liked it when Fobie joined her at work.

'Fobie, you better stay here and look out for the artefacts,' Michel instructed, before leaving the room.

As soon as Michel had left, Greta made for Fobie and gave him a giant hug. 'I've missed you terribly,' she whispered breathlessly.

She stood on her toes and planted her moist lips on his. The kiss was prolonged and meaningful. He echoed her words and his hardened hand crawled up under her jersey. He cupped her left breast and with his finger tenderly tickled her swelling nipple. He could feel the quickening pace of her heartbeat. She allowed him that liberty, then pulled back.

'I must get a move on, half the day is already wasted. Are you sure you won't accompany me?' She began to rub up seductively against him.

'Nope, better remain here, I dare not risk the wrath of Michel.' His hand tried to return to its previous resting place.

'Are you afraid of him?' she teased as she drew even closer, excited by his masculinity, feeling his hardness push up against her.

Fobie paused before answering.

'He has done many a good turn for me and my family.' He hesitated for a moment, and then he continued. 'To be truthful, in one sense I am afraid of him, he is a very rich and powerful man and I certainly wouldn't like to be listed amongst his enemies. Then again, I would trust him with my life,' explained Fobie with childish sincerity.

'That sounds to me like an oxymoron.' Greta sputtered, as she nibbled on one of his cauliflower ears.

He tilted his head, and then he remarked, 'it does seem like a contradiction, but that's the way it is.'
'Do you feel the same away about me?' she growled.
With eyes closed, he squeezed and kissed her. 'My dear, you wouldn't hurt a fly.' Then he lifted her off the floor.
She lingered in the warmth of the moment letting her body wallow in the fondness of his embrace. 'You can put me down now.' Her voice was lilting.
He planted her firmly on the carpet and kissed her forehead. 'I need a shower.'
Her eyes widened, as she remembered the offensive clothing stored in the cubicle. 'Just a moment, I need to clean the bathroom.' She threw herself backwards.
'Don't be ridiculous. Since when have you become a neat freak,' he joked.
He followed her into the bathroom. He laughed when he saw her bent over gathering up her clothes.
'Turn round,' he said softly.
'Give me a moment,' she said.
From behind her she felt his warmth as he traced the plains of her back. He gave her posterior a playful slap. She twirled around, her laundry dropping to the floor, and she threw both her hands around his neck. He placed a hand on her hip, and followed the camber of her waist like the shape of his guitar. She cackled and pulled away.
'I have a mountain of work to do,' she declared, haltingly.
'Are you sure?'
'Yes,' she said, yet more haltingly, 'I am.'
But then she took off her jersey. The tips of her breasts were dark around the nipples.
Then she took off her jeans.
'What about birth control?' he said.
She undid his belt.
'I'm on the pill,' she murmured.

Then she shook off her panties, stepped out of them, and left them on the white-tiled floor.
'Ah. I'd forgotten about that for a second,' he grinned. 'Lucky me.'
She unzipped him.
He propped her back against the sink.
Then he kissed her on the mouth.
She had her hands around his penis. She ran the circle of her fingers up towards the head, back towards the scrotum and up towards the head again. She put it between her thighs, and looked up.
'Now,' she panted, 'how's this for a welcome?'
'It's the best,' he gasped, half inside her.

Helena was waiting in reception with two tackle boxes, two bow bags and two quivers. Michel introduced himself to the young Greek girl, slightly built, yet remarkably striking. Making an impression had never been an issue for her. She had a head of full-bodied shiny brown hair, and wore a pair of black-laced boots, a white pleated skirt and a light sleeveless jumper. Her panoply suited all sports catered for in the complex. As they left the hotel, Michel saw Dmitri jump into a Land Rover. He was carrying an armful of daily newspapers.

The gate was at the bottom of a gentle hill. The archery range, perched on top, was just visible through woven knots of prickly scrub, Tamarisk trees and bushy rockroses. A gravel path edged with boulders of local limestone led in from the trail past mixed beds leading toward a tall Judas tree. They chatted amiably as they walked side by side. Helena, through polite questioning, tried to ascertain Michel's experience, but his answers were vague and unrevealing. She could not fathom why he was so unforthcoming but in order to avoid any nasty surprises she persisted. There had been an incident two years earlier. A guest was badly injured when a wayward arrow struck him. Understandably, Michel made her nervous and she watched him like a hawk.

Approaching the fence, Michel was delighted to find they had the entire range to themselves. Two pillar-like statues acted as sentries on either side of the steps leading into the area. Running the width of the range was a huge protrusion of rock with a smoothed surface, like a natural barrier. With no hurry upon them, Michel examined the bow. He rejected the first string, which had a fluffy appearance, and he took a second string from his tackle box. Helena felt more at ease when she saw him reject the string. He held the bow in his left hand and started to pull the handle towards his body. Keeping the bow in that position, with the assistance of the ground, he slid the loop into the groove. Then he spun each arrow between the nails of his fingers and his thumb, and out of twenty arrows, five hopped out of his hand.

Helena felt a pang of guilt for doubting him.

He smiled knowingly then deftly trimmed the tab to fit his fingers. Finally, he fitted a bracer to his bow arm and fixed the straps securely. Helena led him to the firing line. She stood in the background and waited with interest.

'Helena, would you care to shoot first?'

'Fire away,' came the reply, swift and predictable.

'Very gracious of you.' He took an arrow from his quiver and laid it across the bow, then gently pushed the nock against the taut string. He took aim; his eye studied the centre of the target face. Unperturbed and settled, he loosed the arrow. The steel pile stuck deep inside the red zone.

He slid another arrow from his quiver but paused with the shaft in his hand while a breeze spurted then dropped.

The next shot pierced the gold zone.

'Bravo! A bull's-eye. Fantastic shooting.' She applauded.

'Gold happens to be one of my many vices.' He turned his head and winked, he could not resist the odd gloat.

'Would you like the target moved further back?' she enquired.

He had already started to walk towards the target.

'Yes, perhaps the 50 metre mark,' he suggested.

He let the target fall on the flat of its back, and then, without exaggerated motion, he paced out the supplementary metres. It had been a long time since Helena had attempted such a distance, and she failed miserably to get anywhere near the target. In stark contrast, each one of Michel's arrows found the target with the exception of three flighty attempts. The novelty of his marksmanship wore thin and she drummed up an excuse to leave.

'I think it's safe to say that although this is your first time here, you can continue without supervision,' she said.

Her confidence dented, she gathered her gear and left him to his practice.

'Helena, would you mind leaving your quiver,' he called after her.

She no longer saw the joke. Nonetheless, she left her quiver and set off to cater for guests who genuinely needed supervision.

After a quick inspection, Michel discarded two slightly warped arrows. He spent the remainder of the day on the range. Occasionally, passers-by would stop and guffaw. A gathering of children flocked across a rolling grass path to gawp and shout each time an arrow hit the target. After they had left, three men came sauntering up the path that wound around protruding rocks, scrubby bushes and curved walls. Michel recognised one of them, the shaven-headed man whom he had pummelled outside the bar in Gouves. For a man of Michel's temperament, with his taste for danger, it was an exciting interlude.

The men spoke quietly amongst themselves. Harry clutched his ribs, strapped to reduce the pain, and with his free hand pointed in the direction of the range. Michel reckoned they were plotting some sort of revenge.

'There's three of us and only one of him,' Harry whispered spitefully.

Even in the frantic seconds before he fired, Michel found time to steal an arrow from his quiver and with sleight of hand break the tip. He drew back the bowstring and called out, 'Harry, if I were you, I'd start running. My aim isn't the best today, and look around, there are no witnesses.'

Harry stood defiant, but was dismayed when his friends took flight.

'Come back, he's only bluffing,' he yelled after them. He turned round in time to see Michel, having just shot the arrow, lower his bow.

Like his friends, Harry had started to run and looked up as the arrow climbed higher and higher into the sky.

'He's trying to kill me,' he cried, and then he fell over. He heard the arrow rattle against some rocks nearby. Almost immediately, he checked his body for any signs of injury. He had no reason to believe the arrow was blunted, so when he saw Michel nock another, he sprung to his feet and ran towards the beach. Michel took much delight in watching him, surrounded by sand and flies, lumber through the prickly scrub.

Far from hurrying back, Michel lingered in the gardens. A flight of narrow, winding steps, led down to a shady path edged with aromatic herbs and wild flowers that curved back towards the hotel. It was just light enough for him to make out an old wooden bench set on a gently sloping hillside. He settled back, not to rest, but to open his mind to the notion of history.

A drained Dmitri arrived back at the hotel as dusk settled in. Greta and Fobie were sharing a large bowl of mousaka. Fobie set aside his plate and rose from the floor. In a somewhat hushed voice, he asked Dmitri whether his excursion had been worthwhile. Dmitri nodded, indicating success, and then he glanced sharply in the direction of Greta. She was eating nervously, having found it very difficult to spend the day in uncustomary isolation.

'Come, join us, how many did you get?' Fobie quizzed, keeping his voice low for Greta's sake.

'Two revolvers, and some ammunition, where is Michel?' Dmitri asked in an equally low voice.

'He's still at the archery range. Darkness is setting in, so I guess he won't be too much longer. Have you eaten?' Fobie took a mouthful of food.

'I'm not hungry.' Dmitri, his fortitude stretched to the limit, was beginning to feel the worse for wear, and the stress of the day was catching up on him.

Greta, who had not missed a word of what either had said, pushed her plate away and asked, 'where are the guns?'

'In the boot of the Land Rover,' Dmitri replied.

He sat down on the floor and fell back on the carpet with both hands outstretched. In walked Michel with bow in hand. He commended Dmitri for the way he handled the task.

Reassured, Michel stepped out onto the veranda.

The oars of a boatman plashed across the beach's waters. Afar, a mauve sheet, fused with pale blue, provided a distant backdrop to a solitary sailboat, naked of sail, which skipped to the subtle rhythm of underlying currents discreetly making their presence felt. He went back inside to where poor Greta was trying to guess what next, not yet sure if Michel was hero or villain.

Michel searched in his pockets and pulled out his sat-phone. Returning to the veranda, he punched in a series of digits.

'Hai!' The greeting was abrupt and clear.

'How soon can you send two of your guys to Crete?' Michel asked, disregarding normal formalities.

Chen attempted to organise things on the fly. 'As soon as you're on the plane to London.'

'Fair enough. When they get here they need to contact Dr Greta Cartwright, at the Sun Hotel, in Gouves. Is that okay with you?' Michel knew it would be.

'Hai!' Chen's tone became more submissive.

'Whom will you send?' Michel enquired.

'Hirokatsu and Ichiro.' The names rolled sweetly off his tongue, his imagination brought in to play.

'Great!' Michel, not believing for a moment the names put forward were genuine, was about to hang up.
'Michel, your move.' Chen sensed victory.
There was a pause, during which Michel studied an imaginary chessboard.
'Sorry I almost forgot, castle to queen's bishop four,' he said.
'Are you sure?' Chen visualised the move.
'Yes,' Michel replied, after a moment's deliberation.
'Hai!'
Chen was now busy considering Michel's move.
'Excellent, I'll see you tomorrow night,' Michel said.

As the haze of twilight deepened, Michel beckoned to Fobie to join him on the veranda.
'I'd much rather have you here overseeing the operations of the excavation,' he confessed to him, as the two men discussed the events of the day, 'than have to send you back to Holland.'
Fobie was concerned about his responsibilities back home. Michel dismissed his anxieties out of hand and suggested that his brother, Ube, a seasoned hand, should temporarily take over his duties. Ube was a widely respected employee, and Michel hoped his brother's stewardship might encourage Fobie to remain on.
    The exhausted sun had retired for the day. Far distant from the shore, a star flickered low in the sky. Soon Fobie took his eyes off the nightscape, having thought through what Michel had said. They finalised their arrangements and went back inside. Michel let everyone settle down before he spoke at length, emphasising the need to be inconspicuous.
With a degree of hesitancy, Dmitri expressed doubts about the validity of adding weapons to the excavation's expenses. Michel eased his mind by guaranteeing the exact amount, plus a little extra, would be in his bank account by close of business the following day.

Dmitri returned with the weapons concealed in a blue woollen blanket. When he unrolled the bundle onto the bed, out spilled two pistols. For once the scroll was not the centre of attraction. Michel immediately recognised both pistols. The first was a black-handled Walther P38. He picked up the second pistol, a Mauser automatic in a reddish-brown holster. Greta coughed nervously as Michel slotted a magazine into the base, then felt its weight. Likewise, Fobie cradled the Walther P38.

'Fobie can you hide these,' Michel said, laying down the Mauser, then added, 'and Dmitri, it might be a good idea for you to go home and get some well-earned rest.'

Michel turned slowly to face Greta.

'You've done your work well,' he told her.

On returning to the Elizabethan apartments, Michel noticed that the strand of hair was missing. Stillness hung over the corridor and no explanation could be discerned. He stood there for a while, then, he slowly unlocked the door and carefully entered the pitch-black apartment. He turned on the light. A moment's inspection and his eyes went across the room to the print – it was out of place. He looked around thoughtfully. The cleaners had been in and the bed linen had been changed; he took the print off the wall and removed the back. Unsurprisingly, the decoy envelopes were gone. He could see that the contents of the safe-deposit box were also gone. Then he lowered his eyes and eased his way into the bathroom. When he pulled the chord on the strip-light, he saw the bulb in the main light was missing. Well, he told himself, that's odd. He came back into the bedroom.

That night, after retiring to his bed and reading for a short while, he lit a cigar. Theorising, he confidently ruled out the cleaners as suspects for the vanishing objects. Then he made a mental note to enquire whether his room might have been under surveillance.

Loud music woke him in the early hours of the morning. Without turning on the light, he got up and disarmed the crossbow aimed at the patio, and then he peeked out through the curtains. The laughter and tinkle of glasses affirmed the beginning of a serious knees-up. He spotted the blonde girl who had been watching him by the poolside. She seemed sober, unattached and disinterested. He fought off the temptation to join her and instead returned to his bed. Five minutes later he got up, and again he looked out the window, but the girl was nowhere to be seen.

When dawn came it lit up an empty sky.
Michel was scheduled to fly out at eight but the flight was delayed for half an hour. Finally, the plane left its parked state, and slowly nosed its way to the top of the runway. His time in Gouves had given him a good deal to mull over. On the fruits of the excavation much might depend, he thought. Yet, coming so soon after his arrival, his plan to set off again could not help but leave the group diminished.
Without warning, midway down the runway, the aircraft's electrics died, shedding an eerie dullness right the way through the interior. Back at the terminal, an hour went by as technicians scrambled about the plane like honeybees in a hive. The pilot once again apologised and announced they had to disembark and wait for a relief aircraft, already airborne.

Michel found the terminal sullen and unwelcoming. Some forty passengers stood in a press around an airline representative, demanding satisfaction. Six hours later, the replacement aircraft took off at a low trajectory, passing over a series of local beaches. A flutter of excitement passed through his lower belly as the plane roared over - where once there had been nothing but scuff on clay - the excavation site. At that very moment, Hirokatsu, a huge Japanese man, and Ichiro, a debonair, well-dressed man, vain of his good looks, knocked on Greta's door.
Fobie invited them in. He was surprised by the size of Hirokatsu. Seldom was it necessary for him to look up to make eye contact.

CHAPTER 6

When Pat Hogan, a lanky, vibrant 27-year old with a shock of jet black hair, joined Secure Span, he started off doing small projects, but now he was managing more and more of his own programmes. The main laboratory was near the tail of the open-plan space, just below the empty boardroom and below Richard's office. Most programmers had eight-hour shifts, but Pat's was from 8 a.m. to 8 p.m. – and he always seemed to be there by night too. Sometimes rather than return to his riverside apartment, he slept on the floor.

The software connection was through his parents, Matthew and Andrea Hogan, who opened their own company, Hogan Computers, back in the early nineties in London, before moving it to Eastbourne in the noughties. Pat took his time joining them - he fancied himself the hero of his own destiny. First, he took a year out after college and went to Asia. When he came back to England, he did a diploma in software engineering before heading off again, this time to America. His mother had made arrangements for him to stay with his uncle in California. It was here that he hooked up with the infamous Scallion twins.

After a period of working as an engineer, his life took a sudden turn when he answered an advertisement for accommodation. It was a warm April morning when he arrived at the beach house with all his worldly belongings. The garden was ablaze with reds and pinks, yellows, purples and blues. Parked in the driveway were two matching Ferraris, momentarily blocked from view by a gardener, who was dragging a dried up tree that had capitulated to strong winds. The twins were in their sleeping bags, smoking, drinking, and watching a pirated movie - their faces illumined by a background of cloudy haze. Behind the quiff-haired duo, leaning against the wall, were a pair of nine-foot freshly polished surfboards. Famous for their extravagant lifestyle, Tom and Edward surfed in the Californian sun and, weather permitting, skied on the eastern slope of Squaw Peak. They had become cult figures and their seamy beach parties were notorious along the west coast.

After dropping out of college, the twins had begun a long period of hacking financial institutions. Their names were often mentioned in connection with the criminal underworld. Time and again they had risked their future – and time and again they had emerged victorious. It was inevitable that Pat would be sucked into their lucrative fold. By summer their influence and his own attachment to the daughter of a racketeer at whose tavern he frequented were reflected in his behaviour. Although he at first professed a lack of interest, claiming he was too law-abiding to participate in skulduggery, he quickly shed his reservations and began to adopt a more cavalier bent to those around him. He later resigned from his job and became a fully-fledged hacker. A life of obsession and sexual compulsion brought him instant gratification, but it was not to last.

One afternoon, out of the blue, there was a loud knock on the front door. A Japanese man, sporting a friar-tuck haircut, introduced himself as Mr Hiroki. Beside him stood Mr Okumara, a wrinkled man with thinning hair and saggy jowls. Without invitation they let themselves in. Mr Hiroki spoke at length and insisted that all stolen funds be returned to Peoples Pensions, an estimated US$22 million. Pat stared at him in absolute disbelief, half his mind filled with dread, the other half with naivety.

In the days that followed Pat emptied his bank account, transferring hundreds of thousands of dollars to an account scribbled on the business card given to him by Mr Hiroki, whereas the twins, who had taken refuge in Alaska, absconded with millions. Alarmingly, just a matter of months after the visit, an article appeared in a national newspaper that reported a freak boating accident off Kenai – in southern Alaska. It said: *two American twin brothers were drowned in the Pacific Ocean*. So it was with some surprise that a hapless Pat received an email from Mr Okumara thanking him for his cooperation and, more specifically, inviting him to Secure Span headquarters in London. After spending the autumn in his Uncle's house dwelling on the demise of his friends, which inspired much gloomy moralising, and fuelled by an anxiety to put his recent history far behind him, Pat packed his bags and went. When he arrived in London Mr Okumara took him out to dinner and explained, 'no more need be said on the matter. Would you like to come and work for us?'

After a time Pat began to realise how brainless he had been. He asked himself constantly, why would two rich guys seek a lodger in the first place or, indeed, why did I spend so much time cracking algorithms while others indulged their passion for kicks.

A difficult period in his life, which seemed to be receding, came suddenly, disconcertingly, into focus. But he dare not remember it properly.

The racket was Jenny hammering the vacuum cleaner against the skirting boards and the bedroom doors. May put her feet on top of her slippers and slid them across the floor. Jenny shifted to one side, not looking up, to let May pass. When May looked in the mirror above the sink she saw the imprint of her own watch below the ear where she slept on her arm. With an effort she splashed water over her face and dried it on the towel. She smiled at herself, remembering how she had phoned Larry and accepted Richard's offer. Life was very good. She pulled her slippers on properly and left the bathroom.

'Excuse me, Jenny,' May bawled out, 'can I just ask you something?'

Jenny switched the vacuum cleaner off. 'What's up?'

May lowered her voice. 'What time are you going out?'

'I'm not. Tony can't make it tonight, something came up at work, so I'm staying in,' Jenny responded, a little perplexed by the question.

'Great, I mean too bad. Fancy going out for a drink, after work?' May invited. 'My treat.'

'Sounds good,' Jenny answered without a second's pause.

May went through to the kitchen and broke a croissant in two. On her way back through Jenny turned and looked at her. She shook her head; she closed then opened her eyes. 'Get out, girl!' she yelled. 'I'm cleaning.'

May started to laugh. 'All right! All right!' She turned back into the kitchen.

It was a Wednesday. Jenny and May walked past a building site. Some builders were standing on the scaffolding that covered the outer wall. They shouted something after them. May crossed the road and glanced up at the scaffolding, then down again. Suddenly a Subaru veered round her and she felt the air as it passed and she jumped to the footpath. When she looked back over her shoulder she saw that it was Declan Mills, her former tutor.

Jenny had carried on walking.

'Come on then, if you don't want to be late,' she called without turning. May caught her up on King Street and started to giggle as if she had just finished telling a funny story.

Pat Hogan was uneasy. The mode was one with which he was all too familiar with. He sat in a leather chair in a dark suit with an ID badge pinned to his chest, and next to him sat a fiery-haired colleague. A hushed conversation was going on in the corner of the laboratory, which the red-haired Sid dipped in and out of while also managing to hold his own with Pat. The hub of activity was a wiry structure of 21 screens – five laptops, fifteen PC monitors, and one closed circuit TV that showed everything from errors to alerts to warnings. Pat sensed that this was an important discovery, one that Mr Okumara should know about. Unusually for a man in his twenties, Pat liked opera. He played it on his music system as he thumbed through the firewall logs while repeating in a harmonious whisper, 'We will not let them pass.'

Then he stabbed at the printout with his finger, pointing out irregularities in the logs. 'Look here, and here, and here,' he said.

Someone's phone trilled a chart hit. A colleague in lavender tights dug into her oversize cardigan. But it was Pat who stepped away from the desk and reached into his new overcoat. He spoke into the phone while staring across the city below.

'Okay Declan, tell me when you are ready,' he said.

He walked back to the desk. When he checked his email a message flashed up. He clicked on the attached image. The message was sent from Mr Okumara. For a moment he felt much better. Then the good feeling went. He said her name to himself - May Franks.

Declan, a tall, striking 42-year-old South African man of Afrikaner origin, glinted at May through the darkness of the revolving doors of National Bank; he had a fatherly eye. For her orientation, he brought her on a tour of the building and talked briefly about some of the work that involved him. Upon reaching the canteen, he phoned Pat. Then he spread his arms in a gesture of apology and walked out of the canteen. May smiled a girlish smile, waved goodbye, and waited.

'Please follow me,' Pat told her.

May pushed past the legs of the person next to her and picked her way up the glass-sided stairs. The doors swung shut behind her. She headed up the aisle to Pat's desk, located in a partitioned office at the back of the open-plan space. The partition wall had a little circular plaque stuck on it that said the word Encryption in italic writing with an illustration of a lock next to the word. It was a very plain office. There she met with Larry who went through the formalities and fine points of her contract. There was not really a need for secrecy, but Pat waited outside. He was tossing a tennis ball at the partition by the photocopier, catching it, tossing it again, catching it, and tossing it again. The circular plaque shook as the ball hit the partition.

After May signed the contract, Larry excused himself and left a copy on Pat's desk.

'May, our primary goal is to consistently reduce the time required to read an encrypted message,' Pat said, explaining what they do. 'There are two approaches. The first is to pour more and more cash into quantum computing. However, this is unsatisfactory when assigning a budget. The second approach is to focus attention on mathematical factoring. We've chosen the latter.'

'That sounds smart,' she said. 'I can recall a group of students who drained 60 years of desktop time, while trying to read an encrypted message...' she paused, correcting herself, 'no, 70 years.'

For the first time since they met, she became bashful.

Her mouth was pink, open. She was very beautiful.

Get your mind on the meeting, Pat told himself.

'Yes. Yes, indeed. That's the nature of what we are about at present. I can see from your thesis that you have an avid interest in this area.'

He waited, head cocked, for May to say yes back.

'I have,' she said, with a lingering glance.

He opened a file cabinet and removed a thin folder from a packed drawer. She could see the smooth metal on the underside of the drawer. After scanning several pages, he shook his head.

'An impressive thesis,' he said, pointing to the document in his hand.

A smile adorned her face.

He sat down at his computer and he typed a two-line message on Secure Span's intranet. Then he fixed his eyes on some point beyond

her head and wondered aloud if it was time for breakfast. She started to reply, but he interrupted. 'I'm starving!'
He got up, holding his stomach. Outside the partitioned office he called to Sid. 'Would you like to join us for breakfast?' Sid called back that he would.

The lift doors shut with a pinging noise. May walked into the canteen but all the faces were strange to her. Pat handed her a tray. She took it in both hands so as not to drop it. A thin, bespectacled Malaysian named Abdul joined them. He was dressed in faded blue jeans, a light-red jacket, and a T-shirt emblazoned with an orange tiger head.

Sid watched May put her fork in her mouth and chew and swallow. 'You've a healthy appetite,' he remarked. Then he sat forward, leaned on his hands on the table, and farted. Abdul gave him a withering look.
'Sid, where are your manners. There are ladies present.'
'Excuse me,' Sid eventually conceded.
'May, how are you settling in?' asked Martina, with a Slovakian accent. She sat opposite her. Her dark hair was shoulder length. She was wearing a pink blouse with its lapels tucked into a yellow sweater.
'Finest. How long have you guys been working here?' May directed the question at no one in particular.
'A couple of years...' Martina was cut short by a low-pitch noise.
'Eh! You Wally, that's totally disgusting. Incorrigible. Don't laugh. Come on May. Let's find a table were the air is less polluted.' Martina grabbed May by the arm and led her to a table by the window. There was a vase of flowers on the table between them. She breathed in, deep.
'What's his story?' May nodded towards Sid.
'Sid is a well-known pain in the butt with an obnoxious sense of humour and a massive ego. Flicking through the Kama Sutra is his

idea of light reading,' fumed Martina, tired of Sid's relentless wisecracking and obscene witticisms.

'You can say that again,' Sarah giggled. She was a plump, small woman dressed in a long sarong.

'Hi! My name is Sarah,' she said pleasantly,' and this is my co-worker Lynne.' Lynne was thin and pale. She had a scarlet thong round her neck, and her long fingernails were painted in a bright shade of orange.

'Nice to meet you both,' May responded.

She felt overdressed in her Betty Barclay designed pink dress suit. Gloomily she held her cup out in front of her. She swirled the end of the coffee in it and watched it settle. 'What is Sid's area of expertise?' she asked.

'He is widely considered among the city's best real-time programmers,' Sarah answered, as she cleaned her spectacles with one of the red dinner napkins.

Sid approached the table, accompanied, not for the first time, by strange looks.

'Oh no you don't!' Martina warned him to stay away.

'I'm sorry,' he said and held out his hand. Martina looked at his hand, looked back at him, vacant. He held it out; up in the air for a minute more then lowered it to his side. He cleared his throat. His face was all sweat. He spoke with one eye on the girls and the other on Pat, who had ordered him eat humble pie. Despite Sid's devil-may-care attitude, he did not want to get on the wrong side of Pat. Pat's teams were involved in the most challenging, cutting-edge projects. Sarah smiled. Sid thought she was smiling at him. He smiled back. He smiled at Martina too. She gave him a deadly look and left the canteen. He chuckled.

Sarah had just pushed her plate away, pushed her chair back and stood up and left the table, left the canteen. Richard, accompanied by Chen, passed by the table. Richard turned back to where May sat and congratulated her on her decision to join Secure Span. Sid disappeared back to his own table, uncomfortable in the company of a mercantile heavyweight, only to find Pat in serious conversation with Chen. Sid had never been formally introduced to Chen but he had heard enough to place him high in the category of one-to-steer-clear-of. He promptly removed his tray.

Chen was deceptively boyish looking. He wore big, round sunglasses and had a ponytail, which was flecked with silver. At 52, his face was without anxiety. He had the cultured air of a successful dancer and he spoke with a distinctive pitch contour. His simple manner set Pat at ease.

'Ah!' he said. 'I hope I'm not disturbing your breakfast.' To which Pat replied: 'No Master Chen, please sit down.'

Chen pulled back a chair from the table. 'I'm afraid there has been an upsurge in brute-force attacks on our on-line banking systems. We must look at the situation from the point of view of a hacker.' After a pause, he added thoughtfully. 'Can you spare some time to investigate?'

Indeed, it was Chen who had sent Mr Hiroki and Mr Okumara to the home of the Scallion twins. And it was he who had suggested Pat for the position of programmer with Secure Span.

'I'll sort it out,' Pat vowed.

He was delighted someone like Chen had singled him out to tell him something like that in his ear. For a moment Pat was lost in thought, and he neglected to mention that Mr Okumara had already asked him to look at the problem.

'One more thing.' Chen turned his head in the direction of the seated May. 'Would you be kind enough to let Miss Franks help you?'

Pat was surprised at the request and he too glanced over in May's direction. She was still conversing with Richard who remained standing and seemed to be killing time while waiting for Chen to rejoin him. 'Sure thing.' Pat made to leave.

'Do you mind me asking, why are members of your team sitting at different tables?' Chen quizzed, without emotion.

'Sid farted,' Pat replied at once. He became slightly embarrassed, sensing he had overstepped the boundary of formality.

'Ah yes, that would explain it,' laughed Chen. He rejoined Richard and they left the canteen together. Pat cleared his tray and hurried over to where May and Lynne sat.

'May, have you finished your breakfast?' he asked, and then he continued, 'something important needs our attention.' He looked a little discomfited before racing away. She trotted after him and when she caught up with him she asked what was up. He explained the situation and told her that Chen had requested an input from her.

'Me, why?' she asked eagerly.

'Don't know, but you must be good if Master Chen asks for you personally.' He held open the door and allowed her to step through. He checked his mobile phone. He had missed a message.

'Who is Master Chen and what does he do?' she asked.

'He is head of security and, in the eyes of many, not a man to be trifled with,' he told her.

Pat sat at his desk and May observed him systematically examine, with meticulousness, all the recent change requests. It was he who broke the silence.

'That's really what this exercise is about: troubleshooting,' he said.

She got a pen and a foolscap pad. 'Then we have much to do,' she said softly. After a while, she began to understand things first time around, rather than having to play them over in her mind.

'Here is a little tip for you; configuration changes always effect a network. Nine times out of ten that's where you'll find the source of a problem,' he said, irritably shoving the keyboard out of the way. Then he rubbed his eyes.

'Are you feeling alright?' she asked. She sat beside him at his desk, their knees almost touching.

'Just exhausted.' He smiled jadedly at her. She smiled back. Then he caught sight of Mr Okumara talking to Sid by the water-cooler. May sensed his altered disposition and she casually wheeled her chair to the other side of the desk. At a sudden thought, Pat rotated the screen so that she could see it.

'Let me point out the problem. Do you see here?' His finger touched the screen to highlight the change afresh. 'Change 14003, executed by Daniel Smith and approved by the Internet security manager, Paul Wilkinson.'

Twice May read its description but nothing stood out, and then she glanced significantly at Pat.

'Smith has reconfigured the bank's outer-firewall, allowing external traffic to come in through port 2139,' Pat explained scornfully. 'As a result, the inner-firewall is under more pressure than before,' he added.

'He has increased, among other things, the maximum threshold for authentication failures,' he growled. A small shudder racked him as he moved the keyboard back into place.

'Has anyone gained access?' Her voice was low and mellifluous, her eyes bigger than usual.

'Well, I -.' He began. 'I'll need to trawl the logs, but first things first, I'll need to carry out an emergency change request.' He typed quickly.

Soon after submitting the request an email arrived from Chen approving the change and congratulating him on his discovery. A follow-up email summoned the pair to a war room, to be convened immediately after Pat had completed his forensics.

Watched by Sid, May returned to her desk, where she wrote an email to her friends on the subject of how happy she was in her new job. After she had gone Pat looked at his watch. It was 11.37. He stood for the next five minutes at his window. Then he checked his email. He went through the new emails and deleted without reading the eight messages - sexual in nature - from Sid.

Meanwhile, Sid sank back into his chair, closed his eyes and tried to imagine May straddling him in the boardroom. But he could not picture it. A phone rang and he picked it up clumsily. He looked across at May. The phone went dead.

'May, Pat asked me to bring you up to speed on the work I do,' Sid said, and he stepped up behind her.

'I've only a few minutes to spare, will it take long?' She looked at him, uninterested.
'I can make it as quick or as long as you like,' he replied.
May was not sure if his words held a hidden meaning but she acquiesced. 'Very well then.'

May could only suffer a quarter of an hour in Sid's presence before teaming back up with Pat.
Pat was still at the desk, sitting back and sitting forward, shifting about in his chair.
'I'm back,' she said. Her expression was solemn.
It took him some time to find his own voice.
'Hello, May,' he muttered.
He took out a handkerchief and wiped his brow. Occasionally, he pointed to the screen and explained something that appeared to be out of the ordinary; May sat quiet as a church mouse and remained like that for hours watching and learning, through which diligence a genuine affection was engendered between the pair.

In a hushed voice, so as not to break his concentration, she asked him if he was hungry. He nodded and gestured at a take-away menu on the table. Everyone had left but they worked on together into the evening, only taking a break in order to devour a lukewarm pizza, which they happily shared. Later, they finished their post-mortem, but found no evidence of a breach.
Pat picked up the phone. 'May and I have just completed our investigation.'
May smiled when she heard Pat mention her name. He is definitely not a glory hunter, she thought to herself.
'Excellent! Would you join us in room B4? Paul Wilkinson and Daniel Smith are already here.' Chen's voice was controlled.
'We're on our way.' May trotted after Pat.

Chen opened the door and in they walked. They walked right past him. He had opened the door while he was still on the phone. Hang on, he had said to his wife. 'Something has come up; can I phone you straight back, Matsumi?'

CHAPTER 7

April had been the wettest on record in London, and it had rained overnight. As Tony, Jenny's boyfriend, drove further from the capital, the suburbs began to give way to flooded fields, woodlands and meadows. There were cows in the pastures, birds in the trees: larks, magpies and ravens. Tony, loose-jointed, tall and lean, wore a dog tag etched with a serial number on a gold chain around his neck and tattooed on his right forearm. He tried to calm his racing thoughts, but his mind was preoccupied with the logistics of his current assignment. Certain now that he was not being followed; he flicked what was left of his cigarette out the window.

Half an hour later his jeep pulled up outside an old brick shed. At the back of the shed was a large allotment. He deactivated the alarm and unlocked the weather-beaten door. As his eyes adjusted to the gloom he peered out of a small circular window and squinted. A short, very pale old man, crippled in one leg, was cutting grass with a scythe in an open field.

Tony, still in jeans and a blue-stripped polo shirt, pulled a stool from underneath a makeshift table. He sat down and leaned forward slightly. Peeling back a strip of clear, acid-free paper, he held up a detonator in gloved hands. He attached it to a long stretch

of fuse and opened a one-pound packet of sugar, which he mixed with weed killer. Suddenly his phone vibrated and shifted position on the table. His eyes were fixed on its display. It was Jenny. He carefully emptied the incendiary mixture into a plastic tub.
'Hello,' he said in a deep voice.
'Hi Tony, I hope I'm not disturbing you,' she said.
'Don't be silly,' he said, fingering the container on the table.
'What time do you want to meet?' she asked.
'Nine o' clock,' he said.
'Okay.'
'See you then. Oh! …Jenny, can you bring your laptop with you. It's just …well, mine is on the blink and I want to do up some invoices.'
'Damn! My battery is low.' She murmured a vague obscenity. 'Of course, and I'll give you a hand if-'
'Hello,' Tony said.
She was gone.

He flicked the cap off an empty box and inserted a pack of condoms, which he had pulled from his back pocket. Then he examined the lid of a small jar of sulphuric acid and made sure it was screwed on tightly. Pulling his dreadlocks over his eyes, he went outside. Bent almost double, he forced a mud-coated nozzle onto a cylinder of gas and lit the burner beneath a barrel of water. Back inside, he rummaged through an antique tallboy and found a little memo-park timer. He went back to the table and took a heated soldering iron from its cradle. He carefully soldered two wires, one black and the other red, to the memo-park timer. The free end of the red he left hanging outside the box.
Again his phone vibrated.
Tony answered after only a few vibrations. He had recognised Tom's number.
'Yep.'
'Tom here.' The Californian accent was unmistakable.

Tom stepped out of the lift straight into the Manhattan loft he was sharing with his brother, where over the spring the twins had been running their illegal operation. Edward was sitting on a tall chair. Tom sat down beside him. Their chairs were arranged side by side. The twin's body poses were similar with mirrored crossed legs and hands under chins, suggesting a like-minded purpose.

'What's up?' Tony asked.

Edward's voice butted in. 'We need that job completed by tomorrow morning.'

'When?' Tony quizzed. 'I mean, why?'

'It needs to be brought forward to coincide with another job,' Tom said.

'But you said tomorrow would be fine,' Tony complained. He put down the soldering iron.

'It'll mean an extra ten percent for you,' Tom said.

'Oh,' Tony said. 'Good.'

'Tremendous.'

'Right,' Tony said. He hung up, and then he rang Jenny, but there was no answer. He remembered her battery was spent, so he rang National Bank's switchboard.

'Extension 497 please.' He had barely finished the sentence when he heard the ring tone.

'Hello,' Jenny said faintly.

'Bad news, I've another work emergency and I won't be able to make it tonight.'

'Eh, two days in a row,' she said.

'Sorry!' His tone was apologetic.

'Don't worry.' She hid her disappointment. 'Same time tomorrow?'

'Great, looking forward to it already.' He waited for her to hang up.

Into a plastic container Tony fixed a mercury tilt switch and then he bolted on three magnets. When this was done he tested the device by inserting a light bulb. Next he soldered the metal leads from a receiver on to a printed circuit board. Satisfied, he paused for a moment to think. Very quietly, he slipped out to the field. He held in his hand a baton, like a catapult, with a cord mounted at both forks. The old man was not in the field. His red Citroen was still there, though, at the front of the allotments, so he could not have gone very far. Tony caught sight of someone moving below. But no, it was just a black whippet. There were a few conker-sized stones under a bush. He picked one up. He brushed the soil off the stone and then he gave it a rub on his jeans. A sycamore tree basked in the warmth of the sun. High up in its topmost branches a pigeon cooed. Tony killed the bird with a single shot as it took flight.

He came in from the field and the first thing he did was put the dead pigeon in a freezer bag. Then he stood outside, by the barrel. Using a hunting knife, he scooped some crystals from the surface onto a wooden lat. He began to beat them with a plastic hammer until they had turned to dust.

He pressed the nozzle on a hosepipe. Nothing came out. He checked the tap, pressed again. Still nothing.

The old man hung the scythe in a bush to dry, and then he dithered as he tossed kindling onto a small fire. When he saw Tony, he immediately made his way towards him, and asked him abruptly, 'you haven't on your travels seen my friend Ben, have you?'

With his back to the old man, Tony shook his head. He had just drawn water from a hand pump at the back of the allotments and was carrying a small pail.

In an animated voice, the old man asked, 'where are you going?'

Tony ignored him and continued.

The old man then asked him if he was working for Ben, and he said, 'No.'

Tony had a wild gleam in his eyes, like a tiger ready to pounce. His square jaw tightened, his facial expression was twisted and the golden-brown colour of his skin had darkened.

The old man wagged a bony finger and said, 'you shouldn't be here.' Then he turned round. But as he went he said something. Tony could not quite make it out.

What he said had sounded like: *police*.

Suddenly Tony's decision to come early was looking like a mistake. How many other things did the old man notice? Tony wondered to himself. He put the pail of water down in front of him on the soil.

All at once the old man felt his coat being ripped downwards. He tried to yell but a huge spade-like hand covered his mouth. Then he felt panic shoot out of his chest and up and down his body. A palpable blackness enveloped him.

He struggled to tear himself away, but Tony overpowered him and strangled him.

As Tony lifted the corpse its head tipped back. On returning to the shed he spread the tarpaulin on the ground and placed the body upon it. Then he wrapped the corpse and carried it to the fire. Strangely, he was angry with himself, but he was elated too, he was both.

While it was still light, Tony came across the allotments and knelt down in front of a grain bag full of seed inside the shed. He pulled a mortar and ammunition out. Skilled hands broke the whole lot down into two loads for backpack transportation. Then he patched up a hole in the sail of a sophisticated hang glider buffed up against the wall. He locked up the shed again. After one last look around, he popped the jeep into first gear and roared through the undergrowth, sending a fence post reeling into the vegetation.

A morsel of solid food had not passed his lips since breakfast, so on his way, he stopped off at a takeaway and bought a selection of Chinese dishes: chicken chow mien, pan-fried crispy duck, king prawns and a large batch of prawn crackers.

He parked the jeep at the back of a redbrick apartment block, halfway between Hyde Park Corner and Green Park, and he stood in the air on the corner of Down Street until all was quiet. He could see a man loitering across the street outside the front door. A taxi drove past, reversed, and then stopped. The man got in.

Tony skirted up the stairs to the fourth floor. He readied the key in his hand and sprinted for the door. Swiftly he went straight to the bedroom and placed two sets of clothing into a small backpack. After a quick shower he was on the road again.

Traffic was light all the way to Folkestone and he arrived at Cheriton just in time to catch the next shuttle train as it prepared to leave for Coquelles, near Calais. He purchased a return ticket and drove onto the shuttle, where a girl, blonde, tall, directed him in behind a French registered car. He remained inside the jeep for the duration of the journey, studying a roughly sketched map. When the train came to a stop at Coquelles he swung himself over the front seats into the driver's seat. He disembarked and headed straight for the town of Vosselar. Conditions were good, no rain and little wind. As he drove, he had his elbow out of the rolled-down window in the balmy air of the evening. He had taken the exact same journey three times in the last week.

Warily he steered the jeep through a wide opening, which served as an entrance to a large deforested area used by workers to store heavy machinery. His whole body pulled back taut. When it was obvious that he was alone he stood up to get out, but before he got out he leaned in over the top of the front seats. He opened the backpack containing the two sets of clothing and changed into a mud-caked pair of size ten boots, combats, black hat, and gloves. Under a boulder, behind an iron-banded tube of chopped trees right outside the lumber mill, he hid the keys. As he shone his headlamp onto a wall, a path appeared. He found himself walking in a waist-high expanse of heather. Encumbered by a backpack in each hand, and a heavier backpack hanging off each shoulder, he waded through a narrow streamlet. On the other side was a long ridge, with an abundance of bluebells, foxgloves and ferns, even under torchlight, the fresh tracks of wild boar and deer were highly visible.

    He abruptly stopped when he came to a leafy glade. Ribbons of water fell from his boots and were gobbled up by thirsty roots. Keeping an ear cocked for noises in the dark, he laid his packs carefully on the ground. Looking upwards he could see the gaping hole in the canopy of treetops as the moonlight cast mysterious shadows across the firm patch of dry ground where he assembled the mortar. As he placed the mortar bombs in a nice tidy pile, he recalled the words of his employers: *Hiroki, and his family, must die.*

In ghostly silence, he continued walking, laden free, for another five hundred metres until he reached the edge of a backyard lawn. Quickly he surveyed the isolated split-level house. It was as he expected; Mrs Hiroki and her two children were already in bed. Hiroki himself would not arrive home for another hour. Tony returned to the glade and emptied the rest of his backpacks. Upon a lifeless-looking bunch of twigs, at the base of the tree nearest to him, he set down the device with the memo-park timer. Then he trekked back to the house with the receiver-bomb under his arm and climbed on top of a water butt. From this vantage point he removed a vent. On a previous night he had chipped away the cement holding it in place. He primed the device and put his feet up on the sill then took them off again, brushing down where they had been with his hand. Back at the glade, he devoured a bag of edible mushrooms.

Flat on his stomach, he slid around to the front of the house with the mercury-switch device and immersed himself in a clump of untamed bushes growing in the middle of the garden. Just then a Mitsubishi Gallant reversed up the short driveway. It braked well away from the front door. Full of banter, three Japanese men got out and, without looking in Tony's direction, they went inside. Fifteen minutes later the lights went off but Tony stayed where he was for another five. Then he slunk across the ill-maintained lawn and on his back crawled in under the Mitsubishi. The magnets stuck fast to the metal of the under-body.

A light came on as he shimmied to the end of the backyard. He stopped as though uncertain of the source. Minutes later he heard a toilet flush. He went forward slowly, then paused and surveyed the glade ahead. Everything was as he had left it, so he settled back for half an hour with his feet up.

Nervously, a field mouse nibbled on a pine needle, and then sniffed the air. It sensed something was afoot and scurried off in the direction of the house.

Tony closed his eyes, but not to sleep. Finally he knelt down on one knee and picked up the mortar. He set the base plate on the ground, tilted the long barrel and checked the range finder. He pressed a few buttons on his phone and triggered the receiver bomb. In the same instant, he loaded the first of eight mortar bombs into the muzzle. One after another, each bomb flew above the trees and ploughed into the growing mound of rubble, leaving possessions scattered and body parts shredded.

Smoke billowed from the treetops and travelled on a light breeze. In minutes, Tony had everything packed away. He calculated the time it would take a pursuer to reach the glade, and then he set the memo-park timer accordingly. He stood back, relishing the aftermath, and then he disappeared into the yawning darkness. Back at the lumber mill, he quickly changed into a London Underground uniform and then he piled all the empty backpacks, combats and other accessories into a heap. Behind the jeep he poured sulphuric acid into a condom and lowered the last homemade bomb to the ground. He put the jeep into first gear and slowly edged out of the opening. He turned left, which brought him onto a road, straight as a ruler.

Instinctively, Hiroki grabbed his wife and he threw her through the shattered bedroom window. Chunks of concrete fell all around him as he ran to where his children's bedroom used to be. Frantically, he searched through the wreckage for his offspring but his eyes watered up and the fumes scorched his throat. In hope, he called out their names. He realised all was lost when he heard the whistle of the first mortar bomb. Immediately he covered his head and scampered out through a gaping hole in the front wall of the house. Miraculously, his car keys were still on the hall table. He grabbed them with a bloodied hand, while yet another mortar bomb fell from the sky. Shrapnel smashed into the boot of the dust-covered car as he jumped in. All that mattered to him was finding his wife. But the car would not start. He tried again, and again. His wife, meanwhile, had run into the woods with her arms out. Surging with fear, she had dragged herself to a firm patch of dry ground. At the foot of the tree where she sat, she heard a tiny click; the memo-park timer had turned full circle.

Three-quarter ways down the road Tony came upon the smoke-shrouded house. He slowed down and was shocked to see an empty driveway. As of yet, there were no police cars or fire engines rushing to the scene. Suddenly, his jeep was overtaken by the Mitsubishi Gallant as Hiroki searched up and down the road for his wife, thinking she had run to the front of the house and out on to the road. Tony checked his rear view mirror, there were no other cars in either direction, and so he accelerated. He seemed to be using the whole of his body to sink his foot even more heavily to the floor. The jeep rammed into the side of the Mitsubishi, forcing it off the road and into a jagged gully on the other side of the cycle path. Hiroki, trapped in the bottom, twisted and turned and moaned and cursed. He kicked his legs, but to no avail, then his body went limp. At last the mercury tilt switch levelled out and detonated the car bomb.

London was still in darkness when Tony found a vacant space on a side street, a short distance from the redbrick apartment block. He walked past a newsagent and stopped in front of a façade of oxblood tiles. Instead of continuing down the footpath, he took out an old mortise key and unlocked the door of the disused tube station. Shining his light, he dashed down a short flight of stairs and descended an aluminium spiral staircase. Halfway down he stopped and again used the mortise key, this time to open a fire door. Then he hurried down a slippery passageway with corroded pipes running along the walls until the beam of his headlamp spotted the doorway of an old bathroom.

CHAPTER 8

Buffeted by a patch of weighty turbulence, the antics of the fragile craft mirrored the erratic tones of a nervy captain. Sitting disconsolate, between two airhostesses, a boy flinched nervously as a ball of lightning moved slowly across the sky and burst. Eventually the plane emerged unscathed, much to the relief of aircrew and passengers. An impromptu round of applause served to channel the passengers' nervous energy as the plane resumed its intended course and nosed towards the English capital.

Passengers settled back to frittering away time. Michel yawned. Across from him, there was a group of habited nuns praying quietly - thanking God for the plane's safe deliverance. Behind them, a young couple were at loggerheads, arguing over whose fault it was they had chosen to fly. A row further back, two men sat upright, eyes alert and arms folded. One of them had red hair and a boxer's nose, while the other had a Gallic complexion. Towards the back of the cabin, Michel spotted a woman who looked strangely familiar. She wore her chocolate-brown hair short and curled, and her skin was overly tanned. He racked his memory trying to remember where he had seen her.

The plane landed safely in Heathrow. Michel caught the tube train to Leicester Square. From there he took the tube train to

Camden Town. He asked a taxi driver to take him from the station to Decourcy Street. Taking a sharp right onto Decourcy Street the taxi pulled up outside a house with a black plaque on the wall that said Shengjun. Michel climbed the steps and pressed the doorbell. He looked down the street. Then he looked up the street. There were a couple of people walking around, but nobody he recognised. The heavy black door swung open and Chen stood in the doorway, sporting a wide ear-to-ear grin. He bowed deeply and Michel reciprocated with a bow of lower depth. Chen then smiled and clapped Michel warmly on the shoulders.

To the left of the hall was the lounge and to the right was the dining room. Its bay window overlooked the street. Behind the dining room was the kitchen, which ended in a conservatory leading on to the back garden. Michel was ushered into the lounge. Both men assumed the lotus position with natural ease and sat facing each other on a large tiger skin that Chen had shipped over from his birthplace, Wenzhou, a port city in the Zhejiang province, Eastern China.

Dressed in a traditional kimono, Chen's Japanese wife Matsumi was petite and wiry, with gold earrings shaped like seedpods and a pearl dangling from a necklace around her neck. She served a bitter green tea and a plate of sweet delicacies, and then she placed the tray on the floor by the ebony table. She and Michel exchanged polite pleasantries before she quietly left the room. Engraved on the surface of the table was a chessboard, which Chen had shaped by hand along with thirty-two carved pieces. Michel examined the relative positions of each piece, which corresponded to the chessboard in his mind except for one piece, enabling him to deduce Chen's last move. Michel registered the new position. At the same time, he gave an account of his last few days in Crete.

He revered the man before him; Chen had no airs or graces, and was the only man in the local circuit that could defeat him in both the tactics of free sparring and competition Karate.

Chen then insisted on going to his favourite restaurant. Matsumi entered the room to remove the tray. Michel invited her to join them but she declined without the need to offer an excuse. Just as they opened the door to leave, Chen's only son, Setsu, arrived home from the family-run dojo, where he gave sought after instruction. He had broad, expressive features and the build of a judo champion.
'Ah! Michel san.' Setsu performed a cursory bow.
'Setsu.' Michel replied in like by lowering his head to the same level.
'Kanki deska!' Setsu forced a smile from his weary lips.
'Mushy Mushy!' Michel answered informally.

Whenever Setsu saw his father conversing with Michel an unpleasant feeling, a type of resentment, bubbled to the surface. He suspected that his own achievements were measured against those of Michel and did not cut the mustard. Despite his many victories there was one accolade that continued to elude him, and he regularly brooded over the best way to find favour in his father's eyes. One afternoon, when Setsu was alone with his mother, he vented his frustration to which she simply answered; *your father loves you as his own flesh and blood, whereas he honours Michel as a spiritual son.* Her reasoning, communicated with artful benevolence, appeased him temporarily. In his mind he understood what she meant but in his heart he did not fully understand.
He never broached the subject with his father, convinced he would think less of him.

Chen took Michel to Chinatown. Outside Leicester Square tube station, they veered left and then they took another left, walking past the Prince Charles cinema, and continued on down a thronged pedestrian street. On their way, Michel stopped and gave a busker a pound coin. Chen searched in his pocket for a coin too, to do the same. Between the tube station and the restaurant, Michel stopped and gave away a pound coin to every busker.

They arrived at the Peony Ki at about 8 p.m. Within a half-hour the queue extended out the front doors, down the side of the restaurant, and out into the street. Through an open door on the first landing, Michel had a bird's-eye view of the kitchen. The door had been left ajar to help void the searing heat built up by the huge iron woks, steaming, frying and stewing. The workers were busy cleaving, chopping, plucking, skinning, slicing, dicing and peeling. There were black bins full of scales, feathers, shells and used-fat. Containers of pork, beef and fish were set down on stainless steel counters and underneath there were baskets of chestnuts, mushrooms, seaweed and bamboo shoots. The head chef took a slug of scotch whiskey and snarled a command. Not altogether happy with the abeyance exhibited, he walloped the worker nearest him. On the second landing, waiters laden with clattering delft galloped to and fro.

In the cavernous restaurant, Michel and Chen were shepherded to one of the large circular tables rimmed with basic seats. Six people were already at the table. Once settled, Chen, with a somewhat bemused look, listened attentively to Michel speaking about yet another successful enterprise. He could never fathom his protégé's desire for precious objects or how he managed to merge such desires with an acute awareness of cultural beliefs. When Michel had finished articulating, Chen reported on May's brush with the bomb squad, and then he briefed him on Pat Hogan's audit of the Internet team's change control procedures.

'What do you suggest the correct course of action regarding Mr Wilkinson?' Chen asked.

'Create a project with a nice title, and then move him sideways,' Michel answered.

'Any ideas on who should replace him?' Chen had in his own mind the ideal candidate.

'Who do you think?' Michel enquired out of politeness.

'Pat Hogan,' Chen replied straight out.

Michel did not respond immediately but looked into his small white cup. He took a drink and smacked his lips. 'How would you feel, if I suggested Miss Franks for the position?'

'She's a bit on the young side, with no proven record.' Chen hid his surprise.

'That's true, but what if she had an experienced assistant manager, a mentor to shield and support her.' Michel directed Chen's train of thought.

'Then, who would you nominate for the position of assistant manager?' Chen asked.

'Pat Hogan.' Michel drained his cup.

'Well, who do you have in mind to take over the encryption programme?' Chen asked.

'You can discuss that with Pat, but run it by me before you finalise a decision.' Michel refilled his cup.

'Will do,' Chen said.

'Did you have my room in Crete under surveillance?' Michel asked.

'Of course, and I've arranged for someone to join us who can shed some light on the subject,' Chen said.

'Good,' Michel replied.

He told Chen about the dream he had and asked him what he thought it meant. Chen did not have an answer but promised to consult Matsumi, who from an early age, like her mother before her, was very good at dream interpretation. The waiter, as if conjured up by the essence of conversation, materialised between them and served their usual meals. Laid out in front of Michel was a dish of special fried rice, while Chen, with chopsticks in hand, toyed with a plate of sweet and sour pork. They consumed their victuals in silence, enjoying each sumptuous mouthful, stopping only to replenish an empty teacup from the third pot of Chinese tea. Both plates were wiped clean except for a few grains of rice. Afterwards Michel produced two filtered cigars from his inside jacket pocket and asked the diners sharing the table would they mind if he smoked. There was no objection, so he lit a cigar and passed it, lit, to Chen. Through the cloud of smoke, he asked Chen if there was anything out of the ordinary reported by those still in Crete. Chen assured him things were all quiet on that front and that he would be sending two replacements shortly.

'I hope you'll be sending two replacements of like standard?' Michel demanded.

'To be honest, I hadn't intended to,' Chen replied.

'Please do. This is important to me. I'm not sure why yet, but it is,' Michel insisted.

'Okay,' Chen said.

The waiter appeared with the bill and muttered something under his breath and plopped a small saucer on the table. Michel reached for his pocket but Chen stopped him.

'Michel, my treat.' He handed the waiter a crisp fifty-pound note.

They joined the crowd milling about Chinatown. Painted dragons, floral displays and giant lanterns swayed in the evening breeze. Before long, they took their leave of Chinatown and ambled through Leicester Square, stopping occasionally to merge with ad-hoc gatherings. A procession of Hare Krishna, clad in orange saffron robes, entered the square. Devotees chanted a purification mantra, "Hare Krishna, Hare Rama", ardently supported by sect members jingling well-worn bells. Leaders jumped high in the air and banged on drums that hung from their necks. Ponytails, the divine means of salvation, wagged and flapped to a pulsating beat. Close behind, women clothed in long robes handed out small delicacies. The Krishna held station for a few minutes more, to purify and entertain, then moved off and continued on their circular route, passing the Hippodrome and marching on up Tottenham Court Road.

Further on, a large crowd of spectators surrounded a small unkempt man, wearing dungarees, sitting like a peacock on a peculiar looking bicycle. There were two distinct chalk lines etched on paved stones, separated by a distance of no less than fifty metres. The man on the pushbike spoke in a strong cockney accent, challenging onlookers to ride his bicycle from one chalk line to the other without their feet touching the ground. Challengers were obliged to pay five pounds, and if successful, a prize of fifty pounds awaited. A stouthearted woman, spurred on by her two teenage sons, took up the challenge. She cycled four metres, turned the handlebars, so as to recover her balance, but her foot touched the ground. The crowd laughed and jeered. Again the small hackneyed man threw down the gauntlet, however, after witnessing the ignominy of the opening attempt, there were no takers. Michel decided to take up the challenge and produced a crumpled five-pound note. Chen scanned those in close proximity, searching for suspicious characters. He caught sight of one of the four bodyguards on duty. A red-haired freckled faced Irish man who had won a European boxing middleweight title after buying himself out of the army. While in the army, Sean Ryan had been trained as an explosives expert.

Slowly Michel pedalled, one metre, ten metres, twenty metres and thirty metres. The crowd shouted encouragement and started a slow handclap that attracted two policemen. As the policemen approached, Michel edged past the forty-five metres mark, and the crowd, which had grown in numbers, cheered and clapped loudly. And the hurrahs were deafening when Michel crossed the chalk line. The hackneyed man spotted the policemen and sprinted towards Michel. He jumped on the bike and pedalled off at high speed, like a man possessed.

Michel failed to notice the policemen, and called after him. 'Where's my fifty pounds?'

'Everything all right Sir?' quizzed one of the policemen.

'Fine officer, lovely evening,' Michel replied.

The other policeman spoke with a wry grin. 'If it's any consolation, you're the first I know of who has cycled the full fifty metres, but I wouldn't waste my energy chasing that scoundrel.'

'At least that's something. Good evening to you officers.' Michel acknowledged the compliment and walked back to where Chen was standing.

After a little more dillydallying, they arrived at the family-run dojo centrally located on Lichfield Street. The décor was simple, clean and down to earth. The main floor was composed of spring ash wood and the walls were adorned with a selection of antique weapons. Despite its simplicity, no cost was spared. Behind the arena was the massage room, which provided Chen's cousin Li, a Chinese masseuse, with employment. The stairway, laid with blue carpet, ran up the first and second storeys. On the first floor, behind the changing rooms and the sauna, was a meditation room. On the top floor, along with the two storerooms, was an office.

Chen wore a red cloth belt around his gi, while Michel wore a black belt. Both men knelt opposite each other, in a state of contemplation, eyes closed, inhaling deeply through the nose, down to the base of the belly. Free from material thought, neither man showed any sign of anxiety or any form of restlessness. The meditation room was quiet and tranquil, a safe haven away from worldly pressures. A gong was beaten but no one moved. Finally Michel opened his eyes and stood up. Chen sensed Michel's movement and jumped to a standing position. They left the room in harmony, each man planning his own distinctive approach to what was surely going to be an exacting test. Setsu, the class instructor, skidded to a halt outside the massage room. He watched his father and Michel enter the arena. Hurriedly, he darted upstairs and spoke to his students in a gruff manner.

'Please return to the arena and move in silence. When you enter, sit by the wall,' Setsu warned.

The twelve students took up a position by the wall furthest from the door and bowed to the men in the centre of the arena. Michel and Chen exchanged bows and instantly began to circle one another. Suddenly Michel feigned a left frontal kick, and then he swiftly moved to the outside of Chen's leading leg, he then swivelled on his left heel and brought his right leg up in a reverse roundhouse motion, but his ankle missed. This was the first time Michel had used such an obvious manoeuvre as an opening gambit. Chen, in order to recover his position, performed two successive backward somersaults. Then, suddenly, he leapt forward, coming in low, under Michel's guard. Even so, Michel struck him on the ear with a venomous elbow-strike, and then he grabbed his exposed leg, lifting it upwards and backwards. Chen landed on the flat of his back. In a half-kneeling position, Michel prepared a snap-punch, but Chen swept a foot across his hamstrings and turned him in the air.

Michel was first to his feet but with his back to Chen. He bent forward and dispatched a vicious back-kick directed at Chen's chest, and sent him sliding along the ash floor into the arms of Setsu. Setsu did not move a muscle; if he had his father would have been furious. As Chen regained his feet, Michel leapt high against the wall and snatched from its guardianship a double-sided battle-axe, consisting of an ugly spearhead on a solid wooden handle. The students wheezed in disbelief, but quickly regained their composure after a curt word from Setsu. Michel leapt once more and wrested a spear from its lofty perch. He transferred his body weight onto his right leg and arched his back. Chen ducked as the spear whizzed by him. The flint point penetrated the wall just above the awestruck students. While the shaft of the spear still quivered, Michel wielded the axe then sprinted towards Chen. The speed of the attack allowed no time for Chen to arm himself.

Chen had to exert all of his ability and power to hold Michel off and still he suffered a cut through his gi that grazed his side. He covered the crimson-stained material with his hand, leaving his right side undefended. Michel followed up the axe thrust with a hand chop to the side of Chen's temple. Chen collapsed in a heap and lay motionless on the floor. Then Michel, with a crazed roar, swung the axe high in a sweeping arc and brought the flat of the head downwards. The students gasped. One moved to prevent the blow but was held back by Setsu. Suddenly Chen's eyes opened. He rolled towards Michel's feet, away from the axe's trajectory, knocking him off balance. The axe struck the floor.

Ash splinters flew out in all directions.

Michel had to work hard to retrieve the axe, a task that gave Chen enough time to arm himself. Chen advanced, rotating a sword in a wide helix. He now had the advantage. Michel, who had successfully reclaimed the axe, was forced back by the longer reach of the sword. Chen flexed both knees and lunged just below the saddle line. Now Michel was pinned against the wall. In one motion, Chen whipped up his sword and dispatched a downward cut. He left Michel with no choice but to parry. Michel lifted the axe above and away from his head.

The slashing blade severed the head of the axe and Chen immediately launched a running attack, beating aside the wooden handle before smacking the hand-guard of the sword across the side of Michel's head. Michel tottered and swayed from side to side. Chen then drove the sword into the floor and left it oscillating. He delivered a two-footed aerial kick, directed at the head of the wavering figure before him. The contest was over.

Setsu was both delighted and relieved; his students were dumbfounded by the sheer explosiveness of the blood-spattered session. Groggily, Michel lifted himself to his feet and stood upright. They finished the session in an identical manner to the way they had started, bowing to each other with clasped hands, before retiring to the meditation room. Li was waiting outside with the first-aid kit. He was big and hollow-eyed, his chest tattooed with Shinto symbols. At Chen's insistence, he worked his magic on Michel first.

They took the tube train back to Chen's house, where waiting for them in the dining room was Mary Jane, a senior forensic scientist with Secure Span. Matsumi expressed no surprise when she saw the state of Michel's nose, so Mary Jane followed suit. Matsumi left the room to prepare tea.

On the dining table were a number of items: a disc, a watch and a leaden case. The unrelated items perked Michel's curiosity. Mary Jane clicked the player open, inserted the disc, which happened to be the disc with Michel's apartment on it in Crete. She pressed fast-forward, then pressed play. She turned the volume up. As Michel studied the flickering screen, he recognised the apartment. He watched as a blonde girl stood warily outside the apartment door with a small parcel tucked under her elbow. The cleaning lady was doing her rounds and had just finished cleaning the apartment. She was busily gathering up black plastic bags and was just about to close the door when the blonde girl beckoned her. Boldly, the blonde gave the impression she was staying in the apartment. The cleaning lady sauntered off without suspicion. Shortly afterwards, the blonde emerged with the parcel, now opened, still in her hand. She scurried away looking left, and then right.

Mary Jane pressed stop. For the only time during the viewing, she grew wary. Sitting back in her chair, she gave her head a quarter turn to look at Michel out of the corner of one eye. Then she adjusted her square-shaped spectacles and stood up and brushed down her grey pinstripe suit. A few strands of hair escaped her tightly woven bun.

'The item I was asked to examine is nothing more than an ordinary light bulb. However, the contents are distressing. It contains a thousand gig-beckels of caesium chloride, which is a low-grade radioactive material,' she said.

Her eyes rested on the leaden case. She opened it.

'Can you repeat that?' Michel asked in a nasal tone. The blood-soaked cotton was beginning to harden in his nostrils.

'Caesium chloride: a radioactive material. Even more worrying, under closer inspection, we found a tiny quantity of gunpowder,' she explained, as she lifted the open case for the two men to see.

'Why on earth would someone go to so much trouble?' Michel asked.

She answered in an officious manner, detached from any detectable emotion. 'The gunpowder will blow the bulb and the buoyancy of the heated air will cause the caesium chloride to drift across the room. Then, during the night, as the temperature chills, the radioactive particles cool and begin to drop and settle on the apartment floor. The effect of such exposure wouldn't be immediately noticeable, but it would lead to the mutation of human cells and eventually result in cancer. Unfortunately, radioactive material doesn't go away and the material would remain in the apartment for many years to come.'

'Charming!' Michel quipped, belying his concern.

'I was asked to provide you with a watch, with a built-in radioactive sensor, that will detect the presence and intensity of radiation.' She handed the watch to Michel. 'If you press these two buttons simultaneously, it switches to a mode that displays the level of radioactivity present, a miniature Geiger counter of sorts. One to two milliceverts is the threshold measurement of normal background radioactivity, anymore than that is considered dangerous,' she warned.

'Where would someone find such material,' he asked.

'There are a few places. The most likely spot is in a hospital where it's used in needles essential in the treatment of cervical cancer.' Her cultured explanation complete, she began to gather up her props.

'Thank you Mary Jane, we're most appreciative. As a token of our gratitude, please accept this gift.' Chen handed her a pink envelope containing an itinerary and tickets for a mid-week break in romantic Paris.

Matsumi saw out Mary Jane. The two men sat in silence.

'Any luck in tracing the girl?' Michel asked.

'No, not yet,' Chen answered apologetically.

'I presume you're targeting the hospitals and running background checks on employees with access to cancer wards?' Michel demanded, as he strapped on his new watch.

'In the light of Mary Jane's forensic analysis, we will.' Chen made a mental note.

'That blonde girl featured in the surveillance footage was on my flight back to London. She looked different; her hair was a dark chocolate brown. At the time, it escaped me as to where I had seen

her.' Michel shook his head. 'It was by the pool; she was hanging around with a group of medical students. They called her Tara.'
'Are you sure?' Chen asked.
'Yes,' Michel replied.
'Excuse me a moment, I need to organise a plane inspection.'
Chen left the room and phoned Mary Jane. 'My apologies, I need you in Heathrow, as soon as possible. I'll organise the relevant clearances, and a man, Christophe, will be waiting for you.'
Chen hung up.
While looking at his watch, Chen phoned Christophe, and then he phoned the private line of the shift commander overseeing airport security.
'George, Chen here, I'm sending two people to inspect one of your planes. Depending on the results, it may need to be quarantined.'
There was silence on the other end. 'That's a tall order, but I'll do my best.'

Chen returned to the dining room and waited patiently until Michel had finished playing with his new watch.
'Needless to say I'm very concerned regarding this change of tack. It's an amalgam of brilliant recklessness and a laconic demonstration of foresight,' Michel complained with a hint of admiration.
'It's not your typical approach to eliminating adversaries.' A crestfallen Chen was in agreement. He had made a conscious decision not to inform Michel of the brutal murder of Hiroki and his family. Chen felt it wise not to put him in the picture until those responsible for the tragedy were brought to heel.
'Does Fobie have a sat-phone?' Michel made to leave.
'Yes, he has one for emergencies, but I enjoy daily communication with those assigned to protect him,' Chen answered, putting Michel's mind at ease. 'And you'll be pleased to know that every artefact is safe and accounted for.'
'I wouldn't doubt it for a second. I'm tired my friend, you worked me well tonight.' Michel fiddled with his nose, now gloriously swollen.

'You nearly ended me with that axe.' Chen caressed his wounded side.

'Nonsense. By the way, as a matter of interest, what were Mary Jane's plans?' Michel asked, his inquisitive nature getting the better of him.

'It was her wedding anniversary.' Chen stopped rubbing his side.

'What was in the envelope?'

'A midweek break.' Chen stood up when Michel headed for the door. Matsumi was waiting in the hall and her angelic figure caught Michel by surprise.

'Toyoko is waiting outside, she says there are urgent messages to deal with and they cannot wait until tomorrow. Your bag is already in the car.' Matsumi returned Michel's smile.

'I'll see you soon.' On his way out, Michel poked his head around the lounge door so as to have one last look at the chessboard and then he left the house, venturing out in to the chill of the night.

The passenger door flew open and Michel hopped in.

'Toyoko, what can't wait until tomorrow?' he chided.

'The architect, on site in Warbah, says there's a problem with one of the load bearing formulae, and he needs to speak to you urgently,' she said, as she indicated and swerved out, barely missing the overturned rubbish bin that she had knocked over on her arrival.

She was bright and strikingly cute, with broad cheekbones.

'You're not making any sense, those formulae have been triple-checked and checked again.' His face darkened.

'That may be true, but one of the column supports may not be wide enough because of a modification.' She heard him curse.

'That's it, how many times have I told Sheikh Ra, that any deviation, no matter how small, from the original design, can have dire consequences.' He fumed and the windscreen misted up.

'Don't kill the messenger and what happened to your nose?' She turned on the blower.

'I know, I know. Who's the architect?' He touched her jean-clad knee in platonic fashion.

'Fergus Arnett.' Her knees shivered under his touch and she thought to herself, please leave your hand where it is. She lived in hope, ignoring all other suitors, that one day she would be more than just an assistant to him.

'Ah, the new guy, that explains it.' His equilibrium restored.

There was a light tap on the door. Chen looked up and smiled at his son. He was proud of him and regretted not telling him so. He invited him to sit on the fluffy cushion. Politely, Setsu kept his silence until his father spoke.

'How are you my Son?' Chen smiled.

'Fine, more so with the knowledge that you weren't seriously hurt.' Chen rarely smiled while conversing with his issue and the gesture had not escaped Setsu's cognisance.

'Ah yes, I must confess I was pushed to my limits this evening. His dojo craft is so much improved and he's getting stronger, braver and increasingly fearless. I'm not getting any younger, so I think it's time for someone else to share my responsibilities. How would you feel about working with me, protecting Michel?' Chen asked.

'It would be a great honour to work with you father, but I don't understand why you risk your life shielding Michel,' Setsu replied. Buoyed by an atmosphere of rare intimacy he waited for an explanation.

'I'll tell you in good time but suffice it to say, for now, that your mother would not be with us but for the bravery of Michel.' Chen spoke gravely and with utter sincerity.

'What, mother has never mentioned this to me.' Setsu paused when he saw the hurt traverse his father's eyes.

'I suspect she doesn't remember too much about the incident. It might be better if you didn't ask her.'

'Very well.' Setsu resigned himself to more waiting

Chen changed the subject and the smile returned to his face. 'Now, how do you feel about working with me?'

'I trust you father and because you're prepared to give your life for Michel, then I too pledge my loyalty to this man.' Setsu held his fist over his heart.

'Tomorrow, I'll ask Michel for his thoughts on my proposal. If he agrees, then you may start immediately.' Chen was genuinely pleased with Setsu's commitment.

'Thank you, father. Now please go to bed and enjoy a well-deserved rest.' Setsu's concern was touching.

'Has mother retired to bed?' Chen asked.

'Yes, father.' Setsu nodded.

'Then I'll join her. Good night my son.' Chen lightly punched Setsu on the shoulder and left the room.

'Father, why are your sparring sessions with Michel so dangerous?' Chen heightened his voice from halfway up the stairs. 'It may be the very thing that saves his life.'

Careful not to disturb Matsumi, Chen slipped in under the duvet. Matsumi opened her eyes and placed a soft hand on the small of his back.

'Are you awake?' he whispered, just loud enough for her to hear.

'Yes my love.' Her answer was clear-toned and she began to massage his back. He turned over and sat upright. They discussed and agreed upon the idea that Setsu should take over some of his duties, conditional on Michel's approval. Then Chen recounted Michel's dream and asked her to interpret.

'First thing in the morning, I will meditate upon its essence and seek an understanding. For now, go to sleep and pleasant dreams.' She drew his head back onto the pillow and began to sing a nagauta to help him relax. She waited until his snore was in full swing, and then she slid out of bed and tiptoed to the prayer room.

It was morning but it was still dark. After a lengthy night of recalculations and videoconferences in the Canada tower office, Toyoko and Michel drove through the stirring streets of London.

They stopped off at a small café, near London city airport not far from canary wharf, and he treated her to a hearty breakfast.

'Thanks for your help, Toyoko.' He yawned and rubbed his eyes.

'No problem, that's why you pay me big bucks. You didn't tell me what happened to your nose.' She chuckled in a coquettishly teasing way and tried to touch it, but he backed off. Her light-skinned cheeks blushed a sallow pink, barely detectable. Her discomfort caught him off guard. He put it down to the hot air being spewed out by the fan heaters above the door. 'Ask your father,' he snarled.

'Ah, that would explain it. Have you two been fighting again?' She recalled putting the same question to him four months ago. On that occasion, he wore a bandage on his wrist and walked with a limp.

'Just a little.' He gulped down the last of his coffee.

'Dad rang and asked could you call round to the house at your earliest convenience.' She used a cut of toast to scoop up a runny egg and pop it into her mouth.

'No time like the present.' He waited until she had finished and then paid the bill.

'Did you really have to fire poor Fergus?' She looked in the rear view mirror and turned left.

'Any other time, no, but when you're dealing with the well-being of thousands of lives, an example has to be made.' He thought of the carnage in the wake of the collapse of the Sampoong Shopping Centre and the subsequent incarceration of its owners.

'Fair enough, you're the boss. Should I draw up an advertisement for his replacement?' She pulled up on Decourcy Street, just outside her parents' house. The car mounted the footpath and pushed the same bin into a parking metre.

'Yes.' Accustomed to her driving gaffes, he hopped out and moved the bin. 'Thanks Toyoko, go home and get some sleep, I'll catch you later.'

Matsumi was waiting for him. She swung open the front door and invited him upstairs to the prayer room. Food offerings of rice and fish were arranged neatly on a small pine table in front of a Shinto shrine.

Sublimely poised, she offered her interpretation of his dream.

'I found it difficult to visualise some aspects of your dream, but those that were clear I will now explain. The centurion is your new protector, yanked from a life he knows well, entrusted with a commission he does not yet understand. The warlock is an assailant, addicted to evil doing and corruption, capable of horrific savagery. His actions stem not of his own volition but at the behest of a pronged force, campaigning for power and revenge. His decomposing flesh embodies a mounting spiritual debt, decaying with each terrible exploit. Indeed, it shall come to pass, that he will point a weapon at you, in a place where exiled people have suffered an intolerable misery and where lies a forgotten fortune, which must not be removed from the country of its entombment. The silver bullet represents destiny, and the young seer is a woman who will save you from yourself,' she explained

She suggested that he remain in the prayer room and contemplate her words, while she went downstairs to prepare tea. She hid her disappointment. She had hoped the girl in his dream might have been her daughter, Toyoko, but alas, it was a woman she had never seen. Michel felt very at ease in the prayer room, although not a believer in Shinto ideology he found it a great place to collect his thoughts. He fell asleep but awoke when he heard the handle of the door squeak. Matsumi placed a cup of tea on the floor beside him and shuffled out, quiet as a church mouse. An hour later Chen joined Michel in the prayer room and sought permission to handover some of his obligations to Setsu. Immediately, Michel gave his blessing.

Chen sat quietly in the lotus position at the base of the Siberian tiger's neck. Setsu knelt at the other end. The jewel-toned light, filtered by the drawn net curtains, enhanced the fabric of intimacy between the two men. An atmosphere not disturbed in any way as Matsumi glided across the floor with a bamboo tray laden with a pot of tea, cups and a plate of salted rice cakes. She set the tray down on the rug, in front of Chen, and poured two cups of tea and then left them alone. Chen picked up a cup and handed it to Setsu. He received it with both hands. Chen then picked up the second cup and held it below his nose. He watched the leaves diffuse and darken the tint of water, and then he spoke softly but emphatically.

'Setsu my son, one of my responsibilities, and probably the most important, is the management of the White Sock Guard whose primary duty is to protect Michel. They are rewarded handsomely through the books of our dojo. This is the reason why I never trust anyone other than myself to do the books, that is until now.'

Then he took a piece of folded paper from under the paw of the lifeless tiger and passed it to Setsu. Setsu unfolded the paper and studied the Chinese characters; it was a list of names and dates of birth. Up until now, Setsu had believed that his father did not think him capable of doing the dojo accounts, but now that he understood, his confidence soared.

'What do these names signify. Are they members of the White Socks?' Setsu asked.

'Yes, they are, and I will describe briefly each member. In time, you will meet them.' Chen wondered whether he was placing too much responsibility on his son.

'Thank you, father. You do me a great honour.' Setsu felt goose bumps surface on his forearms as he skimmed the length of the list.

'You have earned it my son. Needless to say, I'll start you off with some basic tasks but as time goes by, you'll assume more and more responsibility for the White Socks.' Chen reached over, but had to stretch in order to pat Setsu on the head.

'The first name on the list is Fukiko, who happens to be a calligrapher by profession, and her main discipline is karate. The second name on the list is a French man who goes by the name of Christophe, a medical doctor, whose main discipline is Judo. The third name on the list is Akiko; she is a housewife and she is married to Christophe. They became romantically involved while working on a White Sock mission. Her favoured discipline is aikido, the same as your mother's discipline.' Chen stopped when he saw the look of surprise on Setsu's face.

'Mother's discipline?' Setsu stuttered.

'Yes, your mother is an exponent of aikido. You should ask her about it. Actually, your grandmother was a highly regarded student of Morihei Uyeshiba, the founder.'

'Amazing!' Setsu was already priming a series of questions to put to his mother.

'I'll continue. The next name on the list is Hirokatsu, a retired professional sumotori who reached the level of yokosuna, grand champion. I usually pair him off with the next name on the list, Ichiro, the son of a wealthy merchant, and an expert in kendo.' Chen's sense of pride grew. As he went through the list of names, he was reminded of how accomplished and worthy these people were. They did not seek glory or recognition but revelled in the knowledge that they belonged to a group that stretched the barriers of normal living. An organisation not strangled by the constrictions of a governing body.

'Father, sorry for interrupting, but how did you manage to assemble such an illustrious membership?' Setsu asked.

'With great difficulty and a lot of travel,' Chen replied, recalling the sleepless nights and countless days criss-crossing continents.

'Is there any reason why they all have different primary disciplines?' Setsu wondered out loud.

'Yes, each discipline lends itself to a different character. For example, the next name on your list is Mayumi, who is a practitioner of Ninjutsu and Shuriken-do, an exemplar for covert work. She has the uncanny ability to blend into any situation.'

There was a gentle knock on the door and Matsumi entered the room.

'Excuse me, Michel is on the phone,' she said. Chen left the room.

'Mother, please join me.' Setsu folded the paper containing the list of names and placed it under his knee.

'Just for a moment, I'm very busy,' she replied.
'Father has told me of your interest in aikido,' he said.
'That's true,' she replied.
'Grandmother was also a student, a student of the founder?' he asked the question rhetorically.
'Yes, she was a student of the great Morihei Uyeshiba.' She smiled as she reflected wistfully on the beauty and grace of her dear departed mother.
'Tell me about him, the founder?'
'Your grandmother seldom spoke of him but when she did, it was to substantiate the constant rumours circulating about his powers. He could read his opponents' minds and predict their actions before they moved. On one occasion, while under his instruction, your grandmother was having difficulty with a complicated pattern of movement. She noticed him looking at her intently; suddenly her body advanced of its own accord and executed the pattern. By all accounts, he was a truly remarkable man.'
Matsumi studied her son's face, captivated by the testimony, his mouth wide open.
'Astonishing to know such a person,' he said.
'Another time, in order to demonstrate the harmony of universal energy, he challenged eight sumo wrestlers, standing in a line, one behind each other, to push him over. The wrestlers showed no restraint and applied all their collective strength. They gave up after fifteen minutes, all their energy expended. Morihei just smiled at them and walked off to give thanks in front of a shrine.'
Mother and son sat quietly for a minute before he shook his head.
'Mother do you still practice?'
'Yes, of course,' she replied with affront.
He continued to quiz, in the manner that every child does, no matter how young or old. 'When? I've never seen you practice?'
'I awake at 4 a.m. every morning and go into the back garden. Usually I stand in the shade of the spruce. Sometimes your father joins me.' She waited patiently for the obvious request.

'Can I practice with you one morning?' he asked.
She bowed to his request. 'You may, next Friday.'
'Why not tomorrow?' he asked.
'I have my own ways and rituals. Your father is only allowed to join me on a Friday, and the same rule applies to you. It's just my way.' She smiled and offered no further explanation.
'Mother, if I may ask another question. You don't have to answer if it rekindles unpleasant memories.' He spoke softly, he did not want to ask, but the nature of youth propelled him to enquire. 'Father spoke of Michel and how indebted he was to him, that in all likelihood you would no longer be with us but for his help.' He stopped when he saw the shadow of hurt drift across the plains of her face.
'Your father has told me of his desire for you to share in his work, so perhaps you should understand why he does what he does. It's important that you never repeat this to anyone.'
She waited for him to agree.
'Mother, you have my word,' he pledged.
'When your father and I first came to this country, we got a job running a small restaurant in Chinatown. You were probably too young to remember but after a few years we took out a lease and started our own little restaurant. It was hard work but we persevered. Your father believed that you and Toyoko were at a disadvantage, since English was not your first language. So we tightened our belts and saved enough to send you and your sister to private school. Throughout all those years, we never had any trouble. Unexpectedly, one stormy afternoon, while your father was at the wholesalers, and I was busy washing rice and preparing food for the night's business, three men from the triad, wearing black capes, barged into the restaurant. One of them had with him a Shar-pei fighting dog. I complained when the dog splayed all over the furniture, but the man just laughed. Everyone in Chinatown had to pay the triad's tariff. But we failed to prepare the brown envelope in the previous week - business was a bit slow. When the man with the fighting dog opened

the till and saw it contained only coins, he became very angry. He began to shout and curse, and then the dog started to growl and bark. Then he hammered shut the till with his fist. One of the other men threw a bowl at me. It hit me on the side of the head and knocked me over. The others laughed, and then the man who had thrown the bowl said he would teach me a lesson to serve as a reminder to never forget the tariff. He shouted at the other two to hold me down. The man at the till released the dog and it went for me. The pain from the dog's fangs was excruciating. The angry man cut through my kimono and then he pulled down his breeches. The dizziness left my head and I began to recover my senses. I started to laugh at the tattoos covering his belly, a fearful laugh, well disguised, as I was petrified. Then I jeered at how small his manhood was compared to a real man like my husband. This made him even more furious. I began to panic and started to yell for help.'

Matsumi stopped for a mouthful of lukewarm tea.

'Mother, you don't have to continue,' Setsu said.

'I want to. Occasionally, it's good to cleanse the cupboard of skeletons,' she answered.

'Where are these men now?' He became angry and impatient.

'Please, allow me to continue.' She collected her thoughts, and then she took up from where she left off.

'He separated my legs and knelt down between them, still cursing and shouting profanities. But he suddenly looked up. A teenager that I had never seen before stood in the doorway, wearing oilskins. The young fellow was only a few years older than you were, and I feared for his safety. Cool as you like, he asked for a drink of water. The evil man stood up and, with his breeches around his ankles, told the teenager to vamoose. Instead of leaving, the teenager unbuckled his rucksack and let it fall to the floor. Then he walked bravely to the counter. One of the men holding me down let go of my arm and slipped a long thin dagger from his sleeve. He sprung to his feet and went to intercept the young fellow. The dog released its vice-like grip and turned to follow the man with the dagger. I struggled to break free and yelled a warning to the youth. He grabbed a wok and struck the approaching man in the face, and then he brought it down heavily on the snarling dog. The man who was still holding me down sprang to his feet and ran towards the youth. He bobbed and weaved before stooping to pick up the fallen dagger. The struggle ran its course, with the dagger lodged in the triad member's gut. The man who was standing between my legs pulled up his breeches and tried to run out the back door but the youth ran after him and tripped him up. The youth caught him in an arm lock and squeezed with all his might. I can still see the man's bulbous eyes staring at me. The man collapsed on the ground, and then the youth sprinted towards the man recovering from the wok blow, and he began to kick the life out of him. The dog regained consciousness, but not for long. The young fellow drove the dagger through his heart. I was in a state of shock; the teenager was none other than Michel. I could not comprehend what was happening, the violence, the outcome, it all happened in a flash, and then he asked me who these men were and I told him. He went into the back kitchen and broke open a drum of cooking oil. He poured oil over the dead men and the dog. He picked me up and moved me to a chair by the back door and then he proceeded to set the bodies alight. He waited until they were burning before he ignited the deep-fat fryers. He set fire to my kimono and then he quickly stamped it out. He flared my hair and then he hurriedly smothered it, leaving me with a singeing head. Then he carried me out into the back lane. I could not stand; so he made a bed out of cardboard boxes. Then he stripped off his oilskins and ran back into the restaurant just as your father returned from the wholesalers.' Matsumi sighed, her energy drained as she relived the terrible episode.

Setsu gulped. He was in a state of shock.

At that very moment, Setsu pledged himself to follow in his father's footsteps. What bravery, he thought, for a teenager to save an unknown woman from the wrath of the triad and have enough forethought to protect her from retribution by making the fire look like an accident.

Matsumi took a deep breath and spoke once more.

'When the dust settled and I told your father what had happened, it was then that he committed himself, in the spirit of the samurai, to Michel.'

She fought back the tears and tried to forget the likely outcome if Michel had not wandered into the restaurant. Chen believed that her ancestors had sent Michel to protect her on that terrible day, a belief that she now shared.

'What courage, now I can see why father treasures him so,' Setsu said. He wanted to scour the capital for Michel, hug him, kiss him, and lie prostrate at his feet. Remorseful and guilt ridden by the many ill thoughts he had fermented when bitterness trickled through his veins.

'Since Michel has come into our lives, a whole new world has opened up for us. Through our association with him, we have become financially secure. We own this beautiful home and a thriving hotel in Wenzhou, your father's hometown, without the heaviness of a mortgage. Toyoko is Michel's personal assistant and owns her apartment outright. In fact, if Michel had his way, our wealth would be increased a hundredfold, but your father and I remain adamantly opposed, arguing that he has already brought prosperity to this family. Now, it's your turn, your father believes you are ready, as do I,' Matsumi said.

She looked into his eyes and saw truth, tribute and trustworthiness. She thought for a moment, and then she left the room.

Setsu could hear his mother and his father converse excitedly. Not long after, Matsumi returned cradling two items, which she laid down in front of him. He focused on the longer sword and began to stroke gently the hilt, admiring the beauty of its artwork. He appraised its true value by scrutinising the calibre of the point. She let him bask in the sword's exquisiteness before speaking.

'These two swords belonged to my father and were bequeathed to me when your grandfather left this world. His ancestral lineage was that of samurai, and the spirit of the samurai is the sword; the long sword is the tachi, and is used for combat, the short one is called a wakizashi, and is used for seppuku - the taking of one's life should the samurai fail his master. My great-grandfather, who was a member of the emperor's police guard, commissioned a weapon-maker to make these swords, using ancient traditional techniques.'

Matsumi watched intently as her son fondled the hilt with reverence.

'Was grandfather a good swordsman?' he asked, his attention now fixed on the smaller sword, egging to ask the question; was it ever used for its intended purpose.

'One year, when I was only a toddler, he and my mother brought me to the island of Kyushu, south of Japan, for our annual vacation. Coincidently, this was the same time as the samurai festival of the Kaseda shrine where swordsmen from all around fought each other with sticks instead of swords. My father emerged the victor and I remember my mother singing joyously while nursing his badly bruised body. You should know that I offered these swords to Michel after I was discharged from hospital, but he refused, saying: *I won't take away your son's birthright.*'

She smiled in the knowledge that her father would be happy that his grandson now cared for his most prized possessions.

Deep down, Setsu felt obliged to offer them again and decided to do so at the earliest opportunity. He stood up with the tachi in his hands and gently coaxed it to trace a small circular movement.

'Son be careful, it's unbelievably sharp,' she warned. Ah! Here is your father.'

Upon entering, Chen beamed brightly.

CHAPTER 9

It was a Friday today. It was getting dark. Hugging the long sweeping driveway, reeled in by an imposing stately house, a taxi nosed over the downslope. Billy, a semi-retired cabdriver, cajoled his grating gears and kept a watchful eye for wayward ramblers. He and May were engaged in small talk. The taxi chugged past a separate thoroughfare that branched off to a one-bedroom mews cottage, used by guests visiting the family.

The driveway curved beneath the maples and oaks to a cobble-locked crescent. Billy parked the taxi in front of a shallow entrance porch. He sounded the horn and a heavyset woman waved to him from the heart of the garden that possessed flourishing growths of sage, basil, oregano, thyme and hyssop. The woman, by means of facial expression and hand movement, gestured to her husband an invitation for tea. He declined with a shake of his head.

The house had survived both world wars and its baronial splendour dominated the three hundred acres listed in the title deeds. Originally, the Franks' domicile had been situated two kilometres north of the current site, but when the daughter of the owner died, it was disassembled boulder-by-boulder and reconstructed on top of a hill overlooking the estate. While it was being rebuilt the Wiltshire house had been extended to incorporate a library and a study room. As part of a more recent renovation, Charles had converted the extension into a tearoom. It had become commercially marketed and widely popular with excursions en route to Stonehenge for the quality of its traditional food.

The East Avon, containing rocks, strong currents and a copious fish populous, flowed swiftly all the way through the outer parklands and was the raison d'être of an annual fishing competition that attracted some of the world's best fishermen. The previous year, the overall winner had hooked a mammoth pike, the biggest ever.

Billy, on first name terms with May, refused to accept the fare on account of the many favours afforded his family by her parents, not least of which was his wife's part-time job serving in the tearoom. May turned the key in the huge brass lock. With a little force it surrendered and she entered the wood-panelled hallway. Its polished timbers kept the hall warm in the winter and cool in the summer. Skippy whimpered with delight. He skidded across the quarry-tiled floor and bumped clumsily into May. She dropped her handbag and lovingly rubbed his ears and allowed him to lick her face with his slobbery tongue. His woolly coat, more brindle than black, added a few kilograms to his powerful body. And the hideous scar on his snout, the result of a vicious encounter with a wolf, belied his good nature.

Charles had been actively involved in a controversial wolf-reintroduction program, and his company, Peoples Pensions, partly funded compensation payments to farmers whose livestock might have been killed or maimed by wolves.

May's face glistened with saliva as she sauntered into the main hall, followed closely by Skippy, who had free run of the house and refused to let her out of his sight, even for a minute. In years gone by, the main hall hosted many a ball and banquet. To get to the kitchen, May had to walk through the dining room, spacious, despite the presence of a long waxed table. As she made her way through, she ran a finger along the lip of a dado-rail and threw an eye over the gallery, which included works by Velázquez, Goya and Tintoretto. A door at the end of the room led to a hallway busy with doors onto the kitchen, scullery, pantry, laundry and the stairs to the cellar. She freed the brass catch and hopped down the single step onto the bright kitchen floor. Dancing along, she passed a series of windows with views across the estate to the rear - the rock garden, wild-flower garden, an orchard, a hothouse, and beyond them goats, horses, and a field of vegetables. She stood by the range and took a sniff. Venison was on the menu - her father's favourite. She returned to the main hall, climbed the wide spiral staircase and went straight to her bedroom. This was her private place, free from intrusion. Even the housemaid was denied access.

She took a shower. Revived and refreshed, her bathrobe wrapped around her, she glanced out the bedroom window. The curtains moved gently, touched by the breeze, the air pure. The view swept down a series of stone steps to an expanse of lush parkland. A distinguished figure scaled the steps. A double-barrelled shotgun, broken at the breech, looped over his shoulder.

Her father had recently grown a beard and, combined with his crimped grey hair, cut the figure of Abraham Lincoln, so much so, that she could visualise him delivering the Gettysburg address.

May waved from the window but Niall, the elderly groundsman, who descended the stone steps, drew Charles's attention away from the house. Niall pointed towards an unused stable block in the middle of an enclosure adjoining the tearoom. On her last visit, her father had been in two minds whether to convert the block into a self-contained apartment, or to buy more horses. The two men spoke in length, and then they turned to climb the steps. Charles spotted May waving from the stone-mullioned window. A smile lit up his face and he gave her a royal salute.

Hurriedly, she picked out a simple frock and a pair of beaded sandals. She could hear her father's hobnailed boots ascend the staircase. He stood on the landing outside her bedroom door and knocked.

'Are you decent?' he asked.

'Come in,' she said. She was brushing her hair.

She smiled lovingly at him. He smiled back.

'Get off the bed, you mutt, or you'll feel the hardness of my boot,' he yelled.

Skippy leapt off the bed and dashed passed him.

'Go easy on him dad,' May entreated.

She pecked him on the cheek. 'What news?'

'One of our wells dried up during the week. The borers had to drill 205 feet.'

He stood by the window.

'How deep was the old well?' May asked.

'Believe it or not, only 35 feet,' he replied.

He folded her dressing gown and made himself comfortable on a chair in the corner of the room.

'Big difference, is that what you and Niall were talking about?' she asked.

'No, he saw some local farmers burning rubbish last Sunday when the helicopter wasn't around.'

He studied her closely. She grew more and more beautiful with each passing day.

'Would you blame them, their fathers used to do it, as did their fathers,' she said.

She sensed he was bursting to tell her something big, for he rarely came to her room.

'Mrs Henson tripped over a cement block and broke her wrist.'

'What?'

'She and her husband were pulling a cow free from the slurry pit. Your mother and I visited her last night in the hospital. Oh, by the way, I bought a few acres abutting the south side of the forest.'

He was looking out beyond the parklands as he spoke.

'Brilliant! You must take me down to have a look. What are you going to do with it?' she asked, wondering if it was a good time to tell him about his briefcase. Perhaps not, she thought, it would only dampen his spirits.

'Extend the forest,' he declared.

'Sounds fantastic.' She was excited for him.

'Even better, there is an old flourmill on the riverbank, and Niall says it wouldn't take a huge effort to get it back working again,' he said.

He was plainly delighted with another potential homespun industry.

'Fabulous, are you thinking about erecting a fence?' she asked.

'No.' He looked at her and smiled.

She noticed a mouse scurrying across the pipe in her room.

'Look,' she said.

Charles clicked his teeth.

'Young lady, what do you expect when you leave breadcrumbs on the floor. No self-respecting mouse can resist an easy meal.' To underline his displeasure, he proceeded to pick up the crumbs one by one.

'Sorry dad, I meant to vacuum but I was running late and mum was in a hurry,' she said.

'I'll set a mousetrap later on.' He tossed the crumbs out the window.

'Ah, leave it be, it isn't doing any harm.' She opened the door. 'Now out you go, I must finish dressing for dinner.'

'Very well, your mother will be home shortly. She went to Salisbury to buy some lilies.'

He left the room and hunted Skippy down the stairs.

    Jane raced to the back door and into the kitchen. Her face was striking, unwrinkled, her eyes like berries. She caught the meat just in time. At the sink, she arranged the lilies in a fusion of petals. Then she saw a tour bus pull up outside the courtyard. She rushed to the tearoom to make sure all was well. The women on duty, accustomed to the erratic nature of the business, had everything under control and sent her packing.

Charles carved and served three lean portions. The Franks enjoyed their food and as a result the conversation was stunted.

'How is Jenny keeping?' Jane asked.

'Never better, her new boyfriend has certainly put a pep in her step,' May replied, her mouth half full.

'What does he do?'

'Not too sure, something to do with carpentry.'

'Mum, the venison is to die for.' May rubbed her tummy. 'But I think I'll have to leave some room for afters. What's for dessert?'

'Banana and custard, and it's your turn to do the wash-up, young lady,' Charles said.

He removed the stopper from the decanter and poured out three glasses of wine. Earlier in the day, he had spent a considerable amount of time selecting a dusty bottle from the cellar.

While her parents swilled the vintage Châteauneuf-du-pape, May stood up and made an announcement.

'Dad, mum, I'd like to propose a toast.' She said it as if she were joking.

After a sharp exchange of questioning looks, her parents raised their glasses.

'I've been promoted.' Her unbridled delight spilled over onto Skippy.

'Quiet down dog, congratulations my dear. What do we call you now?' her father asked.

'I'm the new Internet security manager.' She flicked her hair back in a display of importance.

'The Internet security manager, no less, I suppose that means you're in no hurry to come and work for me?' His uttered words hinted disappointment, yet he was as proud as punch.

'In honour of your promotion, you're excused from the wash-up.' Her mother, swollen with pride, raised her glass.

'Why don't we take a spin and have a look at our new plot,' Charles suggested.

'Why not! Mum, are you coming?' May asked.

'You two go on ahead, I'll close up the tearoom.' Jane ushered them to the door.

Tony, dressed in black from head to toe, scaled yet another wall. The ground was firm and the going smooth. A full moon shed light across the roof of a half-timbered farmhouse and confirmed no major obstacles for another half kilometre. This was the first time he had ventured into Wiltshire since his military days. He travelled light: compass, small torch, water bottle and map. A pair of night-vision goggles hung from his belt and a hunting knife was strapped to his leg. He saw the outline of a ditch, jumped over it, and then he vaulted one-handed over the next. A herd of cattle, flummoxed by his presence, bunched together and formed a barricade. He circled around them.
A wrought-iron gate, already opened, pierced the outlying boundary wall.

A bovine silhouette sidled through the lush grass. Its large head heaved upwards. Tony dropped to one knee. There was no doubt in his mind; he was looking at the head of a bull. The stark silhouette moved towards him.
The bull could see him against the moonlit backdrop of the stars.
The bull gathered pace and his forequarters came into view, shoulder to ground at least five foot, and then he halted and snorted mischievously. The moonlight struck his white woolly head and telegraphed to Tony a simple warning, "RUN".
Unsure of what he was looking at, the bull lowered his head and stamped the ground. Nimble-footed, Tony sprinted in the direction of a circular group of upright stones. The 1000kg bull charged. Tony dived full length in behind the nearest stone and landed in a cowpat. The enraged bull ran headlong into the stone, and then he left the field to chase the herd.

An uneventful kilometre later, Tony heard the sound of gushing water. He followed the riverbank until he came to a narrow footbridge that creaked achingly under his weight. On the other side, he ran parallel to the river, following a winding route to an old mill located at the periphery of the forest. He paused to get his bearings. He stooped and splashed himself clean. Then he heard it – a low humming sound. And then, directly over him, sporadic lights flared from the forest canopy.

Skippy stuck his head out the window as the Range Rover negotiated the hidden lumps and bumps. The headlights burned into the ground one moment and shot up in the air the next. Quality time spent with her father, deep in the heart of the countryside, meant a lot to May and her smile widened with each dip in the trail.

They got out and walked, arm in arm, between the freshly planted yews. Charles pretended not to notice the wolf tracks intersected with the prints of deer that were exposed to the headlights. He returned to the vehicle and dragged the shotgun from under the backseat and rejoined May.

The peaceful silence was interrupted by a singular howl. There was a den not far away atop a wooded hill sheltered by overhanging branches. Charles considered it prudent to return to the safety of the vehicle. At May's behest, he reversed the Range Rover back into some ferns and turned off the headlights. He switched on the interior light and they waited for a possible sighting.

As Tony moved through the trees, he snapped off eye-level branches and repeatedly checked to make sure that he was not being followed. And then, abruptly, he stopped. Easily, he picked out the soft tone of the vehicle's interior light. He slumped into the forest undergrowth. Then he felt his way up the branches of an elm and found a comfortable limb. He peered across the terrain where the vehicle was parked. A million possibilities ran through his mind. He counted two people, and a dog. Perhaps there were others. An eerie yowl stole through the trees.

May and her father were not disappointed. A grizzled grey-brown trotted by on its toes, the back part of its feet rarely making contact with the layer of leaf-litter on the forest floor. It was a male.

The radio-collar in no way hampered him as he moved quieter and faster than any domestic dog. Without taking her eyes off the collared beast, May compared the wolf with Skippy. Although similar in physique, the wolf's legs were longer and his feet wider. She guessed he measured six foot from the tip of his snout to the end of his tail. 'What a magnificent specimen,' she whispered.

The wolf rubbed his neck against one of the newly planted trees, still moist from Skippy's urine. In the back seat Skippy did not bark, instead he growled deeply. The wolf raised a hind leg and squirted a tiny jet of urine. He tasted the air and then he scraped his paws on the ground, churning up large divots of moss. He eyed the vehicle curiously.

Unfazed by his previous encounter, Skippy leapt from the vehicle. Abruptly the moon struck the wolf's golden eyes. Puffed up, Skippy began to posture, his head close to the ground, his hindquarters thrust upwards. The distant hooting of an owl perched on a tree briefly halted the display. The wolf saw no reason to retreat and judged the canine a soft target. Charles grabbed the shotgun and jumped out of the vehicle. He fired one barrel into the air. The wolf lowered his head and flattened his ears, and then he vanished.

On the way home, Charles stopped to report the sighting. As he did, Skippy looked out the window and whined. A large something was running towards them. Charles tapped him on the nose.

'Quiet down boy, you've caused enough trouble for one evening,' he shouted, and then he turned to May and asked her nonchalantly, 'what do you think of a golf course?'

'Any particular golf course?' she quizzed.

'Harvey Thornton is thinking of putting his farm up for sale. He's getting on in years and doesn't have kids or living relatives.'

Harvey Thornton's predicament made Charles appreciate even more his one and only child. He started the engine and drove off. Skippy barked just as the large shadow closed in. May rolled her eyes.

'Shush Skippy.' She hopped into the backseat and closed the window and put the dog's head on her lap.

'So, you'd like to build a golf course?'

What next she said to herself.

'Whom should we get to design it, any ideas?' he invited.

'I don't have a clue about golf courses, but you'll have to do something about the wolves.' They laughed in unison.

'Why is Billy's taxi here?' she asked.

'Oh, I'm expecting someone.' He jumped out, almost stepping on the dog.

'Come here boy,' he ordered. The dog reluctantly obeyed.

May trotted after her father. Billy was still in his taxi, so she stopped to ask him if he would like to come in. He switched off the radio and followed her into the house. She heard someone laughing in the reception room. The door was left ajar and she peeked in. Unable to see the man's face, his back was turned to her, she leaned in a little too far. Her mother noticed her and asked her to join them. May shook her head and mimicked a yawn. She led Billy down to the kitchen.

'Sure you're not hungry?' she asked.

'You don't have to mollycoddle me child. I know the run of the kitchen. Let ye be off now and be about your business. I'll wait here until your father's guest calls for me.' He bit hard into a homemade ginger biscuit and took a mouthful of tea to soften it. 'Strange one, he barely spoke on the journey up here. Then he says: *switch off the metre and I'll pay you double what you normally make for the whole night, as long as you wait here.* It would be nice if that happened every night.'

    May walked quietly to the reception room. Outside the door, she listened for a while but could not make out what they were saying. She was so intrigued that she failed to notice her father coming up behind her. When he tapped her on the shoulder she nearly jumped out of her skin.

'Are you coming in?' he asked.

'No, I'm off to bed. I have had a long day,' she pouted, annoyed with herself for being caught.
'Very well then, good night.' He went to close the door.
'I let Billy into the kitchen,' she whispered loudly.
'Ok, I know where to get him.' Her father closed the door.
May climbed the spiral staircase with Skippy in hot pursuit.

Tony left the forest in full flight just as his guiding lights sped off. He could make out the dotted lights of the stately house and it encouraged him to move even faster through the meadowland. The more distance he ate up, the more open to the elements he became. Uncomfortably exposed, he slowed to a walk and changed to a circular route. He took his time traversing the remaining kilometres. The moon held firm and lit up the stud railings that bordered the stone path. He stopped and filled his senses. Then he came across the mews cottage and hunkered down. The building was in darkness with no sign of life. He left the cover of the mews and edged towards the large house and crouched and crawled along the dewy grass. He slunk into the herb garden and settled down to observe.
There was a muffled sound of light footsteps close by. His heart missed a beat. Every muscle in his body tensed. He gripped his knife.
'Sean, everything clear on this front, I'm moving towards the back of the house, can you see me?' Christophe searched the ground for unusual tracks. He then added, 'Akiko and Fukiko are on their way back towards you.'
Tony, clutching his knife, pulled back slowly. He snuck out of the herb garden and onto a flat rock. An instant later he leapt away into the dark.
    Tony ran past the dell that Charles had used to turn about in and checked his compass. There was a rustle, faint but definite. He scaled the nearest tree and looked across the dell. A wolf with raised tail appeared and sniffed the air. A second materialised from the cover of trees, pulling a fresh kill, a young fallow deer. Tony looked

at his watch and grimaced. He put on his night-vision goggles and hacked a suitable branch. Then he carefully carved a spear, long and straight. To make sure there were no other wolves lurking, he took his time paring a second. He placed the two spears close at hand and assumed a standing position. He was ready.

The wolves were aware that something was amiss. The male rubbed his lips and neck on a tree trunk, while the female squatted and urinated. Tony dropped from the bough with his arms crossed. Scrambling. Moving along the dell's edge. He stood, took aim, tracking the wolves from right to left, a spear in his hand, his arm at full stretch. He hurled the spear at the male. The point took the wolf beneath the spine and went in deeply. The second spear flew across the dell and smacked into the female. She yelped. Tony came up on top of her, and then he used his knife to finish her off. Then he grabbed the male by a front paw and dragged him through the wood. He came back for the female. On his way over the footbridge, he tossed the radio-collars into the rushing river.

A day had passed since the woodland butchery. The sun rose to welcome Niall as he wheeled a barrow chock full of saplings. In soiled, black overalls and a brown hat, he left the barrow by the tractor and set off to clean the stables. After a couple of hours the Range Rover pulled up in the courtyard. Two unhappy faces got out. Niall hurried from the stables to the paddock and made short work of emptying the barrow. In his hand, he held the last sapling, the roots of which were wrapped in sackcloth crammed with nutrient enriched soil.

The side door of the house opened and out ran May. Niall carefully hoisted the young tree over the side panelling and into the rickety trailer. He tossed a spade in, and then he climbed into the tractor cab. When he saw May's leopard-print boots a rare smile crossed his broad, high-cheeked face. There was only one seat in the cab, so May had to stand and hold the crash bar. The tractor sucked in a gullet of diesel and then coughed and wheezed its way out of the

paddock. Peering over the large rear wheel, May kept an eye on the young trees, making sure none toppled off. During the week, Niall had deliberately set aside the saplings so as to give May a chance to become involved in the new plot. Another one of his brilliantly conceived ideas to spend more time in her company. She knew the chore was contrived but she played along.
'How's your Aunt?' shouted Niall, over the roar of the engine.
'Not the best, her memory is deteriorating.' She heaved a sigh.
'Sorry to hear that,' he said moments later.

They bumbled past the dell where the wolves had dragged their kill. Crows and other scavengers, watchful of their presence, waited in the wings. Niall set the tractor in neutral and hopped off to investigate. His seasoned eye thought it strange so much meat remained on the deer carcass. Tufts of fine-haired skin lay strewn about and a cable of entrails snaked through a pod of decaying plant matter.

His eye caught sight of a pared chipping left behind by Tony's blade. He picked it up and examined it. While doing so he noticed the bloodied drag marks leading from the trail into the forest. Stymied, he scratched his puckered brow but did not say a word and climbed back into the cab. May noticed the concerned look on his face and asked him what was the matter. He fobbed her off with some lame pretext but decided to come back later on his own when they finished planting.

As they picked their way across the large tract, Niall cautioned May to walk carefully. He tended to the saplings already planted, pressing disturbed ones back into place. After several hours, May sank the last sapling into a deep hole, and they filled it in together. Niall used his heavy boot to make sure it was well rooted and properly anchored. As they prepared to return, her brand new iPhone pealed noisily.
'Hello.' She made a waspish face and Niall turned off the engine.
'May, fancy a game of squash,' Jenny asked.

'Sure do, but I won't be back in London till this afternoon. Niall has me slaving out here in the woods. Say three bells. How does that square up?' May checked her watch to make sure she had given herself enough time.

'Perfect, I'll book a court right away.'

'See you then.' May gave Niall the thumbs up and he started the engine.

On the larger tennis court it was May who had the edge, but when it came to squash, Jenny was the superior player. Determined to win, May began to flex her wrist. Her arm swung wildly in front of Niall's face. He ducked his head and the tractor swerved. He frowned and ordered her to grip the crash bar with both hands. Eventually, the tractor rolled into the courtyard. She dashed to the house. She packed her bag and nabbed her mother, who was on her way to mass, and asked her for a lift to the train station. Niall shouted after her to be more careful but it fell on deaf ears. He turned the tractor around and set off to inspect more closely the area surrounding the wolf kill.

The harsh calls from a raiding party of crows that had regrouped above the forest canopy seemed to portend a shadow play on the natural order of things. It was not difficult for Niall to hunt down Tony's tracks. The disturbed leaf-litter had formed a shallow basin where the wolves had been dragged through the forest floor. Niall traced the twisted path, throttled by densely knitted trees, until he stepped upon a soft mound. He brushed away the blanket of leaves and discovered the body of the female. Beside the body lay a bloodied spear. He felt vulnerable and backtracked at pace. He did not wish to raise suspicion should someone in the trees be watching, so he slowed right down to a hike. I must tell Mr Franks immediately, he thought, no time to waste.

CHAPTER 10

May reached Paddington station in the afternoon and hailed a taxi to take her to Bayswater. She stood behind a mailbox and got out her iPhone. She keyed in Jenny's number and pressed call. Jenny's messaging service came on.
'It's May. I'm running late. I forgot my charger. Just getting my, uh, gear. I'm at home. If you get this message in the next five minutes or so, can you buzz me back?'
She stuffed her kit into her gear-bag and darted to the tube station and caught the tube.
    She arrived just before half past three and she ran down the corridor and quickly changed into her outfit. The Trafalgar Lawn Tennis and Croquets Club had four squash courts. Jenny pushed open the glass door of court number three. She held it open for May, who had a steely look in her eye.
May wore a one-piece dress, laced with bands of white and brown, and tastefully tethered by a red seam.
Jenny's apparel consisted of a yellow-patterned blouse and a navy skirt.
'You're late,' Jenny said.
'I tried calling you.'
'You're always the same,' Jenny said sardonically.
'Let's not go there right now, Jen,' May said.
Jenny groaned.

May spun her racket to determine who would serve first. Jenny claimed the X and prepared to serve. She flicked her wrist and the ball ricocheted off the front wall, skidded along the sidewall, and then rebounded off the glass.

May moved like a gazelle, with her racket in a ready position, fully prepared to strike as the ball rose from the floor. On the first bounce, she struck it hard, long and straight, down the sidewall, and she immediately ran to the T-junction. Jenny drew back her racket, pretending to strike hard, but she kept the face open and sliced the ball softly. It was first blood to Jenny.

Jenny moved to the other side of the court and served. It was match on, and it ebbed and flowed with rallies of varying lengths.

Michel arrived early at the clubhouse to get some practice in before his game with Richard on court four. To get to court four, he had to pass through the viewing areas of court one, two and three. Unnoticed, he opened the door and walked along the top step. Initially, he paid the girls no mind but when he saw out of the corner of his eye May's beautiful face he sat down on the step. His eyes followed her as she skated about the court; she was evidently healthy and fit.

Invariably, May did more running about the court than Jenny, who always seemed to hit her shots with greater length, and the fabric of her dress was patched with perspiration, revealing her hidden curves. May knew how to move and play. Her shoulders were strong. Michel watched her bare legs as she strove to reach the tin. The words 'natural' and 'gorgeous' sprung to mind. Time passed quickly, he looked at his watch and left the viewing area just as Richard entered. In his eagerness to join Michel, Richard failed to recognise either girl.

The score was levelled at two games all and four points each with May holding serve. Jenny suggested a change of ball and introduced the slower white-dot. May agreed, and they spent a few minutes warming it up. May served and then she moved forward. Bending her legs, she crouched close to the front wall and returned

Jenny's angled shot with an underhand lob, but it did not have the height to clear her opponent's reach.
Jenny jumped high and struck downwards on the ball.
There was a loud shriek.
May put her hand to a point halfway up her spine. Jenny apologised and tried to relieve the hurt by massaging the effected area.
In spite of the pain, May insisted on finishing the match. While she took up her position in the service box, Jenny prepared to receive.
Jenny went on to win the point, with a dainty shot, and then she served out the remainder of the game.

Sweaty and exhausted the victor and vanquished made their way to the showers.
'Are you sure you didn't hit that shot on purpose?' May, shivering in the shower, interrogated the sudsy form beside her.
'On my life, it was an accident. I'm truly sorry.' Jenny, lathered in shampoo, was unable to open her eyes.
'My lob shot was pathetic, but it wasn't as bad as your overhead smash,' May said. She turned off the cold tap.
'Fair enough, but who won the match?' Jenny grumbled.
May, wrapped in a bath towel, slapped Jenny on the bum.
'I've a tub of lotion in my kit, do you want some?' Jenny asked.
'I do.'
After Jenny had towelled down, she applied some lotion to May's back.
'Fancy a gin and tonic?' she asked.
'For sure, could murder one,' May answered.

Located above the squash courts, the plush clubhouse was thronged with members dressed in shorts and skirts. It had a huge fan in its ceiling. And one wall had three windows overlooking the tennis courts. As the girls ventured in, heads turned to follow the new arrivals, paying particular attention to May in a t-shirt and jeans. Jenny went to the bar while May eased herself into a seat.

Jenny placed the drinks on the table. The sound of rattling ice cubes was strangely comforting. May temporarily forgot her pain and kicked off her shoes. She gazed out the big rectangular window and watched a young girl, not even in her teens, getting a lesson from the club professional.

'Tell me something,' May said, 'how did you get on last night?'

'Tony brought me to a fancy restaurant. Then we went to a wine bar. Everything was going wonderfully well until I looked down at my tights and saw a winding ladder. I excused myself and went back to the apartment and changed. However, I didn't tell him the reason for my desertion,' Jenny said.

May looked astonished. 'Was he still there when you got back?'

'Yep. But he said that he was on the verge of leaving, a humbled and broken man,' Jenny laughed.

'Did he? Gosh, you're lucky. He must be eager,' May teased.

'We talked until the early hours of the morning, and then he asked me to accompany him to a rowing regatta.'

'That sounds promising. Is he an oarsman?' May asked, trying to picture his physique.

'He used to row, but now he doesn't have the time. We're going as spectators, wearing the full regalia,' Jenny said.

'What does he do again?' May asked.

'He's a cabinetmaker. I guess that sort of makes him a carpenter,' Jenny answered.

'Oh, then he's probably good with his hands,' May joked.

Jenny looked coolly at her. 'Don't be so cheeky. As of matter of fact, he is.'

'You lucky girl, I want one of those. Has he any friends?' May asked with a twinkle in her eye.

Jenny decided to change the subject.

'How was your trip back home?' she asked nonchalantly.

'Dad and I went to visit my aunt Tracy. The radiotherapy succeeded in reducing the size of her tumour, but the growth is still too large for surgeons to operate.'

May saddened and her tears welled suddenly.
'I'm sorry to hear that. The same thing happened to my uncle Joey.' Jenny's concern was genuine.
'How's he now. Still the same?' May asked.
'My aunt had to put him into a nursing home. He requires assistance in the simplest of things: eating, bathing and suchlike.'
'My Dad is dreading that,' May said. Her smile was one of melancholy.
The girls sat quietly, tired and in sombre mood.

Richard and Michel ambled into the clubhouse. Richard, flushed from his exertions, waved to a couple he knew. Michel, in his shirtsleeves, appeared fresh and relaxed as he trailed Richard across the clubhouse floor.
Richard, a decent club player, had recently sneaked into the club's top ten. He had gone into today's match brimming with confidence, but the three-nil score line put paid to his high expectations.
Michel ordered a bowl of cabbage-cheese soup and a draught beer. He got out his wallet.
Richard ordered a coffee from the girl. She had short spiky hair.
'Do you want something to eat?' she asked.
'No, thanks,' Richard sighed.
'And how do you take your coffee, sir?'
Again Richard sighed. 'White, thanks, no sugar.'
He got his wallet from the inside pocket of his sports jacket and opened it and took out a twenty. The waitress took the money. Richard surveyed the clubhouse. His eyes stopped at the girls seated at the table near the alcove. He waved to May. May waved back at him. Jenny waved too.
'The value of your stock portfolio has dropped,' Michel said. He was holding the newspaper he had bought earlier that day.
'I know. I'm trying not to think about it.' Richard said. He stretched his arms above his head and yawned.

'Don't say you weren't warned. I told you five months ago, four months ago, two months ago and last month,' Michel said softly. He dropped the newspaper on to the counter.

'But its value hasn't dropped dramatically,' Richard said. He stretched again.

'Perhaps you'd have been smarter to accept my advice instead of leaving yourself open to bankruptcy,' Michel said sharply.

'You've heard something. What is it?' Richard asked.

'There's a heavy-hitter getting ready to unload all of his property holdings,' Michel warned.

'Are you sure?' Richard asked. He stared at him, open-mouthed.

'Listen, my friend, nothing is certain in this life,' Michel said.

'But forecasts for the sector, based on our computer models, predict strong demand,' Richard argued.

'Be that as it may, I suggest that you invest your personal savings in diamonds,' Michel advised.

'I honestly don't need a lecture,' Richard said, his heart racing.

There was a sharp silence.

Then Michel said, his voice friendly, 'I hear Paul Wilkinson has handed in his letter of resignation.'

'Afraid so,' Richard said. He sipped the coffee.

'Did he give a reason?' Michel asked.

'He told me that he got a better offer, and said he was unhappy in his current position.'

The cup rattled in its saucer as he put it back on the counter.

'Remind me, what's his current position?' Michel asked.

'Customer Relationship Manager.'

'Make him a counter offer, and see if you can convince him to stay.'

'Are you sure?' Richard quizzed.

'Think of it this way. Everyone is entitled to one mistake. I remember a case study about a guy who messed up with IBM. When he went to work the following day, convinced he was going to be fired, his boss told him: *don't be ridiculous, not after spending ten million dollars on your education*,' Michel laughed.

'Good.'
'How's Miss Franks coping with her promotion?' Michel enquired.
'Great, and I must say Pat is demonstrating a keen willingness to support her. I thought he might have been a tad resentful, which would've been understandable, since no one likes to be passed over for promotion. In fact, why not ask her yourself?'
'Maybe I will.' Michel was uncommitted.
'Well, there's no time like the present. She's sitting over there.'
Richard nodded his head in the girls' direction.
'I can see with my own eyes thank you very much Richard,' Michel said. He thought a moment. 'All right.' Michel gathered his gear.

  May shifted in her seat. She pried her eyes off Michel and Richard, and she looked at Jenny. 'Oh no, look who's coming over,' she muttered.
Jenny lifted her head. 'Who's that guy with him?' Her eyes settled on Michel.
'I don't know. I've never seen him before,' May replied.
'He's good-looking,' Jenny whispered.
  The two men neared the alcove carrying their drinks in front of them. The girls began to busy themselves, as if to leave.
'Ladies, you're not going already?' Richard spoke loud enough for the entire clubhouse to hear.
He smiled, embarrassed a little.
'Yes, we were just about to leave,' Jenny answered.
'Please, might we join you for a drink.' Richard made an exasperated noise.
May nudged Jenny. 'Richard, we're pushed for time but we can squeeze one in,' she said.
'Great, let me introduce you to a friend of mine. This is Michel, and this is…' Richard hoped that May would complete the introduction.
'Hi! My name is May, and this is my friend Jenny.'
'Hello all,' Michel said. He smiled at them, nodding slightly.
Then he slumped down into a chair.

Richard ordered a round of drinks and the group asked after each other's games.

May complained of Jenny's unfair tactics. Everybody laughed.

Richard began to dominate the conversation and guided it towards work.

'May has recently been appointed the Internet services manager, and she's doing a splendid job.'

'Richard, you jest. I'd be totally lost without Pat who should've got the job in the first place,' May said. Her blue eyes narrowing, and her jaw tightening a bit. Then she reminded Richard of their heated exchange. Only a timely intercession by Pat had saved the day when he convinced her that he was genuinely uninterested in the job.

'You're too modest.' Richard glossed over the subject and half-smiled.

There was an awkward silence.

Michel had taken an instant liking to May.

She felt his eyes on her. Those piercing eyes equalised by an easy smile and devilish good looks. Her heart beat strongly and the ache spread from her back to the rest of her body, but it was a different ache, a sweet ache. He had not yet spoken a word to her and she searched for a meaningful question. Abruptly, she asked him, in her well-bred voice, what he did for a living.

'A bit of this and a bit of that.' He brightened, surprised by her directness. He caught a whiff of her perfume. Desiring her, he made a mental list: young, good-humoured, beautiful, cultured, articulate and smart. Definitely worth the effort, he told himself.

'Michel is one of those rare breeds, an entrepreneur,' Richard said.

'Ah, that must be very exciting,' Jenny interjected.

Michel spoke with candour. 'It can be, but it can also be very stressful, risky and lonely.'

The conversation bubbled to the strains of tinkling glasses and the girls agreed to stay for one more drink. Gradually, they became more attentive to Michel. He recounted his experiences climbing Mount

Everest. He described the sheer unpopulated wonder of being on the summit of the highest mountain in the world, climbing up something insuperable, going higher up than most. He told them that he had seen dead bodies on the southwest face. The unburied bodies of people who were killed in a fall, tangled in a rope, trapped in a crevice or for whatever reason just perished.

At times, making a point, he lifted his finger, raised his eyebrows, and an expression of fulfilment passed over his face.

'Oh come on, no way,' May said. She reprimanded him for telling fibs and she laughed with gusto.

Richard, on the other hand, did not doubt the story.

There was a long pause, and then Richard said in a low voice, 'May, if Michel says he climbed Mount Everest, well then, he climbed Mount Everest.'

May and Jenny looked at each other, and then they looked at Michel.

'I wasn't for a moment suggesting you didn't,' May laughed.

'Would I lie to you?' Michel said.

'No. No of course not,' May said.

She was enjoying herself immensely.

'But it's true. You know it is,' he said.

May gave another burst of laughter.

'So is Mount Everest your favourite climb?' Her ache grew sweeter.

'Believe it or not, it isn't. The avalanche gulch route to the summit of Mount Shasta is my number one. It's not a difficult climb, but it is the most memorable.'

He went on to describe the glaciers, steam vents, Douglas firs and a couple of close encounters with black bears.

The girls were suitably impressed.

'Where is it?' May asked. She could picture herself climbing to the summit and then looking down into Shastina's crater.

'Northern California.' Michel checked his watch.

'Another drink?' Richard asked.

'No, not for me, I've a prior engagement and must be off. I'm running late as it is.' Michel got to his feet.

'Let me buy you a drink?' May said.

'No, it breaks my heart to leave such company, but I must bid thee farewell,' he said, 'but thank you, May.'

'Very well then, you killjoy, be off with you.' May gestured with a flail of hands, banishment.

He squatted. 'Would you be interested in a game of squash?'

'I'd love to,' May beamed, her heart quickening. Then her open mouth, her tongue and her lips, were a few inches from his face.

She found a pen in her bag and wrote her number on his forearm. She could not help but feel the strength coursing through his veins.

Her touch was soft, but at the same time sensuously charged.

The hairs on the back of his neck stood up.

'Great, I'll give you a buzz next week,' he said.

He kissed the back of her hand, and then he smiled and waved goodbye.

'Do you need a lift?' Richard asked.

'No. I've a taxi waiting outside,' Michel replied.

May watched him go with a spring in his step, tall, immaculate and self-assured. Inexplicably, the back of his head looked familiar. Don't be ridiculous, she told herself.

May turned to Richard. 'Who in God's name was that. Have you known him long?'

'A few years, crikey, is that the time, my wife will kill me. Must dash. Either of you two ladies need a lift?' he asked. 'I'm going as far as the tube station.'

'No thanks,' May said, 'it's just down the road.'

He stood up, flattened his trouser-legs at his feet, and headed for the door.

In the car park, he sat on the bonnet of the jaguar and called home. Margaret answered.

'I'll be home in about an hour and a half,' he said.

'Have you eaten?' she asked.

CHAPTER 11

Richard stood at his office window with his hands behind his back and watched a cloud of dust rise above a Convent Garden shopfront. Bill Watson doodled with a golf-tee on a book-length contract, while Rasmus fiddled with the usual white-collar fodder: endless reams of figures and percentages. Richard turned away from the window and plopped into his high-backed chair. He checked his emails and dashed off several responses. Larry spoke sharply into the intercom and announced Michel's arrival.
'Rasmus, do you have the projected milestones?' Richard asked.
'Yes, sir,' Rasmus replied, 'here.'
Minutes later, Michel, Toyoko and Setsu marched into Richard's office. Bill stopped doodling, and Rasmus sat to attention. Michel, debonair in a blue suit, white shirt and red tie, apologised for being late and sat down. The unexpected presence of Setsu wrought changes in Richard's disposition. He had not seen Setsu before, and wondered, without rancour, in what capacity he joined the meeting.
When Michel introduced Setsu as the new assistant to the Director of Security, Richard recovered his composure, but his brow remained arched.
For the sake of clarity, Richard gave a short account of the steering-team's latest effort.

'It was brought to our attention that Peoples Pensions were looking for an outsourcing partner, so we put together a comprehensive tender with a view to gaining an influential foothold in the industry…'

Toyoko jotted down in shorthand every syllable. She wore a nondescript cardigan and an unfashionable pair of corduroy jeans. Her hand flew across the page at a rate of a hundred words a minute. Briefly, Richard deliberated on the tender and, with an air of knowingness, he handed a copy to Michel and one to Setsu. Michel skimmed over it and passed it to Toyoko.

Richard curled his lips and straightened his shoulders.

'And I'm delighted to say that our tender for the outsourcing contract has been accepted,' he said.

There was a light round of applause.

Rasmus and Bill tidied up their paperwork. Both men left the office feeling very good about themselves.

Out of sight, in the cloakroom, Richard changed into a new suit.

'Do you mind bringing along Setsu?' Michel asked.

'Are you sure. It'll be pretty high level,' Richard said, as he donned his jacket and made to leave.

'I'm certain,' Michel tolled with a glare. 'Did I mention Setsu is Chen's son, Toyoko's brother?'

'No.' Richard scrutinised Setsu, and then Toyoko.

'By the way, Setsu graduated from the School of Economics, your alma mater.'

'That changes everything.' Richard perked up. 'Larry, can you round up the lawyer boys and make sure Bill is with them?'

'Yes sir, I think they're waiting for you in the car park,' Larry said.

Larry followed Richard and Setsu to the lift.

Richard put his hand on Setsu's shoulder. 'Come on young man. Let's see what you're made of.'

The lift door opened.

'Age before beauty, in you go,' Richard said.

Then he snatched his laptop bag and car keys from Larry.

Chen appeared in the doorway of Richard's office just as Toyoko whizzed by.

'Hi dad,' she said. 'Bye dad.'

Chen strolled over to the window.

'How did the meeting go?' he asked Michel.

'Smooth as you like.'

'And Setsu?'

'Same as you, mouth closed, eyes and ears wide open.' Michel smiled.

'Ha, Toyoko has forgotten her phone. I'll return it to her tonight when she calls over,' Chen said. He recognised the distinctive pink cover and stuffed it into his pocket.

Industrial relations between staff and management had collapsed. Negotiations had failed, resulting in a total suspension of work.

"Down with that sort of thing" one of the placards read, while others explained more clearly the issue in dispute: "No to outsourcing" and "Save our jobs".

Richard's jaguar sped by the column of picketers patrolling the back entrance of a building located in the dreary environs of a Slough industrial park. Bill's vehicle, weighed down with an ensemble of strait-laced lawyers, followed Richard's jaguar from an overly safe distance. About four hundred metres away behind trees there was another building and behind that there was another even bigger building. The dour looking premises, crowned by a saw-tooth roof, housed the Information Technology headquarters of Peoples Pensions.

The picketers' plight had been blessed by a gloriously sunny day. And coupled with plenty of media coverage, the one-day stoppage was going well. The union, which represented the majority of staff, had balloted their members. The result was an overwhelming vote in favour of industrial action. Earlier in the afternoon, the union's chief executive had condemned the systemic erosion of workers' rights and he had urged his comrades to cut free the bonds of repression.

In a second offensive, two orderly lines of picketers, marshalled by a shop steward, marched to and from the service entrance at the rear of the grounds to the main entrance, where the bulk of the picketers rallied in a show of solidarity. Vexed, Richard stalled his jaguar, barely avoiding a demonstrator who had strayed in front of the car. Richard reached forward to start the engine. Deliberately, the picketers slowed their walk to a snail's pace and swarmed about the jaguar. Sweaty under the collar, Richard blew the horn. He was tempted to use the car as a battering ram but Setsu put his hand on the steering wheel and told him to calm down. Unhurriedly, a senior-ranking manager moved towards the barrier and made a call on his mobile to the security desk. The picketers were uncertain what to do next, but as soon as the barrier juddered into an upright position a groundswell of fevered heckling erupted. Richard had every reason to feel irked and for the first time gnawing doubts surfaced. He wondered if Michel had got it wrong.

A mischievous cloud shaded an executive helicopter that flew slowly in from the west. Its arrival seemed to knock the wind out of the picket-line sails. The chopper circled the building once and then landed on a helipad adjacent to the car park. Richard seized his opportunity and sped through the gate.

The Information Technology Director, Mary Taft, welcomed Richard. She was calm but flustered. In her office, a projector purred quietly in readiness to show the solution to the industrial unrest.
Richard was pleased with the planned approach, but he was insistent that Secure Span would not be a party to any mediating talks. After the slideshow, Richard and his entourage were shepherded into the boardroom. Ratification of the seven-year deal required one more signature. On queue the boardroom door swung open and in walked

the CEO. Without saying a word, Charles signed the leafy contract. About three minutes after that, he left the room. A bemused Richard clicked on his pen and pondered on the eccentricities of the super rich.

A heavy shower of rain had fallen. Charles, sporting a peak cap, perched sideways on his head, and a well-worn anorak, hopped into the helicopter cockpit and gripped the control stick. He adjusted the plane of the rotor and the helicopter took off.

Meanwhile, Richard went back across the car park to his Jaguar. He got in and waited for Setsu.

Eventually the jaguar passed safely through the picket line. Richard rummaged through the glove compartment.

'Do you mind if I smoke a celebratory cigar?' He did not wait for an answer; instead he broke the seal and lowered the window.

'Not at all.' Setsu struggled to conceal his distaste for the habit. He put his hand to his mouth and fought back the cough that lurked at the base of his throat.

'That went well,' Richard said happily. He tapped lightly on the steering remote and lowered the volume. The sound of Bach's Suite No. 3 in D major made him feel even better.

'Do you think so?' Setsu asked.

'My good fellow, it's important for a union to occasionally flex its muscles. After all, they represent more than fifteen thousand staff in Peoples Pensions alone and they don't want to jeopardise issues such as training allowances, gender equality, career paths and productivity payments,' Richard explained.

'But it depends on whether or not they back down,' Setsu argued.

'Believe me, they will,' Richard said. 'So tell me about yourself.'

'Not much to say really.' Setsu had inherited from his father an unwillingness to reveal too much.

Not to be fobbed off, Richard continued. 'Where have you worked? The city.'

'I don't have a career as such,' Setsu admitted. 'Instead, I assist my Father in his dojo.'
'Not much money in that,' Richard remarked.
'Anyway, in my new job, Michel has put me on a generous salary.'
'Well, one thing is for sure, you must have promise. Michel only backs winners, which means you've a rosy future,' Richard said.
He returned Setsu's smile, and then he checked the rear-view mirror.
'Do you practice martial arts?' Setsu asked.
'Afraid not, and I'm too old to start now,' Richard said, as he puffed his cigar.
'Nonsense, you're never too old,' Setsu said. 'Do you play any sports?'
'I play squash. There's less chance of injury,' Richard joked.

Preoccupied, Michel sat in Richard's chair and flicked a pistachio nut and then he moved his head forwards. He caught the nut in his mouth and then he cracked it with his teeth. He read through the documentation stacked up on Richard's desk. In the corner of the office, sitting on a black leather chair, facing an elevated bookcase, Chen meditated. Michel threw another nut into the air but he missed and it clacked along the leather inset of the mahogany desk. Chen stood up and made some space for himself and pantomimed a kata in slow motion.
'How was your trip to Athens?' Chen asked.
'It went well,' Michel replied.
'Glad to hear it,' Chen said.
'Any sign of the Mata Hare of the Mediterranean?' Michel asked wryly.
'You mean Tara. No sign,' Chen replied bleakly.
There was a gentle knock on the door.
Chen sat down.
'Come in,' Michel invited.
As it opened, the door creaked, and in walked May. Both May and Michel were caught off guard. She hesitated, still outwardly calm,

but her heart thumped wildly. A whole range of complex emotions percolated her inner depths. She tried to take a step forward but her legs turned to jelly.

A prolonged look drew Michel to his feet. She blushed a shade of pink and shifted her weight from one foot to the other. Her eyes darted to Chen, and then back to Michel.

'May, I'm afraid Richard is still at a meeting,' Chen said.

May addressed Chen, but her eyes were glued on Michel. 'Larry wasn't at his desk, otherwise, I wouldn't have barged in like this,' she said.

She tucked a disturbed tress of hair in behind her ear.

Michel stared firstly at her breasts, flaunted by a loosed silk blouse, and then he watched her pearly white teeth appear and disappear between her lips. Involuntarily, his eyes slid to her legs accentuated by the fine cut of a chastely elegant monochrome dress. Breathtakingly beautiful, his heart quickened and his skin felt chilly.

May made to leave.

But Michel pre-empted her departure and he took off his jacket. He threw it across the office and it landed in front of her. Numbed with shock, she stared at the jacket aghast and then at Michel. Chen watched as Michel rolled up his shirtsleeve and displayed May's phone number, albeit well faded.

May laughed haughtily and told him to behave.

'The truth is, I've been abroad and I just got back today. I took the liberty of booking a squash court for tomorrow evening. I was going to buzz you,' Michel said.

'It's a bit short notice, but I'm free the following evening, if that's of any use,' she hissed in an offhand manner.

Michel ignored the rebuff. 'Great, I'll make the necessary arrangements and pick you up at seven.'

Her smile bloomed and flowered.

'What time do you finish work today?' He walked briskly to where she stood.

'Five-thirty, why?'

'You might fancy an early bite,' he suggested.
There was a cautious silence.
'Ok,' she said. 'Meet you in reception.'
He held the door open.
Chen stood with a hand to his chin, as if in deep thought.
'Something amusing you?' Michel asked airily, as he rolled down his shirtsleeve.
'No.'
'What's keeping Richard?' Michel wondered out loud.
'You know how long these things can drag on for,' Chen said.
'True.' Michel looked at his watch.
'An unusual incident occurred at the Franks estate shortly after your visit,' Chen said quietly.
'What kind of incident?' Michel asked crisply in an equally low voice.
'The Wiltshire office of one of our security subsidiaries got a call from the Frank's groundsman. He ordered a night patrol for the estate. Two wolves were hacked to death on the grounds and their radio-collars turned up downriver, miles away,' Chen said. He tried to read Michel's thoughts, and then he added. 'I dispatched Mary Jane to carry out an investigation.'
Chen judged the moment right to tell Michel about the demise of Hiroki and his family, but spared him the gruesome detail.
'Did Mary Jane turn up anything?' Michel asked.
Sickened by the death of Hiroki's children, Michel adjusted his position.
'As a matter of fact she did. The serological and toxicological tests were inconclusive, but she uncovered a shoeprint that was identical to a print she had moulded in Vosselar.' Chen looked away, his expression grim. After all, Hiroki had been a dear friend.
'Bump up security arrangements on the Frank's estate but keep it low key. It's best not to alarm them. And put a minder on May,' Michel insisted, and then he asked, in a more mellow tone. 'Have you established any tangible links between the two incidents?'

'Debt recovery,' Chen said.

Michel was on speakerphone placating Sheikh Ra. The Sheikh was delighted to hear Michel was coming over and in his own mind he prepared a lavish welcome.

Those that worked with Michel for any length of time profited greatly from his knowledge and determination. And the Sheikh was no exception.

Michel pressed the disconnect button. Richard was sitting on the other side of the desk for much of the call. And, in jubilant mood, he reamed off a bullet-point version of the Slough meeting. Michel offered no outward expression but inside he was ecstatic. He shoved a small number of documents across the desk. Richard was peeved when he saw the number of amendments.

'Did you manage to bulk up Secure Span's share capital in National Bank?' Michel asked.

'Good news, the last transaction went through this morning. Secure Span now owns 63.7 percent of National Bank.'

Richard gloated boyishly.

Michel handed him a crumpled slip of paper with a list of names.

'Here's a list of people who're interested in selling,' he said, 'chase them up. By my calculations, Secure Span should own 69.9 percent by close of business tomorrow.'

In the foyer, Michel stood motionless only an arm's length from the gigantic revolving doors, and he studied the multitude of masked faces that littered the end-of-day exodus. Unexpectedly, a shining smile burst forth from the taut-faced crowd.

May waved and he waved back.

A belted trench coat lay draped across her arm.

As they strolled, she told him of the mishap that had befallen her father's briefcase. Michel inspected the damage, and then he suggested treating it with linseed oil and vinegar.

She said she would.

'Are you hungry?' he asked.
'Starving.'
She licked her lips in anticipation. Then she thought, a high-class restaurant, at least.
'There's a pizza place round the corner.' He noted the look on her face and smiled inwardly.
'I thought you were only joking,' she said.
'It's a bit early for gourmet cooking but you'll be hard pressed to find a better pizza in all of London.'

The chef, Lorenzo, welcomed them with open arms and ushered them to the best seat in the house. He removed the reserved sign and handed Michel a couple of laminated menus. May and Michel sat opposite each other, by a large clean window. After lengthy deliberation, they ordered two house specials. Then Michel went to the salad bar and arrived back with two hefty plates of salad.
She scoffed at the sheer quantity.
'Do I look like a rabbit?' she joked.
'As St Francis of Assisi used to say: *you've got to look after Brother Ass.*' Michel scooped up a handful of raw carrots.
'Brother Ass?' May repeated.
'Yes, St Francis nicknamed his body Brother Ass,' Michel said.
'If you say so.'
'At the risk of sounding bigoted, are you religious?' he asked.
'Church of England, but lapsed,' she replied.
She sucked in a sliver of beetroot and spooled it around her mouth.
He watched her chew and swallow. A dribble of vinegar appeared by the corner of her mouth. He reached over and wiped it clean.
His scent sent shivers down her spine and her early nerves vanished and she felt longed-for.
 The piping hot pizzas were packed with all things Mediterranean. May took a bite and listened. She was captivated by Michel's charm, wit and easy demeanour. He, in turn, was bowled over by her beauty, honesty and warmth.

'What age are you?' she asked.
'I'll be twenty-seven soon,' he replied.
'What does your dad do for a living?' May could not stop herself. She wanted to know everything about him.
'My parents passed away when I was seven years old, a traffic accident.' A tone of melancholy tinged his voice. 'And I spent most of my youth in foster homes.'
She wanted to embrace him.
'Do you have a best friend? They say you can tell the character of a man by the company he keeps,' she said light-heartedly.
There was no menace in her questions, so he answered without compunction.
'No, I consider Chen to be my best friend, but he's more of a father figure,' he said.
'Jenny is my best friend. You met her at the squash club. She works for National Bank,' she said.
May chose the biggest slice of pizza and handed it to Michel.
'Taste this pepper,' she said, 'it's scrumptious.'
'Thanks,' he said. 'Who's your favourite author?'
He took an educated guess. 'Emily Bronte.'
'No. Jane Austin, and you?' She cocked her head and lowered the tip of a slice of pizza into her mouth.
'So you're a romantic.' He reached across the table and wiped a splodge of tomato from her cheek.
'Thank you.' She liked the idea of him fussing over her. Each time he reached across, her heart fluttered.
'Ernest Miller Hemingway,' he said.
She bit into a chilli and her cheeks turned a scalded red.
'Lorenzo, a glass of milk,' Michel yelled.
Lorenzo darted into the kitchen and returned with a frothy glass. She gulped it down and fanned her face with both hands.
'I should've warned you. Lorenzo doesn't hold back, he throws everything into his house specials.'

Michel waited until she had cooled down, and then he followed up with a soft question. 'Do you like living in London?'
'No, not at all,' she said, 'give me the countryside any day.'
She sipped a second glass of milk, a tall one that Lorenzo had brought to the table straight from the fridge.
'I love London, the hustle and bustle. Don't get me wrong, I love the countryside too,' Michel said.
He finished his pizza and watched as May struggled to finish hers.
'Where do you live?' May offered him the last slice of her pizza. He gratefully accepted and made short work of it.
'Lancaster Gate.'

Michel found himself distracted by an odd-looking man. The man glanced at him from outside the window. Michel recognised him. It was the small-dishevelled man who had done a runner in Leicester Square. And his peculiar bike was slung over his shoulder. It had two flat tyres. Michel leapt from his chair and bolted out the door. Frantically, May searched her pockets but found no cash.
Lorenzo came out of the kitchen.
She shrugged her shoulders.
'No pay, on the house,' Lorenzo said. His wide smile was friendly and honest.
'It was a beautiful meal,' she said. 'I can pay you tomorrow.'
She was very embarrassed.
'It's ok, Michel is owner.' He chuckled and his huge stomach wobbled over his apron.
'Are you sure?' she gasped.
Lorenzo nodded, still chuckling.
May gave Lorenzo the thumbs-up sign.

She passed a side street but backtracked in horror. Appalled, she thought her eyes deceived her. Michel held a man, dressed in scuffed dungarees, up against the wall. The man's legs were dangling. A strange bike was leaning against the wall and by the front wheel there was a long-pointed knife.

'Michel, what on earth are you doing?' May was totally flabbergasted.

'Sorry about running out on you like that, but this guy owes me fifty pounds; worse still, he tried to stab me. If he doesn't pay, he forfeits his bicycle. It's as simple as that.' Michel tightened his grip.

A group of students strolled by, but they were too frightened to interfere. On the opposite side of the street, Hirokatsu ambled past. A voice in his earpiece instructed him to assess the situation. That he did. And when he saw the knife on the ground he knew Michel had the situation under control, so he kept walking.

The unkempt man feigned innocence. 'Miss, I've never seen this man before. Call the police.'

'Do I look like a fool. If Michel says you owe him money then I believe it to be true. Now, Michel, put him down, please.'

May surprised herself and was delighted to see her words had effect. Michel's eyes lost their intensity and he smiled.

'Very well then.' He ground his teeth and put the man down. 'But I just want to make it clear that the next time I see you, I'll collect.'

'Okay.' The unkempt man grabbed his bike and ran off as fast as his legs could carry him. Then, out of harm's way, he gave Michel the finger and swore at him.

Michel stooped and picked up the knife. He dropped the weapon between the grilled teeth of a drain. There was a loud splash. They stood facing each other. Michel was annoyed with himself for losing his temper and May was perplexed by his antics.

Suddenly, he burst out laughing, barely able to contain himself. His laugh was so infectious that it succeeded in making her laugh so much that she cried. When at last they managed to contain themselves they walked and talked their way to the tube station.

'I must leave you here,' he said.

They stood at the station entrance.

'Don't you use the same tube train?' A red-eyed May trilled in a sweet voice.

'I do, but I'm flying to Holland this evening.'

He took her hand, invitingly.
Then he pulled her closer.
'I enjoyed myself, immensely,' she said.
She moved forward and pushed her hips against his. She kissed him on the cheek and shuddered when his hand brushed off her posterior. A delightful hotness suffused her body.
'Listen, I know you've plans for tomorrow night but I've two tickets for the last show in the Comedy Club,' he hinted.
She radiated a childlike aura. Her cheeks were still a little flushed and her eyes watery.
'Sounds lovely, I'll meet you in this exact spot.' She gave a demure little laugh.
'Ten bells.'
Michel watched her slowly disappear down the escalator.

Jiang stood behind May, protecting her without her knowing, all the way to Bayswater. He had long black hair and was dressed in blue denim. May hopped out of the train and she moved off quickly. Jiang followed her out of the tube station and onto the street. Then, in Queensway, he stood at the door of the supermarket and waited for her. When she came out again, he gave her a head start and then he walked behind her past the shops. May did not slow her pace. She turned off the street and took a lane at the rear of the Little Flower restaurant.
Dogs were scavenging among the bins, and they fled at the approach of Jiang. At last May paused beside a gate that emerged from a low arched opening. She disappeared into the opening and then she turned abruptly into a narrow walkway. She climbed up a series of tiled steps and then she punched in the code and put her shoulder to the backdoor and it squeaked open. Now Jiang had his first clear view of the apartment block. He checked his wristwatch and he squatted on his haunches to wait. Suddenly, the Blackberry under his denim jacket rang.

CHAPTER 12

On a hot summer day, around five o' clock – it was June - Jenny arrived home earlier than usual. No sooner had she closed the door behind her than May turned the key in the lock. Jenny loped from view and ducked inside the kitchen. She stuffed a glossy pink bag inside the dishwasher and hid behind the door. It was not until she heard the faint drone of the bathroom fan kick in did she retrieve the bag and dart to her bedroom.

It was unusual for either girl to leave the workplace so early. May had decided to down tools an hour before time. In the early hours of a busy afternoon, Michel had disturbed her at work when he phoned from his office in Canary Wharf to verify the squash match was still on. One-sided as the game promised to be, she entertained the thought that there might be an outside chance of victory. The wait was agonising. She missed her suitor's manliness and felt an almost puppyish desire to know that he missed her in turn. In an attempt to take her mind off the game, she peeled a banana and chopped it into little pieces. She tasted the sweet fruit, and then she tipped a fresh carton of custard into the bowl.

Jenny shuffled into the kitchen, and the first thing that caught her eye was the banana skin on the kitchen table. Playfully, she flicked May's ear and pointed to the skin.

Since noon, Jenny had found herself increasingly distracted by events elsewhere. Although smitten, she now occupied the moral high ground after insisting that both Tony and herself undergo an AIDS test. She had been nervous that he might think her mistrustful, but it was a risk she had been willing to take.
Her results confirmed she did not have AIDS.
On the stroke of midday, Tony had sent her a celebratory text: *All clear. Need you. Can't wait.* But it was a tissue of lies.
Deskbound, it was difficult to suppress her libidinal energy, so she told her boss that she was feeling poorly and needed to go home. As a reward for Tony's patience, she spent two hours on a shopping spree and had bagged the sexiest lingerie.

Jenny brewed some coffee and nibbled on a chocolate whirl. Then she turned to May.
'How was the Comedy Club?' Jenny asked.
'It was brilliant!' May exclaimed.
'Did you go anywhere afterwards?'
'No, like a proper gentleman, he brought me home,' May told her in wistful tones.
'Too bad,' Jenny said.
'No floozy here,' May said, pointing to herself.
'More fool you.'
'Bringing your work home,' May said. 'That's so not you.' She pointed to the laptop resting on the counter-top.
'Tony's computer is still on the blink,' Jenny told her, shaking her head. 'He became so animated when I turned up without the laptop last time that he promised to cook me dinner.'
'So you're feasting in his place tonight?' May asked.
'Yes, eight o' clock. What're you up to?'

'As a matter of fact, Michel has finally plucked up the courage to take me on in a game of squash,' May said.

Jenny shrugged. 'I should think so. He has twice stood you up,' she pointed out, ever pragmatic.

'He's an extremely busy man,' May argued.

'Really,' Jenny said, 'best of luck.'

'Can I borrow your yellow sports skirt and black jersey-top?' May asked.

Her glamorous blend of style and eloquence seemed at odds with her request.

'It's a tad long,' Jenny answered wryly. 'Besides canary yellow isn't your best colour.'

'It'll be fine.' May was adamant.

'Very well, but before you return it, make sure that it's washed, dried and ironed,' Jenny insisted.

'I will,' May promised.

'What time is your game of squash?'

'My God,' May blurted out in astonishment, 'seven. I better get my skates on.'

'Hold you horses,' Jenny said. 'Let me show you Tony's picture.'

She held up her phone.

'He doesn't look like the shy type,' May considered, 'does he play squash?'

'No, he's not a racquet man.' Jenny thought for a moment. 'Fancy meeting up for a drink next weekend; you, me, Tony and Michel?'

'I'll run it by Michel,' May said. She doubted Michel's availability, second-guessing he would be abroad on business.

'There's a new wine bar just opened near Burlington house in Piccadilly,' Jenny suggested.

'Fingers crossed,' May said. Jenny toddled off.

May decided to have a bath, even though it made no sense to wash before a game.

At six-thirty, there was a loud rap on the door. May was squelched up in the bath filing her toes with a pumice stone. She cried out in lyrical form.

'Jenny, I'm still in the bath. Can you let Michel in?'

Michel knocked again but this time the thwack was louder. Jenny peered inquisitively through the peephole. She opened the door.

He was wearing a designer shirt outside his jeans.

'I believe you're early,' she said with a pale-skinned smile.

She stood aside and let him pass.

'Would you like something to drink?'

Under his mercurial gaze, she became self-conscious and a little embarrassed.

'No you're fine. I'll just sit here and wait for May,' he said.

'You'll have to excuse me,' she said, 'I'm being wined and dined tonight, and I must get ready, you know how it is with us ladies.'

'I'd say you scrub up well,' he quipped.

Jenny did an about turn and lingered in the hallway. She had exchanged her work suit and heels for jeans and boots. Emboldened, she put her hands on her hips and confronted her flatterer.

'You rogue.' Her voice was filled with mirth.

May giggled as she listened to the brazen exchange. Michel laughed.

After waiting for what seemed like hours (although it was probably nearer to 25 minutes) May entered the lounge in the canary-yellow skirt and black top. Her skin was still damp from bathing and her outfit clung to her body. She curtsied in an appealingly innocent manner.

'Wow! I've seldom, if ever, seen a lady so closely resemble a goddess,' he charmed, 'without doubt you belong in the celestial realm, not down here amongst mere mortals.'

'Seldom seen or ever seen?' she asked.

She folded her arms impatiently and tapped the carpet with her foot.

'Ever seen,' he clarified.

'Shall I ring for a taxi?' she asked.

'I've one waiting outside,' he told her.
They looked into each other's eyes. In daring to imagine, she pulled herself away.
She asked herself, could this be love?
'Give me a moment,' she said.
She grabbed her bag and yelled in the general direction of Jenny's bedroom. 'Jenny we're hitting the road, see you later.'
'Have a great time you guys,' Jenny called out.
Jenny waited by the bed until she heard the door close. She retrieved her shopping bag from under the bed and emptied out the sexy lingerie.

Tony, wearing a denim shirt and black jeans, got his wok really hot, threw in his oil, then beef, then vegetables with a couple of tablespoons of water. Then he put a lid on it and let it steam. He used soy sauce, manuka honey, and some lemon juice and sesame seeds to make the sauce. Then he took onions, garlic, ginger, turmeric and chillies – sweated them up in a frying pan, and then added in some chickpeas, vegetables and potatoes. He uncorked a red Don Diego Escolano and let it breathe. Jenny preferred red.
The doorbell shrilled annoyingly. He grabbed the remote and changed the channel. On the screen, a shady character, wearing a black hat with a neck flap, stared blankly at the door. His grotesque appearance, sharpened by his slanted forehead and pained expression, was enough to unsettle even the most hardened criminal. Tony opened the door and handed him a large parcel. There were no words exchanged. Ten minutes later, there was another knock on the door. Tony checked the screen and was relieved. It was Jenny, but more importantly, her laptop was hanging from her shoulder.

They embraced. She could feel his strong hands crumpling her lemon-coloured skirt. Rhythmically, his hands pushed and pulled her buttocks apart. They kissed and his mouth excited her. It tasted of hot aromatic spice and she savoured the tang. He pressed his mouth hard against hers and his tongue flicked like a reptilian. She broke free and told him there would be plenty of time for that. He reluctantly acquiesced. He hung her jacket on an antiquated coat stand and placed her laptop at the base of the stand. He pulled out a chair. The lights were romantically dimmed and the sound of Sade permeated the room. He ventured into the kitchen and poured out two glasses of wine and then, standing on a kitchen chair, he opened the top cupboard. Behind a tidy pile of unopened letters, addressed to Bill Neville, he located a small bottle with a torn label. He popped the cap and shook several tablets into the palm of his hand. Using a nutcracker, he crushed the tablets. With a rub of his hand, he deposited the resultant powder into one of the wine glasses. He held the glass up to the light and inspected its texture. Still a little cloudy, he gave it another shake and placed the glass on the draining board. While he waited for the powder to dissolve he hid the pill container. He returned to the living room with the two wine glasses in hand.

'Jenny would you care for a drop?'

He offered her the glass containing the adulterated wine.

She accepted the tendered glass.

'Don Diego Escolano, no less,' he added.

The conversation was light-hearted.

The starter was delicious. The meat, falling from the bones of chicken wings, was tender and succulent in a broth thick with lentils and herbs. The dinner was even better.

'That was amazing!' she said.

She gobbled up the last of the brown rice, and then she washed down the straggling grains with a gurgle of wine.

An air of melancholy surrounded Tony as he speculated on how long it would take for the narcotic to kick in.

'Thank you for bringing your laptop, I'll print out some invoices later,' he said in a voice that betrayed no real accent.

'You're welcome,' she said.

'What's the password?' he asked.

He refilled her empty glass.

'Queensway1, with a capital Q,' she told him.

'And the boot-up password?' he asked, lightly touching her lips.
'Queens2,' she replied.

In silence he busied himself, placing the leftovers in plastic bags, scouring the wok, sponging the hob clean, and sweeping the floor. Jenny helped him. He appeared sad, always seeming to focus the gaze of his amber eyes somewhere off in the middle distance.

On the couch, they sat nestled together. She grinned at him with a lecherous smirk and then she burrowed her head in under his arm. Her third glass of wine rested precariously on the arm of the sofa.
He placed a hand on her knee. His melancholy appeared totally gone now.
She drained the dregs of her wine and used her tongue to squash the tiny deposits lodged at the base of her gums. Her mobile chirped.
She read the text: *Michel hammered me 3 nil, so much for chivalry. We're out on the town. Hope you have a great night, XXOO May.*

    Jenny switched off the phone and pushed aside Tony's dreadlocks.
'Thank you for dinner,' she said. 'Now, it's time for dessert.'
She started to nibble playfully on his ear, scarred from fighting. With strained arms, she pulled him close. They locked lips. He thrust his tongue deep inside the walls of her mouth. Drawn to the damp warmth of her pink crotch-less panties, his spade-like hand edged upwards. He lifted her to her feet and plopped her standing, with legs parted, on the couch. Aroused, he popped the buttons of her blouse and nuzzled her scented cleavage. He teased out a heaving breast and left it momentarily unattended. Encouraged by her moans, with his grizzled tongue, he pinched her nipple and rasped her bellybutton. Her legs began to tremble. He unhooked her bra and threw it across the dim-lit room. Then he unclasped her skirt. It fell to her feet. He pulled off his shirt and kicked off his shoes. His fingertips slid upward between her thighs. Afraid he might stop, she clamped his

head with both hands and pulled in hard. With a single movement, he ripped off her panties.

'They're edible, you know,' she murmured.

She grabbed his hand and guided a finger deep inside her.

His forefinger played roughly on her clitoris.

'Ouch!' she said. Her head grew fuzzy. Her momentum unstoppable, she unbuckled his belt and slipped her hand along the full length of his phallic identity.

'Do you want me?' She knew it was a ridiculous question.

'Yes.' Whatever she wanted to hear he would say.

'Even my love handles?' It must be the hormones, she thought to herself.

'Yes.' It must be the drug, he thought to himself.

'Tony I want your cock inside me, do you have protection?' Her voice tapered off to a slur.

'Give me a sec,' he gushed.

He bounded into the bedroom. He pulled out the top drawer of the bedside cabinet and pushed aside the Desert Eagle pistol. He tore open the box of condoms and shook a few into his hand. Then he covered the pistol with a vest and closed the drawer. He stripped off the remainder of his clothing and ran stark naked from the bedroom. His appendage swung like a lance primed for battle.

Infuriated, he sat down on the couch and stared venomously at Jenny's unclad body. She was out for the count. One foot was on the floor, the other was on the sofa, and a cushion propped up her head. His blood-filled member refused to shrivel. Standing over her naked body, he contemplated self-masturbation, but not for long. He twisted around and made himself comfortable - his belly against hers. He eased himself in and began, slowly at first, but then faster and faster like some deranged incubus. Despite the odd moan, her tightness slackened. Frustrated, he brought her knees up to meet her breasts and then pushed her thighs closer together. He began again.

Beads of sweat formed on his brow and his eyes rolled in their sockets and his back arched. Suddenly he roared, spurting his seed deep inside her caverns. It was the primal sound of a mating beast. Utterly exhausted, he stayed inside her until his firmness returned. Again, thrust after thrust, his powerful manhood invaded her limp body until his force was spent. He bundled her up and carried her to the bedroom and set her down on the bed.

Awakened by a pig-like snore, Tony roused himself and shoved the unopened condoms back into the box. Jenny had stopped breathing and her face had turned a dark purple. He stood and watched the spasm abate. Then her lungs filled up with air and the colour of her face normalised. He opened the bottom drawer of the bedside locker and wheedled out a rusty metal box. Sitting on the bed, he substituted a number of parts in the Desert Eagle pistol. He exchanged the standard 152mm barrel with a 203mm barrel and loaded a 10.92mm cartridge, and then he engaged the safety. He stepped into a Kevlar bodysuit and put on a pair of ankle boots. He stuffed a black ski mask, the pistol, night-vision goggles, phone and Jenny's laptop into a black shoulder bag. When he opened the freezer, a blast of cold air nipped at his face. Using his knife, he forced the frozen pigeon into a cooler-bag. The knife, he slipped into a sheath around his ankle. He pulled on a long black overcoat and threw the bag over his shoulder. He left a note on the dresser, the last part of which read: "Called away by a valued customer. I'll return ASAP".

 He switched off the lights and closed the apartment door behind him. He paused for a moment and then he hurriedly descended the staircase. By now the evening shadows stretched long and thin, and he saw a huge cloud forming over the capital. Adrenalin surged through his veins, weeks of planning about to reach fruition.

It was already dusk when Tony turned off the headlights and allowed the jeep to freewheel towards the front of the shed. A middle-aged man in a golf cap was digging down around Bill Neville's allotment.

Christy Moore moved quickly and quietly around a small fire. He stopped to look at Tony, and then he turned right back to his work. Moving from patch to patch on the allotment, Christy hoed potatoes from long drills of earth, pulled up carrots, picked parsley and rosemary. Satisfied that he had taken enough, he loaded the produce into a battered wheelbarrow parked by the dirt path.

Tony loaded everything that he required into the back of the jeep. He latched the glider securely to the crash bars and then locked the shed. The air was filled with birdsong and the smell of eucalyptus. Suddenly, to the right of the shed, a faint but distinct rustle arose from the undergrowth. Tony stopped and listened. Unnerved, he was not sure what caused the disturbance. Briefly, he spotted a tiny glow through a mass of broadleaf shrubbery. His every sinew tautened.
Then it dawned on him: it was a mobile phone.
He came up like thunder and slammed into Christy. Shaken and bruised, Christy yelled. There followed a petrified silence.
Tony went straight for the jugular. He carted the weighty body from the undergrowth to the fire, still burning. He reflected moodily on his bad luck. A body discovered in a fire is one thing, but when a second turns up, with a broken neck, the whole place will surely be sealed off, he said to himself. He hoisted the body over his shoulders and trudged from the undergrowth.
A vibration broke the silenced night. It was somewhere close. Tony swivelled, much too quickly, and his ankle boots got entangled in the ropey undergrowth. He stumbled and fell.
Christy's phone had an incoming call, but try as he might, Tony could not pinpoint its location.
Then there was silence.
Careful not to extinguish the flames, he set the body down charily on the fire. He scattered a bundle of twigs onto the flickering flames. The composition of human fat and synthetic clothing crackled and hissed. As he walked back to the jeep, the rank attar filled his

nostrils. He locked the shed door and nailed a piece of plywood across the front.

He sat into the jeep and flipped open a small notebook. He marked off each item before having one last look around. Everything seemed to be in order so he started the engine and moved off slowly. A slight fog descended. He breathed a sigh of relief, glad to be on his way.

The full beams of an oncoming vehicle almost blinded him. As Tony jammed the gears into reverse, the jeep jolted violently.

A branch had got caught under the back axle.

When the approaching vehicle came to a halt, two of the uniformed occupants got out. One of them, the younger of the two, adjusted his chequered cap and advanced towards the jeep.

'Good evening sir, we received a call from a worried man regarding a Mister Ben Neville. The caller also reported an unsavoury character lurking about Mister Neville's hut. Did you see anyone wandering about the allotments, or better still, have you seen or spoken to Mister Neville?' The bearded policemen asked.

As he spoke, the second officer, a veteran at first glance, shone his torch through the back window, and then Tony saw his gaze switch towards the hang glider.

Fascinated, the officer was unable to keep his eyes off the glider.

'Terry, come here,' he said 'what's this?'

'A hang glider,' Terry said. He moved back towards the driver's side of the jeep and tipped his hat.

'Sir, isn't it late to be going hang gliding?'

While weighing up his options, Tony thought for a moment and considered his reply. He noticed an obscure movement in the police car up ahead. There were at least two or maybe three other officers in the vehicle. He made up his mind.

'It was I who phoned in the report. I mistook Bill for an intruder. I spoke to him no more than five minutes ago,' Tony said.

'I can take you to him?' he added.

'That would be most helpful,' the bearded policeman said. Then he stood back in order to give Tony enough room to step out of the jeep.

But the veteran officer noticed that Tony seemed to be almost rigid with anger.

The two policemen exchanged knowing glances. They were in no doubt that Tony's appearance and physique fitted the description of the trespasser.

The heat gave way to dismal rain. Tony led the two men through the rows of vegetables towards the burning fire. The older officer walked directly behind him, while the bearded, energetic Terry used the fire as a beacon and blazed a trail across the corrugated earth. Beams from the officers' torches crisscrossed the unworn path and cast an eerie unnatural shadow. As he neared the fire, Terry cursed loudly for he could not believe his eyes. Amongst the flames, he glimpsed a human figure. Without forethought, he started to run. His reaction was so impulsive that it surprised both Tony and the older officer. Tony reached down to his ankle and withdrew the knife from its sheath. In one sweeping movement, he brought the knife upwards in an arc and seared the throat of the veteran officer.

His victim collapsed in a heap.

Amazingly, the dead officer still held the torch in his hand. The beam shone straight up into the sky.

Then Tony rushed towards Terry.

Terry had witnessed the attack and he stared blankly at the crumpled bundle that was his superior. Tony closed in on him. Terry panicked. He turned and ran. His only allies were the settled darkness and the lightsome fog.

He reached the safety of the undergrowth and slid into a water-filled gully. His elbows sank and he buried his face in soaking wet hands. Alone, so alone, he could not bring himself to lift his head. He tried to think but every thought was void of hope. Then there was a loud splash and seconds later he felt ripples of water wash up against his face. His heart thumped wildly in his ears, so wild that he believed his pursuer must surely hear it. Tony paddled through the shallow water but moved in the opposite direction to where his quarry lay.

'Where are you?' Tony sang softly.

Granted a reprieve, Terry wiped away from his muddied cheek tears of despair. Tony had doubled back towards the police car.

As he neared, Tony dived onto a peaty loam not five metres away. Unseen, he opened the backdoor of the jeep and retrieved the shoulder bag. Crawling along the well-trampled vegetation, he circled the police vehicle and crept up on its unsuspecting occupants. Two officers sat in the back seat, a woman and a slightly built man. A crown of curls adorned the young woman. They chatted convivially to each other, not yet alarmed by the no-show of their colleagues. Tony put a gloved hand on the door handle and counted to three. The officers were taken completely unawares and stared with huge rounded eyes. Tony shot the policewoman right between the eyes. The bullet shattered her skull. She died instantly. Tony grabbed the surviving officer's limp hair and ordered him to radio the control centre and report all was ok. Tony promised to spare his life, but only if he cooperated fully. It was a lie. The second shot was as accurate as the first.

Upon hearing the second shot, Terry, still hiding in the gully, strengthened his resolve and pulled himself out. Under the cover of darkness, he inched blindly towards an old Sunday school, which was behind a hedge where a farmer's goats, let loose to fend for themselves, were grazing peacefully.

Tony smashed the radio, and then pushed the blood-drenched vehicle off the dirt track. He trotted back to the jeep and opened a storage box full of weapons. He selected two grenades, and then he closed the box. With no time to waste, he put on his night-vision goggles and dashed back to where he last saw Terry.

Tony stood on an enormous compost heap and adjusted his night-vision goggles. A hungry vole, no bigger than a mouse, ran along the lip of the gully. It scurried past the compost heap and ran towards a cabbage leaf unearthed by Terry when he fled. Tony's head swept a 180-degree arc. Abruptly, his head jerked backwards when he spotted a tiny movement by the old Sunday school. The slow moving policeman, agonisingly close to the school entrance, looked back in trepidation. In the headlights Terry glimpsed the shadowy shape.

Tony lobbed an armed grenade. The projectile bounced off the school's orange-tiled roof and rolled back along the pitted surface to where the helpless policeman cowered.
Terry took evasive action, but in doing so, he inadvertently wriggled over the grenade. His body muffled the explosion.

Tony opened the storage box. Carefully, he handled a steel pipe, a foot in length. The pipe had a round cap welded to both ends and a long strip of wire that protruded from one end. He left the driver's door open and the engine running. He nipped around the back of the shed and placed the pipe beside the gas cylinder. He cut the hose and flicked the cylinder switch. Then he chucked the last of the grenades into the backseat of the police vehicle. He scrambled headfirst into the jeep. Its deep threaded wheels span violently, dislodging the branch under the back axle.
The grenade exploded first. Then the pipe bomb detonated. The omni-directional blast rocked the jeep but Tony managed to keep it under control.
Safely away, he overtook a bus on the main road. As he did, he felt the steering wheel shudder. The shuddering worsened and forced him to pull over to the grassy verge. He stuck his head out the window and cursed when he saw the front tyre. It was as flat as a pancake. A shard of glass had ripped the tyre wall. He slapped the steering wheel with both hands.
He found the jack and changed the wheel as fast as he could. With one eye on the road and the other scanning a map, he overtook the same bus. Soon after, he stopped as a shepherd herded his bleating flock across the road. Then Tony continued his journey through rolling farmlands to the outskirts of a small village.

It was one of those muggy, miserable nights. The journey lasted no more than an hour. He parked the jeep along a secluded dirt track and unloaded the vehicle. Close to a chalky ridge, the sophisticated hang glider rocked in the breeze. A sudden gust of wind caught the sail-wing as he clipped a fixed camera to the alloy frame. He strapped on the shoulder bag. Strips of Velcro secured his knee-guards and on his head he fastened a crash helmet with a long peek. Under the swing-type seat, he trussed a large leather pouch. He settled his helmet and pulled down the visor.

Initially, the apparatus was cumbersome. It wobbled over the first few metres of the graceful sloping hill. At last the gusting tailwind lifted the sail-wing. The glider veered left, and then right, as Tony shifted his body weight. His thighs safely clamped. He took a quick look at the GPS display and adjusted the course accordingly. For the most part, he remained in a prone position, gliding on up-currents towards Woking at an altitude of eight hundred metres. Again, he checked the GPS display.

At last he reached Woking, a distance of twenty miles south west of London. He flew parallel to the railway lines until he passed over the racecourse at Sandown Park. Then he changed direction and skirted Hampton Court and sailed towards Richmond Park. The wind dropped as he flew over a high-roofed rectangular building, forcing him to swerve round a flame-topped chimneystack. But the wind picked up again at Barnes reservoir. He turned east to follow the Thames. Over road bridges, railway bridges and streetlights, he maintained a steady as she goes height until he came to Battersea.

Tony pulled gently on the aluminium lever. Descending quickly, he circled the rooftop of National Bank Headquarters. He reduced the wingspan further, taking into account the unpredictable shifts of converging airstreams. He slowed to a stalling speed just above the roof garden that crested the building. At the base of a flagpole, he landed with precision. A camera swept across an area cordoned off by a chain-link fence.

Packed between two massive air vents, the sail-wing was well camouflaged. He left the alloy frame intact. There was no telling when a quick exit might be needed. He popped the pistol and knife into the shoulder bag. He unfurled a brace of high-strength polymer ropes from the leather pouch hanging under the swing-seat and tied the alloy frame to a girder jutting out from the concrete ledge. Then he lowered the frame and, using a much shorter length of rope, dropped the shoulder bag over the side.
He slipped through the tiers of chain-link and peered over. It was a steep drop. Superbly balanced, muscles taut and arms twisted, he gripped the forked girder and climbed down the rope that held the shoulder bag. He swung acrobatically, and then he eased himself into the alloy frame.

    The fog was not overly dense. Pleased he had secured a good hiding place, Tony climbed back up and drew in the shoulder bag. He circumvented the roof garden, running along the concrete ledge. He ran with the confidence of a steeplejack. There was a long row of pots, each one decorated with a different country scene. To his left there was a Japanese-style decorative bridge that spanned a water lily pond. On the other side of the bridge, there was a gravel path that led to a metallic door. His next spurt was synchronised with the sweep of a second camera perched on a steel spire. A nesting peregrine falcon squawked angrily.

Tony waited for the bird to settle. Then he opened the side pocket of the shoulder bag and extricated the newest in high-tech gadgetry. Crouching and weaving, he timed his crisscrossing run to perfection and galloped over the bridge towards the metal door. He attached a RF device to the underneath of a shiny keypad. Then he retreated to the cover of the potted trees and removed the dead pigeon from the cooler bag. There he waited until both cameras were at the end of a sweep. He held the thawing bird in his hand, and then he hared towards the metal door and his foot slammed violently against it. An impact so severe, it sent vibrations up his leg and chattered his clenched teeth. He dropped the pigeon and retraced his steps back along the ledge. He slid down one of the climbing ropes and lowered himself into the alloy frame.

Steve, not at his most sententious, closed his eyes. In the control room, located directly behind the front desk, he groomed his walrus moustache with the tip of his tongue. Then the alarm sounded. Shocked into vigilance, he punched Colin on the shoulder
'Colin, wake up,' he shouted.
Colin, a courtly man of around 50, flicked his cap and tried to focus.
'What what's wrong?' he stammered.
'The alarm, can't you hear it? The roof. You stay here and alert Master Chen,' Steve said. He grabbed his walkie-talkie and torch and hightailed it for the lift to wait for George.
George ran eagerly down the corridor, cudgel in hand. His wraithlike figure, the product of a lifetime working graveyard shifts, was lost in the oversized uniform.
The lift journey seemed to take an eternity. Vulnerable and nervy, neither felt courageous enough to exit the lift. Self-preservation was foremost on Steve's mind, so he pushed George out of the lift and into the corridor. The ousted expression on George's face was one of sullen submission. Furtively, he looked up and down. Relieved by the marked absence of danger, his narrow shoulders miraculously squared up. In grandiloquent triumph, he signalled Steve to follow him as he marched down the corridor. Shamed into action, Steve raised the walkie-talkie to his mouth and addressed Colin in the control room.
'Colin, can you give me an update please?' he asked.
'Everything looks normal here. Nothing peculiar showing up on the monitors,' Colin replied.
'Did you manage to make contact with Master Chen?' Steve asked.
'I left a message with his wife,' Colin said.
'Did you try his mobile?' Steve demanded.
'No, not yet, I'll try it now,' Colin said.

'Roger that, over and out,' Steve said.

He produced a hipflask and took a swig. Then he passed it to George.

George was slow to bring it to his mouth. When he did, his face reddened.

'What the hell is the matter with you?' Steve barked. He wrenched the hipflask from George's trembling hand.

'I only drink beer,' George said, 'I'm not used to spirits.'

'Come on, let's get out onto the roof,' Steve said, his finger poised over the touch-sensitive keypad. He entered the four-digit code but nothing happened, save for a red light blinking. He muttered the code under his breath, and then he tried again. This time the green light blinked and the metal door sprung open, but only narrowly. Steve, with both arms extended, pushed firmly. Nervousness, along with a marked difference in temperature, caused him to shiver. He raised his jacket collar and blew hard into cupped hands. George took a few steps back, just in case Steve press-ganged him into going out first.

Reluctantly, Steve ventured out and toe-poked the pigeon, an action that exorcised his fear. When George heard Steve laughing, he sauntered up beside him. With the top of his boot, Steve pointed out the headless bird and then he kicked it across the rooftop.

Steve's convulsed bulk settled down. In exultant mood, he raised the walkie-talkie to his mouth.

'Colin, false alarm, cancel that call to Master Chen. It was a bloody pigeon. The bird must have collided with the door,' Steve said. 'The fog is clearing, so we'll have a quick look around up here.'

As he turned to his colleague to yap an instruction, Steve spotted the peregrine.

'There's the culprit. It must have chased the poor bugger. George, take a dekko down that side. I'll check this side,' Steve ordered, pointing with his walkie-talkie at the ledge.

George moved cautiously, still coming to terms with the interruption in his nightshift ennui. He peered behind a grille of Rose Dusky

Maidens. Out on the periphery, screened by a long line of potted conifers, he stood near the ledge. Directly above the forked girder, he urinated. Tony covered his head. While he waited for the golden shower to end, he drew his legs up into the foetal position.

From behind the bank of conifers, Steve bellowed, 'what in God's name are you doing?'

He plodded up behind George.

George covered up his tackle. 'I needed to relieve myself.'

'Pathetic, there could be pedestrians down there?' Steve said.

The luminescent face of Tony's wristwatch caught Steve's eye as he glanced over the ledge. George, embarrassed by his actions, did not catch the pale shadow stealing across Steve's face.

'There's nothing up here, let's go back inside,' Steve said.

He prised George away from the ledge and gave him a toe-poke up the backside.

He shoved him in the direction of the roof door.

Choosing not to enlighten George, Steve shut the door and told him to stand guard until he returned.

The instant Steve got back to the control room he phoned Chen. On tenterhooks, he described the intruder and how they had discovered him.

Colin listened to every word. Perhaps, he thought to himself, this could be an opportunity to show everyone, in particular Master Chen, how brave I am.

'Who else is in the building?' Chen asked.

'Pat Hogan and Sid Roland - Roland is in the bunker working on the mainframe and Pat is at his desk,' Steve answered, his tone fretful.

'Good, ask Pat to meet me in the foyer, and make sure Sid doesn't leave the bunker.'

'What about George,' Steve asked.

'Tell him to return to his usual post,' Chen intoned gravely.

'Consider it done,' Steve said.

'I'll do it,' Jason, a portly guard of 30, said.

Chen then instructed Steve to remain where he was and not to do anything rash, that he himself would be there in person within twenty minutes.

Chen arrived with Setsu and Mr Okumara. Sat in the foyer was Pat Hogan. Sid's absence and Steve's bee-like energy were beginning to play tricks on Pat's mind. Convinced his past had somehow reared its ugly head, Pat reminded himself that Mr Okumara was fully au fait with all that he had done before joining Secure Span.

Mr Okumara nodded and smiled.

Then Christophe and Akiko entered the building. They had spent most of the previous month as part of Michel's elite bodyguard unit. Chen liked to rotate members of the unit on a regular basis, so as to keep them on their toes. Recently, Christophe and Akiko had been reassigned to a taskforce headed up by Mr Okumara. A taskforce entrusted with a very specific assignment - to hunt down Hiroki's killer.

'Master Chen, shall I call the police?' Steve asked.

The phone slipped through his sweaty grasp.

His shirt had the appearance of a field being drained.

'No, not yet, we'll wait until he makes his move. Keep your eyes on the monitors,' Chen insisted.

'Should we deploy someone to the top floor?' Setsu asked.

'No, I need to establish what exactly the prowler's intentions are, and the best way to do that, is to allow him to proceed unimpeded,' Chen insisted.

'What about Sid, in the bunker?' Steve enquired.

'Reactivate his access. But phone him first and tell him to report to the control room,' Chen ordered. 'And patch me through to Pat in the foyer.'

'Pat, can you join us in the control room.' Chen hung up. 'Steve, Pat will need temporary level-seven security clearance.'

Colin ushered Pat into the control room. There were three security guards sat at the long table facing the computer screens.

For the next two hours the weather freshened as the front wave of an approaching storm sent cool winds and occasional rain to London. Hazardous location aside, Tony remained motionless for a further hour or so, long after Steve and George retired to the comfort and safety of the building. Even Chen began to doubt if Tony was still there. He was on the verge of sending Setsu up to have a look.

Tony climbed about 20 feet up the girder along the steep glass-wall and reached the ledge. Gazing up into the nighttime sky, he hoisted himself over the ledge. He scampered along the perimeter and knelt down behind the potted conifer nearest the bridge. Satisfied that neither camera had their line of sight adjusted nor sweep interval altered, he pulled out Jenny's laptop and attached a communications-pod. He hid the bag behind the conifer and darted for the door. Crouched down, he raised his hand and, with a delicate touch, located the RF device. Using his fingernails, he peeled off the Velcro strip. Brightly displayed, on a narrow pane, were four flashing digits. Out loud he rehearsed the numbers and stuffed the device into his pocket.
Watched closely, not by the cameras, but by the peregrine falcon, Tony tapped gently the keypad and the door sprung open. He flitted inside. Armed with nothing but the memory of the building's blueprint he went straight to the fourth floor via the staircase. He paused at length outside the swing-door.
A scattering of chairs and presses forced him to plot a course through the passageway. Apart from the singular hiccup of being mistaken for a urinal, his smooth unobstructed progress left him feeling uneasy. Despite his misgivings, he arrived at Jenny's desk. He made sure it was the correct desk by cross-referencing the phone extension with an internal phone list dated the previous day. This was when he noticed the photo stuck to the handset.
His eyes widened, it was a picture of him.

Annoyed, he denounced the photograph as a betrayal of trust and tried to guess on what day Jenny had taken it. Almost forgetting where he was, he regrouped and slid the laptop into the docking station. He powered it on and entered the boot-up password. Finally, he switched on the communications-pod and speed-dialled the sole entry in the dial list. 'Tom, we're on,' he whispered.
The reply was just as quiet. 'Ok. Good work.'
Tony terminated the call and reset the communications-pod. A blue fluorescent aurora appeared above the pod's display.

Inside the sweltering building, sweat was running in rivers down Hirokatsu's massive chest and across his enormous belly as he lumbered past the control room. Ichiro trailing along.
'Who usually sits at that desk?' Chen asked. He had been following Tony's every step. A whole host of cameras, the size of pinpricks, interleaved in the perforated panels of the building's suspended ceilings, were relaying crystal clear images back to the control room. Colin scrolled down the console menu and used the mouse to mark the destination on the computer screen, and then he clicked on the icon representing the camera directly above Jenny's desk. He manipulated the joystick and zoomed in.
'Jenny Ferdinand,' Pat piped up after pulling up the floor plan on the bank's intranet. He was apprehensive, knowing Jenny to be May's best friend.
'She works on the Secure Span account,' he added.
Chen was also aware of the girls' relationship but his anguished disquiet focused on how this turn of events may impinge on his protégé.
'Where does she live?' Setsu demanded impatiently.
'Give me a moment. I need to access her personnel file. There we go?' Pat printed out Jenny's address.
Setsu palmed out the printout from the tray and handed it to Akiko.
'You and Christophe go and bring her here. NOW.'
But Chen pulled rank and overrode Setsu's directive,

'No, Akiko you go alone. Jiang is already in Bayswater. Christophe you stay here and marshal the front desk. Pat, switch Miss Ferdinand's LAN port over to the honey-pot network, and then decommission the lifts. Setsu, you take the emergency stairs, the rest of you, follow me.' Chen and Mr Okumara moved swiftly to the fourth floor. Steve and Colin lagged far behind.

Now that the bank's firewall had been physically bypassed, the Scallion twins were free to implant a worm. At risk were bank account details of businesses, depositors and employees.
In order to fulfil Chen's request, Pat had implemented a subtle change to the configuration of the hub wired to Jenny's access point. Although the hackers had breached the bank's vanguard, they were being rerouted to a ring-fenced dummy network, identical in every way to the production environment but populated with fictitious names, accounts and personal information.
In a frantically intense manner, Pat picked up the hackers' trail. The hackers were computer hopping between India, Korea and Russia. He wondered how long it would take before they realised that they had been hoodwinked. Once the subterfuge was up, their trail would quickly run cold.

Oblivious to the consternation he had caused on the ground floor, Tony readied himself and prepared to leave. Suddenly, the lights were toggled on and off. He lay crouched on the floor, behind Jenny's desk, like a sprinter on starting blocks geared up to spring. He spotted Chen and Mr Okumara through a slit between two partition panels. They were guarding the far doorway and Mr Okumara had his finger on the light switch. Tony sprung to his feet and sprinted for the near door. Setsu burst through the door and cut him off. Tony craned his neck and saw that Mr Okumara was almost upon him. He adopted a defensive pose and took measures to minimise their advantage. Positioned with as many objects between him and his enemies, he stood with legs apart and fists clenched. His jutting jaw served as a heady reminder to those stalking him that he was not a man to be trifled with.

Setsu and Mr Okumara exchanged conspiratorial glances, and then they fixed their eyes on Tony. Setsu nodded then let fly a straight punch. Tony altered his stance and executed a low block.

Meanwhile, Chen was analysing Tony's every move.

Mr Okumara came on like a force of nature. But his forward momentum carried him smack bang into Tony's fist. Tony, having held their combined offensive, chambered his left leg and let loose a kick aimed at Setsu's ribs. Then he launched a furious slapping and pushing attack.

Unbalanced, Setsu struggled to break free. Tony yanked him close and delivered a lethal uppercut that lifted him up off his feet. Setsu had barely recovered when Tony finger jabbed him. But, with a powerful kick, Setsu sent Tony tumbling over an office chair.

Mr Okumara charged forward with a combination of fierce short hooks and then, with the back of his fist, he landed a ferocious blow on Tony's temple.

After five seconds, a couple of good uppercuts, and hooks left and right, Tony punched Mr Okumara into a corner. Then he forced Mr Okumara's head downwards, so that it met his rising knee. Those standing at the far door heard the bone-crunching thud. Tony lifted Mr Okumara over his head and flung him at Setsu.

It was a demonstration of raw power that sent both men crashing into a long bank of filing cabinets.

There was a certain thrill in viewing raw power unleashed.

Steve looked on in awe and he silently questioned why Chen had not rushed to his colleagues' assistance. In answer to Steve's unspoken doubt, Chen turned to him.

'To defeat one's enemy,' Chen told him, 'one must know one's enemy.'

Chen produced from inside his jacket a blowpipe, and then he popped what appeared to be a black bead into his mouth. With surprising casualness, he brought the mouth-hole to his lips and gulped a lungful of air and ballooned out his cheeks. He extended his elbows, and then he aimed at the towering figure. Tony felt nothing. Quickly, Chen concealed the blowpipe. Confidence restored in his boss, Steve watched with expectation, wondering how long it would take before the intruder buckled. However, Tony did not falter. Instead, he waited for Setsu and Mr Okumara to launch a counter offensive, but an attack never materialised. The crushing weight of the metal filing cabinets had effectively immobilised them.

All of a sudden, complete calmness descended.

Tony turned his attention to the three men standing at the far door. He ignored Steve and Colin but stared intently at Chen. Chen stood with his arms folded. Driven by a natural curiosity, he speculated on the intruder's next move. Then Tony strode forward with dubious intent.

Blank-eyed, Steve and Colin hastily retreated and sought refuge in the shadows. Chen did not budge. Tony feigned an approach but veered away and sprinted towards the emergency exit. The race was on, yet Tony was ready to turn in a flash. At each landing, he paused and stood his ground.

Pat scrambled over to Jenny's desk and disconnected the communications-pod. The hackers had already disappeared into cyberspace. Chen and Steve hoisted the filing cabinet from off Setsu's ankle. Just then Colin crashed through the emergency exit and set off after Tony. He ran with a braggadocio born from an innate desire to impress rather than to actually catch and apprehend the intruder. George joined him.

Whoops and shouts echoed up the stairwell. Half-expecting the door to be rendered inoperative, Tony punched in the code. Much to his surprise, the latch gave way and the door sprung open.

Before closing the door he took one last look down the stairwell. Some flights below, he heard hurtling footsteps.

He dragged two of the biggest conifers, screeching, across the bridge and set up a barricade.

'That should slow them up,' he mumbled to himself.

Someone had turned off the roof lights. Tony stared blankly into the darkness. Then, out of the black, came a shimmering presence.
Hirokatsu looked a lot like Tony from the neck down, but his body was more powerfully built. The initial clash brought the gladiators flying toward a thunderous embrace. With their fiercely muscled arms wrapped around each other's backs, they carried on a struggle that lasted more than a minute. Finally, Tony got Hirokatsu backed up against the roof door. But Hirokatsu jabbed his palms under Tony's armpits. With a display of brawn, he shoved, slapped and tripped Tony. Then he doled out a vicious stamping kick. Tony rounded on him with fire in his eyes. Slapping, pushing, tripping and wrestling-style flips sent Hirokatsu rolling to the ledge, and out under the chain-link fence.
Hirokatsu fell to his death.
Tony fixed a baleful stare at Ichiro.
Tony jumped nimbly away from Ichiro's initial charge, and then he sent him sprawling to the synthetic turf with a powerful shove in the back.
Short but intense, the fight lasted less than a minute. With a look of determination in his eyes, Tony grabbed Ichiro and sent him flying wildly from the rooftop.
Tony sprinted to the far corner of the ledge, fully aware that both cameras were following his every move. He reeled in the alloy frame and quickly assembled the glider.

Chen was in the middle of bringing some semblance of organisation to the floor, so he asked Steve to go after Colin. He truly believed the chances of Colin catching such a formidable foe were slim at best.
Somewhat reluctantly, Steve gave chase.

Tony could hear the excited rumble of voices entrenched on the other side of the door. The stockade slowly surrendered to the combined weight of the guards. Tony placed the knife between his teeth and released the safety on the pistol. The wind cranked up as he exploded into a powerful sprint. The gravel stones crunched with applause as he raced down the path. The girder functioned as a take-off board and helped him jump away from the building.

Disorientated, George and Colin stumbled through the weakened stockade and caught a glimpse of Tony's heels. The hang glider slowed its rate of descent until a strong gust of wind whisked it upwards and away. Tony could see the guards swarming over the roof. From the wrong side of the bridge, Steve and Colin hurled a volley of gross insults.

As soon as Steve saw the pistol he ran for cover.

Tony discharged a full round. Atomised pockets of gravel were strewn in every direction and Colin was hit in the midriff, not by a stone, but by a bullet. A fatal shot.

Steve heard Colin screaming. In an attempt to rescue his stricken comrade, he stopped running and returned to the spot where his friend lay mortally wounded. Surprised by his own bravery, Steve knelt down beside him.

At last, Chen and Setsu arrived on the scene. Chen had seen this type of wound before and immediately applied pressure so as to stem the flow of arterial blood.

Colin's life force ebbed away through the gaps in his uniform and it was not long before Chen and Steve were kneeling in a pool of thick blood. Steve produced the hipflask and dribbled a drop of whiskey over Colin's lips. Disconsolate and distraught, Steve lifted the walkie-talkie and spoke in a hoarse voice.

'Jason, call an ambulance, Colin has been hit and is in a bad way,' he said, kneeling and scraping away the stones.

Under Chen's disciplinary gaze, Steve took a swig of whiskey, and then looked upwards. He could see the man-bird shrink in the darkness. A gloomy silence filled the air.

After a nap, Tony pulled up a chair and carefully considered the curled up bundle. With every act of wanton destruction and human finitude, the more blurred his perception of right and wrong. In a profession where human life is held so trivial, guilt and remorse had long been replaced by impassiveness. He had grown fond of Jenny. Nevertheless, in his line of work loose ends ought to be tidied up. Along with Bill Neville's apartment, Jenny was a needle-sharp loose end. Tracing his finger across her back, he asked himself, would Jenny have the same feelings for me if she knew my profession? Could I risk opening up to her?

His mind harked back to the aftermath of an assignment in Beirut, where he faced the exact same predicament with a local girl, who had fallen in love with him, and he with her. In his heart, he knew Jenny would ultimately suffer the same fate as the Lebanese girl, if not sooner, then later. In a trance-like state, he took the pillow from under her head and placed it over her mouth. There was neither struggle nor sadness. He wrapped a dressing gown around her wilted body and stuffed the folds with candles. He lit a candlewick that poked out from the overlap, and then he set fire to the bed. He closed the bedroom door and went straight to the kitchen.
The escaping gas hissed with menace, each hob was turned to max.
He unplugged the microwave and inserted a digital analogue timer with a backup battery.
On his way out of the building, he nipped into the basement and removed the mains fuse.

CHAPTER 13

On a day when the early morning sun was filling the mist-shrouded waterway of the Wiltshire estate with a shining glow, Michel snipped two of three hooks and skewed the remainder. A subtle flick of his wrist catapulted the lure across the river.
Although he had instigated the meeting, it was Charles who had chosen the location.
The anglers stood within talking distance of each other, on the estate's choicest berth, not far from the flourmill. Both men were locked in solitary thought. Suddenly a long, lean salmon shot up from the deep and lunged at the artificial fly. Its jaws snapped shut in a squall of bubbles. Charles looked on approvingly as Michel worked the line with a touch of élan, reeling in the 20lb wild salmon. In the shallow water the fish suddenly rolled onto its back in surrender. Jubilantly, Michel waded forward and he grabbed the hook with his fingers and after several sharp tugs, he yanked it free. He carried the fish to the bank and dropped it into the net. It was the first catch of the day.

Michel whipped the fishing rod back and forth and looked across at the freshly planted trees, and to Charles astonishment, he said, 'I've a blank cheque in my back pocket, how much do you want for the Tintoretto self-portrait?'

Charles thought for a moment.

'Say, eight million,' he answered.

Michel did not balk at the inflated valuation.

He propped his fishing rod between two huge boulders and signed over the cheque.

'Thanks, you can take it with you this evening, once you've had dinner,' Charles said.

'I can't stay for dinner.' Michel's tone was bordering on the apologetic.

'Nonsense, you know how Jane loves your company.' Charles was persuasive but unavailing.

'We'll see.' Michel flicked his rod. 'There's something else.'

'I'm all ears,' Charles said.

He was well softened up.

'I'd like to buy out your block of National Bank shares,' Michel said, deadpan.

'What?' Charles exclaimed. Initially, he thought Michel joking, but when he saw the seriousness of his gaze, he knew that he meant business.

'If you agree to sell, I'll own 91 percent of National Bank shares,' Michel said. 'As a consequence, I'll be in a position to cancel its listing and force all other shareholders to sell.'

Charles took a step back.

'I don't know what to say.'

Charles, severely shell-shocked, found it difficult to believe that Michel owned nearly 70 percent of National Bank share capital.

'Oh, and one more thing: I'd like to offer you a position on the board,' Michel said. He measured Charles's reaction, and then he added, 'you'll need time to mull it over.'

'You caught me off guard,' Charles said bluntly. 'But I would like to hear how you propose to guide the company over the next decade.'

Charles, stupefied by the scale of Michel's ambition, recovered somewhat, but not for long.

'I don't want to come across as the proverbial bull in a China shop, but I believe the time is right to forge ahead. It's all about short-term yield.' Michel paused, keeping the ferment off his face and out of his voice. The next throw of the dice was pivotal. 'Once I've secured National Bank, I'd very much like to orchestrate a takeover bid for Peoples Pensions. The price on the table is one hundred and eighty-five million pounds cash on signature. But that is open to discussion.'

Michel felt a slight tug on his fishing rod, but then the line went limp.

Outraged, Charles fought to moderate his temper but his patience gave out and he yelled angrily, 'you're delusional, I've no intention of relinquishing control.'

Charles, after a moment of hand wringing, felt weak at the knees. He leaned against a boulder and tugged on his beard. With obsessive dismay, he listened intently to Michel's every word. So glad and confident a few minutes before, now he was tormented by self-doubt and questions, and he thought, this guy is going to chew me up. How could I have been so wrong about him? He must have been planning this moment for years. Fretting miserably, he found it hard to accept the fact that this upstart had outwitted him so easily. Emasculated, his world had been turned upside down and he began to ponder the unthinkable, the end of everything he held dear.

'I know what you're thinking; perhaps I've not explained myself clearly. Let me quash your fears,' Michel said.

He expounded his machinations in a forceful style and, slowly but surely, Charles came round. Surprised by Michel's in-depth knowledge of the elements underpinning pension models, he realised that this minion was neither vindictive nor greedy, more like a reviewer dissatisfied with the trammelled expectations of tradition.

'Go on.' Charles swallowed his resentment when the realisation hit home that he was looking at a carbon copy of himself in his halcyon days. Full of extraordinary game plans, ideals and empirical designs. Michel carried on.

Charles, convinced that there were no more surprises, re-baited his hook and listened with bated breath.

'To see and understand the big picture, you've got to start thinking about this as more than a business. We both know that you're not getting any younger, and at some stage control for Peoples Pensions will be wrested from you,' Michel said. 'Your life's work will become a plaything for some high roller. As it is, the company's portfolio has become conical and needs to be broadened. My intention is to appoint a quality person, sympathetic to your achievements, who is capable, with your guidance, of steering Peoples Pensions in the years ahead. The person whom I see at the helm is your daughter, May.'

Michel witnessed Charles's mood transmogrify from misery to elation.

His imaginative suggestion had struck a chord.

Charles, wearing a determined expression, asseverated, 'May, why on earth May. She has no knowledge of the industry?'

Although joyous, Charles probed Michel's motivation.

Michel gave him an odd sideways glance.

Ever since Jenny's death, May had become distant and self-absorbed, so much so, that she failed to attend her aunt's funeral.

In recent weeks, only once had she visited her folks, and that was but a fleeting visit.

'That's a valid point,' Michel said. 'I know I can't force you to sell or coerce you into lending support to the takeover bid, but the picture will become a little clearer when I ask your daughter for her hand in marriage,' he added. His countenance betrayed no sign of anxiety throughout the entire conversation.

'You've no idea. For years, I've been trying to convince her to come and work for me. Not alone that, but my daughter is not one to suffer fools lightly, and let me state, in no uncertain terms, that love will be the presiding reason for her to accept a proposal of marriage. She is a romantic creature imbibed with starry-eyed notions.' Charles pointed out, in mingled bitterness, believing he had gained the ascendancy.

'True, but let me give you the lie of the land. May and I have,' there was a short moment of utter stillness, 'formed, what I hope, will be a lifelong friendship. Since Jenny's death, May has become more serious and introspective, searching for the meaning and the purpose in her own life. Listen, I know in your eyes no man living on this planet is good enough for May, but allow me to set your mind at ease. I'll treat her like a queen. I'm no womaniser, not for the want of opportunity, but rather an adherence to my belief that there must be a purpose to everything I do. And I fear no man, other than myself. One more thing: don't underestimate your daughter's talents, she is a quick learner, earnest, dutiful and ridiculously intelligent,' Michel said.

He reeled in his line and strolled over to where Charles sat. He placed a hand on his shoulder.

'I wish you no ill will. I've no desire to cut through your family or your life's work,' he said. 'I trust you'll not speak of this to May.'

'What would I say. She probably wouldn't believe me anyways. Besides, I'd run the risk of alienating her. This is the first time in my life I've been bullied, and let me tell you, it doesn't sit well.' Charles wondered quietly to himself, he is ambitious, strong-willed, formidable, intelligent, ruthless and financially independent.

'By the way, you could never do or say anything to alienate May,' Michel said, his voice deceptively soft.

'And how is she, health-wise?' Charles enquired.

'Finest, she twisted her ankle playing squash, but other than that, she's fighting fit,' Michel answered.

'Good,' Charles said quietly.

'We can discuss the golf course at a later date.' Michel offered his hand artlessly.

'Okay,' Charles said.

'Are we Okay?' Michel asked.

'You're some operator. Answer me this, how on earth did you discover that I own shares in National Bank? Those transactions were meant to be hush-hush,' Charles said.

He grabbed Michel's hand and squeezed hard.
'I own the company that manages your portfolio. Listen, I'll walk back to the house and give you some breathing space,' Michel concluded, 'before I go, let me remind you that May will be the primary beneficiary.'
In a tumult of emotion, Charles watched Michel leave. There was much to encourage him. He put away his frustration and became pragmatic. In the final analysis, his mind raced through the criterion of a perfect son-in-law and Michel ticked all the boxes.

The next morning, in Lancaster Gate, sitting at a round table, Michel, dressed in a grungy tracksuit, perused the Financial Times. Smartly, he folded the newspaper and left it neat and tidy on the glass-topped table. Directly above him, there was a faint movement. Next door to Michel's bedroom, May had spent the night in the most palatial of spare rooms.
Cheerfully, Michel whistled as he descended the tiled stairs. He was not a regular visitor to the basement kitchen and it took a few minutes of opening and closing cabinet doors to locate the necessary ingredients: oat flakes, cranberries, cinnamon, and milk. He stirred the mixture and left the saucepan to its own devices, cooking at low heat.

Up with the lark, May drew back the curtains. She squinted as a flare of sunlight deflected off the Serpentine and sizzled along a blanket of trees, in Hyde Park. She stretched and yawned, her porcelain complexion still creased by the pillow. She wanted inspiration, so she adjusted the tripod-mounted telescope in front of the large sash window. Peering through the eyepiece, she observed a group of tourists carrying picnic baskets and walking briskly through Speakers' Corner. She spotted a red fox skirting a hedgerow as it returned from its nocturnal forage. The magnificent image she was now presented with fetched little comparison with the impoverished view from her Bayswater apartment. She felt an added sense of comfort being so close to nature. It reminded her of the family estate. Although captivated by the view, she turned away to inspect the room.

Late last night, before retiring, she thought the bedroom spacious, but now as daylight raided its four corners and emphasised just how big, 4,000 square-foot, it took a moment to register. The walls and floors were decorated with Greek mosaics. The bed could comfortably cope with four or five people, six at a squeeze. In the far corner of the room, to the left of the walk-in wardrobe, three white Parisian chairs encircled a coffee table with legs of intertwined bronzed leaf. As she limped towards the Victorian writing desk, she ran the palm of her hand along the mantelpiece - stencilled with African carvings. The opulent beige carpet massaged her dragging foot. She stopped in front of a gilt-edged mirror, hung in a satin covered recess, and smoothed her hair. Beyond her own reflection, she caught sight of a painting, which had hitherto escaped her notice. The visual detail seemed to capture how she felt when she slept alone. She examined closely the hard-nosed depiction of a dark rural landscape and she recalled that her father had at one time a similar painting. She tried to make out the signature, El Greco, and she wondered if it was an original. At loggerheads with herself, she continued to explore the room's grandeur, not sure if she was being nosey or just exercising a woman's prerogative.

    Her clothing lay draped over a dual-sided sofa. She slipped on her green blouse and stepped into her Balenciaga wrap-floral-print skirt. A leopard brocade jacket, tied with an embroidered scarf, saw her fully dressed. Her sore foot objected when she tried to put on her boots, so she decided to leave them for later.

A nagging disquiet resurfaced. Granted, their shared kisses where both romantic and sensual, yet she wondered what was preventing Michel from challenging her sexual boundaries.

Perhaps, she silently adduced, since Jenny's death I convey a sense of vulnerability.

Already, she had exhausted many hours of quietude, weeping in grief for her dear departed friend; all the same, a fresh tear welled in the corner of her eye.

Even hunger pangs could not prevent her from having a snoop. She wandered off, filled with inquisitiveness. She passed a room dominated by arches and alcoves that bore the hallmarks of a west-end bar. She regarded with a sense of awe the spectacular ceiling and studied each one of the mythical characters. The mural, of epic scale, depicted gladiators fighting in the coliseum. Before leaving the room, she asked herself, how could one so young afford such a home, in the heart of Lancaster Gate, normally reserved for organisational headquarters and landed gentry.

Discountenanced by niggling doubts, she brushed them aside; it would be downright boorish of me to offend him with such an enquiry, she said to herself. Gripping the banister, she hobbled down the flight of stairs. Her progress was stumped by the coldness of the hallway tiles. A chill travelled up her spine but she bested it and ploughed on. The tempo of her motion produced an irregular pat on the unforgiving floor.

In keeping with the rest of the house, the dining room was large, modern, clean and tidy. A bowl of steaming porridge awaited her. Michel ran to intercept her. He put his hand on her arm and ministered to her until she was comfortably seated.

'How's your foot?' he asked.

'It's just an ankle twist, and as my father says: *it'll be better before you're married.*' After blurting out her dad's dictum, she penitently bit her lip. She hoped he would not conjecture, in anyway, that she was dropping a hint.

'That's not to say that I'm in any hurry to get married,' she stated.

He grinned widely.

'Will you at least go to the hospital?'

'No, it's just a sprain, believe me,' she demurred. 'I must say this is top-notch porridge.'

'One of my foster mothers gave me the recipe,' he recalled, unaccustomed to discussing themes of a personal nature.

'How long have you lived in this beautiful house?' She looked at him openly.

'A little over four years,' he replied.

Then he passed her a tall, clear glass. 'Have a glass of melon juice.'

They did not speak further, until both bowls were licked clean. Michel hurried to the kitchen.

He returned with a bubbling brew of coffee.

May rose from her chair and reached over for the jug of milk. The colour glowed in her cheeks. In order to balance herself, while pouring, she touched him on the arm. She adopted a twisted pose so that he could admire her breasts. She was not disappointed.

Teased by the texture and scent of her skin, he intuited her want and fingered her hair.

Her heart fluttered at the thought of him wanting her.

He could no longer resist her charms.

He put his hand around her waist.

She melted into his bear-like grip. Her heart quivered and her person trembled.

Immersed in the smouldering sinuosity of an embrace, she inveigled his hand and placed it inside her loosed blouse.

Her lips moist, she placed her mouth over his and hunted his tongue. They clung together.

His heart thumped.

Her heart raced.

Far from restraint, she gathered her breath and pressed hard against him. She willed him to whisk her off his lap and lay her across the table. She let her fingers stray and ease down his tracksuit bottoms. He was helpless and exhaled a tense gasp. She wriggled off his lap and kissed his bellybutton and peered up at him, her eyes wide and anxious. He smiled and waited. She used her fingers and lips, searching and stirring and retreating. Encouraging her, he grasped her hair and stroked the nape of her neck. She heard him sigh above

her. Hard as a bone, he cried out. Her lips stayed on him, not leaving while the last residues of ecstasy lingered.
She stood up and with a saucy smile, lifted her skirt and opened wide her jacket and blouse. She spread herself and straddled his leg.
He wondered, what next.
Rhythmically, backwards and forwards, she rode his leg as if riding her mare. She moaned as if in agony, wild and uncontrollable. He seized her buttocks. They were firm, yet soft.
He murmured encouragement to her.
She could feel her vulva becoming liquid.
He suckled her and praised the size and shape of her breasts.
Triumphantly, she sang out and then slumped against him. Tongue-tied and shy, giddy with the sensation of being naughty, she found warmth curled up in his arms.

A female voice bawled out from the basement. 'Yahoo!' Followed by the sound of a slamming door, and then the echo of yips and yodels.
May looked aghast. She jumped off Michel's leg and fixed herself. In her haste, she knocked over the jug. Her mind in consternation, she rebuked herself, it could be his girlfriend, even worse, his wife. Her emotions seesawed from jealousy to guilt. She imagined herself as the dreaded other woman.
Michel sensed her unease and reached out.
He held her hand and raised his voice. 'Good morning Hanna.'
May regained some degree of decorum, helped in no small measure by Michel's composed countenance.
'Relax, May, Hannah is my housekeeper. Sadly, she only speaks a little English. One more thing: she never smiles,' Michel said, pulling up his tracksuit bottoms.

Hannah, a big woman with long brown hair, bustled into the dining room carrying three shopping bags. At once, armed with a handful of tissues and a bottle of cleanser, she made a beeline for the spilled milk.

May sat uneasy.

Hanna clucked as she mopped. Her Popeye-like forearms made quick work of the cleanup. Suddenly, she looked up and gave May the once over.

Michel grabbed May by the hand, and they withdrew to the hall.

Her limp forgotten May walked with perfect grace.

Still holding hands, Michel invited her to sit on the antique two-seater. She sat cross-legged. After a while she tugged on his hand and whispered, 'Michel, I should've asked you this before, but somehow I took it for granted. Are you married?'

He sharpened his voice. 'What do you take me for, a scoundrel?'

'Sorry, but I had to ask. I fretted when I thought Hannah was your wife, or girlfriend. How on earth have you managed to escape the claws of a predatory woman?'

He shrugged. 'I've not met the right girl.'

He squeezed her hand and caressed her soft fingers. For the next few minutes, they huddled together in comfortable silence.

'Michel, I'd really like to confide in you something of a very personal nature, so that you may understand me better.'

Michel watched her chest rise and then, sensing the significance of the moment, he encircled her waist. She responded to his tightening grip by looking directly into his eyes.

Leaning forward, her mouth was close to his ear.

She whispered to him, 'Michel, I've never known anyone in the biblical sense. As a girl, I made a promise to myself to treasure my virginity until the day I marry, and it's my intention to honour my future husband with this precious gift.'

A droplet of cold perspiration formed on the tip of her nose.

He was full of admiration for her forthrightness. He compared her virtues with those of his former girlfriends, none of whom were virginal. He reassessed the implications of becoming seriously involved. Then he thought, on the other hand, a man could go through his entire life without ever meeting a girl he could truly love, unconditionally, and in turn; ford the prospect of reciprocating that love.

At this early phase, he knew he could walk away emotionally, selectively compartmentalise any simmering feelings, and continue to look upon her as an instrument of business.

Unobserved, his fingertips slid along the lowest sill of the Victorian stand. He found what he was looking for and presented her with a brightly coloured box. The box was too deep to contain a pair of earrings and too wide to enclose a necklace. Carefully, she opened it. It was a box of knobbly-black French truffles.
She fought to keep her disappointment in check.
She nibbled on the flesh of the smallest truffle.
In a change of heart, she whispered, 'I must confess, since Jenny's death, I've reassessed my stance on sex. No one knows what tomorrow will bring, and I don't want to go to my grave without experiencing the act of love.'
Michel bided his time before replying. 'Of course, my selfish side is in accord with your wishes. However, I firmly believe you should keep your promise. Have no fear, for as long as you're with me; nothing will happen to you, I'll make sure of that. That's my promise to you, and I never break a promise.'
Again his eyes became piercing.

Hannah had finished cleaning up the mess. She switched on the Dolby and turned up the volume. Strains of the Tales from the Vienna Woods trickled out into the hall. In the absence of words, May's underlying loneliness bubbled to the fore. As the minutes passed, the awkwardness of revealing her innermost thoughts threatened the informality of the setting, but her misgivings were soon dispelled. Michel stood up and, with ease, swept her off the two-seater. She anticipated a kiss, so she closed her eyes and parted her lips.

'Miss Franks, may I have this dance?'
They waltzed the length and breadth of the hall, with May giggling like an adolescent girl, melting in and out of his arms. They both forgot her injury, which had miraculously healed. In the middle of a twirl, she noticed Hannah discreetly leaving the dining room.
May, with effort, pulled back from Michel.
'We must allow Hannah to do her work, and I must go and do my work. What are you up to today?' she asked.
'What I'm doing is flying to New York.' Michel studied her for a moment. 'Listen, how would you feel about accompanying me on a trip?'
'To New York?'
'No.'
'Where to, somewhere exotic?' Her face brightened up even more.
'The destination is a surprise but let me give you a clue; it's in Europe, and you can count on plenty of sunshine,' he said.
Her imagination clicked into top gear. She conjured up visions of herself and Michel running hand in hand along a sun-kissed beach, carefree. Long leisurely walks, leading to refined dinners on the promenade, and her being serenaded by local musicians.
'I'll have to run it by Richard. When, exactly, are you planning to go?' May queried enthusiastically, while her mind plotted shopping excursions that would fill her suitcase with travel essentials.
'Before the end of the week, assuming all goes according to plan,' a delighted Michel answered.
May's exuberance waned. She put her hands on her hips and said importantly, 'you're very sure of yourself Mr Trebeh.'
'I'll call a taxi?' Michel said, smiling.
'No, I'll walk.' And, as an afterthought, she added jovially. 'Michel, with all your money, how is it that you don't own a car? A girl like me is used to being ferried about in the greatest of style.'
She pouted her lips.
'I enjoy public transport. Besides, it helps keep my feet on the ground and in touch with normal folk whose lives revolve around

ordinary jobs. I hope I don't sound too condescending, but it provides a glimpse into all aspects of human existence, in particular, the resourcefulness of people,' he replied.

May, satisfied with the cryptic nature of his explanation, kissed him on the cheek. 'Give me a moment; I must get my boots and bag. Oh! You're a miracle worker, my foot doesn't hurt anymore.'

She scurried upstairs.

On her return, she begged the question. 'That painting, in the spare room, is it an original?'

'I hope so, I bought from your dad,' he replied softly.

'From dad! I do declare,' she paused, 'I thought I recognised you, well actually, the back of your head. Did you visit, say, within the last two months?' she asked, flabbergasted.

'As a matter of fact, I did, and since that visit I've purchased another painting.' He smiled at her shock.

'Which one?' she looked pained.

'The Tintoretto self-portrait,' he replied, his voice placating.

'Well, I'll be. Dad didn't say a word,' she said helplessly.

The grandfather clock standing by the door coughed up a chime as she left with food for thought.

The dark-suited Richard, in a generally relaxed mood, tapped his fingers on the steering wheel. He scratched his head and yawned. The cogs of an inventive mind, greased by the voice of Jose Carreras singing Puccini's Nessum Dorma, warmed. Abruptly the car-phone cut short the interplay of mind and timbre.

'Hello,' Richard said.

'Hi Richard! This is Michel.' He seemed upbeat. 'May Franks needs some time off, can you arrange it?'

It was an unambiguous command.

'No problemo,' Richard said delicately and hazarded a guess as to the real reason for the early morning call. Most likely a buyout or yet another takeover bid.

There was a short silence.

'Merlin foods is bankrupt and up for grabs,' Michel said.
'Really,' Richard said.
'I'm going to buy it,' Michel announced.
'What are you going to do with it?' Richard asked.
'I intend to sell the buildings in Manhattan, Jakarta and Windhoek. And I'm going to get rid of the baby food division then cash out the pension fund and replace it with an annuity from Peoples Pensions,' Michel declared.
'I'll need you to take care of the paperwork,' he added.
'Of course,' Richard said. Michel hung up. He then rang Chen.

Chen was standing on a hot, sunny tee, watching with pride as Setsu teed up.
'Chen, how are you on this fine and beautiful morning?' Michel enquired, as he wandered about the spare room.
'Fine, Setsu and I are enjoying a game of golf,' Chen answered, almost apologetically.
'Good for you, that reminds me, you owe me a rematch,' Michel said. 'I'm just ringing to let you know that I'll be leaving for New York in the afternoon.'
Restless, he sauntered over to the window and looked through the telescope.
'I'm taking the jet,' he said.
'Ok, I'll make sure it's ready,' Chen said.
'Now, get back to your game.'
    Chen stuffed the sat-phone into his golf bag, and watched his son take a practice swing on the championship tee. Setsu, who only graced the golf course annually, addressed the ball. Concentrating, he reminded himself of the rudimentary principles: keep your head down, left arm straight, slow back-swing, keep your eye on the ball, hit down on it and follow through.
But, he forgot the golden rule; let the club-head do the work. And he ended up trying to take the skin off the ball.
The wayward shot swerved and headed towards a cluster of trees.

Chen lost sight of the ball when it bounced off a tree, lodged in the rough, and refused to come out.

He reprimanded Setsu.

'Swing your hips, transfer your weight from your left foot to your right foot,' he said.

Setsu, although frustrated in his ambition to master the art, showed no signs of petulance.

With their bags slung over their shoulders, they set off in search of the ball.

Suddenly an angry voice yelled out from behind a clump of hawthorn bushes.

'That tee is out of bounds.'

A low-sized, scrawny man peered out upon a nearly unbroken expanse of fairway with one clear-cut bunker barely visible to the west. Lesley Grain had been making his way to the practice range, adjacent to the ninth hole, when Setsu caught his eye.

Lesley, wearing retro shades and a straw hat, approached the pair with a shuffling gait.

'Do you mind if I ask you a couple of questions?' he croaked out, waving his right hand like a conductor. 'What club are you a member of?' he asked accusingly.

'As it happens, I'm a member of this club,' Chen answered unflinchingly.

'What's your name?' Lesley put his full attention on Setsu.

Chen replied with measured politeness, 'Chen Shengjun.' Only for Lesley to quip, in a ponderous tone. 'I've never heard of you.'

Chen became impatient.

'I've been a member here for six years or so, and this is my son, Setsu.'

For the first time, Lesley smiled.

'You must think me an interfering busybody. It's just that your son was holding up that four-ball, and one of them happens to be an ex-president of the club.' His manner was contrite and his posture stooped.

'What's your name?' Chen asked.

'Lesley Grain.' His coarsened voice stretched to the limits.

Chen recognised the name. 'If recollection serves me, you're a former amateur international,' Chen said. 'In fact, a few years ago, a friend of mine had lessons with you - Michel Trebeh.'

'Ah Michel, an absolute natural. I seldom see him out here though…' Lesley began to reminisce, and then he spotted a hickory-handled golf club in Setsu's bag.

'That,' he noted, 'is a beautiful club. Whatever you do, never sell it.'

Setsu pulled out the rustic club, the handle of which was covered in mud-stained bandages. He offered it to Lesley for closer inspection.

Lesley glanced over at the eighth green.

'I think they have a beginner with them as well. They seem abnormally slow,' Lesley said.

Setsu was highly indignant at being referred to as a beginner.

Lesley toddled off to the practice range and Chen waved through the ex-president's four-ball.

A gangling youth topped his drive.

Setsu beamed with delight. He looked after Lesley and wondered if he had marked that woeful shot.

Unfortunately, Lesley was busy negotiating his way over the old lady's mounds.

    Chen made up his mind and delegated the organisation of the next mission to Setsu.

'Michel is going abroad. As soon as we're finished here, can you put together a team? Chen asked.

'Of course,' Setsu said.

'It might be a good idea to select yourself,' Chen suggested.

'Where to father?' Setsu asked. His anxiety drowned his excitement.

'New York,' Chen answered.

CHAPTER 14

Rarely sleeping or eating, Michel paced the house in his slippers, downing cups of coffee. Due to a decipher breakthrough, enthusiasm coursed the veins of all involved in the Gouves excavation.
He settled down to watch some television. He had put his laptop on charge and left it on the arm of the chair and as he got up to make a cup of coffee, he inadvertently knocked it on to the floor.
'Oh shit!' he grumbled.
He picked it up and powered it back on to check it was still working correctly. It took longer than usual but eventually the display lit up.
Just to be certain there was not any internal damage, he logged on to his email.
A message flashed up.
He clicked on the attached file. It was a brief excerpt from the Gouves scroll.
The message was sent from Greta.
He sent off a response.
While he sat in his socking feet, debating whether to make ready the jet, Hannah fussed busily about the dining room. She plopped his heavy canvas bag on a chair and began to massage his neck and shoulders. At times, the power in her hands amazed him.

She pummelled his shoulders until they ached.
'You should take more care of yourself,' she said. 'You work too hard.'
It was a challenge for her to translate into English, but she persevered.
She could perceive from his aura a restless spirit.
Unlike most women that came into contact with him, an infatuation never developed nor did her eyes ever betray a lustful thought.
Only when the doorbell rang did the pummelling stop. Michel stifled a yawn and rubbed the tiredness from his eyes. He slipped on his shoes and heaved the canvas bag over his shoulder.
He swung open the door.
There May stood in all her top-to-toe elegance.
'Mr Trebeh, you promised me a holiday?'
'Indeed I did Miss Franks,' he said. 'You're just in time.'
When she spotted the canvas bag she hooted, 'we're not leaving right now, are we?'
'Yes we are, and here is our ride.' He pointed to the black cab.
'But we were supposed to fly out this afternoon,' she complained.
'There's been a change of plan,' he said.
'But I've no stuff,' she lied. She had spent the previous evening shopping until closing time.
'We're in no rush,' he said, 'we'll swing by Bayswater.'

May scampered around the apartment, tossing in random fashion the contents of a dozen shopping bags into a new designer suitcase. Then she crammed a half-empty box of tampons into an oval straw bag; then her cleansing lotion, manicure set, toothbrush, hairbrush and a handful of knickers.
In the taxi, she suddenly realised she had forgotten to pack her purse.
'Damn, I forgot to bring my cards and cash,' she screeched.
Michel stroked her knee gently.
'Don't worry, I've enough for the both of us,' he said. 'Are you hungry?'

'Starving,' she said.
'Cabbie, pull in over there,' he said. 'And keep the meter running.'

May slid onto the barstool next to Michel at the luxury hotel, just off the M25.
'How was New York?' she asked.
'Fruitful,' he said.
'So, where are we going?' she quizzed.
'It's a surprise,' he said, shaking his head.
'Ah, go on,' she sighed.
'Crete,' he said.
As they spoke, one or two guests drifted in for a drink. Next to the bar was a brightly lit area with a pool table and jukebox. Beyond was a small stage and dance floor, dark but for the glow of red and blue lights strung along the ceiling. On the stage a jazz band with two saxophones, trumpet, and piano were playing to a sparse crowd. The pianist, sweating heavily, eyes closed, crooned, "My baby just cares for me".
'Do you know Richard well?' May asked in an offhand manner.
'For some years, why?' Michel, slight still, wondered what prompted the question.
'Is he happily married?' she asked with a girlish innocence.
'He and Margaret have had more than their fair share of marital problems, like most couples, but they're back on track.' Michel, composed as ever, took a sip of soda. 'He hasn't hit on you by any chance?'
She leaned over and kissed him lightly. Then she sniggered and scrunched up her nose.
'I was just wondering, that's all,' she said.
'Ah, here he is,' Michel said.
'Who?' May asked, frowning.
'Our co-pilot.'
Michel shook Gerard's hand.

He was 52 years old; stalk thin, with an orange goatee and lively brown eyes, exaggerated by silver-rimmed glasses. He was wearing a long, loose shirt, a black skullcap, and black khakis.
'Who's the pilot?' May asked, while shaking Gerard's hand.
'You're looking at him,' he said.
'Where?'
'Me.'
'What!' she exclaimed.

The cockpit instruments of the silver Gulfstream jet were lit up like a Christmas tree. Gerard manipulated the dials, screens and controls.
'Power-plant,' Michel said.
'Check,' Gerard said.
'Flight.'
'Check.'
'Landing.'
'Check.'
'Navigation.'
'Check.'
'All systems go,' Gerard said, in his deep, gravely voice. 'We're cleared for take off.'
The plane taxied along the runway. Michel turned to May and smiled. He pulled on the wheel column and lifted the nose of the plane.
All seemed right with the world.
After flying for a time, May, seated between Michel and Gerard, asked, 'Michel, why Crete?'
'I've visited the island four times over the past two months, always with my dive gear, and every time I've strapped on a scuba tank and stepped off a boat, I've been excited. Not only is the diving tough and demanding – open-sea currents that swirl around underwater archaeology can be strong and unpredictable – but it usually serves up a surprise or two,' he said.
'Sounds idyllic,' she said.

'I've begun days watching dolphins leaping out of the sea,' he added, 'then swum with shoaling fish near reefs, seen seals toy underwater...'

Their fuel was running out when Michel spotted a long wake made by a cruiser speeding south-southwest. Forty miles beyond the island, he dived, putting the plane just above the wave tops.
'Oh, my god.' May covered her eyes.
Michel and Gerard burst out laughing.
'Pull up,' she shuddered, screaming.
As Michel pulled away, he wagged the plane's wings.
May swung around to photograph the cruiser. Minutes later, they zoomed across the island, flying at low altitude.
As the plane nosed toward Heraklion, Michel told May to buckle up.
She surveyed the city and remarked, 'it's beautiful.'
The plane dropped down to 70 feet and skidded in for a landing.
'Ger, take over,' Michel said.

Camera affixed like a prosthetic device, May started shooting as soon as she put her feet on the runway.
Michel switched on his sat-phone.
There was a call coming through. It was Chen.
He sounded perturbed and hard-edged.
Instinctively, Michel moved an acceptable, but not an offensive, distance away from May. He stood alone at the nose of the plane, looking down at the ground.
'What's the problem?' Michel bellowed, forcing his voice above the din.
'One of the daily broadsheets has got wind of some damning information and the bank's court are convening shortly to deliberate,' Chen said.
Michel waved to May, pointed to the phone, and he threw his eyes up to the heavens. At the same time, he moved a little further away.
May smiled and nodded her head.

'What type of information?' Michel asked.

'Well, in a nutshell, the article claims that Richard violated corporate policy by accessing pornographic web sites. Not just once, but on a number of occasions. They have dates and times of each visit, along with the IP address of the computer used to visit the sites.' Chen waited for a response.

'We need to smoke out the leak immediately,' Michel said. 'Exactly what kinds of site?'

'Escort agencies,' Chen told him.

Michel dropped his voice. 'Call out the sites visited.'

He recognised one of them. 'That'll do, were there any transactions?'

'There was one request for an escort and a single transaction,' Chen said.

'Have you spoken to Richard?'

'I spoke to him not more than half-an-hour ago, and he admitted there was evidence to suggest that he acted in breach of corporate policy. Furthermore, he said his resignation would be penned first thing in the morning.'

'Who called the meeting?' Michel enquired quietly while giving May a wink.

She was still out of earshot and she wondered what was so important that it could not wait.

'That old stick-in-the-mud Peter Sussman,' Chen replied.

'Okay, where's Richard right now?' Michel demanded.

'Probably at home making peace with Margaret.'

'Are the sites visited legal?' Michel glanced over at May.

'Absolutely, nothing you wouldn't find on the top shelf of a corner store,' Chen said.

Michel continued. 'Who has access to the proxy-logs?'

'Only a handful of people, I can forward you their names, but you know how quick rumours spread,' Chen said as he jotted down a list of names on a napkin.

'Who reported it?' Michel had already settled on a plan of action.

'Pat Hogan reported it to May Franks, and she duly informed personnel,' Chen said.

It saddened him to implicate May.

Michel's temper flared. 'Confiscate all laptops, workstations and servers used by anyone who had access to the logs. And scan for documents or emails containing Richard's name.'

'Okay,' Chen said flatly.

Michel hung up.

He walked past May towards the terminal. His anger thinly concealed by a strained smile, and then he asked her to be patient while he made an urgent call.

It had come as a bolt from the blue. Richard had started the day like any other day, skimming over the leading dailies. But his mouth dropped when he read the acidic headline, "BANKER ESCORTED". A sick nervous sensation welled in the pit of his stomach. Shocked by the level of detail, he slammed his desk with coiled fists. In a fit of rage, he tore the broadsheet to shreds, and then he stormed out of the office. Crestfallen, he instructed Larry to clear his morning calendar. Then he drove off at high speed.

Days earlier, a collusion of high-powered investors had launched a campaign of scare mongering against a heavily leveraged financial institution. They had orchestrated misleading rumours that the Anglo-Aus Bank was in difficulty, which caused a huge drop in the institution's share price. The adverse hype caused a run on the institution and its shares were temporarily suspended.

As a result of investing heavily in Anglo-Aus, Richard was on the verge of bankruptcy.

Ahead of him, there was an oncoming bus.

There's a bus, Richard told himself; just nudge the steering a fraction.

'Oh! Can't do that, there are passengers onboard,' he muttered.

Then, approaching a treacherous bend, he hugged the inside curve. At almost the same moment he swung out on the wrong side and overtook a slow-moving truck.

He took the next corner poorly. The tyres screeched as he overcorrected and skidded along the hard shoulder. 'At last, an easy way out,' he thought out loud, 'the next truck that comes along - truck drivers never get hurt, just treated for shock.'

He could see the winding road ahead of him empty, but no more trucks crossed his path.

Fed up with bourgeois pretensions, he no longer indulged in the grotesque vanity of make-believe accidents. He arrived home safely and accelerated up the empty driveway. A change of wind sent a dustbin toppling.

He jammed his foot on the brake.

The jaguar skidded and knocked the dustbin for six. The bin landed in the middle of a shrub-bed planted between the rambling Tudor country house and the tall-detached garage.

Richard got out and opened the boot.

Disgrace and pride bolstered his nerve. He unzipped the emergency breakdown kit and extracted the unused towrope. Deep down, he did not want to die, not just yet anyway. His mind worked overtime; perhaps he could sell up and emigrate, a new start where no one knew him. Then he pictured his meltdown becoming front-page news, and Peter Sussman gloating over his grisly comeuppance. His determination to end it all waned further when the phone in his jacket pealed.

Michel moved further away from where May stood and stalled a few minutes, and then he tried again.

'Hello,' Richard wheezed as he strode to the garage, rope in hand.

Michel spoke with force. 'I've just one thing to say to you, are you listening?'

'Yes, I'm listening,' Richard croaked with self-contempt.

'DO NOT RESIGN,' Michel barked.

'How can I not resign?' Richard asked.

'Because all you were doing, whether you know it or not, was processing a venture capital request made by a company trading as Skintingle. You treated the application, from the outset, as you would any other petition for funds, by thoroughly examining the company's product and its competition,' Michel said, his words measured and calm.

'How on earth can I back that up?' Richard asked, not wishing to brand himself a liar and make matters worse than they already were.

Michel spoke with calm authority.

'Fortunately for you there exists a relevant application filed only six weeks ago. Skintingle is the parent company of the escort agency you used,' Michel explained.

There was a prolonged silence.

Michel was uncertain, but he believed that he heard sobbing. Only then did he realise the unbearable pressure brought to bear on his right hand man. Nothing worse than a family man embroiled in a seedy scandal, he thought.

'Nee nee needless to say it won't happen again,' Richard stuttered plaintively, 'you've saved my bacon. I owe you my life.'

Richard blabbered on relentlessly.

Michel grew impatient.

'Just tell me you're not resigning,' Michel said.

'Absolutely not,' Richard said. His flamboyant air had returned in no small measure. He waxed lyrical about how he was going to sue the newspaper for libel.

'That's great,' Michel said, 'I must let you go now, so that you can flesh out a formal reply and argue your case before the bank's court.'

'I don't know what to say,' Richard mumbled, 'how can I ever repay you?'

'That's a first,' Michel said. 'One more thing: I intend to cover your Anglo-Aus losses. You can sign over the shares whenever the suspension is lifted.'

Michel hung up, another crisis thwarted.

He rejoined May, linked her arm and apologised for his rudeness. On the other side of passport control, Fobie waited with a fulsome grin that filled the terminal building. Greta, dwarfed by her lover, was also excited by Michel's arrival.

'Allow me to introduce, Miss Franks,' Michel said. 'She's here in an observatory capacity, as my guest.'

'There's no need to be so formal, please call me May,' she insisted.

The dirt-smeared Land Rover, parked just outside the airport entrance, stood tall with a jet ski stuck fast to its roof. Attached to the tow bar was a metal trailer with a submersible resting on a thick layer of foam-beads. In pairs, they walked to the vehicle.

As the women got to grips with each other, Fobie brought Michel up to speed.

Fobie, in the driver's seat, pulled on a pair of leather gloves and put on his wrap-around sunglasses. The Land Rover moved slowly through Heraklion. On the outskirts of the city they passed a fleet of three cargo trucks.

The two girls got along like a house on fire, glowing with conversation, barely stopping to draw breath as Greta conveyed the adventure of archaeological discovery to her newfound friend.

'Truly unbelievable,' Greta told May, as she held a piece of rock in her outstretched hand.

May gazed at it as if mesmerised. While they chatted, the vehicle picked up speed and barrelled down the precarious E75. They overtook a taxi, but as they did, a red Lamborghini jumped them. Back in line, Fobie remained sharp-eyed. They raced through the town of Gournes, and then, in the blink of an eye, they sped through Hani Kokkini. Fobie changed down gears and squeezed off the E75. Then he cut right and sped towards Gouves.

Pulling in at the excavation site, they were welcomed by Dmitri.

May joyfully exclaimed, 'look over there.'

She had spotted a turtle edging towards the seaward side of a pebble beach dipping away from the roadside.

Dmitri introduced himself, and then he told her that she was looking at a loggerhead turtle. Then he assumed the role of driver, an altogether safer approach, and he banished Fobie to the backseat. Instead of rejoining the E75, Dmitri decided to follow the coastal roadway.

The large commercial town of Hersonisus, a hub for road traffic, slowed them down but they made good time thereafter. They drove through Stalidha, and then they dissected Malia before turning off for Neapoli. The roads began to whorl sharply and undulate, up and up, with few places to pass. A severe unprotected drop shelved out into the gulf of Mirabello. Their four-wheeled drive courted the mottled coastline of rocky shores punctuated by deep gorges and spectacular coves until the road angled downward towards the sea. Greta pointed excitedly to the picturesque village of Eloundas sited on the shore of a salt-water lagoon. The turquoise-coloured waters, filled with fish, were calm and inviting. Dmitri's sense of adventure picked up when he realised where they were. He slowed the vehicle and drew Michel's attention to a concealed road sign that pointed to the sunken city of Olous.

Michel whirled and leant forward, his hand out. As May watched closely, Greta took a sealed envelope out of her handbag and offered it to him. He took it but was hesitant about opening it. Weighing the envelope in his hands, he looked uneasily at May. She noticed his fingers were trembling. He opened the envelope and immersed himself in the magical tale of ancient origin. The blood drained from his face. He gawped at the first page, and then he skimmed through so rapidly that May doubted he was reading it. From where she sat, she could not see what was written.

'What? What is it?' she blustered with childish excitement.

'A translation of the scroll unearthed by Dmitri,' Michel answered incredulously, his voice chilling.

'What does it say?' she gasped.

Michel cleared his throat and read aloud. '"In praise of the most holiest of emissaries and protector of the imperial bloodline, the eunuch that bears this scroll is both deaf and dumb. A division of five thousand men - archers in chariots and foot soldiers with spears - has besieged the island stronghold of Long Thorn. The invaders have incurred the wrath of Triton, causing him to raise an almighty storm. For three days and four nights the winds have been unrelenting. Alas, Triton grows tired and the storm abates. As twilight deepens, we face imminent attack. The island shakes to the thunder of hooves and the rolling of war drums, while officers ride back and forth, and squadrons dig up the ground. Huge banners flutter above their infantry and their spearheads shimmer. Even though we glory in the fact that the Dodecanese, Mycenaean, Romans, Byzantines and the Arabs have all failed to annul our heredity; our ancient order, customs and traditions may be lost forever, consigned to the depths of forgotten history".'

Silently Michel handed May the sheet. The content was split in two. The letters, numbers and symbols of the script were meaningless. As were the golden lines that connected the hieroglyphics.

She studied the imagery and it tugged at her heartstrings.

She swallowed and declared, 'the artistry is beautiful, but at the same time fear-inspiring.'

She read the commentary in the top left portion of the page.

There was a long silence. She handed back the page.

At length Michel raised his eyebrows and continued with his oratory. '"We thought ourselves secure in our stronghold but our position has become weakened by the capitulation of Candia. Monstrous warships amass beyond the horizon whilst galleys tow pontoons across the entrance. On the peninsula, hordes of ever-thirsty enemies weave through gore-spattered piles, once exquisite landmarks. It seems that an even more brutal oppressor will vanquish our Venetian conquerors. Batteries of many cannons keep them at bay, but for how long. Princess Carme, the secret heiress and direct descendent of our nation's greatest monarch, King Minos, is in mortal danger. It tortures me to think that a dowry fit for a king, held in reserve for the enthronement of the first she-child, might end up in the hands of the barbaric horde. Like a plague of locusts, they swarm forward. Even so, there is still a chance for us to slip into the open night, but the Princess, hardened before her time, refuses to abandon the fortifications. Our highness awaits you in the chamber of kings. If anything should happen to me, Britomartis will show you the way through the labyrinth of the ancient acropolis, your servant, always, Daedalus".'

No one spoke until Dmitri pushed the Land Rover into first gear and drove slowly to the village. One by one, their scholar-weary spirits came alive to the authenticity of the letter.
'Incredible,' May beamed, and then she added in a more restrained manner. 'Michel, I wonder whatever happened to Princess Carme?'
Michel pondered the question.
'To be honest, her predicament is farfetched, yet possible. Time will tell. At least the carbon dating inconsistency has been resolved,' he said.
As they drove through the village, he shuffled the papers together and handed Greta the envelope. She clasped her handbag.
'It beggars belief to think that an ancient tradition and culture could be preserved without the ruler's knowledge. Truly amazing,' she said. Yet, to her chagrin, two questions remained. To whom was Daedalus writing? Secondly, could it be that Daedalus and Princess Carme were real people, or simply borrowed figures from mythology?
'Where is Long Thorn?' May asked softly.
'The Venetians christened Kalidon "Long Thorn" because of its thorny shape. To confuse matters, locals refer to the island as Spinalonga, while others dub it the "Island of Tears",' Dmitri explained. Fobie glanced at his watch and coughed lightly.

'Michel, I've booked us into the Elounda Beach Hotel and chartered an ocean-goer, the Trophy. It should be moored in the marina and ready for us as we speak,' Fobie then added, 'however, as per your instructions, I only booked four hotel suites.' He turned apologetically to May.

'Doctor, I'm sure you won't mind sharing with May?' Michel smiled, showing a courteous interest in her answer.

Greta gave Fobie a fleeting look, she had been looking forward to sharing the lap of luxury with her man mountain, but in response to Fobie's glare she forced a smile and nodded, but it soon faded. Michel stretched, an ache now in his neck. The Land Rover pulled up in the car park of one of the most luxurious hotels on the Aegean. A uniformed doorman opened the door for Dmitri. The five adventurers piled out of the vehicle. In next to no time, a small army of porters carted off their luggage. An impassive concierge showed them to their seafront villas and introduced them to their respective butlers. Each villa came equipped with a separate swimming pool and a private entertainment centre. Never one to rest on his laurels, Michel suggested walking the two kilometres back to the village. He set a steady pace, stopping now and again to give the others a chance to catch up.

At the causeway to Kalidon, guarded by two windmill towers, he let his mind range with the same single-minded intensity he brought to the planning of all his ventures. This was because the project was not something distinct from his latest undertaking but an extension of it. Reaching down, silhouetted against a brown dune, he tossed sand in the air. In the silence of the beach face, he readied himself for a journey filled with possibility and risk. An extinct culture beckoned.

The surface of the lagoon was tranquil and serene. It reflected the sky like a giant mirror. He inhaled the subtle wind-borne scents, and then he followed Greta behind a low wall, built entirely of stone. It concealed a splendid dolphin mosaic that once was the floor of a Byzantine basilica.

The vast square, in the heart of the village, was surrounded on three sides by shops, bistros, hotels and cafes, which reeked of opulence. The group of five trailed off towards the fishing harbour. Fobie leant against a balustrade and cast his eyes over the vessels moored in an orderly fashion. The pictorial setting, half in the shadows, and somewhat tarnished by the large coach park located next to the marina, seemed to elevate Michel's thoughts to the tincture of Princess Carme's plight. The threads of intrigue that the scroll had spun now entangled the whole harbour and gave him pause.

She was hard to miss. Big, sleek-bodied and streamlined. A flagpole to its aft from which a gaudy pennant fluttered. The Trophy's metal hull, painted green and yellow, looked powerful enough to circumvent the globe. A wooden gangplank invited them on board. Michel skipped across without any hesitation. He ducked warily under some ropes and wandered the length of the boat. The boat smelt of fish and sea salt. Her one-eyed skipper was showing a young boy how to mend a sail. May and Greta rambled along the gangway in his direction.

Greta was nosing under the cover of the lifeboat when she felt the skipper's eye on her. For a long moment she stood motionless. She could feel her temperature rising and she went a bright red. He had the haggard look of an old sea pirate, with his head shaped like a cannonball and a black patch covering his empty eye socket. His good eye glittered with menacing geniality.

The women found themselves trapped, his bulk blocking the gangway. Greta folded her arms across her breasts in a protective gesture, and the skipper inspired in May a rare dread that made her distinctly nervous and her flesh creep. She blushed and kicked off her sandals, ready to run. Dmitri rushed to their rescue.

Rankled, the skipper swung around, his eye fierce. Michel joined Dmitri, an additional distraction that allowed the girls to slink away. The skipper had no English so Dmitri conducted the conversation.

Michel expressed his desire to leave early the next morning, no later than five-thirty, and stated his preference to sail without the skipper. The request did not sit easily with the skipper. After a furious debate, he asked Michel some seafaring questions. Michel answered them perfectly, after which, the skipper visibly relaxed, believing his precious yacht to be in safe hands. Still, he hiked up the rental cost. Michel turned his stare on the old seaman and half-smiled. Piracy, he thought, is alive and well. Without bothering to bargain, Michel nodded. The skipper followed them to the gangplank and watched them leave.

The party of five toured the promenade in search of a nice place to eat. As patrons of the Marlena tavern, located on the harbour front, they were treated to a bird's eye view of the boats going to and fro between the harbour and Spinalonga. Dinner was laughter-filled, the banter first-class, and the mood upbeat. Replete with food, they talked of nothing else but Princess Carme.

By now twilight was beginning to close in, but the night itself failed to engender any mystery or intrigue, separate villas and separate beds for all concerned.

The next morning, after a substantial breakfast together, they arrived at the village centre. All was quite except for a few local fishermen intent on ignoring the newcomers. Fresh-faced and nimble-footed, Michel boarded the Trophy and mobilised his crew. With brisk efficiency Dmitri and Fobie started to bring on board the high-tech equipment, while the girls resigned themselves to unpacking and storing food supplies. Michel inspected the lifeboat, bow roller and then the wind-glass. Traipsing along the tacky deck, impeccably maintained, dotted with jackstays, he stopped and began to apply force to the quad-rails. He paused to gulp in the sea air and found refreshment. The words of Daedalus snapped at him as an imaginary whiff of the past clung to the tails of the freshening wind.

Sitting on the rail, Michel reckoned the wind was strong enough to employ the inner and outer forestay. Down below, he inspected the diesel engine hidden away under the cockpit companionway. There was fuel in the remote tank and the filter was free from impediment. Back on deck, he watched Fobie join forces with Dmitri to lug the submersible across the gangplank. Almost everything else was secured in the unusually long keel. He made his way to the cockpit and switched on the echo reader. It revealed the depth of the marina - a little over thirty metres.

Michel convened a meeting in the galley. He insisted the confined space of the galley be kept free of clutter. He told them of his plan to journey westward along the coast of Crete, as far as Dhia, before turning about and sailing back to Spinalonga.

After the meeting, they changed quickly into appropriate clothing. Michel, with his authority now firmly established, cut an impressive figure. On his head, he wore a blue nautical cap with a hand-stitched emblem of a wooden steering wheel. His blue shorts exposed scars left by combat.

May had donned a smart one-piece swimsuit, covered by a red windbreaker. Thoughtfully, her arms wrapped around herself, she watched Michel stretch his hands over his head. She glanced over her shoulder. Greta and Dmitri were having a spirited discussion about what they might find in the chamber of kings. Greta, dressed conservatively in a crumpled white blouse and a pair of flowery linen slacks, carried a basket of fruit. She showed a mix of excitement and nerves. A clean-shaven Dmitri, on the other hand, seemed completely unfazed by what lay ahead. Wearing cut-off jeans and a red sweatshirt. He appeared to be the more comfortable on water. He tied a sweater around his waist and trotted to the cockpit.

'Dmitri, have you done much sailing?' Michel asked.

'My uncle has a twenty footer, square-rigged, and he lets me borrow it whenever I want,' Dmitri said.

'Great. Reel in the ropes? Fobie, can you help him free the boat?' Michel boomed.
Fobie seemed equally at ease on water. He loosed the locking turns and jumped back on board. He staggered and almost lost his footing. Michel used his hands as a loudhailer.
'Okay, prepare for cast off,' he hollered.

    The towering cumulus clouds that filled the sultry sky foretold fresh conditions out at sea. Michel, at the helm, put the diesel engine into slow astern. The Trophy reared itself up from the disturbed surface. Cradling easily, she exhibited an affinity with the choppy water. Deftly, he put the muted engine into quarter-ahead and applied the gentlest of touches to her steering. She responded instantly and purred her way out of the marina. On the jetty, at the entrance to the quay, stood the Trophy's skipper. The eyepiece of a telescope placed to his eye, as he watched Michel pilot the boat from the harbour. Michel slipped her into full steam ahead. Once clear, he brought her about and headed out to sea.

    Upon reaching the north tip of the Spinalonga peninsula, Dmitri took over the steering. Michel waited until the yacht was head to wind, and then he busied himself finding the foot of the main sail. He located the clew with dizzying speed and fed it through the gooseneck end of the boom. Greta and May looked on. Pulling a face, he stretched out the foot of the sail and then he looked over his shoulder. Idly, May touched her hair and smiled at him. How handsome and competent, she thought. He gave her a glorious wink. With his powerful limbs, he tensioned the outhaul from the eye on the clew to the end of the boom. Then, making sure the battens were leeched, he eased the mainsheet, and then, with the aid of a winch, he hoisted the main sail. He lashed the halyards securely to the mast and gave the thumbs-up sign to Dmitri, who in turn cut the engine. The wind wrenched control of the craft. Michel swayed easily with the motion of the boat as the joyous sails propelled her along the soft fluffy surf. He sprinted with great sure-footedness to the cabin.

'I'm going to goose wing the jib. Can you handle the steering?' Michel asked.
'No problem, go for it,' Dmitri said.

The boat was moving comfortably at a rate of twenty knots and slicing through water thick with salt. The peninsula faded with loss of outline as they overtook a chartered fishing vessel. Some tourists flopped their hands in the air, and Greta gestured with a sweep of her arms. Michel watched as Dmitri handled the boat with the aplomb of an experienced helmsman. With practiced ease, he nursed the wheel, his black mullet ruffled in the wind. Certain the yacht was in good hands, Michel went below to see how Fobie was getting on. The fruit of his labour was evident in the arrangement of apparatuses. Nicely grouped together were facemasks, fins and weight belts. Alongside him, leaning at angles, were four blotched aqualungs. Near the corner of the galley, chained to a vertical pole, stood a compressor brought along to refill scuba tanks as they emptied. Behind him, a pneumatic drill and a cylinder of foam were propped up against the wall.
'How's it going?' Michel asked. He stood amongst the four diving suits, hanging from plastic pegs.
A rubber-handled knife fell to the floor. Michel stooped to pick it up.
'Okay,' Fobie said.
'Where are the explosives?' Michel snapped.
'Here, beside me,' Fobie replied, his face strained.
'Everything seems to be in order,' Michel observed, his voice a monotone.
Fobie accepted the faint-praise compliment with a grunt, but he knew well enough that preliminary checks did little to satisfy Michel.
'Be a good sport and check everything again,' Michel said.
  May descended the stairs at the back of the galley. Anxiously she gripped the banister, her eyes fixed on Michel. She hurried in the hope there would be a brush of contact; every pore yearned for his

touch. She missed his closeness and could not bear the thought of a rift developing between them. Since leaving the airport they had not found themselves alone, either by design or chance. It seemed that he was avoiding her. She wondered with a sinking heart whether she had done something wrong. Perhaps, she thought back to the runway, it might have something to do with that phone call. Whatever the reason, she decided the best slant would be to confront him before darkness fell. Being a half-full kind of girl she still managed to keep a smile on her face. Michel backed away from the stairs to let her pass, but not before putting out a helping hand. He held her gaze. She accepted the gesture with an innocent's charm, but she pretended to slip and fell into his arms. A trice passed between them, a cementing.

It left May soothed.

Michel realised it would take time and effort on his part and, he thought hopefully, patience on hers. The more time he spent in her company the greater his desire to protect and cherish her. It was wrong of him to judge her. After all, reporting Richard's misdemeanour was part of her job.

He set her upright.

She thanked him with a smile.

'Have you found your sea legs yet,' he whispered, still holding her hand. 'I hope you're gelling with this beautiful boat.'

Their faces were only inches apart. She looked at him and her warmth melted him.

Fobie caught the sizzle of electricity between them. Momentarily, he let his eyes wander from the mouthpiece in his hand to the beautiful couple and he watched the moment tingle between them.

'You're right, it's a gorgeous boat and the sea air is so refreshing. Anyway, as long as I'm with you, then I'm happy.' May's eyes brightened, energised by the tick of intimacy.

A silence fell between them.

'Would you care to join me on bow. We can dangle our legs over the side,' Michel said.

She pulled a wry face and her eyes flickered.
'Will you save me if I fall overboard?' she asked.
'I'd risk life and limb. Let's go and leave Fobie finish his work.'
He gave her a gentle slap on the bottom.

Michel read the barometer. The atmospheric pressure had risen three millibars. He stared at the sky, growing cloudier by the moment, and then at the log. Lastly, he peered at the depth finder, 120 fathoms. He charted the yacht's position, and then he used a divider to measure the distance they had sailed.
Hurriedly, he joined May and they walked to the bow of the boat. They clambered over the wind-glass and made themselves comfortable. Slowly, he slid his arm around her waist. She noticed how relaxed he looked, his legs dangling in the midst of salt spray. The yacht dipped and twisted. Gripping the rail, she raised her voice in glee.
'It's so beautiful here.'
As she spoke, the boat carved a wave and the breaking surf engulfed the bow. Drenched to the bone, they laughed and pointed at each other.
He clamped his fingers around her arm and announced with a
perfectly straight face, 'I'm planning a trip around the world, would you be interested in joining me?'
She thought he was kidding and chuckled, but she could see from his face that he was not. She continued to look at him and became serious.
'I'd go to the ends of the earth with you,' she said.
She squeezed his hand and placed it between her legs, glistening with salt water. She tightened her thighs to keep it there and felt a rush of pleasure and dropped her gaze.
'Dad told me to keep an eye on you and not to be sucked into your fanciful schemes,' she said.
'Does he think me a dreamer?' His face was cold.

'On the contrary, he admires you, in spite of your swashbuckling style,' she smiled. Her clear creamy skin seemed at one with the sea. A strand of damp hair, anchored to her forehead, took on the guise of kelp. She rested her head against his shoulder. Tenderly he touched her cheek and stroked the length of her back.

Unnoticed, Greta slipped noiselessly down the galley stairs. Fobie had just finished his inspection. Reassured by his beaming smile, she went up on her tiptoes and kissed her man mountain.
'I missed you last night, why didn't you come to my villa?' she asked.
Guileless, he laughed and shook off her grip.
'Behave,' he muttered with a smirk.
She ran her tongue down his chest.
'Don't worry, Michel and May are nuzzling each other, and Dmitri is steering, so I'm at your mercy. Take me if you dare.'
She smiled seductively, and then she unfastened the buttons of her slacks and wriggled free. She was greedy for him. His mind said no but his manhood said yes. Pleasured by her appetite and daring, he laid her down out of sight. She moaned, caught hold of his hair and pulled him to her. He ran his hands over her body and they began. Gently, his fingers nudged her legs apart, and they coupled to the rhythm of the waves. Overwhelmed by a profound feeling of euphoria, he rolled off her and pulled her on top.
The flow of moist air drifted a yawning sleep upon the lovers.
Greta, awoken by a raised voice, waggled into her slacks.
'Ahoy, Dmitri we'll drop anchor,' Michel howled.
He began to lower the sails. Eventually, a guilty looking Fobie came to his assistance. Greta went in search of May with the intention of preparing dinner.

Attracted by the commotion above, the women deserted their self-imposed duties and came up on deck. An athletic spectacle greeted them, men in shorts perched on top of a rail ready to dive.

Michel yelled, 'on your marks, get set, GO.'
Fobie's dive was the longest and helped him to an early lead, which Greta took much delight in applauding. However, halfway to the buoy, Dmitri had taken the lead. The women became animated and neither felt the slightest bit embarrassed about their display of favouritism. Rounding the buoy, Dmitri tired in a crosscurrent and began to flounder. Fobie and Michel were neck and neck, matching each other stroke for stroke. A beleaguered Dmitri, having accepted defeat, switched to breaststroke. Still level with thirty metes to go, May was sure the bigger man would win. With less than fifteen metres to go Michel kicked his legs explosively. He increased his stroke rate and drew away from Fobie. Michel touched the yacht first. May pursed her lips and whistled loudly.

They ate heartily. Stew washed down by a dry red wine. Fobie and Michel moved up deck. On their way, they collected an overflowing jug of wine, two glasses and a couple of cigars.
'I bet you're aching to get back home,' Michel said.
'On the contrary, I'm enjoying the experience. The more time I spend here, the more time I'd like to spend here,' Fobie answered, puffing out a perfectly formed smoke circle.
'I need a trustworthy man, based here in Crete.' Michel exhaled.
Fobie's reply was both enthusiastic and immediate.
'Look no further. Count me in.'
'What about the good Doctor?' Michel asked.
He waited for a reaction.
'I'm not sure what you mean.' Fobie lowered his stare, preferring to follow the swirl of the wine.
'Nothing, just wondered if you knew how she might feel about a permanent move, that's all,' Michel said.
'Well, she likes Crete and from the way she talks of the place, I'm sure she'd have no problem.'

CHAPTER 15

The road leading to Wimbledon was lined with red maple trees. Whether at the celebrated lawn tennis club or at a football match, the town offered an idyllic glimpse into British society. It was this that made Wimbledon such an attraction for well-paid young middle-class professionals. Nevertheless, the commuter town was also a perfect cover for less salubrious activities.
In the front room of a semidetached house, nestled on a quaint cul-de-sac, Tony sat with his back to the wall. He reflected on the silence of the evening as he watched neighbours come and go. He was tired. Even so, he pushed himself to stay alert.
Long after midnight, when most of the world slept, the sound of a door closing was amplified. In place of night-scented freshness he detected the smell of baked bread. An ambient atmosphere pervaded the room, with streetlights adding a warming hue. The scheduled drop was late. In a world touched by evil, where the super-wealth and the Mafiosi coalesced, mental endurance was as fundamental as physical prowess. Behind the scenes, drug gangs had joined forces in order to finance and establish a sophisticated retail, supply, and distribution chain. As a result, drop-off points that served as outlets for narcotics ringed London. Tony, wearing his

Kevlar armoured jacket, waited in a calm frame of mind, lost in thought.

Excitedly he stood up. He could hear it lustily now. There was a beating noise, which resembled the roll of a distant drum, a far-off construct that gradually became familiar. Tony, a former SAS commando, recognised the distinct hum. His heart almost stopped, excitement possessed him. He harked back to his dark days onboard a military prison vessel. Increasingly, conglomerates had been lured by greed into war-torn economies, and they behaved like androids in their pursuit of wealth and power. They exerted pressure, intimidating and bribing those they wished to influence. Assassinations of nationals, as well as foreigners, had become an integral part of Tony's remit and cut across every political boundary. The man who had spent four punishing years in the Middle East had been drained of patriotism. Something inside of him seemed to have snapped. He had abandoned the combat zone to others, and he had surrendered his sniping services to the super-wealthy. The skills that had once been dedicated to the service of his nation were now used in the low-art of spilling civilian blood.

Tony shivered in spite of himself. Sadly, he thought, not much has changed. An alternate arena, remote from reality, matted with long hours of boredom and unrepressed violence. He spat the vile taste of incarceration from his mouth and looked at the phosphorous digits on his watch. The time was 01:56. Once, he had lived by the ethics of a warrior. Now, a mercenary, he trampled on them. But it was no longer the need for tribute that motivated him. Rather it was self-preservation. It was as though, poisoned by the loss of honour, he had turned his contempt upon all of humanity.

While the helicopter lorded it over the estate, Tony moved deliberately about the front room, step by careful step, like a rabid animal, wild and caged, half in odium, and half in gloom. His eyes traced the darkness with growing impatience. Bamboos and grasses danced restlessly. After spending the last few hours in darkness, his eyes were attuned to the dim. From his vantage point, he spotted a flicker of light coming from a bedroom window across the road. A restless occupant pressed her nose hard against the cold glass, disquieted.

Tony paced the room, looked outside at the darkness, sat down, and then he stood up again. The helicopter was moving away, leisurely and purposefully, over a patchwork of playing fields. Intent on locating its whereabouts, Tony tried desperately to catch a revealing glimpse. There, in the muddled dim, his feet balanced comfortably on a log box, he felt the invigorating thrill of danger surrounding him. He could see no sign of the helicopter but he registered that its hum still sounded strong.

Suddenly there was an ominous silence, nervy and shrill. With his head cocked upwards, he half-expected the next shadowy form to be that of a snatch-squad seeking retribution for his killing of four police officers. After all, the police force was full of ambitious young men, many of whom were anxious to make a name for themselves. Perhaps, he conjectured, a marauding assassin hired by a rival faction might cast the next long shadow. Despite such gloomy forebodings, he remained confident. No longer pacing, he allowed his pistol to fall softly against the windowpane.

He remained motionless.

Suburban serenity had been restored, albeit shortlived.

A nondescript car rocked up the narrow cul-de-sac. A young hoodlum leapt from the moving vehicle and landed gracefully. Tony needed more light to be able to see the face of the small hooded figure.

Sporting a sparse beard, enormous sneakers, and baggy trousers, the low-life kept his head at windowsill level. He produced a sealant gun and squirted pure, unadulterated, high-grade heroin through a narrow transparent tube. In a matter of moments, the tailor-made windowsill had grown 30 mm. There was a gentle tap on the windowpane, indicating the process was complete. The hoodlum left his crouching position and shrank away. Tyres gnawed into the tarmac and the driver sped flat out over the verge.

Tony recalled the very first delivery to the area. It had been a total cock-up. The merchandise had been delivered to the wrong house. The unsuspecting owners, thinking the mess was the result of a window-smearing prank, had washed down the window with bleach. Money, literally, down the drain.

Patiently, Tony bided his time, concentrating on the layer of white paste. Through the open window he scraped the hardening substance into a container. He stored it away in a fire safe concealed under the floorboards.

After the deed, Tony treated himself to a glass of Scotch malt whiskey. He opened the drinks cabinet and poured. He inhaled the vapours before sipping, then, with the tip of his tongue, he pushed the golden syrup between his clenched teeth, and then he tumbled his taste buds. The burning flavour left a distinctive smoky aftertaste. Standing with his back to the window, he took another sip.

There was a tap on the window, barely audible. Tony swore at himself for dropping his guard and immediately slumped to the floor. He craned his head, but there was no one at the window. The golden-red liquid spilled over the rim of the glass and made its way into the tiny crevices in the floor.

He took care to avoid the fifth step. Upon reaching the landing, he scaled a ladder, permanently propped against the attic entrance, and then he felt around for his head torch. His long legs spanned the insulated parts. He moved aside a large wooden crate stamped from top to bottom with foreign export lettering. There was a similar crate on the other side of a large circular hole. By pushing past this crate, he was able to gain access to the attic next door.

With economy of effort, he lowered himself down through the attic-door and thudded onto the carpeted floor. He descended the stairs, holding his pistol at head height. At the end of the stairs, he edged closer to the front door. After a short delay, he unlocked the door and eased it open. When he saw the curvy outline of Tara skulking alone in the shadows, he relaxed. At 28 and five feet seven, Tara looked stunning. Excited and amused, he closed the door. At the top of the stairs, he leapt off the banister, only a few inches wide, and swung from the attic entrance and pulled himself up and made his way back to where he came from.

He opened the door and, without uttering a word, waved her into the hallway. The lights remained off. Decked out in a vintage lace dress, she followed him into the front room. He was exceedingly wary of Tara, once a British soldier herself, now she ran a strong-arm crew in the East End of London. She had the allure of the femme fatal, bristling with self-importance and bold enough to get into a fistfight if the situation called for it.
But is she as brass-necked as she seems? Tony asked himself.
Still not a word passed between them.
'What's your poison?' he asked.
'Bacardi and Coke,' she said.
He fought to control his drooling appetite and fixed her a drink.
She accepted the proffered beverage. 'Thanks Tony.'
She stepped over the shiny patch of spilled whiskey.
'This is an unexpected visit. What brings you to this neck of the woods?' Tony gave her a quizzical look and searched her face for clues.
Tara tried to make herself comfortable.
'Tom has been trying to get in contact with you,' she said, perched on the arm of the sofa, not yet at ease in his company.
'Damn, I forgot to switch on my phone,' he said.
He got to his feet and went in search of his phone. He found it, hidden under a cushion, and he turned it on. A text message popped up.
He read the message: *You're needed in Northolt. Tom.*
'Gee! That's strong.' Tara smacked her lips.

'There's Coke in the cabinet. Help yourself.'

'No, it's fine. Bloody hell, it's warm in here.' She took a sip and coughed. 'Tony, we're off to Crete. There's a Cessna waiting for us at Northolt aerodrome and Tom is sending someone to look after this operation while you're gone. Hermione, the twin's contact in Crete, assures me the tools you need are already in place.'

She stirred and rested on one elbow.

His debauched streak – ironically – was what she liked most about him and sat well with the seediness of her own character, depraved and wanton. Aware of Tony's sinister reputation, savage and cruel, she knew this trip was a calculated risk. The twins trusted her but they esteemed Tony. Even her own gang feared Tony more than they feared her. Spine-tingling stories that linked him to disembowelled bodies and decapitations had spread like wildfire through London's criminal underground and had made him into a figure of fascination. Her future cachet was dependent on her being able to manipulate him and cultivate a common purpose. Except she knew that she was taking a big chance. Too dangerous, considering what she had to lose. After all, she had spent years making a name for herself in an extremely violent business. She wanted to be queen, run the whole show, but Tony had other ideas.

He smiled but it did not reach his lips.

'The two of us.' Tony, who was keeping a careful eye on Tara, was willing to travel with her even though he preferred to work alone.

'Yes. Here's a photo of the mark. Not so long ago I engineered an assassination attempt, but he survived.' She opened her handbag. 'It's hardly surprising the twins want you and your rifle to finish the job.' She handed him the photograph.

Tony spotted the Walter PPK revolver in her handbag.

'A failed attempt?' Tony asked rhetorically.

'Yes. Because he's so well protected I tried a more scientific approach, caesium chloride.' She went on to explain her method of choice.

'Did you bring the usual gear?' he asked witheringly, while peering out the front window.

She produced fake passports, cash and freshly cloned cards.

'We're travelling as man and wife, Mr and Mrs Breen,' he laughed indulgently.

'It seems so.' Once she heard the innuendo-laden laugh, her defences came up.

He reached out and touched her gently. 'Man and wife, that sounds lovely. It has a nice ring to it.'

'I'll say,' she said.

He gave the passports back to her. He put his hand on her knee. She did not pull back, lulled by the rum. He gave her a hard long look, searching and conniving. Is it possible, he began to wonder, that she likes me. The prospect filled him with lust. He came nearer. They stalked each other.

She had never smooched a man with dreadlocks before. His matted locks flopped about her neck. He wrapped his tonsils round her tongue.

'Now's not the time, we've a plane to catch,' she said, her voice hoarse. 'The pilot won't wait forever.'

'We've plenty of time.'

'We can't, sorry. No time.'

She took his face in her hands and kissed him lightly on both cheeks. He held her at a distance and she saw his wolfish eyes studying her.

She held her gaze for as long as she could, angling to tease, adding to his mounting excitement. An animal lust lay behind his expressionless face. She reached for his hand and held it tightly.

'In Crete, perhaps in Crete, surely you can wait until then?' Her heart was beating, her palms sweaty.

In one stroke, she felt an arm firmly around her. Before she realised what was happening she was on the sofa. He pinioned her with his forearm, and he lathered her with kisses, wild and slobbery. He sneezed violently into her face. Her cheeks, eyes and nose were pasted in mucus.

She turned her face away.

'No Tony, I'm serious,' she shrieked. 'The pilot has been waiting ages.'

'Don't worry, the plane won't leave without us,' he growled.

Crete seemed an age away. His fingers wandered over her, groping, pinching, squeezing. She rallied and fought back, but he grabbed hold of her upswept hair. Smirking, he tore her dress to below her waist.

'You're dead,' she cried.

'Don't threaten me,' he muttered through gritted teeth, as the red mist descended. He ripped off her bra. She affected outrage. He stared at her as though he was measuring her up for burial. Wriggling beneath him, she worked an arm free and clawed for his eyes. He caught her hands in a vicelike grip, crushing her wrists, and then he forced his knee between her thighs.

'So, you like it rough.' With a sneer, he gnawed on one of her nipples.

She screamed at the top of her voice.

He adjusted his grip and pulled down his fly.

'Bastard,' she shouted.

The pain was excruciating, but electrifying, and it made her flesh tingle. Fierce passion combined with heated rage drove her on. She sunk her teeth into his neck. He exploded with fury and unleashed a violent punch across her chin, and then another. Blood gushed from her mouth, a mixture of his and hers.

He mauled her in such an uncontrolled burst of aggression that she feared he might kill her. Each successive blow left her momentarily dazed. Shocked by how quickly the violence had escalated, she convulsed and vomited. He flipped her over, buried her face against the soft couch, lifted her dress, and yanked down her satin knickers. She nerved herself for what was to come.

He examined her in all her glory. Her buttocks, pearl-shaped and firm, glistened with sweat.

She was shaking so much that he thought she was going to burst into tears. He had not expected this from her: usually she was as tough as nails.

There was no more resistance. For an ordinary woman, this grim and grimy act would be humiliating, but for Tara it was an intoxicating experience. For an ordinary society, this slavish behaviour would be repellent, but amongst the seamiest circles, it was acceptable.

She was trumped, tamed, wanting it, his dominance established. He knew there was no going back after something like this. Their toxic relationship had been torpedoed into uncharted territory. Now he took his time. At leisure he used his tongue to prime her upper orifice. She was about to lose her anal virginity.

Though silent, the helicopter had not left the locality, having landed nearby in the centre circle of a school's rugby field. Earlier in the night, Sean had dropped Mayumi close to their intended target. The utmost stealth was crucial. Mayumi wore a tight-fitting cap and a wraparound garment. Armed with a shuriken belt, she moved into position, unseen, unheard.

Before it had expired, the biodegradable bead had done its job. Tony's patterned movements had been fed back to a Secure Span tracking system. The company had gone to incredible lengths to develop this bead using a living material made from mineral substances secreted by marine worms.

Sean remained behind in the helicopter, with his finger on the start button. In harmony, Chen, Fukiko, Christophe and Akiko, moved swiftly through a long row of back gardens. They wore helmets fitted with a radio, and a GPS transmitter that supplied real-time location data to a computer housed in the helicopter. A barking hound, jumping around like a bucking bronco, interrupted their progress. Christophe, alarmed by the dog's feverish yaps, reacted quickly to the hindrance. A tranquilliser dart quelled the canine protest.

Akiko and Fukiko were armed with Browning firearms. But Chen was unarmed and so relied on his mental, physical and spiritual faculties. Likewise, Christophe was equipped with nothing more than a tranquilliser gun, knife, pocket torch and a handheld thermal-imaging device.

They wanted to take Tony alive.

Keeping close together they crept towards No. 7.

Chen stood upright from a squatting position; a rope and a grappling hook draped around his shoulders. They had been huddled together in a small group behind the common wall that separated No. 7 from No. 8. Chen gave a hand signal. Christophe hurtled into the overgrown grass, flattening it as he crawled. Sprawled out like a reptile, he studied the two shapes on the screen of the thermal-imaging device. He pressed the capture button and fell away. Behind the wall, he showed Chen the captured image. Chen gave a soft whistle. They moved as one. To have any hope of success, they needed the element of surprise. Chen gripped the rope with both hands and hurled the grappling hook at an acute angle. The hook slid backwards along the far side of the roof, and then it wedged itself between a tile and the chimneystack. With the soles of her feet firmly planted on the wall, Akiko tested the rope before shooting upwards. She immediately began to prise away some roof tiles, allowing Christophe to saw through the underlay with the serrated edge of his blade.

Chen joined Christophe and Akiko on the roof. Fukiko stayed below in the back garden, slipping away amongst the bushes, while Mayumi covertly watched the front of the house.

When the hole was big enough Chen funnelled the rope into the dark attic. Christophe switched on his pocket torch and rotated it in a circle. Grasping a wooden beam, running lengthwise down the centre of the attic, Chen swung his arms left over right toward the water tank. He let his feet rest on the tank's lip before stepping down onto a lower beam. The trio came to a sudden halt. Much to their surprise, the attic-door was open and there was a ladder extended above the ledge. Chen stood back and deliberated for a moment before signalling an advance. They climbed down the ladder. Chen led the way down the stairs, stopping every few seconds to listen to the snorts and whimpers coming from the front room.

The brutal attack on Tara had left her with bruises, loose teeth and injuries to her upper and lower body. In a transport of lechery, Tony continued to thrust his hips forward, oblivious to the drama being played out on the stairs. The front room door stood open. Disaster struck in one frozen moment when Chen's foot found the fifth step. Much like the sound of a tree being felled in a forest, the creak resonated throughout the house. In a sea of uncertainty, they had lost the element of surprise. If confirmation were required, the grunts could no longer be heard in the front room.

The crackling noise came like a bolt from the heavens. Tony reacted immediately and rolled Tara aside. He shook his pistol from its holster, and then he buckled up. At the same time, Tara reeled in dismay to her feet. She looked around her wildly. Her belly twisted. She could not comprehend what was happening. Frantically, she covered up. Aching all over, she searched the floor for her purse and found it. She pulled out her revolver and inched along on her stomach. But as she crawled Tony trod on her wrist, and he wrenched the purse from her hand. She filled her mouth with spittle and spat after him.

 Gambling that no one was lying in wait, Tony slipped out of the open window and turned a somersault. At that instant a star-shaped object struck him with a force that drove the air from his lungs. He used his arms to cover his head and protect his throat and face. Acting as a shock absorber, the Kevlar armoured jacket bore the brunt of a stream of missiles thrown by Mayumi in quick succession. Try as he might, he was unable to determine from whence the missiles came. He cudgelled his brains for what to do next.

Suddenly he saw a shimmer of light glint off his jeep. There was movement. Then it ceased. He looked for an escape. He zeroed in on the window of house No. 7, and he struck hard with the butt of his pistol. The glass shattered into tiny pieces. As he dived, the prong of a shuriken pierced the heel of his boot. Mayumi rolled out from under the jeep and charged after him.

It was decision time. Poised on the fifth step, Chen was faced with a dilemma: should he abort, yet by doing so allow Tony to escape ensnarement; or should he give the order to continue, and risk the lives of his team. His momentum pushed him onward and downward into the hall.

Tara's compact revolver was pointed directly at the open door. She was stretched out behind the sofa and the range was point blank. Abruptly a red beam scythed the wall above the open fireplace. Fear began to well but she pushed it back. Christophe signalled that he was ready and, without any hesitation, he stooped through the doorway. Akiko provided cover, and she skipped in after him. She remained in an erect position, her handgun arcing over the vague forms and objects.

There was an eerie silence.

With great care Chen crept into the room and knelt down beside Christophe. In sympathy with the deafening silence, his keen sense of hearing picked up the rapid breathing of a fourth person. Suddenly his eyes narrowed, and in an attempt to divine the source, he tilted his head forward.

Meanwhile, Tony had threaded his way through both attics and had bought himself some time by blocking the hole in the wall before Mayumi slithered in through the attic-door. Without a sound, he stole down the stairs - skipping the fifth step - and waited beside the front door; the palm of his hand turned downward, ready to open the lock.

Chen touched Akiko on the hip and she followed the direction of his stare.

The radiator was boiling and had begun to make life uncomfortable for Tara. Her nearest leg was getting hotter, and in the event of being discovered, she was unable to adjust her aim or discharge an effective shot. Confronted by the odds that she now faced, even Tony would have been hard put to break free. The inevitable could be postponed no longer. She came to her senses. She scrambled to her feet with defeat in her eyes.

'Don't shoot, I'm throwing out my weapon,' she cried.

It was more like the bizarre-sounding cry of a stricken animal than the pleading of a human voice. Chen was caught unawares, expecting a man's voice and not the shrill voice of a woman. A noisy shuffling accompanied by raised voices followed Tara's surrender, thus allowing Tony to exit unheard.

Christophe was sceptical at first. He removed his helmet.

'Slide your weapon across the floor, and then slowly place your hands behind your head,' he ordered.

The pocket-sized firearm spun across the wooden surface and glanced off Chen's knee. Akiko fumbled about for the light switch, while Chen dismantled the weapon. Christophe approached Tara. Then, to his astonishment, two loud blasts rang out, forcing Christophe to prostrate himself before the sofa. Tara, who clung to the back of the sofa as if falling from a cliff, sucked in a gurgled breath. An artery had burst and splattered blood in haphazard patterns across the magenta-coloured wall. She was lying face up on the floor and arterial blood trickled down the side of her mouth.

Mayumi stood in the doorway trying to make sense of what she saw. It was a sad spectacle. Unsteadily, Chen came to his feet and pulled Akiko up after him. At a word, all heads twisted around. Sure enough, there were two bullet holes left behind in the glass.

Chen covered the distance to the window in two quick leaps and shoved with force. In an attempt to tag him, Christophe exited the house through the front door and sprinted after him.

Akiko examined the inert heap behind the sofa. She felt for a pulse in Tara's pale, cold wrist but there was none evident. The first bullet had entered the flattened side of her cranium, while the second bullet had passed clean through her neck and scarred the wall. Mayumi stood undecided.

Tony kept close to the pavement; the soft grass muffled his footfall. As the gradient increased, the grass became thicker. He repeatedly looked back to see if his pursuers were gaining on him. Much to his surprise and annoyance, Chen was matching him stride for stride. Tony redoubled his efforts and speeded up. His head was hunched down as he veered away from the path and rounded the far corner of the avenue. In a driveway, edged with low-growing plants, he observed a diminutive woman carrying her baby to the family hatchback. He dragged the woman from the idling car and he left her crumpled and shrieking on the front lawn. The colour had drained out of her face. Her squealing infant had fallen just short of the lawn. Careless for her safety, she tried desperately to gather her baby. In dread she jumped to her feet and plucked the baby from the jaws of death. She stood alone in a shock-like state, the infant safe and sound in her arms.

Tony did not even bother to reverse; instead, he thundered down the long row of open plan gardens and surged into the path of Chen. Even in the face of the frenzied headlamps, Chen took time to assess the situation. And he evaded narrowly the looming vehicle, which looked likely to go out of control at any minute, and he barrelled into a thick clump of spiky grass.

Christophe was less fortunate. He was thrown seven feet into the air, landing awkwardly, and his head smashed off the roadside kerb.

Tony kept his foot on the accelerator. Recklessly he steered the car through the network of long avenues. When he pitched the hatchback through an unforgiving hairpin, two wheels briefly left the roadway. Somehow, he sensed that he was not alone. He eased his foot off the accelerator and adjusted the rear view mirror. Two pale-faced children, a boy and a girl with pixie haircuts, were staring wide-eyed at the back of his head.

They had never seen a wild-haired giant before. Tony brought the car to a screeching halt, got out, and he opened the backdoor.

'Get out,' he ordered.

The children were a bundle of nerves inside and could not bring themselves to leave the vehicle. Tony did not ask a second time. To expedite matters, he grabbed the little boy by the scruff of his neck and set him down on the footpath. The little girl recovered her senses and clambered out of the backseat to join her brother.

Tony looked down at the children. Then his thoughts shifted to the Cessna waiting for him at Northolt. He got back into the car and dumped the contents of Tara's purse onto the passenger seat. Then he threw the beaded accessory out of the car window. It landed between the feet of the little girl. She - full of excitement - picked it up. The colour bloomed in her cheeks.

'Mister, can I keep this lovely purse?' Her tiny voice was hopeful.

Still, Tony could see the fear in her eyes.

She brushed clean the purse with her little hand.

Tony heard the small boy whisper. 'We're not allowed to speak to strangers.'

Then, in the full of the moon, the children withdrew unhappily.

After a moment, Tony put his hand on his pistol and looked about him.

There was a short pause of indecision.

With a heavy heart, he pointed the pistol at the little girl, but he did not squeeze the trigger.

The siblings watched him take the road, weaving from side to side, and vanish into the night. As soon as the car disappeared they turned on their heels.

Akiko bawled out, 'Why!'

Then added in a whisper, 'I love you.'

She cradled her still breathing husband, ahead of the arrival of Sean and the helicopter. Christophe fell in and out of consciousness. She heard a police siren. Then, almost magically, the helicopter descended.

Chen glanced at the injured body laid out stiffly on the stretcher, then at Akiko. Also onboard was Mayumi, who put her arms around Akiko and tried to console her. Chen had his own contentions. He nursed a sickly feeling that the man who continued to elude him would ultimately become Michel's nemesis. And he was in two minds whether to search for the hijacked vehicle, or to fly directly to a hospital. Faced with such a choice there was only one course of action.

Fukiko was last in. Avoiding panic or undue haste, Sean flew to a private hospital funded by Michel.

Tony was driving along and thought the car behind him had been there for a while. He pulled into a filling station and stocked up on convenience foods. He phoned for a taxi and waited outside. The taxi dropped him at the entrance to the Northolt aerodrome. To his surprise the gate was open and unguarded. Normally RAF sentries would be standing there. A lean, long-faced, squadron leader, who frequently turned a blind eye, ushered him in through a side door. Tony then boarded the same aeroplane that had taken him on his last flight: London to Los Angeles.

Tony passed the hours resting and sleeping, waking with a start when the plane blazed in to Heraklion. He checked in at the Holiday Inn, using the pseudonym Ken Breen. After settling in, he showered and shaved, and then he changed into attire pressed and hung in the freestanding wardrobe. His attention turned to the bed. Absently, he pulled back the duvet and dragged a white flowerbox from between the sheets. He placed the box on the floor and broke the seal. A moment's inspection and he rummaged through the box. Warily, he pushed the flowers aside and whistled involuntarily. He touched the butt of the Galil sniping rifle, which had been folded forward so as to fit neatly into the box. An additional poke around revealed a Glock self-loading pistol, and a perfumed white card. The concealed message, hidden in standard text, was not difficult to decipher. Idly his eyes went from word to word.

He read aloud. 'Target is aboard the yacht Trophy. Off the Spinalonga peninsula.'

He scanned the room before sliding the Glock inside his belt, and gathered up the flowerbox.

The Cretan taxi-driver took no prisoners. He sounded the horn indiscriminately and gave the finger to overcautious tourists. Occasionally, he glanced in the rear view mirror, hoping for a sign of approval. When he realised that there was none forthcoming, the taxi lost much of its impetus.

Intent on ignoring the driver, as well as the scenery, Tony sat upright with a forbidding expression on his face. Arriving at Elounda, he tipped generously the driver, a gesture that merited a sharp blow on the horn, and then he entered the tourist information bureau. He procured a simple map and browsed a touch screen computer. With the flowerbox tucked beneath his underarm, he stopped at a fanciful kiosk, on the harbour, and he hired a speedboat with a long-range fuel tank. He purchased binoculars, an upmarket bomber-jacket, and a small picnic hamper, which he duly stocked with juices, crackers and chocolate bars.

The well-weighted speedboat was put through some punishment, as Tony's reconnaissance took him into a phalanx of local boats and pleasure cruisers. He circled the island of Spinalonga three times, in an eastwards direction, at full throttle. Despite patrolling incessantly, only stopping to nibble on a snack bar, there was no sign of the Trophy. In the course of time, he cut the engine. Strategically placed, with an excellent view of the island's main entrance, he noted, with the aid of binoculars, the name of each vessel leaving and mooring.

Time was ticking by. The speedboat breasted the undulating current as it rolled further away from the islet. Disappointed but not disillusioned, Tony yawned and lowered his binoculars. He was about to turn the key in the ignition when he noticed a far-off spec on the horizon. As he waited for the sail-born spec to grow in dimension, he snapped a salty cracker and washed it down with cranberry juice. Eventually he made out the thick, italic lettering: Trophy. Soon afterwards, the tiny figures onboard became lucid and life-size.

The yacht's sails had been lowered and Dmitri manoeuvred towards the jetty. A bespectacled guide, full of years, caught the rope and helped Michel to tie up the yacht. He then offered his services. Fobie, Greta and May trundled onto the jetty, leaving Dmitri behind to act as guardian of the boat. Having arrived in Spinalonga at the same time as boatloads of tourists from Plaka and Ayios Nikolaos, the wooden platform was thronged with people. Consequently, a combined stream of sightseers filed through the main entrance jostling for position. Michel walked at the head of the procession where he soaked up the fascinating but appalling history of the island.
His sat-phone rang. It was Chen.
'What's up?' Michel asked.
Chen reported the events in Wimbledon.
'Thanks for the heads-up,' Michel said, and he hung up.
Fobie tapped him on the shoulder.
'Did you see that Rasta man in the speedboat taking note of our arrival?' He spoke quietly, but very seriously, not wishing to alarm the two women.
Michel frowned. 'I've been expecting him. We should set sail for Elounda and ask Dmitri to take the women back to Gouves, where they'll have the protection of the guards minding the artefacts. We'll wait for Dmitri to return, and then we'll set sail.'
'Easier said than done. I'm sure the women won't appreciate their adventure coming to an abrupt end.'

CHAPTER 16

The tunnel served as one of just two entrances leading to the strongly fortified centre of the islet. At the big stone entrance Michel found himself jostled by the crowd. Peering into the tunnel, he could glimpse, in his imagination, the haze of glittering armour and the glint of steel-tipped arrows. As the crowd splintered, he felt the sweat running down his back. Coming up behind, the tour guide held aloft a black wooden cane, a marker for his small party to follow. Then the guide shouldered his way into the front row of tourists, and he led them through the tunnel and on to the old castle gate bearing the lion of St Mark. Beyond the gate, Michel could see clearly across the water to Elounda. He took May's hand and they walked out together. She felt privileged to be sharing in his adventure.

As they clattered out through the gate, the guide drew their attention to the old town of Turkish buildings and winding streets that had grown up around the base of the castle. There was a strong, tarry smell drifting across the inner bailey. Then, as they proceeded past the castle walls, Michel's shrewd eyes turned to the guide.

'Who fortified the island?' Michel enquired.

Even as he asked, his mind was elsewhere.

'The Venetians did,' the guide replied.

He pointed a blunt finger at the walls. As so often before, he was playing to the crowd – and as a stage, he had the entire fortress.

'The Venetians were a maritime power, and to protect their sheltered anchorage they built these high walls and those two circular bastions. The strength of the stronghold's defences was tested on numerous occasions, but proved so impregnable, that the islet was never captured,' he explained, and he was very pleased with his knowledge.

'Are you sure?' Michel asked. By such a reckoning, he thought to himself, Princess Carme might have escaped after all.

'Yes! I'm certain. These walls were built to withstand attack, and did so.' The guide assured him.

In spite of the multitudes, the islet evoked an unnerving sense of isolation. Inside the fortress Michel and May walked along a row of stores and small houses. From time to time dust cascaded as local craftsmen removed rubble from renovation works.

Attentive listeners were enthralled by the historical account.

The guide's audience badgered him for more and more detail. Rather than draw a veil over the islet's colourful past, he gave them a guided tour of the agonies and disappointments of a colony stranded on the periphery of normality.

'The islet's mythological history has been the subject of many tall tales, but its latter days have often echoed to the cries of pain. Nowadays, inquisitive visitors like yourselves flock to Spinalonga, but not so long ago, a healthy person dare not set foot on this tormented ground. It was a leper colony. And leprosy was one of the most feared diseases of the time, terrible beyond compare, and it preyed on man's ease of mind,' he proclaimed.

To such an accompaniment, then, did Michel touch one of the washboards used by lepers to clean bandages, and, once more somewhat reluctantly, he handled a surgical tool. He nodded to May, kept his eyes on her and he saw a slight shiver of nervousness go through her as she placed a finger in the crack of a cooking utensil. Fobie was taken aback. Others began to toy with similar commonplace items. Then something changed in the mood of the audience. Their whisperings could not be quietened, as they paraded down a rubble-strewn street amid the ruins of houses. Rounding the corner, Michel smiled and pointed at the tapestry hangings lining the wall. He stepped through a doorway and into a courtyard. The guide, pinned down by persistent questioning, finally continued with his script.

'Supported financially by relations and welfare payments, the industrious lepers were in fact quite well off, whereas residents of the now wealthy Eloundas were among Crete's poorest, rowing out regularly to the jetty to beg for alms.'

'Were there any children?' May, through her tears, enquired politely. She put a tissue to her face. The distress of the lepers had moved her deeply.

Back came the answer. 'Twenty babies were born during this period.'

The guide, surrounded by a wall of tourists, then thundered, 'the leprosarium was marshalled like any other town, with its own administration, school, hospital and jailhouse.' His speech delivered, he purred with satisfaction at a job well done.

Michel and May stood hand in hand at the base of the mountain. Allowed to roam freely, they set out in a northeasterly direction, towards the seaward side of the islet. The path twisted upwards through barren gardens and old Venetian buildings. They strode past the leper hospital converted from a mosque built by the Turks. High enough to have kept the stench of infected flesh at bay. An eerie silence cloaked the building. It was then that Michel remembered the leper-like mystic who had haunted his dreams. And images of amputated limbs crowded his mind.

  Far above sea level, along the fortification wall, the couple stopped for a breather. May threw her arms around Michel's neck and hugged him with all her strength. He leant forward and, half serious, half smiling kissed her. They looked back and saw Greta and Fobie coming on apace. Michel loosened his grip, and then he took May's hand and led her along the ramparts. There they sat, perfectly content. He stood up and peered down through a slit in the top of the battlement. May was breathing quite hard.

'Be careful!' she exclaimed.

He smiled calmly and told her not to worry.

'What are you looking at?' She mopped her brow, and then she got to her feet.

He did not turn his head or raise his eyes. 'Can you see the graveyard?'

'Yes!' May nodded. Her face was only an arm's length from his.

'Good! Can you make out the reservoirs?'

'Yes!' Her tone was subdued.

'The Venetians built those reservoirs because there was no natural water source.' He lifted his right hand and pointed across. 'The water level was supplemented by rainfall trapped in those rooftop basins,' he said, and then he touched her on the arm. 'Greta is convinced that Princess Carme is entombed in a chamber beneath those reservoirs,' he said.

May looked amazed. 'Is there some evidence to suggest that a chamber exists?'

Michel thought for a moment.

'By and large, archaeological excavations work from the top down, but what if Daedalus built a labyrinth from the seafloor up. According to the Gouves scroll, the chamber is accessible via the sea.' He smiled, and then he blandly added. 'In Greek mythology, Daedalus built a secret labyrinth for King Minos beneath an ancient acropolis surrounded by porticoes. However, contrary to ancient texts, historians doubt whether an acropolis ever existed.'

He wrenched a flake out of the face of the wall, and then he continued. 'Subsequently, the Venetians built on the site of the acropolis, reusing the foundations – or so the myth claims.'

To May this supposition straight out of legend appeared laughable, but Michel believed it all the same.

High on the wall-walk, Michel found himself listening to Greta's commentary on enduring ruins spaced around the small islet. Each one represented an important milestone in Aegean history. No one could listen to her without feeling a rush of verve and excitement. May was as excited as any one. Graceful and refined, she sat on the parapet and shaded her eyes. Michel gazed down upon the reservoirs below and studied the seaward approach. The sea spanned out until it passed into the limits of the horizon and could be seen no more. Michel turned his thoughts to Princess Carme. In the map of his mind, an underwater route was being plotted.

Tony looked up at the sky. In the distance, at the top of the mountain overlooking his speedboat, he caught a flare of crimson red: May's windbreaker. He turned the key and the speedboat jumped forward. Then, without warning, a pleasure-craft cut across her bow. Tony slid around the obstruction, with a few metres leeway, but into the path of a fishing boat bearing down fast, its captain half-asleep. Tony swung away to avoid a collision and slammed the throttle forward. He sped towards the coast of Plaka, and, 250 metres from the beach, he stopped.
Be cool, he told himself.
The wind had freshened considerably. He kept his patience, looked uninterested, and bided his time.

The quartet scrambled back down the mountain and clambered aboard the Trophy. The crew was abuzz with excitement. It was late afternoon when they raised the mooring lines and set off from Spinalonga, sailing at 15 knots. Michel's plan to offload the women had been dashed when they refused to disembark at Elounda. Touched by boldness, the mutineers threatened to chain themselves to the mast. Michel, struggling to maintain control of the situation, looked at Fobie and spread his hands helplessly.
'I told you so,' Fobie said in a tone of half regret.

Michel's anger with them did not last for long. He explained the situation and the danger they were in. Grim-faced, he proposed as a compromise that they remain below deck during daylight hours. This was a sensible precaution for the speedboat was on the move. Fearful that he might change his mind and bundle them off the vessel, Greta and May rose to their feet and hurriedly went below deck. Even this lack of harmony did little to dampen the general mood of optimism. If anything, it rose to new heights. Dmitri tacked the yacht around, and then, with bow waves curling, he headed seaward. Michel's eyes ranged the sea and studied the flight of the birds. At the same time, he kept a close eye on the speedboat, appearing and disappearing below the sleek skyline. It remained a buoyant menace, incomparably faster than the Trophy, but Michel had grown accustomed to seeing off high odds. He knew when to hold fast and when to tack fresh winds. The wind veered and the chasm between the two vessels grew a little wider. The course they sailed took them through an empty stretch of sea, which became rougher, the further north they sailed.

Michel took one last look across the sea before going below deck. He offered Fobie a filter-tipped smoke. They sat in silence. Fobie looked thoughtfully at the burning ash.

He took a deep drag, and exhaled.

'Tell me about this demon that shows such feverish interest in what we do,' he drawled.

Without realizing it, Michel found himself marvelling at Tony's abilities and good fortune. 'He is elusive, cunning as well as lethal, and he employs many tactics and wiles to get the job done. Apart from his guile, he's a time bomb primed by bitterness and rage. It seems that he was subjected to some sort of racism while in the SAS. But the assassin's problems really started when he struck a senior officer with enough power to break his jaw. Obviously, he is working for someone who holds a bitter grudge against me.'

As the day drew to a close, Michel gave an account - characterised by a grudging respect - of Tony's exploits.

The tale, rather than gripping Fobie, left him numb.

'He sounds to me like the devil incarnate. Guard your back, for the only way to stop this one is to send him to the other side,' he warned, and then he thumped his hand into the palm of his other hand.

Fobie's grisly warning made Michel think.

'I agree, but all in good time. Timing is everything,' Michel said.

He relished the prospect of meeting his adversary face to face.

Once on deck, Michel noticed the sails were flaccid. Quickly he furled them before joining Dmitri at the helm.

'Power her up and bring her around, take her slow. By nightfall the wind will pick up – fingers crossed,' he intoned.

Dmitri gulped the sea air and he opened the throttle.

Michel was chatting with him as though he had not a care in the world. A small trawler nosed into sight; her two side-booms hoisted upwards. She soon vanished and they were alone once more. Twenty minutes later, Dmitri switched off the engine and dropped anchor, well away from the busy sea-lane. The sun was halfway down the sky when Michel and Dmitri hurried below to join the rest of the crew.

    Michel turned his attention to Greta and May. He saw Greta smiling at May and then both of them looked over. In a condescending manner, he clapped his hands over their heads.

'Everybody, we need to revisit our plan of action. That includes you two,' he said.

Michel laid out a sketched copy of the islet, courtesy of Greta's penmanship, and let them study it for a moment. He went through the plan carefully.

'I, along with Dmitri, will leave the yacht and proceed underwater to the base of the islet. If all goes well, our placement of charges will give us access to the soft rock beneath the reservoirs. Since Fobie has a sure grasp of the logistics involved, he'll be responsible for the safety and support of the underwater equipment. Greta and May, you two stay onboard with Fobie. However, if we need an extra pair of hands, Greta will slip on a diving suit and join us,' he said.

Greta was bitterly disappointed at not being chosen for the initial dive. She stood up and complained about it, but Michel turned from her and began issuing orders to Dmitri, and then he glanced round to make sure Fobie had everything in hand. Eventually, Greta resigned herself to staying behind. She closed the drapes then went over to help May prepare a meal.

After they had eaten, Dmitri climbed the stairs to reach the deck. He studied the chart using a flashlight. Then, with the help of a rising tailwind, he steered south towards the island of Spinalonga and its Venetian fortress.

As Tony left the peninsula in search of the frustratingly elusive yacht, the fuel-light winked brightly. And when he checked the spare tank it seemed that his fortunes had taken a further turn for the worse. It was almost empty. He killed the engine and the speedboat floundered well out to sea, but he remained as determined as ever.
With the help of the pale moonlight sifting through the clouds, he watched the waves slop against the topside of the hull. Then he fixed his eyes into the sea ahead, and waited.

The Trophy with her lights doused sped through the darkness and passed within a kilometre of the unlit speedboat. Eventually, Dmitri manoeuvred the yacht to within 50 metres of the coordinates marked on the chart. He could not wait to strap on his scuba tank, so he hurried below to fetch his wetsuit. Michel helped him to get ready.
Fobie cut away a marker buoy and tossed it overboard. A shiver went through Michel. He approached the dive with a solemn sense of mission. It was as though, peering over the rail, gravity was tempting him to jump. Then the Trophy dipped into a slip of the gathering swell and there was a landing splash on the starboard side as he went overboard.

The Aegean Sea was as dark as ebony when Dmitri jumped in. When his eyes adjusted he saw the submersible extended over the side of the vessel. Through an open rail on the port side of the yacht Fobie lowered the heavily laden submersible. It appeared to be precariously balanced, although trussed with cables. With outstretched arms, as if embracing it, Michel guided the submersible down to the chop. He unhooked the winch-link, while Dmitri attached the two buddy lines to the back. Then he fitted an underwater camera to an external mount and tested the mechanical arm. Fobie reached down and hoisted the winch-link into place. The entire operation had been done in minutes.

The wash kicked them around as they sledged, so when they reached the marker buoy, they descended as quickly as possible. Michel kept an eye on the navigational instrumentation. Even with the submersible's high-power incandescent beams he could see nothing but the line from the marker buoy going down. The deeper they went, the murkier it felt. An inquisitive Mediterranean monk seal sped through the darkness on an intercept course. The seal joyously weaved in and out through the trolled buddy lines. Dmitri stretched out an arm, but the seal backed away and, with a powerful whoosh, vanished into the deep.

Finally the seabed emerged from the darkness. Underwater currents pushed the submersible off course, but Michel gently nudged her back on track. The rock rise from the seafloor was suddenly floodlit. He took a good look at the sea bottom, scanning it with sonar, and found a suitable place to set down. Both divers switched on their heavy-duty flashlights. Michel turned back to Dmitri, and waved him toward the islet. They swam across a natural bridge over a deep trough on the seafloor. Michel studied the strata of this section and saw that someone had engraved marks on several rocks. The divers looked at each other puzzled and uncertain. They began to probe the base for loose stones, and then they set about strategically placing explosives. Once all the devices were armed, Michel and Dmitri retreated from the slope, the fuse wire unravelling in their wake. They found cover behind a wedge-shaped boulder. Moments later, the softer portion of rock imploded. The power of the seawater surging through the ruptured hole was so tremendous that it swept away every loose stone, leaving just spiky projections. The resulting debris drifted downwards through the clouded water and settled on the seafloor.

Quickly Michel examined the hole, tapping its margins with his torch. When he looked inside what surprised him most was the bareness. He was wary of becoming entangled in the sharp-edged spikes, so he struck each one a hard blow with a hammer. Now the hole was broad enough for a full-grown man to enter. He prised out a large stone, and then he scraped out the sediment that lay behind it. Next to him, Dmitri waited by the opening. Suddenly, they found themselves confronted with eel-like creatures making good their escape. No sooner had the creatures emerged from their asylum than they disappeared back into crevices between rocks.

The water grew cooler. Michel began to explore the nooks, crannies and recesses of the underlying bedrock. Further exploration of the cave revealed a skeleton, propped up by a cairn of stones, standing guard over an aperture. The discovery was astonishing, barely believable. Michel could only shake his head in astonishment, for the skeleton clasped a corroded sword in one hand and a dagger in the other. As Michel stood before him, half expecting the string of vertebrae to come to life at any moment, he studied its bony head assiduously. Dark watery eyes moved in the skull's sockets to look from side to side. A small fish had taken up residence.

With wonder and reverence, Michel removed the hand from the sword and placed it over the other hand that held the dagger. He crawled through the aperture, contorting and angling so as not to damage the air hose. He stared up at the heights. The cave interior was thick with stalagmites and stalactites.

He emerged from the water and climbed the steep stairway of uncut stone. It did not take him long to discover what lay beyond.

The floor of the entrance chamber was strewn with droppings and fragments of animal bone, the build up of centuries. Perched above the water table, where the air was dank and chilly, he peeled off his diving gear. It was then that he noticed the grilled gate. He took up the flashlight and went over to it and saw that both ends were eaten away. Above the lintel, stones formed an arch filled by two bulls carved in relief on either side of a tree. With a sudden movement, he grabbed the bars of the gate and shook it open. He glanced down upon the slippery steps below. Dmitri had arrived. Michel hopped down the steps to welcome him.
'Give me your hand.' He pulled him to his feet. 'Get a load of this.'
Dmitri whispered, 'amazing!'
'Check out those bowls,' Michel said softly. He was looking at marble bowls stacked on top of one another. Dmitri whistled, and then he removed his diving suit. A waterproof pouch dangled down his chest as he shouldered a bag of light tools. Michel smiled, slapped him on the back and closed the gate after him. The two of them were dressed in shorts, their feet bare. They proceeded slowly with flashlights down a corridor that seemed to lead upward. At the end of the passageway they scaled a broad double staircase to a large landing, then up another staircase to an anteroom five stories below the reservoirs. Michel led the way into the first large chamber of a three-room vault hollowed out of solid stone, treading carefully so as not to disturb the bones lying upon slabs. He found a spiral staircase leading down. At the bottom stood a pair of gilt-bronze doors that swung open on hinges that groaned.
'Are you all right?' Michel asked.
'It's marvellous!' Dmitri answered nervously.
The doors closed behind them.
'Good.' Michel smiled to himself.
They traced the mysterious descending corridor decorated with frescoes and glittering mosaics. The sound of dripping water grew louder.
It turned out to be a dead end awash with water.

Undeterred, they tried again. This time, however, they inspected the mosaics. Then, abruptly, Michel pointed out a false door built into the body of a mermaid, which marked the opening to a secret stairway leading to another vaulted room.

A shallow exit forced them to stoop.

The corridors were designed to be confusing, but small-scale markings conveyed quickly and accurately the right path. Soon they found the end of the main passageway and, to the west, the way down to a vestibule below. They stood in a wide shaft with a curved ceiling where the air was dry and warm. Deep in the labyrinth they turned left at a junction. Shortly after this they veered right at a fork, later turning left at another mermaid carved into the rock. With the torch held above his head, Dmitri trudged ahead of Michel, but their way was blocked. An earthquake had sent building stones and timbers crashing into the corridor. By torchlight they prised out each wooden plank, then dug out the loose debris. It was hazardous work. Clouds of chalk silhouetted against the torchlight rose up around them, and soon their upper bodies were powdered with it. Michel, with more enthusiasm than training, pulled some slats aside and exposed an arch-like opening – the top of a doorway. He saw there was a small space between some shattered stone. Thrilled, he got his flashlight, and then he shone its beam into the darkness.

'Do you see anything?' Dmitri called.

'Yep,' came back excitedly. With great care he squirmed headfirst out of the narrow space. The ossuary floor was littered with human bones, amulets, bracelets and necklaces. In an inner narthex, clay models prostrated themselves before a sacred column. To the west, there was a long two-aisled nave with a gaping maw. He made his way down some narrow steps to yet another unprotected stairwell. Dmitri was close behind him.

Silently they climbed up three flights of stairs and finally they reached the summit guarded by two ivory statues of winged lions. Sealed shut by beams, joists and stonework, the chamber remained as the earthquake had left it. Using hammer and chisel, Dmitri struck a blackened chunk of cyclopean masonry. A hairline crack split the stone from top to bottom. He struck again, then stepped back. There was a dull sound, like the slamming of a door, and the two stones collapsed at right angles to each other.

Almost immediately they began to excavate. After digging a channel, Michel heaved open the bronze door. At the entrance to the principal chamber lay a clay tablet with inscriptions in the same script as the Gouves scroll. He wiped the sweat off his brow and began to carefully pick his way through the gold ornaments and other artefacts. In the farthest corner of the room, the skeleton of a woman was seated on a stone bench. A gold diadem in the form of a garland crowned her skull. He drew off a gold ring from her finger and put it in his swim shorts.

On the floor lay hundreds of relics, including a gold-head with jewels from the cane that held it and a seal in precious stone. In another corner, a statue caught his eye - a reclining goddess, the body carved of ivory and the head in sculptured gold. As he tiptoed across the dirt, he spotted a rhombus-shaped object. It was a padlocked trunk. Dmitri handed Michel the flashlight, knelt down and he closely examined it. There was no doubting its function. Its design was in the Minoan imperial style, and the image tooled into the lid was Minos, the legendary king of Crete. Dmitri knelt a while longer in thought.

Back on deck Greta was agog for news. She harrowed and harassed for every detail. The only way Michel could shut her up was to tell her to go below and put on a diving suit. Even she who had long been suspicious of his ambitions and sharp practices now had her own reasons for acknowledging his integrity. As she turned to hug him, there were tears in her eyes.

'Make sure you wear a swimsuit under your wetsuit,' he said sharply.

Both his agendas, the commercial and the scientific, needed a respected archaeologist to compile a credible account of the labyrinth. Thoughtfully, he glanced at May, then back to Greta. For no apparent reason, he felt a vague sense of evil and a fear of enemies concealed within history, as though a great power was watching him. These feelings grew so intense that he stood motionless on deck and closed his eyes. He purged his mind and spirit to emptiness. Almost at once the thoughts, memories and sensations that once belonged to Princess Carme took hold of him. He opened his eyes and insisted that the woman's skeleton, and the gilded trunk, should sail with them to Elounda - a suggestion that sparked a full-scale argument amongst the crew.

Greta was walking up the gangway toward the cabin, seething. She noticed Fobie was holding a diving suit with a grin she read as a smirk. To register her protest, she tried to avoid her duty of documenting the find, but Fobie reasoned with her.
'We cannot stop it happening. Michel is resolute,' he said.
She took off her clothes and changed. She closed the cabin door behind her and came on deck feeling itchy and tied in by the wetsuit.

Dmitri remained outside the tomb as Michel led Greta to where the woman's skeleton sat. Greta was not surprised to find that there were no booby traps; the Minoans must have felt no threat when they built the labyrinth. Michel switched on the rack of tube lights that they brought with them.
'Dah-daaah!' he droned.
It took all her decorum not to bellow with delight.
'Unbelievable,' Greta said. She had never seen so much treasure in her life. Her gloved hands trembled. She stroked lightly a little arrowhead of gold, her eyes wider than usual, before she lifted it. When she came to one of the unusual ceremonial accoutrements she stared at it. A knowing smile flashed over her. After five complete rolls of film, she removed the diadem and wrapped the skeleton in a winding grey sail.

Dmitri and Michel laid a makeshift cask, fabricated from materials salvaged in the labyrinth, beside the stone bench and lifted the sail-wrapped skeleton respectfully into it. Between them they carried the coffin to an area near the grilled gate. They hurried back to the tomb and lifted the trunk by its handles and moved slowly through the torch-lit corridors with it balanced on their shoulders. They laid it on the first dry step of uncut stone, and then they sprayed it with a protective waterproof coating.

Back outside, Michel showed Greta how to use the submersible controls. Then he attached a rope, pulled almost taut, to one of the loops on the back of the craft. Greta understood that two short flashes from Dmitri's flashlight meant stop whilst a single flash signified go. Michel returned to the cave, moving along Dmitri's line of sight. He ventured onward, his flashlight seeking the aperture and his hand wrapped with the trailing rope. For several tense minutes Dmitri waited anxiously in the darkness. Greta remained with the submersible, where she kept an eye out for his signal.

Michel raised his head above the water's surface in front of the stairway and looked around. After several failed attempts, he threaded the unwieldy rope through the handles of the trunk, drawing it tight. At once he went to the aperture and flashed a signal. Dmitri relayed the signal. The submersible yanked the trunk into the water. It slid towards Michel and rotated and smashed into the edges of the aperture. The collision triggered off a minor boulder fall. Confused, Michel fought the falling stones away. The trunk, meanwhile, gathered renewed momentum and rushed past the skeletal figure guarding the aperture. Then it continued on its downward path across the slippery cave floor. Michel swam to the point of exit and, letting go of the rope, he flashed a stop signal.
Dmitri had seen the flash and relayed the signal to Greta, whereupon the trunk finally came to a halt. Next, after another short signal, Dmitri scrambled out of harm's way. The trunk moved forward in the direction of the exit hole, toppled sideways and jammed itself against a protruding rock. Not only did it plug the only way out, but also, as a result of a tiny puncture, it caused Michel's air supply to fall to a dangerously low level.

As Michel's predicament became steadily graver, his concern mounted. Now he was on his knees, pulling away some loose stones. Frantically, Dmitri groped his way over the exposed part of protruding rock, but he was unable to dislodge the trunk. Although he had a rough inkling of Michel's whereabouts, he could not see him. Careless for his safety, Dmitri worked his way under the rocky outcrop, then, holding the chisel carefully, he began to hammer.

The possibility of becoming a companion in death with the brave soldier who must have suffered a similar fate all those years ago now loomed as large as the labyrinth. With the flashlight, Michel searched the cave until he found the corroded sword. His fingers took hold of the hilt and, with the point of the blade, he pared away at the edges of the hole. Sadly, after many jabs, the sword snapped in half. Having discarded the pointed end, he continued to chisel away with the blunted upper half. With ever-increasing amounts of rock being whittled away, the unstable edges began to crumble. Then, in one last-ditch effort, he wedged the sword between the trunk and the edge of the hole. At this point his blood had turned colder than his watery surroundings. A trickle of debris spilled into the cave, followed by a large chunk that fell on his foot as he adjusted his grip on the hilt. He put his weight and might on the sword. Simultaneously, he flashed a signal.

Unaware of how little air Michel had left, Dmitri was uncertain whether he should relay the signal, or continue to chisel. At the last moment, advancing straight to the spot where he had last seen Michel's flashlight, he sent the signal.

The slack was taken up and the rope became taut once more. Michel's air supply was now spent.

'Move, damn you, move,' he gasped as he bore down on the sword. Breathing only vapours, he tilted the trunk and shoved with all his strength. He found himself teetering on the edge of an abyss. Even so, the sword yielded to both pressure and determination, snapping just below the hilt, but not before it fulfilled the purpose for which it was salvaged. Suddenly the trunk took on a life form of its own and tore out of the cave. Despite burning lungs and failing strength, Michel let the rock face settle back. His liberation seemed to him to be the working of a miracle, but his continued existence was also a matter of teamwork. Before he had a chance to indicate his need for oxygen, Dmitri had replaced the redundant mouthpiece with his own. Michel sucked in the mixture of compressed air and oxygen, and allowed his body to recover gracefully. Realising the rope had lost its purchase Greta came about. In doing so, she saw what was happening. With little hesitation, she readied the spare tank.

Having recovered from his ordeal, and with Dmitri's assistance, Michel strapped on the spare tank. He was delighted to see the trunk was intact, but its lid was badly scratched.
Greta sprayed polyurethane foam around the trunk and Dmitri attached a self-inflating airbag to prevent further damage. As soon as the foam was set, the trunk secure alongside, Michel took control of the submersible. Dmitri ignited the airbag, and the trunk slowly left the seafloor. Taking their time, Dmitri and Greta swam on either side of the trunk, unwilling to let it out of their sight for a second; fearing the rope would snap.

After a heated exchange, all parties agreed not to open the trunk until it was safely housed in Gouves. Armed with the rock-drill, Dmitri and Greta set off to recover the woman's skeleton. Michel stayed behind. May led him to the cabin.
Once the door was closed, she kissed him.
'I was worried about you,' she said.
She made him a cup of tea and he related what had happened.

Dmitri and Greta returned to the Trophy before dawn. Fobie leant out from the deck. The submersible, with the coffin onboard, was hoisted and set down on deck. Inevitably, the crew's tiredness led to mistakes. When Michel came on deck to marshal proceedings, he saw the submersible's lights were still on. He let out an almighty roar and sprinted as fast as he could.

'So so sorry, I forgot…' Greta began shakily.
It had taken him all his will not to vent his anger. He shook his head and warned of the danger of being seen.

Tony unfolded the butt of his rifle and clipped in place the night-sight with brisk and military efficiency. After a fruitless wait, he was about to return to Eloundas when he spotted the light of the resurfacing submersible. It offered him a tantalising opportunity. Now, suddenly, everything seemed to be moving his way. The crosshairs of his scope settled on the huge seated figure of Fobie. Then the beautiful form of May filled his lens.
Why are they sitting around in a circle? Tony asked himself,
His scope zoomed in on Dmitri, then on Greta and finally on the mark who was coming ever more clearly into focus.

The heavy barrel of the rifle was aimed at Michel's head. Now at last Tony's moment had come. He knew nothing of the mark as an individual, other than the fact that he was a businessman of sorts. Instinctively, Tony pulled his head back; for he was certain the mark looked straight at him. Unsettled, he peered through the scope. The yacht appeared to be moving, but there was nobody on deck.
Tony turned the key, but the engine spluttered – out of fuel.
He muttered to himself, 'you lucky devil, the gods are smiling on you.'

Michel sat in the locked toilet and shone his torch. He examined closely the gold ring of spiral design, exquisitely inlaid with flawless emeralds. It was the most impressive piece of jewellery he had ever seen.

CHAPTER 17

In only a single day their world had changed and history was upon them. Fobie lifted the trunk wrapped in a blanket high upon his shoulder. A bead of sweat trickled down his forehead and Greta wiped it off. They disguised their purpose with touristy and glib words. Since most everyone else was asleep, the grand foyer at the Elounda Beach Hotel was deserted except for a silver-haired night porter who offered to help, but Fobie declined. A phone rang repeatedly. Quietly, the porter shimmied away. All the while, on the other side of the foyer, hidden from sight, a tousled woman with sharp eyes scrubbed the floor. She was watching them with a sly smile.

Dmitri was last to enter the bedroom. There he joined the rest of them sitting on the bed with their eyes half-closed, tired and exhausted yet unable to sleep. Michel, who had been urging more resolution on them, checked his watch, five minutes past four.
'Come on, come on, chop-chop,' he barked.
An hour later they were on the move and made good time along the sleepy road, only a lane and a half wide. They wound their way up a mountain where wild goats grazed among the shocks of thistle and the small patches of vegetation. Just below them, a dark-clad

motorcyclist arrowed across the lower slopes, while in the distance, a plane flew low over the plum miasma of the Mediterranean Sea. Each time a car came toward them, Dmitri swerved off the road. Even so, they travelled in buoyant mood, and played a guessing game: "what's in the trunk?"

By the time they reached Gouves the consensus arrived at by the weary but jaunty travellers, diamonds and other jewels. All the while, the motorcyclist trailed unseen along the road behind them

Michel turned to Dmitri. Then, with a twinkle in his eye: 'Oh! By the way, all your personal belongings, as well as the artefacts, have been moved to a new location overlooking the excavation site.'

'You did what?' Greta asked incredulously.

Michel nodded.

She shuddered.

'I hope the movers were careful. This is the history of the Minoans we're talking about,' she sniffed.

Michel sought to explain: 'Merely a security precaution. It's not wise to stay in the one place all the while.'

Greta was soon fretting. The fact that everything had been relocated in advance, without any reference to herself, was an outrage, but one which, for the moment, she was prepared to swallow.

On the fringes of the village, a hefty man with broad beard and abstracted gaze unlocked the entrance gate leading to the large villa. The recently finished building was set against a bay of tawny hills that framed a narrow shingle beach. In the sky loud hollers were heard, along with the clash of bolts and the pounding of unseen feet. Before them, arrayed in uniform, two men, one young and one old, patrolled the grounds.

Dmitri parked near the fountain. Not far from where they parked, a slender man with a designer's stubble and an unapproachable demeanour squatted by the pool.

Michel stepped gingerly over some broken slates. Piles of granite blocks and bags of sand were stacked by the walls. He jumped down to the porch and May followed him nimbly, her laugh just bubbling under the surface and regularly breaking through.

'Look at the two birds,' she said, pointing at a pair of sandpipers swimming in the pond.

A compact man, with grey hair, a small paunch, and wearing plain clothes, opened the door. The interior was furnished with dark-wood furniture. The walls were covered with Turkish rugs and prints in dark wooden frames.

They left the doorway and went inside.

The ground floor, except for the kitchen, was open-plan, with two sofas: velvet and leather. An unusual steel staircase was painted blue. Upstairs, the bedrooms were decorated in a chestnut shade. It was, however, a bright darkness, lively with the brilliance of the early morning sun.

At the same time, beside the last house on the road, the dark-clad motorcyclist veered left to a narrow lane running up a nearby hill.

Fobie and Dmitri ferried the trunk and then the improvised coffin to the folding glass door that linked the garden to the kitchen. Safely ensconced, Michel drew the curtains. Then, along with Dmitri, Greta got right to work. Always on the move, with her apron swirling around her, she took out her camera. Fobie groaned and with a shoulder spin he lifted the trunk so that she could take a picture of the underneath. Drawing inspiration from the example of Greta, Dmitri began work on cataloguing what they found. From memory, he drew up a list of the numbers of tunnels and chambers in the labyrinth. Satisfied he had missed nothing, he turned his attention to the mud-caked coffin. There was something peculiarly poignant about the skeleton's mouth. Dmitri drew back the curtains. From the clean light of the window, the heir to a famous title appeared to want to whisper. Of the group, it was Michel who sensed this most clearly. And, when he reflected on her demise, visions of tragedy swirled through his imaginings. He leaned toward the open coffin and gazed at what in all likelihood were the lifeless bones of Princess Carme. The shelf-like ridge over her eyes was flecked with fine mud. There was no sweet smelling scent in the air, only some bitter tang that seemed infused during the centuries she had spent in the labyrinth. Together, with nothing left undone, they lowered her into her new coffin hidden beneath the long table, and closed the lid. Michel pulled shut the curtains.

Distracted as he had been by his thoughts, Michel turned his gaze back to Greta. After what seemed like an eternity of making observations, taking notes, and drawing sketches, she was ready to open the trunk. Assuming a kneeling position, her gloved hands carefully pushed the lid upwards. Little by little, the trunk involuntarily creaked as it relaxed its hold on history. Nesting snugly within she discovered a gilded box with openwork panels. She asked Fobie to carefully extract it. Only when she had finished examining the box was she willing to open it. With watering eyes, she brushed back her apron and laid her hand on the wooden lid, which was sheathed in gold and ivory. Anxiously the other four watched. Much to their surprise, it contained yet another box. Having completed her initial inspection, Fobie lifted it towards her taking it steadily. It differed markedly from the previous strongbox. He recognised its composition, quartzite, usually employed in the prevention of weathering. After he set it down, he took off his navy baseball cap and wiped his brow. It looked as if he was going to launch into a description of quartzite.

Instead, he sighed and said, 'this box was made to protect something precious.'

The sense of expectation within the room was further heightened. Not hesitating for a moment, Greta, with Fobie hovering protectively by her side, opened the box. Gob smacked and speechless, they stared in disbelief at yet another nested box, a stunning coffer cast of solid gold.

Greta punched both gloved hands in the air. Fobie had never seen her quite so joyful. From the superb quality of the gold, the fine engravings, the amount of adornment, she immediately saw that it was a key find.

'No wonder it was so heavy,' Fobie quipped.
He grunted as he raised the coffer high enough for Greta to take her photographs. She used up a whole roll of film and then she replaced it with a new roll before taking measurements. In a similar manner she took more time drawing it, and produced a sketch that underlined her unerring sureness of hand. Satisfied with the result she asked Fobie to return all boxes to their original position. She stretched her legs as the group whispering urgently held their eyes steadfast. The menace of disappointment magnified with every second that passed. Perhaps the coffer contained nothing more than stones or sand. It may have been a decoy stash. Both optimism and sanguinity served to steel their fluttering nerves. Greta took a deep breath and crouched in front of the chest. The only sound in the room was the ceiling fan's whooshing.
'Wait,' Dmitri warned, then added, 'there could be something nasty inside.'
Greta nodded and said, 'good thinking, can you pass me my facemask.' She placed the mask over her face and twiddled her fingers. For the last time, she girded herself for what she was about to uncover.

A much greater danger, and one that cast its shadow over the entire proceedings, was the presence of the motorcyclist waiting on the hill. Hermione was 36, a thin, reserved, somewhat hostile woman with dark glasses and shaggy brown hair streaked with grey. She sat on her motorcycle, her phone at the ready.

Greta opened the solid gold chest and was amazed to see it full to the brim of gold coins along with a few clumps of coated muslin that contained silver coins as well as bronze. She placed her hand over her heart and beamed, for their reward was spectacular. Michel looked away for a moment, gathering himself. May broke into joyful giggles. Fobie threw his head back and laughed. Dmitri gasped excitedly, lost for a word to capture his feeling.

Greta's numismatist skills were now called upon as she fingered a handful of coins. She recognised that the gold coins were not all of the same mint, nor were the silver or the bronze.

'Ok! Let's get to work. We'll sort out the different sizes and weights, and then we'll count them out,' she said, excitedly.

'Sure.' Michel's face settled.

Greta, with Dmitri's aid, rolled out a number of sheets of greaseproof paper, one for each stack of coin type, and to every one of her eager helpers she handed a pair of surgical gloves. First, she positioned a pair of scales on the travertine floor for easy access. Then she invited the others to join her on the Persian rug. Excitement bound them together. They sat beside each other in a narrow semi-circle.

'I'll write a brief description of each coin, and then I'll start off a stack,' Greta said.

She had already begun jotting down a few lines on cut-cardboard, folding it so that it would stand. In a thin logbook, she recorded the weight, 8.7g and diameter, 1.79cm, of the first coin. She gradually segregated other pieces of the puzzle, trying and discarding ideas about the identity of the coin portraits until they fitted nicely into the overall gist of an ancestral dowry.

'How old is this beauty?' Michel asked. There was a feeling of tightness in his throat as he read Greta's description: *GOLD; obverse: Athena wearing a helmet and decorated with snake; reverse side: Nike with wreath in right hand and the extolled word Alexandrou.*

Greta reached out to take the coin from him, and she inspected the size of the flans.

'This Stater was minted under Alexander the Great, whose coins were struck throughout the Persian Empire,' she said, warmth in her tone, 'indeed, a hundred years after his death, mints were still producing this coin.'

'Amazing, considering his brief reign...' May halted, flummoxed at the thought of someone dying so young. Then she thought of Jenny.

'That's right, he reigned for 13 years and died at the age of 33,' Dmitri piped up.

Pulling his cap down low over his eyes, Fobie plucked out a large gold piece. 'What about this one?' he asked.

'Let me see.' Greta leaned forward. 'Ah! Yes, the head of Apollo,' she paused, then flipped the coin, 'two horses pulling Nike's chariot and bearing the inscription Philippou. This coin was minted during the lifetime of Philip II, father of Alexander the Great, most likely in Macedonia,' she told him. It was then that she examined the reverse symbols more closely before starting a fresh stack. Counterfeiting at the time was rife, so while the others counted and sorted, she sampled the coins in detail. The hours sped by, sleep and food were forgotten, and the stacks grew in size.

When Dmitri placed the last coin on top of a teetering stack, there was a collective sigh of relief.

Greta picked up her logbook and read aloud, '4,951 coins in total.'

Her voice was trembling slightly.

'Comprising 2,941 Alexander gold staters; 1,449 Philip gold staters; 412 silver tetradrachms; and 149 bronze drachms.'

She used a full roll of greaseproof paper, wrapping and taping the coins in quantities of one hundred. She made pertinent remarks on each pouch in her logbook, and then she announced that the hoard was in fact the real deal. As she lifted each pouch from the rug she counted them, making sure that she overlooked not a single one. When at last they were all packed into the golden coffer, she gently closed the lid. Then she closed the two remaining lids and fell back with joyous fatigue.

'Now, what are we going to do with them?' Fobie volunteered the question on everyone's mind.

'There is, in my opinion, only one course of action: hand them over. We can't keep them,' Greta said, sitting upright.

Michel stood up and went to the window. He pulled back the curtains and leant on the sill.

'Well we can't keep them, that's for sure,' Greta repeated slowly, claiming no more sway than was due to her by virtue of her profession, emphasising each word. Her voice thickened and her lips involuntarily twitched. She placed her arm protectively over the trunk, and then she glared over at Fobie. Fobie shrugged his shoulders and looked up at Michel who was now standing by the folding glass door.

Michel sighed theatrically.

'I want all the particulars clear before making a public announcement, because I expect the labyrinth to receive a lot of international attention. Don't worry, the coins will be handed over to the authorities in due course,' he said.

May went across to join him at the folding glass door. His firmness melted away in a broad smile. He stepped out on to the terrace, beneath a cloudless sky, and he lit a cigar. The tranquil garden rolled down to the beach; in the distance, a flotilla of yachts floated. Every so often, a bird flew overhead. He dropped his cigar on to the slabs of the terrace and ground it under his sole. Then he ducked back inside and climbed the steel staircase.

'I don't believe him. Do you?' Greta muttered under her breath, vacillating over what to do.

Fobie leaned over.

'Don't worry, don't worry,' he repeated.

When Michel came back downstairs he was wearing shorts, white sneakers and a cotton shirt. By now it was late in the morning, and he could at last start to flesh out his plans. An engineer and his crew were already on their way to clear a helicopter-landing site and to construct an airstrip.

He held his sat-phone in one hand and a plastic bag in the other.

'Toyoko that's great news! Can you let Bill Watson know - he needs to touch base with his Greek counterpart and tie up some loose-ends?' He hung up, and then he stepped into the kitchen and closed the door quietly behind him.

Forced into action by a worsening hunger, Greta and May rustled up a tall column of pancakes stuffed with tomatoes and mushrooms. Fobie, seated at the far end of the kitchen table, offered Michel a plate.

They ate slowly, savouring the brunch, and their banter concerned the affairs that absorbed them all: the hoard of coins.

His appetite satiated, Michel opened the plastic bag and extracted a green folder, and then he turned to Greta.

'Would you mind accompanying me to the living room, there's something I'd like to discuss with you?'

Then as an afterthought, he added. 'Fobie, can you join us?'

May watched him rush off, Greta and Fobie following.

Dmitri stood up with a belch.

'I'll clean up here,' he said.

'Thank you.' Badly in need of a rest, May stole upstairs in search of a comfortable bed.

Michel shifted the folder in front of him.

'How would you feel about a permanent move to Crete?' he asked Greta directly.

'Doing what exactly?' Her astonishment was plain to see.

'Only today, I was granted planning permission for the construction of a private museum,' Michel beamed.

'How on earth did you manage that?' Greta exclaimed, who was understandably startled by the idea. Yet her suspicions of him lingered.

She herself was too obvious, too independent, to be bought, but simple compliance was not what Michel wanted from her.

He did not answer at once, and then he said, 'it lends itself nicely to a coup d'état of sorts.'

Instead of downplaying his aspiration, he underscored it.

'Recently, a company of mine was granted licenses for oil and mineral exploration. However, in my opinion, this goes hand in hand with archaeology and other disciplines,' he said.

Greta sank back on the velvet couch, and Michel went on.
'With this in mind, I'd like you to accept directorships on the board of a newly formed company KOME, which will oversee the enterprise. You'll receive a five percent share in KOME.'
Thoughtfully Greta let her eyes stray to the folder.
Michel waited patiently.
He saw her turn her eyes back on him, and then he continued.
'Needless to say, the hoard of coins and Princess Carme will take pride of place in the new museum. Cynics may argue that the museum is a publicity stunt, fostered for selfish ends, but the company's charter will harmonise any conflict of interest, placing archaeological importance above mining exploits. And I've decided that the museum will merge with company headquarters. Let's take a look at the plans?'
'Oh, please!' Greta replied, and her voice quivered.
'I'm sure that both of you will need some time to consider my proposal.' Michel waited for a response.
They could well have afforded to bide their time.
Instead, holding Fobie's hand, tears leaking out of her eyes, Greta managed to utter the words: 'You've got to be kidding.'
How could they snub the promise of forging a life together, doing something they both love?
'Excellent.' Michel paused, then suggested airily, 'one other thing: the museum will need a curator, and I see Dmitri as the ideal candidate for the post.'

Composed as ever, Michel unclasped the green folder and spread the architectural drawings out on the floor. At first though, Greta could not find her glasses, and Fobie followed her around the room as she looked for them. He found them on top of the windowsill. Holding each other's hand, they eagerly pored over the drawings. Michel sat back in the couch. Both the scale and the form of the proposed campus were awe-inspiring. The tilted roof of every building, completely covered with solar cells, could produce up to four megawatts of power, enough to satisfy most of the electrical demand of the structural complex. Greta, nonplussed by the sheer magnitude of the project, felt so guilty for misjudging Michel. His vision could only be described as overwhelming, his energy resolute, his determination staggering. Doubtless he needed these qualities to win through as he did, for she knew first hand the tangle of red tape that spewed out from the wheels of ponderous bureaucracy. Now, she understood how gifted people, like Fobie, came to admire and respect Michel.

Nothing to offend a time-hallowed tradition here, she said to herself.

Fobie, so engrossed in the drawings, did not realise he was laughing until Michel passed him a second set of drawings that were of a floating wind farm driven by warmed air, initially located on a shallow continental shelf, off the eastern coast of Crete, far enough away so as not to be invasive.

Michel's finger stabbed at the top drawing.

'That, my friend, is the source of distributed energy for the whole operation. Every wind turbine is 560 foot tall and has three blades 180 foot long. Each turbine will be capable of generating up to four megawatts.'

Michel returned the drawings to the folder.

'The scale of the undertaking is something else. Truly amazing,' Fobie whistled, and then he asked, 'did you encounter many obstacles?'

'To get the go ahead, I had to secure licenses from over thirty different services and engage the involvement of seven different ministries,' Michel replied.

Before standing up to leave, he shook their hands to seal the deal.

'Would you mind if I take another look at the plans?' Greta asked, showing symptoms of shell-shock. She stood up. 'I'm so excited …'

She halted, startled as Michel held up a hand and said with polite authority, 'no problem, just one thing, keep this close to your chest; I don't want anything turning up on the web. I've managed to steal an edge on my competitors, and I want to keep it.'

They both nodded and Fobie reopened the folder. They had clearly decided that there was nothing left for them to question.

'When do you want us to start?' Fobie asked.

'Tomorrow if that suits,' Michel answered, then added, 'Greta, your contract is upstairs should you like to sign. Also, I've a contract for Dmitri if you'd like to make him that offer now.'

'I'd be delighted,' Greta said. 'He deserves it after putting a lot of hours in without complaint and taking care of all the donkeywork.'

'And you Fobie, are you ready to put pen to paper?' Michel asked.

He saw the wide smile burst through.

'Try and stop me,' Fobie said.

Michel left them down in the living room, and he darted upstairs. He approached May who had rolled into the double bed naked. He looked at her and his eyes caressed her neck and shoulders. Her tiny little snores, barely audible, were the only noise in the room. He kissed her gently on the forehead and stroked her hair. Then suddenly there was movement. Her eyes opened and she grumbled, 'I missed you.'

She sat up in a flexed position, with her knees drawn up to her chin.

'Sorry I've neglected you but I had something important to sort out with Greta and Fobie,' he said.

He patted her on the knee consolingly.

She felt a twinge of disappointment when he took away his hand. Coyly she swayed towards him.

'I love you, and I want to make love to you. I don't want to end up like Princess Carme, to live and die a virgin,' she said, hoping to still the hunger she so long endured, a certain angst in her voice.

He whispered into her ear, 'No! You're not ready.'

Then he marked her inadvertent response, and he smiled. 'Wait until your wedding night, after all - an oath is an oath.'

'For God sake, hush, and make love to me,' she pleaded, suddenly heedless of any consequences. She blushed as she said it and carried on in a rush over what he was going to preach.

'Michel, I'm desperate and need some proof that you find me desirable,' she said.

His heart wrenched at her distress. 'It's OK, it's OK, it's OK,' he repeated, consolingly, reassuringly.

While he padded off to the bathroom, she was left on her own – perched on the bed, legs crossed, surveying the bedroom. He returned naked, and aroused. In front of her as he stood on the Chinese rug her eyes were at the same level as his waist. Shyly she touched his swelling member, caressingly, and pushed the foreskin back. Before she could pleasure him, his hands snaked out and he laid her on her back and moved her feet apart. Then he raised her knees and knelt between them. It was some precious moments before she realised what he was about to do. He touched her glistening mount and gently parted its outer lips. Silently he lowered his head. She felt his warm breath on her skin.

Her lips were moist and she felt his tongue slip between them. She grabbed a pillow and covered her head to gag herself; then, finally, her womanhood exploded. She clenched her thighs to stall the flow, but it streamed silkily down her lover's face.

She felt alive, sensational.

'Oh! Yes, yes, yes,' she moaned.

She gathered herself hastily and took a deep breath. Then she grabbed his arm and spun him towards her.

'Your turn,' she said. She tapped him in the middle of the chest to indicate her readiness.

Tentatively she lowered her head, and then she encompassed him with her mouth. At first she was slow and methodical. But then he urged her to increase the rhythm of her movements. Soon she felt him throb and jump, and when his hand drew her closer still, she swallowed quietly and swiftly.

While she drifted back to shallow sleep, he slid out of the bed and into his shoes. He moved quickly and noiselessly around the bed. Rummaging through his canvas bag he found three envelopes, and then he left the bedroom, pulling the door closed after him. At the top of the staircase he phoned Chen who was in a car with Sean, Akiko and Mayumi.

'Listen, Chen, I know you fear for my safety, but can you step back from this one? I want to deal with this guy myself.'

He waited for Chen's measured response.

'How about a compromise.' Chen broke off, searching for the right words in which to articulate his proposal. 'Setsu joins you for the duration of your stay in Crete.'

Michel was taken aback. 'Is Setsu here?' he asked.

'Yes. I saw fit to despatch him.' Chen anticipated an objection.

'I'm flattered. This gives me an opportunity to get to know him a little better.'

Michel heard the bedroom door open, then close. He moved aside to allow May to pass by. She blew him a kiss and he smiled.

'Any other news,' Michel asked.

'We've identified the assassin's employers - the Scallion twins. They want you gone – dead. And it's not just past debts they're trying to renege on. They're tired of being on the run – and they have big plans to expand their criminal network. So they want you, and Secure Span, out of the way. Your name is at the top of their kill-list,' Chen emphasised.

Michel had been well briefed on the havoc wreaked on Peoples Pensions. 'That makes sense, where are they now?' he asked.

'Holed-up in slab city close to Niland,' Chen said.

'Are you going to pay them a visit?' Michel enquired.

'We're on our way there now,' Chen said. He sought to put this problem away for good.

'When I get back to London I want to be able to speak to the twins,' Michel said. He was adamant that they be kept alive.

'Okay.' That will make it a trifle more difficult, thought Chen.

'Cheers.' Michel hung up. He wondered to himself how long it would take for Setsu to arrive. He noted the time. Back in the living room the mood was joyous. Dmitri, Fobie and Greta, huddled together on the blanket, had already begun to make plans and preparations for the museum. Michel took pleasure from their commitment. He distributed the envelopes among the group. May, stretched out on the leather sofa, watched with growing interest as they studied their contracts.

There were words of encouragement on the tip of Michel's tongue when a light knock on the door stopped him from speaking. Fobie stood up and took out the Mauser from under his shirt. He set the selector to single fire and wrapped it in a glossy brochure. He followed Michel to the door.

Setsu stood on the porch and he immediately reached out for Michel's hand.

'Welcome!' Michel said.

Thoughtfully Greta slid a drawing alongside the others in sequence and then she set the folder on the long table. She paid little heed to this latest Asian visitor; she had finally placed her trust in Michel. If he felt it necessary to use guns, she thought, justifiable reasons must exist for taking such measures. And it was likewise her opinion that if he deemed it appropriate to bring in more security, she saw no reason to risk disruption by passing snide comment.

As Michel and May strolled up and down the beach, the fresh sea air seemed to make them more playful and relaxed. They kept their heads close as they joked and laughed with one another above the roar of the waves. Suddenly, Michel got down on bended knee.

'Will you marry me,' he asked.

'Yes, Michel, of course I will,' she said.

He slipped the Minoan gold ring onto the third finger of her left hand. It was a perfect fit.

Then he stood up.

He held her hand, stroked her hair and kissed her cheek.

She hugged the ring protectively to her breast. 'This is the most wonderful ring I have ever seen. I adore it! I adore it!'

CHAPTER 18

La Quinta, less than 200 kilometres from San Diego, bustled busily with retirees. Chen waited in a white convertible with Akiko and Mayumi. An open map and a satellite image of the Imperial Valley were cradled in his lap. Inside a car-hire office, Sean spoke blarney to a young girl wearing a gold nose ring. She was in a basic dress, long bare legs outstretched in front of her. Her voice was squeaky, her eyes bleary.
'I might have some free time later. Where is the best off-road action?' Sean asked in his winning Irish brogue.
'Lake Cahuilla,' she replied.
'Thanks.' He left the dingy office and collected a green silver off-roader from the lot. Akiko got out of the convertible and joined him. They drove along the narrow car-lined road with the radio on playing Hotel California, and a golfer, a woman in her seventies wearing light blue slacks, stepped between two cars on to the road in front of them and Sean swerved round her.
'Bloody hell!' he gasped.
'You could have knocked her down,' Akiko complained.
'Sorry!'

The two vehicles drove along the San Andreas Fault line towards Salton Sea. Abandoned buildings served as landmarks along the stretch of road between North Shore and Bombay Beach. Withered palm trees patrolled by algae blooms served as lookout posts for pelicans, blue herons, gulls, stilts and many more species of migrating waterfowl. The temperature tipped 110 degrees. Chen decided they should stop at a roadside bar to quench their thirst.

Sean looked in all the windows, but the bar was empty. A lady of Hispanic origin was in the yard. She was sitting under a parasol. Cigarette smoke curled up into the canvas above her head.
'Want one?' the woman asked. She shook one out of the box and held it out.
'No, I don't smoke, but I'm really thirsty,' Sean gasped. 'Four lemonades, and four more to go, please.'
'Ah. Right,' she replied.
She shuffled over to the bar and opened it. She brought out some lemonade, poured it into four glasses.
Sean finished his lemonade.
'I needed that.'
He took out a fifty-dollar bill, glanced at it, and then he handed it over.

Despite the sulphuric smell, the water looked inviting. Sean tiptoed along the beach, a lasagne of barnacles and fish bones. He was about to wade in when he heard Chen shout out.
Sean looked at the water and then at Chen.
'Surely you can tell by the smell it isn't suitable for swimming in,' Chen bellowed with all his might. As he yelled, the lady of the bar breezed by, picked up a stone and threw it into the water. It took two minutes for the stone to sink. She smiled grimly to herself, sipping a beer.
'If you want to swim, wait until you get to the Fountain Of Youth Spa further on up the road. It's much better,' she called out. Then

she went back inside and plopped four bottles of lemonade on the counter.

'I've swam in a lot worse, believe you me,' Sean bawled with a laugh. Nevertheless, he was glad he had been warned off.

Chen took a last sip, and then he got up. 'Let's go. Come on.'

As they journeyed, Sean pointed to a salt-embalmed car wreck. Akiko shook her head in disbelief.

Her mouth was dry.

She opened the glove compartment and got out a bottle of lemonade and the tang of it made her feel better.

They passed the Fountain Of Youth Spa, thronged with elderly bathers, but neither car stopped. Instead, they kept going until they reached Slab City. They took a right before entering and headed for Niland, three kilometres southeast of the sea. Chen studied the map as Mayumi drove, he could see the logic of the twin's choice of base. A short dash from Niland would take them over the Mexican border. We need to cut that route off first before we go in, he told himself, and the best way to do that is to render their transport useless.

They circumvented Niland and came upon a little back road. Waiting for them was a pickup truck. The man at the wheel tipped his Stetson and the three cars hit off in the direction of the Coachella Canal. After touring for twenty minutes the man in the pickup signalled the two vehicles that followed him to halt. They stopped in the shade thrown across the sands by a large manmade bank.

Hank hopped out of the pickup and approached the convertible, as did Mr Okumara.

'Howdy,' Hank said. His jaws continued to move as he chewed on a cut of tobacco.

He was a tall, wiry man.

Chen got out. 'Have you been waiting long?'

'Oh, half an hour or so,' Mr Okumara said.

'Any sign of them?' Chen asked.

'Yes, the twins are a mile further on, water-skiing. You can't miss them. Their SUV and trailer are parked on this side of the bank.' Hank tilted the broad brim of his Stetson forward and carried on. 'No one usually ventures this far up the canal so you should be free from interruption. Everything you need is in the back.'

Sean went to the back of the pickup. Underneath a sack of grain he found a Smith & Wesson and a Colt Python. Along with the guns, he discovered two sets of leg irons and an amputation saw - relics from the American Civil War. Under Chen's supervision, he wrapped them up in a large tear of oily rag.

Hank watched them leave on foot.

When they reached the bend they could see the twin's SUV. The sunlight shimmered on its body and was reflected like a sheet of metal into their eyes. Akiko scouted ahead and returned. She stooped and gave her report.

'They've just loaded a speedboat onto the trailer, and are messing about fully clothed in the canal,' she said.

'Sean, you disable the SUV and, if you can, hide in the speedboat. Akiko, you conceal yourself in the backseat of the SUV. As soon as the twins get in, detain them,' Chen ordered.

Dynamic, effervescent and inexorably buoyant, Tom and Edward splashed about in the canal, and then they sat on a sandy bank in a clump of reeds, smoking a joint, blissfully unaware of what was to come. To his delight, Sean spotted the car keys in the ignition and removed them, saving him the trouble of disabling the engine. Peeping out of the speedboat, he could see the twins sliding down the bank towards the SUV. After a while, the twins jumped in and Tom went to start the engine.

'Where're the keys?' He rummaged about.

'I left them in the ignition.' Edward checked his pockets.

'Damn, they must be in the canal.' Tom opened the glove compartment.

'Don't move,' Akiko yelled.

Tom turned around and could not believe his eyes. Akiko held the Colt in his face. He gently opened the door but as his foot searched for ground, another voice echoed.

'I wouldn't do that if I were you lad.'

With the Smith & Wesson, Sean motioned the fair-haired twin out of the vehicle. Now Tom was wearing jeans but nothing else.

'Kneel down and put your hands behind your head,' Sean barked, and he took hold of one of Tom's wrists and angled the hand up behind Tom's back and forced his face into the sand.

'There's some cash in the SUV,' Tom spluttered. 'Take what you want.' He was convinced they were being mugged or car-jacked.

'Keep quiet,' Sean shouted. Then he pushed Edward, who was wearing blue shorts and a checked shirt, forward into the sand and stamped hard on his foot.

Why are you doing this? Edward's look said.

Sean stared back.

But Edward had no idea what the stare meant.

'Believe me I'm your worst nightmare,' Sean said.

'Ed, look who's coming.' Tom nodded in the direction of Mr Okumara. He was striding out across the sand, walking straight through all the brush growing in it.

'That's the guy who left his calling card in Capitola.' Edward looked bewildered.

'Ah, gentlemen, did you forget about my request to repay all the monies you stole from Peoples Pensions?' Mr Okumara asked.

He projected a menacing physical presence.

'We wanted to but found ourselves in financial difficulty,' Edward answered. Akiko stood right behind him with her hands on his shoulders.

'Oh,' Mr Okumara said. He rolled his eyes and looked at Tom.

'Hey! Leave me alone.' Edward struggled as Akiko tried to clasp the leg irons on him. Sean slapped him hard across the face. Tom was next to feel the force of Sean's hand. He too was shackled to prevent escape. Meanwhile, Chen poked round the SUV and found passports, phones, cannabis and a couple hundred dollars inside a small zip-up pocket inside the glove compartment. He looked at the phone in his hand. Then he scrolled through the contact list but it was in some sort of code. The whole time he did he was looking over Mr Okumara's shoulder at the twins kneeling. Chen folded and unfolded his arms. Then he asked Mayumi to go back and collect the off-roader.

The twins knelt together on the verge with the off-roader back up to speed behind them. Any further attempt to speak was met with a slap. Chen thought of a plan that could kill two birds with one stone. He made three short international phone calls. Then he called Sean over and whispered an instruction in his ear. Sean jogged away and unfurled the oily rag in front of the twins, exposing the amputation saw. Chen got out of the SUV and stood behind Sean, watching them.

'This is insane. HELP,' Edward shrieked in a real state of fear. He tried to stand up. Again he was met by Sean's boot. His legs buckled from under him and he toppled over.

'Sean, that's enough,' Chen said. He looked down at Edward for a long time through eyes half-closed against the sun.

Chen smelt fear.

'We'll pay back the monies, honest. I swear on my mother's grave,' Edward declared.

Nobody responded.

Mayumi arrived back and threw two shovels on the sand beside the amputation saw. She dusted herself down and stretched.

'You want us to dig our own graves?' Tom asked.

'I'd like you to dig two holes, here, and here.' Chen scraped an x in the sand and then another close by.

'Our bodyguards will come for us shortly,' Tom mustered a pathetic look of defiance.

'Ah, the bodyguards, look into it,' Chen said glancing at Akiko then at Mayumi then at nobody.

'Hank will show you the way,' he added.

There was a silence, except for the noise of the off-roader.

Chen went back to the SUV. He tried to remain focussed but every now and then an image flashed before him – the charred remains of Hiroki's children.

There was something broken about the way the twins dug. The leg irons proved cumbersome but an occasional reminder from Sean's boot helped maintain a steady work rate. Chen leapt suddenly like a mad man from the vehicle and yelled at the top of his voice.

'It's too long; the holes you're digging are much too long.'

He wiped his hands on his pants, and then he crouched on the sand for a minute.

'What I want are holes this deep.' He put the flat of his hand on top of Tom's head. 'And this long.' He pressed an index finger into the base of Edward's neck.

'No way, you're not going to chop us up,' Edward said. He started to run but he tripped over the leg irons.

Tom caught him as he fell down.

'Too much in the sun,' Chen said.

'They could do with a shower,' Sean said.

Mr Okumara laughed.

Chen glanced at Edward.

'Sean's father was a butcher and as an apprentice he learnt the art of cutting carcasses into parts. He's so accustomed to the sight and smell of blood that he can just as well cut a live animal,' he said.

Chen spotted Sean picking up the amputation saw.

Sean looked straight at Edward, raising one eyebrow.

'Needless to say, he'd prefer a carving knife or a meat cleaver but all he could find was an amputation saw that last tasted human blood during the American Civil War,' Chen said softly.

Mr Okumara was urinating.

'I suppose my name is next on your hit-list.' He smiled a lopsided smile at Edward.

Edward looked away and shut his eyes.

When he opened his eyes again Mr Okumara was zipping up his pants.
It was too hot sitting there in the sun. Chen and Sean retired to the shade of the SUV and watched the sand cake the sweat on the faces of the twins.
'It's hard to believe that those two are so dangerous,' Sean said.
'Indeed.' Chen yawned without covering his mouth.

There were not very many people in the isolated house even though there were all those vehicles parked outside. Akiko looked all round her to see that no one had seen her. Surprisingly, there were no security cameras on the porch. She tried the door of the house. It was unlocked. Three men in suits were standing in the hall almost as if they were waiting for the twins.
Akiko was standing at the door with her eyes narrowing, scanning the inside of the house. Everything in the hall smelt clammy and hot. The roughest-looking man stared directly at her. But he did not do anything or say anything. Akiko took a step forward. He took three steps back. She pushed her hair back off her face with the colt. The man nearest the living-room door looked at her. Although in his sixties, portly, and balding, Akiko turned her head as if he might become a problem. He moved his hand slowly under his jacket. His fingers touched the grip of a Steyr machine pistol. Akiko did not see it, but she knew it was there.
A door across the hall opened and closed. From nowhere Mayumi dispatched a vicious chop. The machine pistol fell from the man's jacket before he hit the floor. His body was at an awkward angle. He looked dead. Suddenly, he was breathing again with the whole of his lungs as if he had been for a long time dunked in water. The third man helped him roughly to his feet.
Akiko marshalled them through the kitchen where all the laptops were. There were several more pieces of equipment around the house – a server in the backroom, a communications cabinet in the living room and, back in the kitchen, a giant printer with a flashing

light. The three men walked round Mayumi giving her a wide berth and let themselves out the back door. Mayumi let the door slam shut behind her. Akiko started forward again, and then she stopped unexpectedly. Once again she gestured. Suddenly, the rough-looking man bolted, but Mayumi was so light on her feet she caught him up before he reached the long shed. She knifed him, striking deeply between the shoulder blades. Then, with a lethal throw, she cut down the portly man running across the garden. When Akiko saw what was happening, she flayed the last of the men over the head with the colt.
He fell to his knees and covered his head with both hands but the blood spurted up between his fingers.
Mayumi tried to restrain Akiko, but she rained down blows on the man's head until he collapsed, and lay dead.
'That's for Christophe, my husband,' Akiko said, in her native tongue, and she lashed out with all the strength of her left leg. She stood over him for a long time before she moved.
They dragged the slain to the shed and hid them.

Chen could see Tom's back disappearing, then his shoulders, then his head. He got out of the SUV and approached the twins with steady purpose.
'That'll do.' He stepped back to give them room to climb out.
'Is their anything we can do to change your mind?' Edward pleaded.
'Afraid not.' Chen looked away and wiped the sweat from his brow. He narrowed his eyes against the glare. For long moments no one spoke. Then, suddenly, Tom and Edward were struck blows to the back of the head. Chen went to each in turn, felt for a pulse then drew back a lid to check the eye of the unconscious twin.
Chen's eyes were fixed ahead, unseeing, as he tried to choose between Tom and Edward.
'Ok, Edward is the weakest one. Tom isn't entirely broken,' he said. After removing the leg irons, he undid the buttons on Edward's shorts and slid them down his legs. Finally he nodded to Sean.

Sean hesitated, and then he put the Smith & Wesson to Tom's heart, and squeezed the trigger. Chen and Mr Okumara watched in silence as the body bag was sealed. Sean dropped the bag into one of the holes.

Mr Okumara was patting down the bloodstained sand when Edward regained consciousness. When he could hear again Edward could hear Sean, Mr Okumara too, laughing like they thought this was a big prank.

'You're awake,' Mr Okumara bellowed.

'Where's my brother?' Edward shrieked. Tears ran down the side of his head down into the sand. He stood up.

'Tom is dead.' Sean said in his ear.

'No,' Edward cried. He stepped back a foot. Then he realised he was naked. He tripped over one of the shovels and fell flat on his face in the sand.

'Yes.' Sean looked completely unbothered, like nothing horrible had happened, like he had not done anything even vaguely alarming.

'I'm burning up,' Edward said. He had gone a red colour.

Ravaged by guilt and anguish, he blamed himself for Tom's death.

'Oh! It's a hot one all right.' Mr Okumara nodded to Sean.

Edward tried to protest, but his throat was dry and his vision distorted.

Sean lifted the amputation saw to shoulder level and placed his knee on the small of Edward's back.

'Hold still,' Sean shouted.

'Wait.' Chen judged the time right and held up his hand. 'Maybe there's something you can help us with it.'

'Anything, anything, anything.' A dash of hope flashed across Edward's sand-covered face.

'I need to trace the whereabouts of,' Chen sat down beside Edward and placed a photograph on the sand. Then he moved a little closer. As much as he longed to rid himself of Edward, he longed much more to neutralise Tony.

'In return for what?' Edward asked disbelievingly.

He spat some sand out of his mouth.

Chen waved his finger back and forth. 'Somehow, I don't think you're in a position to bargain.'

'Okay, Okay.' Edward lay down on his back exhausted. Just then Mayumi arrived in the off-roader.

'Hank is waiting for you,' she whispered in Chen's ear.

Chen studied Edward for a moment, and then he smiled.

'This is what's going to happen. Mayumi will bring you to your house where you'll shower and put on some clean clothes. She will give you a pad and a felt pen. You will write with the pen on the pad of paper everything you know about this man. When I arrive, you'll turn on your computers and we'll go through all your correspondence. Once we've done that, you'll decode your mobile phone entries. If I feel you're cooperating with us in full, you'll then travel to England. Our IT guys will inspect your computers and determine what other kinds of skulduggery you and your deceased brother are involved in. After you've spoken with Michel Trebeh, you know, the man you want dead, you'll then be expatriated to South Africa where your passport will be confiscated; a home of modest proportions will be provided. All your bank accounts will be closed but you'll receive a monthly cheque, which will allow you to live just above the bread line. How does that sound?'

Edward nodded uncertainly.

'Come on then,' Mayumi said. 'Ready when you are.'

'Off you go.' Chen waited until the off-roader was out of sight.

'Do you want me to get rid of the SUV?' Sean seemed to read Chen's thoughts.

'Good idea.' Chen nodded. 'Then you're off to Cape Town to meet Hans Moeller. Drive carefully.'

'Grand,' Sean said, and he drove off.

'Come on then, let's go.' Chen broke sweat jogging back to the pickup. Mr Okumara trudged after him on the opposite side of the bank, his eyes fixed on the sand moving beneath his shoes.

The pickup pulled up outside the car park. After a bit, the convertible screeched to a halt and Mr Okumara got out. Chen stepped over the small wall round the dilapidated-looking house. From the front he saw that the house was an expensive one, though now it was quite derelict. Akiko and Mayumi were in the living room thumbing through magazines. Akiko had finished her coffee and got up. Mayumi hurried to her feet too.

'Well,' he said.

'We had to take out the bodyguards,' Akiko said uneasily.

'Hmm,' Chen said leaning on his elbow at the console table. He flicked through an address book letting his eye stop on random numbers. He closed the book and looked Edward in the eye.

Edward felt the colour drain out of him. He crouched by the skirting board, cup of tea in one hand.

Chen said sharply. 'Tell me about your friend.'

With an effort Edward calmed his mind. 'We made initial contact over the Internet and met him only once, in a ski lodge not far from Geneva. Here's his number.'

He wrote down Tony's number on the pad.

'Do you have a screwdriver set?' Chen asked. He tore the page out and turned it over.

'Yes.' Reluctantly Edward opened the drawer and handed it to him.

'Mayumi, can you help Edward remove all the hard drives and pack any other media into boxes,' Chen said.

When Chen went upstairs and locked the door behind him in the bedroom, he caught sight of himself in the mirror and his face was so sandy that he had to look twice. He sat on the bed looking away from the mirror. He took out his sat-phone and scrolled and rang.

'I need to trace a number,' he said.

'Sure, no problem,' the voice said.

Chen read out Tony's number.

'Ok.' At once the phone clicked off.

Chen rang Michel's number.

'Michel, how are you?'

'All the better for hearing your voice.'

'Mission accomplished,' Chen said. He went on to describe in detail what had happened and then he outlined a plan for capturing Tony.

'Excellent, that sounds great, but I'd like to change one or two things.' Michel spoke at length and when he was sure everything was crystal clear he hung up.

Akiko was sitting on the top step waiting for Chen when he opened the door.

'Is everything packed and loaded?' he asked.

'Yes, Master.'

'Thank you.' He quickly descended the stairs. He walked into the sunlight at the front of the house, Mr Okumara following. Then his phone rang.

'Hello,' Chen said.

'Master Chen, the number you asked us to trace is presently located off the Northern coast of Crete,' the voice said.

'Ok, track it by satellite and keep Setsu informed,' Chen ordered.

'I'll call him right now,' the voice said.

Chen looked at Mr Okumara in total surprise. His first concern was for Michel. He seemed to gather himself. 'We need to keep an eye on the time.'

'Is there a problem?' Mr Okumara asked.

Chen nodded. He looked at the phone then rang Setsu. He waited and waited.

'Hai!' Setsu said.

'Guard Michel with your life,' Chen said.

'I will,' Setsu promised.

Chen went back inside.

'Edward, call off your hitman,' he said simply.

CHAPTER 19

In the shadow of a streetlamp, Hermione was waiting for Tony on the pier. She wore a long coat and could feel the sweat on her back as she watched the muscular figure with dreadlocks climb the rusty ladder.
Somewhere in the distance dogs began to bark.
Hermione's pace gradually increased as she led the way to a nearby path. She began to whistle no particular tune just a desire to break the eerie, unnatural stillness. Behind her Tony walked along the tree-lined path, tired and hungry. With the flowerbox under his arm, he turned the corner and picked his way carefully in the pre-dawn darkness and almost stumbled into a motorcycle that was parked in front of the modern residential building. The door had been left ajar, so he went inside. Conveniently, the apartment was on the top floor, the sixth. The door was open and Hermione stood there. Before she could say or do anything, he brushed her aside and crossed the corridor of the big, plush apartment and went into the lounge. He looked around the room and went over to the window.
A gust of wind rattled the panes.
He flicked open the flowerbox and groped for the rifle.
In silence he waited.

Hermione sipped her whiskey, her eyes fixed on him. She went towards the kitchen for some water. 'Tony?'

'I'm fine,' he muttered.

'I think it'll be dawn in half an hour,' she said.

'I know.'

'Do you want sex?'

After a moment he said, 'later.'

'Okay.'

Still, he patiently focused, his forearm and elbow comfortably positioned beneath the barrel of the rifle, his wrist aligned and solid.

Michel and Setsu stood mutely in the middle of the beach. The two men glanced at each other. That morning, for reasons he himself was not sure of, Michel had decided to swim.

'I don't like this one bit.' Setsu bit his lip and fiddled nervously with the earpiece, his face lined with worry.

Michel finished drying himself off.

'We're very exposed, and the assassin is not far from here,' Setsu complained, the strain still showing on his face.

Tony's view was hampered. He stared from the window, cheek pressed firmly against the thumb of his right hand. He swung the gun barrel over a lofty, wide dune covered with brown sand and dancing grass, then across a gap in the bank. Patiently, he waited.

Suddenly he felt a hand on his trouser fly. He looked down.

Hermione was kneeling. She grinned expectantly and moved closer. He grabbed a handful of her shaggy brown hair and twisted her head back. Then he struck her across the face.

'Not now!' he yelled.

Unexpectedly his mobile phone vibrated, startling him. Hermione tried to keep the surprise off her face. She dabbed her cut forehead with a thin paper napkin. Tony took the phone and went outside.

'Tony can you hear me?' Edward asked.

Tony held the phone closer to his ear. 'Yes, yes, I can. Just about.'

'Abort mission,' Edward said in a tense, level voice. 'And can we meet in London, say, three days' time? Trebeh appears to be more useful to us alive than dead.'

There was a moment's silence.

'You rang in the nick time. Where in London?' Tony's stomach twisted uneasily.

Edward hesitated for only an instant. 'The Ritz, and I'll send a plane. Sorry, got to run -' Chen reached over and cut him off.

Three days later, in Heathrow, nervous eyes jumped from screen to flickering screen as George, balancing a plate of chips in one hand and a coffee in the other, barked out an instruction. He was a tall, handsome man of 53. But his face was taut. He had surveillance cameras trained on the many thousands of commuters passing through the five terminals, along with high-tech detectors looking for conventional explosives, bio-weapons and chemical weapons.

'Sir, there is an anonymous caller on line two, says he has some information regarding a security threat,' the excitable airport officer raised his voice unnecessarily for all to hear.

'I'll take it in my office.'

Stowing his gun beneath his seat, George loosened his necktie.

'Yes, you have some information for us.'

'George, this is Chen.'

'Ah, Master, just a moment.' Very concerned, he got up. 'Smith, is this call being recorded?'

'Yes, Sir,' Smith shouted back.

'Well turn it off.' There was urgency in George's voice.

'Turn it off,' Smith echoed, shocked.

'Listen, I won't ask again,' George said pointedly and Smith felt the blood flow into his face.

'Yes, Sir.' He clicked on the icon.

'Sorry, Master, how can I help you?' George closed the door.

'Did you receive an email from Jiang alerting you to the danger posed by a passenger onboard a flight from Crete?'

'I did,' George said worriedly.
'I want to question the passenger.'
'I've received orders to hand him over to MI6,' George said in a rush.
'Those orders may shortly change,' Chen said confidently.

He had already made arrangements with a senior agent of MI6. His meeting with Geoff Flanders had been brief and unexpectedly blunt. Chen smiled to himself, thinking about what was said.
'Under no circumstances is this guy to be processed by our penal system.'

Outside the hanger was deserted, except for four armed officers waiting near a green Humvee. The Cessna appeared out of the grey haze just within the range of George's binoculars. For fifteen minutes she circled, waiting for clearance to land. Stocky and pink-faced, the pilot was listening to the tower on the plane's radio. 'Still some issue with visibility,' he told Tony. 'Wait a second... she's cleared!'
The pilot tipped down in the direction of the runway.
Inside the terminal building George watched her come on. The Cessna nosed her way earthward on a perfect approach, and then she touched down.
The Humvee rushed to intercept her.
Now Tony could see the approaching vehicles that were racing along the road joining the terminal to the runway.
He could make out two cars and a truck.
Without warning, the airplane door burst open.
'Hands in the air,' an angry-looking officer told Tony arrogantly.
'Let me get my bag,' Tony growled.
'Quiet! Show me your hands,' the officer leaned over and belted him backhanded across the face.
Instantly Tony's knife was in his hand and he moved with catlike speed between the officer and the door. But another blue-uniformed

officer, safely away, raised his machine gun and let off a burst into the ceiling.

Tony froze.

The officer, sweating, shoved the gun barrel at Tony's face. For a moment it looked as though he would shoot, but he just lifted the gun and slammed Tony on the side of the head and knocked him over.

Tony's knife crashed to the floor.

He opened his eyes and stood up and raised his hands.

From the plane, Tony walked through the twenty or so airport officers and was quickly bundled into a truck full of SAS commandos bristling with assault rifles, which headed for the terminal. He recognised one of them, a member of his old unit. The driver opened the door and slid out fast. He raced to the back and released the bolts.

The commandos fanned out, all rifles trained on Tony.

As Tony walked across the asphalt, he felt vengeful eyes on him.

When he was five yards from the gate, a MI6 agent signalled to the agent beside him. There were six of them, all big men, all armed, all except one, Geoff Flanders.

Two former military men – Bernard Seville and Todd Richards – sprang out and grabbed Tony, and then, with a third agent, they pinned Tony to the floor.

Both Bernard and Todd were related to the rookie policeman murdered by Tony at the allotments.

They were holding Tony hard against the ground when someone belted Tony across the mouth and the others started punching and kicking him.

Tony tore himself free, bloodying his hand in the process.

'Ok,' George commanded, 'that's enough.' He turned on his heel and stomped off, Tony and the six agents following quickly.

It was not until much later that Chen and Akiko pushed their way through the crowds. They went into the terminal and up the stairs, past two airport officers, and into the control room. Scattered around the room were a few of the MI6 agents who had been told to stand by.

Glen, a lanky, blond young officer, raised his hand. 'Halt!'

'Glen let them through for God's sake, and point that Uzi downward,' George hollered.

'Sorry Sir, I didn't get a clear look at their badges.' Glen hung his head.

Chen and Akiko came into George's office.

'Please sit down.' George waved at the empty chairs opposite his desk.

'How're things?' Chen asked.

'Good.' George came closer. 'He's travelling under the name Edmond Benitez and swears he's a freelance travel writer.'

George handed Chen the seized hunting knife. Chen passed the weapon to Akiko.

'We fed his photo into the face-recognition system,' George said quietly. 'And it came up with a match. His real name is Tony Blake, Ex SAS. He struck an officer during a tour of duty in the Middle East, was imprisoned, but then he escaped. Been missing ever since.'

In the observation room George poured out three coffees and offered Chen a jam donut. Standing in front of the reinforced one-way mirror, Chen could see that Tony, his clothes badly torn, his face deeply bruised, knew he was being observed.

Tony glanced towards the door. No change: it was still guarded. The commando – with his heavy gear, body armour, and high-tech equipment – looked alert. Tony went back to staring at the steel table. He smiled to himself and let his mind drift. The walls and the ceiling were painted dark red with murals of disjointed characters; on the floor blood red tiles cemented the mood. And the absence of clocks or windows contrived a sense of timelessness.

Tony burrowed deeper into his chair, trying to settle himself more comfortably.

'George, would you mind leaving?' Chen politely asked.

'You've got it.'

'Thank you, commander,' Chen said.

Chen edged opened the door. There was a long pause before he placed two cups of coffee on the table and sat down. He glanced at Tony, still slumped in his chair, his hands behind his neck, steeling himself.

'Hello, Edmond is it,' he spoke calmly, not wishing to be confrontational.

'Yes, that's what's on my passport,' Tony replied gamely. 'What do you want?'

'Or should I call you Tony?' Chen asked simply and smiled.

Tony laughed out loud. 'Where's my lawyer.'

Chen's smile vanished and his stare was cold. 'There'll be no lawyers. Your only chance of survival now lies outside the law. Do you get my drift?'

'What the hell's going on?' Tony asked impatiently and his eyes bore into Chen.

Chen, striving to understand Tony's essence, searched for his next words.

'Ironically, the man you were, for the want of a better phrase, contracted to terminate, has expressed a desire to save your life.'

Tony looked at him. 'Why should he do this?'

Chen tapped the table with his right forefinger.

'And yes, he's aware of the nature of your relationship with the Scallion twins.'

Tony just stared back and Chen felt the man's hatred strongly.

'Enough chit chat, the man you were asked to kill invites you to take up arms, so to speak.'

Chen saw the puzzled expression.

'Bloody hell,' Tony burst out. 'Are you suggesting he wants to avail of my services?'

'No, no, you're mistaken. He'd like to challenge you to a duel…' Chen stopped when Tony burst out laughing.

'You're kidding me!'
One half of Chen wanted to smile while the other half was locked into the nightmare possibility that he may be arranging Michel's death.
'You're crazy,' Tony said. He shivered, finding it curiously enticing. 'Although in the world we live in, nothing should be too surprising, eh!' He then added, 'what if I emerge victorious?'
'You'll be sent abroad and given a period of grace of about a week. After that, you will be hunted down, executed, and your body brought back to this country.' Chen ripped his eyes away and looked at his watch.
'You've got it all worked out, haven't you?' Tony said quietly.
Chen shrugged, wanting to end it.
Tony stared at him, even more unsettled. 'Mr Trebeh must be very confident indeed.'
'No more so than you.' Growing impatient, Chen frowned and stood up.
Tony also stood up. He took the last swallow of his coffee.
Chen stepped to the front of the room and said, 'come with me.' He then added, 'you promise you won't try to escape?'
Chen put out his hand.
Tony just stared at him.
'Please.' Chen's voice was dangerous.
Tony gawked at the hand.
Chen forced himself to wait.
Then Tony conceded, shrugged and shook the hand firmly. 'Sure.'
Chen measured Tony's reply and believed him.
The commando – his rifle slung across his belly – lifted his weapon. Using the gun's barrel, he motioned Tony outside the room.
Grudgingly Tony came forward.

Early the next morning as the darkness rapidly unravelled, May looked at Michel. He was lying on the bed in what was now May's room in Lancaster Gate. His eyes were closed and she saw his chest rising and falling.

She bent over him.

'Michel,' she called softly.

His eyelids flickered. For an instant, his pupils seemed to focus on her face, and then drift away.

She called again.

He awoke.

'Like some coffee?' she asked, in a rush, her voice bubbling.

'Great idea.' He got up.

She danced over to the writing desk and found the small box. 'This is just a little engagement gift,' she said and laughed at his look.

'Oh, thank you, darling.' His eyebrows arched. The pendant was entwined with an eighteen carat gold chain.

'St Christopher, the patron saint of travellers,' she explained. 'To keep you safe.'

He put his arm around her and kissed her.

She hugged him. 'Breakfast?'

'Yes, please, in ten minutes,' he replied happily. 'But first I need to phone Gerard.'

'Going somewhere special?'

Michel grinned back at her. 'No, no, not yet.' He decided not to mention the rendezvous with Jenny's killer.

She gave him a kiss and left.

He lifted the old-fashioned handset and dialled. 'This is Michel.' A pause, then, 'Gerard, I need the chopper.'

Michel replaced the handset. Lost in thought, he sat on the edge of the bed.

May stuck her head in, smiled when she saw he was practicing his breathing techniques. 'Five minutes,' she said.

Eventually he ambled down the hall, stopped at the doorway and stared. May was chasing a bluebottle around the dining room.

'It's as big as a golf ball,' she roared, the laughter in her voice brought a smile to his face.

She blew him a kiss. 'Shall I serve breakfast?'
'Yes,' Michel replied.
'Busy day?'
'Very.'
She regarded him. 'Oh?'
He changed his mind about not telling her. But it took a while for it all to register because she was very emotional.

Setsu was waiting at the helipad. Michel, wearing jeans and sneakers, searched the skies, along with May. The blue Eurocopter came over the wharf at a hundred feet and touched down. Immediately they hurried under the rotors and jumped in. Setsu locked the door and gave a thumbs-up to Gerard.
Once airborne, May, dressed in green, leaned closer to Michel.
'I love you,' she said.
'I love you too.'

On the blustery heights, mosses and other plants worked their way into the crannies. Giant drops of rain fell, splattering dark grey rock, followed by driving sheets of rain that slashed across the Cornish shoreline of cliffs and beaches. The helicopter followed the cliff road. Beyond the road the ground was bare, and beyond that stony paths rose to the cliffs. Moodily Michel looked down at the sea. He was trying to marshal his thoughts for the task ahead. The helicopter made a reconnaissance loop around the area and veered in over the mountainous terrain, across a walking trail, back across the walking trail, and then past a hollow just over the mountains.
Gerard put her down on a large patch of furze.
'Shut her down, Ger!' Michel opened the door and slid out quickly. He led the way out to a monastic tower perched on the tip of a sheer cliff. As May walked behind him, she was still pondering whether to avenge her friend's death. She suddenly felt angry. The wind tugged at them as they trekked past the lookout tower. While the others kept moving, Setsu nipped inside the tower to check on Akiko. Ahead

now were the ruins of a small monastery that appeared to cling to the cliff. Matsumi was waiting on the terrace. She had a view of the open-air theatre, which had been adorned with brightly coloured banners and flags. It was a setting that evoked a surreal atmosphere. She clasped the shoulders of Michel as if he were Setsu and ushered him through the monastery, past the Shinto shrine, to join Chen, who was barefoot and wearing a long cotton cape. Then she grabbed May's hand and escorted her to one of the cushions thrown on the wet flagstone floor.

'I've food to prepare,' Matsumi explained. Then she glided down the flight of stone steps leading to the theatre.

Elsewhere a kilometre or so to the north was a town and coming from that direction was a black Mercedes. It travelled slowly. Ahead on the road appeared a fringe of large trees, the windbreaks of the town. In the car were four men. But as the road began to twist and climb, the tarmac ran out. Near the cliff edge the car stopped. A man with cropped, bleached hair, Lennon glasses, and a blue fleece jacket got out from the front seat. His eyes went over the cliff top and the pockets of soldiers here and there. He gave a signal. Straight away the two men in the backseat, with their battered camouflage jackets, blue jeans, and mud-spattered boots, came out swiftly, Tony between them. He was blindfolded and handcuffed. A thought filled his mind. I am going to die.

Before he knew what was happening, they grabbed him and dragged him over to the theatre. There they removed the blindfold and handcuffs, and then they returned to the car.

The dirt-carpeted rock was impressed with the tracks of birds and wildlife. At one end of the semicircular viewing area, hacked into the mountainside, stood an old wooden table bounded on either side by a stone bench. On the table was bottled water that bore the name Trebeh Wells. After his night in captivity, Tony drank the water thirstily. He watched Matsumi as she kneaded a lump of dried dough, and then she rolled it out to a length of about two feet. Then

her arms crooked upwards, her fingers twitched, and suddenly the dough cylinder doubled. She flipped the ribbons into a hot wok on the propane-fuelled stove and minutes later dipped out a bowl of soup – noodles, chillies, and a bit of chicken.
It made for interesting viewing.

Tony was drinking his soup quite sparingly. Suddenly Michel jumped up onto the low wall bordering the lip of the cliff, the wind filling his salmon jacket so that it flowed out over the abyss.
'Sorry, I didn't mean to alarm you,' Michel apologised, seeing the look on Tony's face.
'You didn't,' Tony said, his voice rising over the wind. But he could feel his heart pounding.
Michel hopped lightly from the wall and walked with threatened purpose across the dirt, kicking up chips of stone, carrying an iroko box as if to hurl. He sat down and opened the box.
Tony gazed at the pair of 18th century duelling pistols.
'Are they loaded?' he asked.
'Yes,' Michel replied.
Matsumi moved around the table, serving beef with rice, peas and carrots.
Michel fished out a brown morsel, dipped it in sauce and ate.
Tony cleared his bowl first. 'I don't understand why you would risk your life.' His tone was sarcastic.
Michel scooped the last measure of rice, which he swallowed without chewing. Then he nodded thoughtfully. 'It is time to put down the moral compass and take up the sword, so to speak.' He took one long swallow and then lowered his cup and said, 'it's also about controlling fear.'
Tony laughed, liking him. 'You're afraid?' he asked.
'You cannot escape death.' Michel's eyes widened as he spoke. 'But you can conquer your fear of death. Those who are reluctant to give up their lives and embrace death are not true gladiators.'
'Perhaps this time death will win,' Tony said.

With her flowing green dress, fierce eyes, and her engagement ring on her finger, May emerged from the mist-shrouded entranceway. She took up a large stone. 'This is for taking the life of my best friend,' she hissed.

Furiously she flung the stone at Tony, but missed.

Tony's fists slammed down on the table, the sudden violence making Michel flinch.

May cursed and stormed off.

Tony's jaw stuck out. 'I've had enough of this nonsense,' he bellowed with rage.

Michel got up and stared at him angrily. 'Let's get this over with,' he growled and handed him a pistol.

Tony got up to his great height and projected a confidence gained through a lifetime of marksmanship.

'We'll walk in opposite directions exactly twelve paces. We each have a single shot. Matsumi will count.' Michel gestured at Matsumi. Then he pointed to a sharpshooter on the mountaintop above the theatre. 'Shoot too early, and...' he warned.

Now, with his back to Tony, Michel nodded his head in Matsumi's direction.

She began. 'One, two, three...'

Tony's heart was in his mouth. The broken skin over his knuckles made it difficult for him to grip the curved butt of the charcoal-grey pistol.

Matsumi continued. 'Six, Seven...'

A sick feeling welled in the pit of Michel's stomach.

'Nine...'

The duellists strode the remaining paces.

'Twelve.'

Michel was first to turn. In one fluid motion, he aimed the pistol at Tony's head and pulled the trigger. The hammer struck the flint and produced a pop of sparks. The ball hit Tony's cheekbone, just below the left eye, ripping an ear off and knocking him backwards onto the ground.

Momentarily blinded, Tony rallied the rest of his senses and regained his footing and wiped the blood from his face.

Squinting, he saw Michel standing before him.

For an instant there was silence. Then May shouted, 'the murderer is up. Shoot him, someone. In God's name, shoot him!'

Michel was helpless, and it was a new feeling. For a moment he thought he was going to faint but he fought off the light-headedness. He cast his eyes in the direction of the viewing area to where May, held back by Setsu, watched in horror as Tony took aim.

'Michel, RUUUN!' she screamed.

Standing on the low wall, one misstep from a fall of four hundred feet, Chen whipped the hunting knife from his sleeve and cocked his right arm. As he threw, he thought of Hiroki's mulched face.

The knife whistled through the air, handle over point, coming in from Tony's blind side. The point struck deep into Tony's neck.

Tony reeled drunkenly, then, without pulling the trigger, he collapsed. Chen rushed to where he lay.

Kneeling on both knees, Chen eased out the blade. The blood spurted sideways, staining his cape. He pried open Tony's jaw and wedged the blade between the two bottom middle teeth.

'This is from Hiroki.' He sawed the blade down to the gum, and then with a yank of his shoulder, he twisted it.

Blood filled Tony's mouth and his rasping breaths filled the small theatre.

'And this is from Hirokatsu, and Ichiro.' He positioned the point of the blade just above the heart and plunged it deep into Tony's chest.

    Michel sat cross-legged on the earth and studied the body. May ran to him, dropped on her knees and threw her arms around him. The relief on her face was so emphasised that it was only then that he realised how close he had come to death's door.

'Oh my God, I thought I was going to lose you,' she sobbed.

'No way.' He gave her a kiss. 'It's not going to be that easy to get rid of me,' he joked nervously.

CHAPTER 20

It was a cold brisk day. Blanche, standing a few inches over five feet tall with a thin build, calmed May's nerves with a gentle hug. Just one of many duties expected of a wedding planner. At last everything was prepared even down to the colour of leather selected for the greys chosen to pull the horse-drawn carriage. His effeminate mannerisms, combined with tender tones, put at ease the most nervous of prospective brides. After all, he had been through this ordeal many times before. He found May's innocent charm captivating and was fully intent on making her special day a most memorable orchestration. His brief had been to mark the occasion as simple and low key, yet fit for a princess.

Normally based in London, this was Blanche's first time planning a wedding outside the capital. He had found his feet quickly, and he had decided upon a heraldic theme. The wedding reception itself would take place in the fantastical surroundings of a castle situated on the banks of the East Avon. Beneath the turrets, the newly weds would be treated to a spectacular view of the river flowing southwards to the English Channel.

The rehearsal day not only marked the shortest day of the year, it was in fact the penultimate day for life as a singleton for Michel and May. The crisp evening ambience greeted the jittery bridal party. The vicar, a big man with a lined face, no stranger to Charles's generosity, spoke to each person in turn, and then he looked sternly at his watch. The church doors opened and in walked the best man, Setsu. Michel entered minutes later and his eyes settled on May's blissful face. After rehearsal, the couple kissed their goodbyes. Adhering to tradition, they would not see each other until May, linked by her father, would walk down the aisle.

After months of planning, May's big day had finally arrived. She woke early at her parents' house and took a hot shower to calm her nerves. Her make-up artist came with a metal case crammed full of cosmetics. Blanche then joined her.

Invited guests, in their finery, trickled in. On queue, the light fog dispersed, allowing the winter sun to squeeze through the fluffy clouds. Outside the church, Michel, with Setsu by his side, waited patiently for the blushing bride. On the balcony, members of a string quartet, borrowed from the national ensemble, tuned their instruments.

May did not have far to walk. The church built in 1874 towered high above the roadway directly opposite the entrance to the family home. She wore a simple white wedding gown made from silk taffeta and decorated with pearls. Her bridesmaid, clad in burgundy, college-friend Rosy Neville, a shy woman with frizzy red hair, busied herself sorting May's train. The enthused photographer, Brad Fogarty, a refined-looking man, put his camera through its paces, kneeling here and crouching there. The wedding party slowly made their way into the church with May on the arm of her father as he prepared to give her away. Stylishly dressed in a mauve Paul Costelloe creation, the mother-of-the-bride could not have looked more pleased.

The entrance antiphon, Give Me Your hand, resonated throughout the church.

As the congregation turned to admire the veiled figure, May held fast on her father's arm. And in her hand, she gripped a small bouquet of wild flowers. Flickering cameras captured each graceful step.

'Take care of my little girl,' Charles said with a watery eye as he transferred May's arm to Michel.

'Thank you Charles.' Michel, in a black Magee suit, silver waistcoat and matching tie, took May's hand and led her to the altar. He wore a white carnation in his lapel that complemented May's bouquet.

Chen read from the Book of Sirach: "A loving partner is a safe shelter, whoever finds one has found a rare treasure".

The platinum rings, rimmed in gold, were blessed and exchanged.

With the ceremony complete, the couple exited the church to be greeted by roars of approval from well-wishers.

The glass-enclosed carriage was not Blanche's idea, but May's Cinderella childhood dream. She pinched herself, just to make sure she was not dreaming.

She planted a kiss on Michel's cheek. 'My handsome Prince, thank you for making this day possible.'

'My darling, you deserve it and much more. This too is the happiest day of my life.' He kissed her full on the lips.

After a while she sat back and relaxed.

In the entrance hall, dominated by a gigantic Christmas tree that glowed with fairy lights, the reception guests were greeted by an elegant harpist, biscuits and free bar - no expense spared. The wedding party had retired to the library. It was decorated with perfumed wreaths of holly and a tree decked out with gold bows, crystal baubles and glittery roses. An endless ream of pictures later, the guests clapped in accord as they welcomed the new Mr and Mrs Trebeh to the gallery hall.

Already seated at the top table were Charles, Jane, Chen, Matsumi, Setsu and Rosy. A photograph of Jenny, wearing a blue graduation gown, was given a place of memory beside Jane.

Blanche hovered about the table, catering for the couple's every need. Meanwhile, at the next table, Richard, Margaret, Fobie, Greta, Dmitri, Toyoko and her boyfriend, Pat Hogan, were getting along swimmingly.

A spicy parsnip soup followed the first of the three starters.

Between appetisers, palettes were cleansed by a passion fruit sorbet.

The main course was served: fillet of Irish beef topped with foie gras, shallot and wild mushrooms.

Throughout the meal, glasses were topped up with Chateau La Fauconnerie and those who preferred white were treated to Haut Poitou.

The large number of staff ensured no delay between courses.

Halfway through the dessert – apple tart with cream and brandy – the sommelier uncorked the bottle of champagne that he was holding in his hand.

For the toast, Charles had selected the most expensive Dom Perignon from his cellar. Also, he had stayed up all night preparing his speech and the moment of truth was nigh.

Setsu turned on the microphone. Once he had everyone's attention, he invited Charles to say a few words.

Charles summarised May's many accomplishments since childhood, punctuating with the odd joke. At long last, when he folded the tract of paper, there was a collective sigh of relief.

Then, after a short speech, Setsu proposed the toast.

'We pray that you'll have a lifetime of happiness and fulfilment. Salute.'

The band finished at midnight, at which point festivities moved downstairs to the dungeon bar where a grand piano took centre stage. Those that could play were invited to do so. Michel and May made it their business to speak to each and everyone of the guests before the celebration concluded. As the hours of night dwindled by, people got braver and more confident in their ability to sing.

Michel bumped into May while doing the rounds and whispered, 'this could go on until daybreak, how about us two slipping away quietly, I'm sure, at this stage, no one will even notice?'
'One more hour, and then we'll bid everyone adieu. How does that sound?' May kissed him on the cheek.

The log fire in the spacious bathroom was ablaze. Stoking the roaring fire that crackled comfortingly, May gazed contemplatively into the flames. She straightened up, returned the poker to its cradle and opened her night bag. 'I'll be a few minutes.' She smiled mischievously.
She draped her wedding dress over the chair. Barely able to contain her excitement, she slipped into a pink tunic style nightdress and sprayed a dollop of perfume about her cleavage and belly. She left the bathroom and, without taking her eyes off her husband's naked body, she skipped across the bedroom and fell into his open arms. She buried her face against his chest and moved gently against him. A yielding murmuring noise caused him to lift her head. Her nervous lips joined his. The heat off their embrace rose a degree while his hands travelled up and down her back. His hand followed a form of natural progression as it moved to her hip and then to her firm and rounded buttock. His other hand traced the same path, making her skin tingle. Now gently squeezing both buttocks, he felt his loins engorge and harden. His experienced fingers skirted her, probing the soft hair and gently squeezing through her swollen lips. She encircled his member with thumb and finger, and placed it at her doorway. When he felt her ready, he began to propel, deeply. She met his thrusting drive with her own supple movements. They became one, scaling the heights of ecstasy, no longer male and female but a solitary creature. Next, they cried out in deliverance.
She stroked his head. 'I'm glad I waited for you my love.'
She nuzzled his ear and felt him harden once more. 'Again my love, love me.' Her rite of passage was reaffirmed three more times before the first shimmering of dawn.

May woke first and went to the bathroom to relieve herself. Michel pulled back the sheets and took note of her virginal blood. It left an almost perfect floral pattern and he interpreted it as a sign of good things to come.

'What pray tell are you up to?' she demanded.

'Nothing, just admiring your artwork,' he joked, as she lavished kiss after kiss upon him.

'So you doubted me, you cad. For that transgression I'll have to punish you most severely.' She pushed him backwards.

Her playfulness aroused him. He laughed as she found her rhythm.

'I could get to like this very much,' she said.

'That's fine as long as you don't become a nymphomaniac,' he joked.

There was a discreet knock on the door.

'Sir, Madam, your breakfast is ready.'

'Just a moment!'

It was long after midday when at last the bride and groom bade farewell to Charles, Jane and Matsumi at the foot of the Gulfstream jet's steps. Wearing festive red and snowy white, May wore the kind of glow that suggested the wedding night had been a happy one. She looked admiringly at her husband wrapped up in a white woollen jumper.

'Merry Christmas! You are now my son,' Charles told Michel.

'Look after her, won't you?' Jane looked at him over May's shoulder as she hugged her daughter. Tears were running down her cheeks.

'Of course I will,' Michel said with a smile, and he nodded his head.

At last the honeymooners climbed up into the jet and it sped them across the English Channel. When they landed at Leonardo da Vinci International airport in Italy a chauffer-driven limousine was waiting on the tarmac to take them into Rome. At the Napoleon hotel the duty manager ushered them up to the honeymoon suite. They did not emerge for three whole days. On the fourth evening they went to

Rossini's most popular opera: The Barber of Seville. The next morning, they were holding hands when May tossed a coin into the Trevi Fountain. She and Michel then climbed the Spanish Steps that brought them to the 15th-century church of the Trinita dei Monti where they knelt side by side and said a short prayer. They spent the afternoon wandering through the Forums and then the ancient tunnels beneath the city and that evening dined in an exclusive restaurant in the Piazza Navona. There followed four short days of lovemaking, sightseeing and general happiness.

Michel flew out to Istanbul to attend an art auction and take care of some urgent business, while May returned home on the Orient-Express to take on her new post at Peoples Pensions as Charles's vice-president. Michel rang her at every opportunity over the next few days to offer guidance. Initially she took no active role in corporate matters. Rather she observed and she listened. Charles was so glad to have the apple of his eye beside him.

For a fortnight she had been sitting so mutely in the boardroom that the other new young directors had almost forgotten that she was there, but now she began to stamp her authority on the board.

Three weeks later both May and Charles were waiting to meet Michel when the Gulfstream jet landed at Gatwick airport. May rushed up the steps to embrace him. Charles gave them a minute before he followed her up to the plane.

'Oh, Michel!' May whispered huskily. 'How heartless of you to have forsaken me all these lonely weeks!'

'Never fear, you're coming with me now,' Michel said. 'Sorry Charles, must dash, but we'll send you a postcard.'

Charles stood alone and watched the silver aircraft taxi to the end of the runway then turn around and with the roar of its engines dart back towards him and rise into the sky over his head. In the cockpit May was waving her red beret at him. Then she was gone.

Made in the USA
Lexington, KY
16 June 2012